Nebula Awards Showcase 2019

Edited by Silvia Moreno-Garcia

www.ParvusPress.com

Parvus Press, LLC
PO Box 224
Yardley, PA 19067-8224
ParvusPress.com

Nebula Awards Showcase 2019

ISBN 13 978-1-7338119-7-2
Ebook ISBN 978-1-7338119-6-5

Cover Illustration © Tiffany Dae
Cover design by R J Theodore
Designed and typeset by Catspaw DTP Services

Table of Contents

Introduction
Silvia Moreno-Garcia

WHEN I BEGAN SELLING short stories in 2006 the speculative fiction landscape was radically different. For one,
I had to purchase international reply coupons to send along
with my manuscripts. I'd dread each and every time the ac-
ronym IRC appeared in the submissions guidelines. Not
every postal outlet carried these coupons. Often, you'd have
an irritated postal worker rummaging through a drawer and
muttering to themselves until, at the bottom, they found the
precious slip of paper. Nowadays, most budding writers don't
know what an IRC is.

There was something else that was different back in
2006: I was alone.

When I first harnessed the courage to start sending my
stories out in 2006, it truly was a frightening prospect. I had
never seen a Latina writer in any of the fantasy and science
fiction magazines I read, nor at the bookstore. Yes, I knew
that Latin American magic realist writers existed, but they
sat on the literary shelf. The science fiction and fantasy section was virtually devoid of people like me.

There were the odd names which popped up here and

there. Ernest Hogan had published *High Aztech* in the 1990s, but he was the only Latino writer under a science fiction or fantasy imprint I could name. And that had happened more than a decade before and he seemed to have gone out of print. Was there anyone in print, in bookstores?

I found a handful of black speculative writers: Octavia E. Butler, Samuel R. Delany and Nalo Hopkinson. Hopkinson was Canadian and I had immigrated to Canada, so the discovery of this author was exciting. But that seemed to be the end of the list of writers of color I could reliably find at my local store.

I had few role models to emulate, no person to ask for advice, no one to talk to at all. I did not know if I was even *allowed* to write. Fantasy was still the world of Medieval castles and science fiction futures did not include any Mexicans. There was no point in even considering horror, either. It was quite depressing.

In a tiny magazine by the name of *Deep Magic*, I bumped into Aliette de Bodard. She was the first writer who I thought was a little bit like me: a woman of color who was about my age, who was also starting her writing career. She lived in France, to boot, which meant she was an international writer.

For a long time I looked for de Bodard's name in publications, as a sort of guiding light.

If she exists, I might exist, I told myself.

In 2007, Nnedi Okorafor was about to publish her second novel, *The Shadow Speaker*, when she discovered that the cover of the book would feature a white woman instead of the black protagonist of the story. Okorafor had written the novel because she wanted to "see Africa in the future." She fought back against this imposition and the cover was changed. She didn't tell the story of the whitewashed cover until 2017, but I saw the cover long before knowing this tale, ten years before, and thought that it was visually striking. It was another beacon.

In 2009, Lavie Tidhar edited *The Apex Book of World SF*, which reprinted stories by writers from around the world. I don't think anything like that had been attempted before. There was a story by de Bodard and a bunch of writers I had never heard about. Today, this anthology series has five volumes.

New magazines began popping up and they were mostly online. The move to electronic submissions, which occurred in parallel with the creation of more and more online magazines, had a profound effect on the science fiction and fantasy short story landscape. For one, it allowed international submissions with ease and therefore increased the presence of writers of color.

Around this time there also began to be an interest and an appeal for diversity in fiction. I still didn't know very many fellow writers of color, but Twitter was now a thing and I joined this social network. Online, at a distance, I became more aware of others like me. I even interacted with some of them through Twitter. I began to look for their names on shelfs, in tables of contents, as beacons, just like de Bodard had been a beacon.

There, right there, was proof I wasn't alone.

In 2010, Justine Larbalestier's YA novel *Liar* was published. It originally was supposed to have a white woman on the cover, despite the fact that the heroine is black. Echoing Okorafor's struggle, Larbalestier managed to have the cover modified. In ensuing online talks about this, someone mentioned that Octavia Butler's covers had also been whitewashed back in the 70s.

It seemed that publishing worked like a wheel and people of color were trampled under it. Why, they were not even allowed on the cover. If Butler had been whitewashed—Butler, who was the first science fiction writer to win a MacArthur Fellowship—what chance did people like me have?

I wondered if publishing would ever welcome people of

color, if I'd ever have a book published, if I'd ever meet another Latina writer at a science fiction and fantasy convention.

Then, something happened. Because that same year Nora K. Jemisin published *The Hundred Thousand Kingdoms.*

I began hearing all kinds of buzz about Jemisin, who had already netted attention with her short fiction. The next year, Jemisin was nominated for so many awards I can't even list them all. The Nebula, the Hugo, the World Fantasy. She won a Locus for *The Hundred Thousand Kingdoms* and would go on to win multiple awards, including the 2018 Nebula for *The Stone Sky.* She was also the first writer to win three Hugos in a row for her Broken Earth trilogy.

The publishing world is different from when I started writing. Jemisin's success will surely serve as a beacon to a new generation. But she is not alone. In 2018, Fonda Lee was nominated for both the Nebula adult and young adult novel categories. Cindy Pon also netted a nomination in the Nebula YA category. Vina Jie-Min Prasad (who appears in this volume with the story "Fandom for Robots" and the novelette "A Series of Steaks"), Caroline M. Yoachim ("Carnival Nine") and Rebecca Roanhorse (winner of both a Hugo and Nebula for "Welcome to Your Authentic Indian Experience™," which opens this showcase) and JY Yang (shortlisted for her novella *The Black Tides of Heaven*) are only but a few of the writers of color that are popping up in the arena of speculative fiction. Beyond the 2018 Nebula finalists, there's also Yoon Ha Lee, Cixin Liu, Victor LaValle, Kai Ashante Wilson, Alyssa Wong, and many others.

Comparing the 2006 Nebula finalists and the list of finalists in 2018, it's also evident there's many more women, including relative newcomers such as Kelly Robson, winner of the Nebula for Best Novelette ("A Human Stain," which closes this volume), and established authors such as Martha Wells, of the Murderbot series (another double winner, her novella *All Systems Red* was awarded a Nebula and a Hugo and is the longest work in this showcase).

There's young queer writers, like K.M. Szpara ("Small Changes Over Long Periods of Time") and more established authors, such as Lambda-winner Richard Bowes ("Dirty Old Town"). And because life is intersectional, like kids say these days, some of these identities overlap like Venn diagrams even if I'm lumping them in a pile right now.

There are twin questions that people ask me sometimes. One, does it matter who writes a story? And two, have things changed in your field, is it better now?

The answer is, yes, it matters. It used to be that I had only a couple of writers I identified with to look at and follow, and now a constellation of writers seems to be revealing itself. It doesn't mean that all the other stars in the sky cease to exist, only that you can see more shapes in the night sky. I'm sure others are having this same experience.

Question number two: has it changed? Is it better now? As you can obviously see, it has changed for the better. Thirteen years ago I wouldn't have thought I'd be writing this introduction, nor that you would be reading some of the stories contained here.

However, this doesn't mean that there aren't more changes that must take place. I recall, still, not so long ago, editors telling me I should modify the names of my characters to be less Mexican or that my characters were not relatable because they were Latin American.

The 2017 #BlackSpecFic Report showed that 4.3% of the stories published by speculative fiction publications were written by Black authors. The Cooperative Children's Book Center's statistics on the number of children's books by and about people of color show that even though 40% of people in the US are people of color, Black, Latino and Native authors wrote less than 6% of the new children's books published in 2016. In the field of romance, the 2017 Ripped Bodice's Diversity Report indicates that 6.2% of all romance books were published by authors of color. The Ripped Bodice is a bookstore and it's also worth noting that 60% of The Ripped Bodice's 2017 bestsellers were written by authors of color.

So, yes, the publishing landscape is changing, but it is easy to overestimate our successes.

It is easy to declare that diversity is a done deal, or even worse, that diversity is a trend, a fad, which has run its course. It is easy to churn lists that purport to contain the 10 Best Science Fiction Novels of all time and find out that the only woman who made the list was Mary Shelley. Or to find threads with people saying that women can't write Lovecraftian fiction because women are able to give birth and therefore cannot understand cosmic horror (I am not making this comment up).

It's also easy for me to get hate mail for publishing an all-women anthology, including a comment which I screen-caped and kept on my desktop for a long time which said that I, and all the women I had published, should be led to the gas chambers, complete with a picture of Hitler.

So, yes, all of this is easy.

What is hard is to build a better, more inclusive publishing community. It's hard to read widely, to read beyond the things that you are used to, to organize events which feature a broad variety of guests, to write lists which go beyond the usual suspects. It's hard, but it's not impossible. Librarians can make displays that highlight the diversity and variety of genre books available, people in charge of concoms can research new and different speakers, writers can go beyond the customary with their list of Best Science Fiction Novels so that they don't end up only with Mary Shelley as the lone woman in the field.

We call speculative fiction the literature of the imagination, so why not imagine a future in which a young writer can find plenty of authors to emulate? A future in which that author is not silent and scared and feeling like she has no stories to tell, as I was 13 years ago when I began my writing journey.

If you are reading this volume, perhaps it will give you hope for the future of our field. All these tales—whether they be short stories, novelettes or novellas—show you a beautiful and dazzling sky. We live in an ever-expanding universe. This can also be true of speculative fiction.

Tlazohcamati. Gracias. Thanks. Merci.

—Silvia Moreno-Garcia, November 2018

The 2018 Nebula Award Finalists

Best Novel

- **Winner:** *The Stone Sky*, N.K. Jemisin (Orbit US; Orbit UK)
- *Amberlough*, Lara Elena Donnelly (Tor)
- *The Strange Case of the Alchemist's Daughter*, Theodora Goss (Saga)
- *Spoonbenders*, Daryl Gregory (Knopf; riverrun)
- *Six Wakes*, Mur Lafferty (Orbit US)
- *Jade City*, Fonda Lee (Orbit US; Orbit UK)
- *Autonomous*, Annalee Newitz (Tor; Orbit UK 2018)

Best Novella

- **Winner:** *All Systems Red*, Martha Wells (Tor.com Publishing)
- *River of Teeth*, Sarah Gailey (Tor.com Publishing)
- *Passing Strange*, Ellen Klages (Tor.com Publishing)
- *And Then There Were (N-One)*, Sarah Pinsker (Uncanny 3-4/17)

- *Barry's Deal,* Lawrence M. Schoen (NobleFusion Press)
- *The Black Tides of Heaven,* JY Yang (Tor.com Publishing)

Best Novelette

- **Winner:** *A Human Stain,* Kelly Robson (Tor.com 1/4/17)
- *Dirty Old Town,* Richard Bowes (Magazine of Fantasy & Science Fiction 5-6/17)
- *Weaponized Math,* Jonathan P. Brazee (The Expanding Universe, Vol. 3)
- *Wind Will Rove,* Sarah Pinsker (Asimov's 9-10/17)
- *A Series of Steaks,* Vina Jie-Min Prasad (Clarkesworld 1/17)
- *Small Changes Over Long Periods of Time,* K.M. Szpara (Uncanny 5-6/17)

Best Short Story

- **Winner:** "Welcome to Your Authentic Indian Experience™", Rebecca Roanhorse (Apex8/17)
- "Fandom for Robots", Vina Jie-Min Prasad (Uncanny 9-10/17)
- "Utopia, LOL?", Jamie Wahls (Strange Horizons 6/5/17)
- "Clearly Lettered in a Mostly Steady Hand", Fran Wilde (Uncanny 9-10/17)
- "The Last Novelist (or A Dead Lizard in the Yard)", Matthew Kressel (Tor.com3/15/17)
- "Carnival Nine", Caroline M. Yoachim (Beneath Ceaseless Skies 5/11/17)

The Ray Bradbury Award for Outstanding Dramatic Presentation

- **Winner:** *Get Out* (Written by Jordan Peele)

- *The Good Place:* "Michael's Gambit" (Written by Michael Schur)
- *Logan* (screenplay by Scott Frank, James Mangold, and Michael Green)
- *The Shape of Water* (Screenplay by Guillermo del Toro and Vanessa Taylor)
- *Star Wars: The Last Jedi* (Written by Rian Johnson)
- *Wonder Woman* (Screenplay by Allan Heinberg)

The Andre Norton Award for Outstanding Young Adult Science Fiction or Fantasy Book

- **Winner:** *The Art of Starving*, Sam J. Miller (HarperTeen)
- *Exo,* Fonda Lee (Scholastic Press)
- *Weave a Circle Round,* Kari Maaren (Tor)
- *Want,* Cindy Pon (Simon Pulse)

Welcome to Your Authentic Indian Experience™
Rebecca Roanhorse

> *In the Great American Indian novel, when it*
> *is finally written, all of the white people will be*
> *Indians and all of the Indians will be ghosts.*
> —Sherman Alexie, *How to Write*
> *the Great American Indian Novel*

YOU MAINTAIN A MENU of a half dozen Experiences on your digital blackboard, but Vision Quest is the one the Tourists choose the most. That certainly makes your workday easy. All a Vision Quest requires is a dash of mystical shaman, a spirit animal (wolf usually, but birds of prey are on the upswing this year), and the approximation of a peyote experience. Tourists always come out of the Experience feeling spiritually transformed. (You've never actually tried peyote, but you did smoke your share of weed during that one year at Arizona State, and who's going to call you on the difference?) It's all 101 stuff, really, these Quests. But no other Indian working at Sedona Sweats can do it better. Your sales numbers are tops.

Your wife Theresa doesn't approve of the gig. Oh, she

likes you working, especially after that dismal stretch of unemployment the year before last when she almost left you,
but she thinks the job itself is demeaning.

"Our last name's not Trueblood," she complains when
you tell her about your *nom de rêve*.

"Nobody wants to buy a Vision Quest from a Jesse Turnblatt," you explain. "I need to sound more Indian."

"You are Indian," she says. "Turnblatt's Indian-sounding
enough because you're already Indian."

"We're not the right kind of Indian," you counter. "I
mean, we're Catholic, for Christ's sake."

What Theresa doesn't understand is that Tourists don't
want a real Indian experience. They want what they see in the
movies, and who can blame them? Movie Indians are terrific!
So you watch the same movies the Tourists do, until John
Dunbar becomes your spirit animal and Stands with Fists
your best girl. You memorize Johnny Depp's lines from *The
Lone Ranger* and hang a picture of Iron Eyes Cody in your
work locker. For a while you are really into Dustin Hoffman's
Little Big Man.

It's *Little Big Man* that does you in.

For a week in June, you convince your boss to offer a
Custer's Last Stand special, thinking there might be a Tour-
ist or two who want to live out a Crazy Horse Experience.
You even memorize some quotes attributed to the venerable
Sioux chief that you find on the internet. You plan to make
it real authentic.

But you don't get a single taker. Your numbers nosedive.

Management in Phoenix notices, and Boss drops it from
the blackboard by Fourth of July weekend. He yells at you to
stop screwing around, accuses you of trying to be an artiste
or whatnot.

"Tourists don't come to Sedona Sweats to live out a god-
damn battle," Boss says in the break room over lunch one
day, "especially if the white guy loses. They come here to find

themselves." Boss waves his hand in the air in an approximation of something vaguely prayer-like. "It's a spiritual experience we're offering. Top quality. The fucking best."

DarAnne, your Navajo co-worker with the pretty smile
and the perfect teeth, snorts loudly. She takes a bite of her
sandwich, mutton by the looks of it. Her jaw works, her
sharp teeth flash white. She waits until she's finished chewing to say, "Nothing spiritual about Squaw Fantasy."

Squaw Fantasy is Boss's latest idea, his way to get the
numbers up and impress Management. DarAnne and a few
others have complained about the use of the ugly slur, the
inclusion of a sexual fantasy as an Experience at all. But Boss
is unmoved, especially when the first week's numbers roll in.
Biggest seller yet.

Boss looks over at you. "What do you think?"

Boss is Pima, with a bushy mustache and a thick head
of still-dark hair. You admire that about him. Virility. Boss
makes being a man look easy. Makes everything look easy.
Real authentic-like.

DarAnne tilts her head, long beaded earrings swinging,
and waits. Her painted nails click impatiently against the For-
mica lunch table. You can smell the onion in her sandwich.

Your mouth is dry like the red rock desert you can see
outside your window. If you say Squaw Fantasy is demeaning, Boss will mock you, call you a pussy, or worse. If you say
you think it's okay, DarAnne and her crew will put you on
the guys-who-are-assholes list and you'll deserve it.

You sip your bottled water, stalling. Decide that in the
wake of the Crazy Horse debacle that Boss's approval means
more than DarAnne's, and venture, "I mean, if the Tourists
like it . . ."

Boss slaps the table, triumphant. DarAnne's face twists
in disgust. "What does Theresa think of that, eh, Jesse?" she
spits at you. "You tell her Boss is thinking of adding Savage
Braves to the menu next? He's gonna have you in a loincloth

and hair down to your ass, see how you like it."

Your face heats up, embarrassed. You push away from the table, too quickly, and the flimsy top teeters. You can hear Boss's shouts of protest as his vending machine lemonade tilts dangerously, and DarAnne's mocking laugh, but it all comes to your ears through a shroud of thick cotton. You mumble something about getting back to work. The sound of arguing trails you down the hall.

⊛   ⊛   ⊛

You change in the locker room and shuffle down to the pod marked with your name. You unlock the hatch and crawl in. Some people find the pods claustrophobic, but you like the cool metal container, the tight fit. It's comforting. The VR helmet fits snugly on your head, the breathing mask over your nose and mouth.

With a shiver of anticipation, you give the pod your Experience setting. Add the other necessary details to flesh things out. The screen prompts you to pick a Tourist connection from a waiting list, but you ignore it, blinking through the option screens until you get to the final confirmation. You brace for the mild nausea that always comes when you Relocate in and out of an Experience.

The first sensation is always smell. Sweetgrass and wood smoke and the rich loam of the northern plains. Even though it's fake, receptors firing under the coaxing of a machine, you relax into the scents. You grew up in the desert, among people who appreciate cedar and pinon and red earth, but there's still something home-like about this prairie place.

Or maybe you watch too much TV. You really aren't sure anymore.

You find yourself on a wide grassy plain, somewhere in the upper Midwest of a bygone era. Bison roam in the distance. A hawk soars overhead.

You are alone, you know this, but it doesn't stop you from looking around to make sure. This thing you are about to do. Well, you would be humiliated if anyone found out. Because you keep thinking about what DarAnne said. Squaw Fantasy and Savage Braves. Because the thing is, being sexy doesn't disgust you the way it does DarAnne. You've never been one of those guys. The star athlete or the cool kid. It's tempting to think of all those Tourist women wanting you like that, even if it is just in an Experience.

You are now wearing a knee-length loincloth. A wave of black hair flows down your back. Your middle-aged paunch melts into rock-hard abs worthy of a romance novel cover model. You raise your chin and try out your best stoic look on a passing prairie dog. The little rodent chirps something back at you. You've heard prairie dogs can remember human faces, and you wonder what this one would say about you. Then you remember this is an Experience, so the prairie dog is no more real than the caricature of an Indian you have conjured up.

You wonder what Theresa would think if she saw you like this.

The world shivers. The pod screen blinks on. Someone wants your Experience.

A Tourist, asking for you. Completely normal. Expected. No need for that panicky hot breath rattling through your mask.

You scroll through the Tourist's requirements.

Experience Type: Vision Quest.

Tribe: Plains Indian (nation nonspecific).

Favorite animal: Wolf.

These things are all familiar. Things you are good at faking. Things you get paid to pretend.

You drop the Savage Brave fantasy garb for buckskin pants and beaded leather moccasins. You keep your chest bare and muscled but you drape a rough wool blanket across your shoulders for dignity. Your impressive abs are still visible.

The sun is setting and you turn to put the artificial dusk

at your back, prepared to meet your Tourist. You run through your list of Indian names to bestow upon your Tourist once the Vision Quest is over. You like to keep the names fresh, never using the same one in case the Tourists ever compare notes. For a while you cheated and used one of those naming things on the internet where you enter your favorite flower and the street you grew up on and it gives you your Indian name, but there were too many Tourists that grew up on Elm or Park and you found yourself getting repetitive. You try to base the names on appearances now. Hair color, eye, some distinguishing feature. Tourists really seem to like it.

This Tourist is younger than you expected. Sedona Sweats caters to New Agers, the kind from Los Angeles or Scottsdale with impressive bank accounts. But the man coming up the hill, squinting into the setting sun, is in his late twenties. Medium height and build with pale spotty skin and brown hair. The guy looks normal enough, but there's something sad about him.

Maybe he's lost.

You imagine a lot of Tourists are lost.

Maybe he's someone who works a day job just like you, saving up money for this once-in-a-lifetime Indian Experience™. Maybe he's desperate, looking for purpose in his own shitty world and thinking Indians have all the answers. Maybe he just wants something that's authentic.

You like that. The idea that Tourists come to you to experience something real. DarAnne has it wrong. The Tourists aren't all bad. They're just needy.

You plant your feet in a wide welcoming stance and raise one hand. "How," you intone, as the man stops a few feet in front of you.

The man flushes, a bright pinkish tone. You can't tell if he's nervous or embarrassed. Maybe both? But he raises his hand, palm forward, and says, "How," right back.

"Have you come seeking wisdom, my son?" you ask in

your best broken English accent. "Come. I will show you great wisdom." You sweep your arm across the prairie. "We look to brother wolf –"

The man rolls his eyes.

What?

You stutter to a pause. Are you doing something wrong? Is the accent no good? Too little? Too much?

You visualize the requirements checklist. You are positive he chose wolf. Positive. So you press on. "My brother wolf," you say again, this time sounding much more Indian, you are sure.

"I'm sorry," the man says, interrupting. "This wasn't what I wanted. I've made a mistake."

"But you picked it on the menu!" In the confusion of the moment, you drop your accent. Is it too late to go back and say it right?

The man's lips curl up in a grimace, like you have confirmed his worst suspicions. He shakes his head. "I was looking for something more authentic."

Something in your chest seizes up.

"I can fix it," you say.

"No, it's alright. I'll find someone else." He turns to go.

You can't afford another bad mark on your record. No more screw-ups or you're out. Boss made that clear enough. "At least give me a chance," you plead.

"It's okay," he says over his shoulder.

This is bad. Does this man not know what a good Indian you are? "Please!"

The man turns back to you, his face thoughtful.

You feel a surge of hope. This can be fixed, and you know exactly how. "I can give you a name. Something you can call yourself when you need to feel strong. It's authentic," you add enthusiastically. "From a real Indian." That much is true.

The man looks a little more open, and he doesn't say no. That's good enough.

You study the man's dusky hair, his pinkish skin. His long skinny legs. He reminds you a bit of the flamingos at the Albuquerque zoo, but you are pretty sure no one wants to be named after those strange creatures. It must be something good. Something . . . spiritual.

"Your name is Pale Crow," you offer. Birds are still on your mind.

At the look on the man's face, you reconsider. "No, no, it is White"—yes, that's better than pale—"Wolf. White Wolf."

"White Wolf?" There's a note of interest in his voice.

You nod sagely. You *knew* the man had picked wolf. Your eyes meet. Uncomfortably. White Wolf coughs into his hand. "I really should be getting back."

"But you paid for the whole experience. Are you sure?"

White Wolf is already walking away.

"But . . ."

You feel the exact moment he Relocates out of the Experience. A sensation like part of your soul is being stretched too thin. Then, a sort of whiplash, as you let go.

⊗   ⊗   ⊗

The Hey U.S.A. bar is the only Indian bar in Sedona. The basement level of a driftwood-paneled strip mall across the street from work. It's packed with the after-shift crowd, most of them pod jockeys like you, but also a few roadside jewelry hawkers and restaurant stiffs still smelling like frybread grease. You're lucky to find a spot at the far end next to the server's station. You slip onto the plastic-covered barstool and raise a hand to get the bartender's attention.

"So what do you really think?" asks a voice to your right. DarAnne is staring at you, her eyes accusing and her posture tense.

This is it. A second chance. Your opportunity to stay off the assholes list. You need to get this right. You try to think of something clever to say, something that would impress her but let you save face, too. But you're never been all that clever, so you stick to the truth.

"I think I really need this job," you admit.

DarAnne's shoulders relax.

"Scooch over," she says to the man on the other side of her, and he obligingly shifts off his stool to let her sit. "I knew it," she says. "Why didn't you stick up for me? Why are you so afraid of Boss?"

"I'm not afraid of Boss. I'm afraid of Theresa leaving me. And unemployment."

"You gotta get a backbone, Jesse, is all."

You realize the bartender is waiting, impatient. You drink the same thing every time you come here, a single Coors Light in a cold bottle. But the bartender never remembers you, or your order. You turn to offer to buy one for DarAnne, but she's already gone, back with her crew.

You drink your beer alone, wait a reasonable amount of time, and leave.

White Wolf is waiting for you under the streetlight at the corner.

The bright neon Indian Chief that squats atop Sedona Sweats hovers behind him in pinks and blues and yellows, his huge hand blinking up and down in greeting. White puffs of smoke signals flicker up, up and away beyond his far shoulder.

You don't recognize White Wolf at first. Most people change themselves a little within the construct of the Experience. Nothing wrong with being thinner, taller, a little better looking. But White Wolf looks exactly the same. Nondescript brown hair, pale skin, long legs.

"How." White Wolf raises his hand, unconsciously mimicking the big neon Chief. At least he has the decency to look embarrassed when he does it.

"You." You are so surprised that the accusation is the first thing out of your mouth. "How did you find me?"

"Trueblood, right? I asked around."

"And people told you?" This is very against the rules.

"I asked who the best Spirit Guide was. If I was going to buy a Vision Quest, who should I go to. Everyone said you."

You flush, feeling vindicated, but also annoyed that your co-workers had given your name out to a Tourist. "I tried to tell you," you say ungraciously.

"I should have listened." White Wolf smiles, a faint shifting of his mouth into something like contrition. An awkward pause ensues.

"We're really not supposed to fraternize," you finally say.

"I know, I just . . . I just wanted to apologize. For ruining the Experience like that."

"It's no big deal," you say, gracious this time. "You paid, right?"

"Yeah."

"It's just . . ." You know this is your ego talking, but you need to know. "Did I do something wrong?"

"No, it was me. You were great. It's just, I had a great grandmother who was Cherokee, and I think being there, seeing everything. Well, it really stirred something in me. Like, ancestral memory or something."

You've heard of ancestral memories, but you've also heard of people claiming Cherokee blood where there is none. Theresa calls them "pretendians," but you think that's unkind. Maybe White Wolf really is Cherokee. You don't know any Cherokees, so maybe they really do look like this guy. There's a half-Tlingit in payroll and he's pale.

"Well, I've got to get home," you say. "My wife, and all."

White Wolf nods. "Sure, sure. I just. Thank you."

"For what?"

But White Wolf's already walking away. "See you around."

A little déjà vu shudders your bones but you chalk it up to Tourists. Who understands them, anyway?

You go home to Theresa.

⊛   ⊛   ⊛

As soon as you slide into your pod the next day, your monitor lights up. There's already a Tourist on deck and waiting.

"Shit," you mutter, pulling up the menu and scrolling quickly through the requirements. Everything looks good, good, except . . . a sliver of panic when you see that a specific tribe has been requested. Cherokee. You don't know anything about Cherokees. What they wore back then, their ceremonies. The only Cherokee you know is . . .

White Wolf shimmers into your Experience.

In your haste, you have forgotten to put on your buckskin. Your Experience-self still wears Wranglers and Nikes. Boss would be pissed to see you this sloppy.

"Why are you back?" you ask.

"I thought maybe we could just talk."

"About what?"

White Wolf shrugs. "Doesn't matter. Whatever."

"I can't."

"Why not? This is my time. I'm paying."

You feel a little panicked. A Tourist has never broken protocol like this before. Part of why the Experience works is that everyone knows their role. But White Wolf don't seem to care about the rules.

"I can just keep coming back," he says. "I have money, you know."

"You'll get me in trouble."

"I won't. I just . . ." White Wolf hesitates. Something in him slumps. What you read as arrogance now looks like desperation. "I need a friend."

You know that feeling. The truth is, you could use a friend, too. Someone to talk to. What could the harm be? You'll just be two men, talking.

Not here, though. You still need to work. "How about the bar?"

"The place from last night?"

"I get off at 11p.m."

⊛   ⊛   ⊛

When you get there around 11:30 p.m., the bar is busy but you recognize White Wolf immediately. A skinny white guy stands out at the Hey U.S.A. It's funny. Under this light, in this crowd, White Wolf could pass for Native of some kind. One of those 1/64th guys, at least. Maybe he really is a little Cherokee from way back when.

White Wolf waves you over to an empty booth. A Coors Light waits for you. You slide into the booth and wrap a hand around the cool damp skin of the bottle, pleasantly surprised.

"A lucky guess, did I get it right?"

You nod and take a sip. That first sip is always magic. Like how you imagine Golden, Colorado must feel like on a winter morning.

"So," White Wolf says, "tell me about yourself."

You look around the bar for familiar faces. Are you really going to do this? Tell a Tourist about your life? Your real life? A little voice in your head whispers that maybe this isn't so smart. Boss could find out and get mad. DarAnne could make fun of you. Besides, White Wolf will want a cool story, something real authentic, and all you have is an aging three-bedroom ranch and a student loan.

But he's looking at you, friendly interest, and nobody looks at you like that much anymore, not even Theresa. So you talk.

Not everything.

But some. Enough.

Enough that when the bartender calls last call you realize you've been talking for two hours.

When you stand up to go, White Wolf stands up, too. You shake hands, Indian-style, which makes you smile. You didn't expect it, but you've got a good, good feeling.

"So, same time tomorrow?" White Wolf asks.

You're tempted, but, "No, Theresa will kill me if I stay

out this late two nights in a row." And then, "But how about Friday?"

"Friday it is." White Wolf touches your shoulder. "See you then, Jesse."

You feel a warm flutter of anticipation for Friday. "See you."

⊛   ⊕   ◈

Friday you are there by 11:05 p.m. White Wolf laughs when he sees your face, and you grin back, only a little embarrassed. This time you pay for the drinks, and the two of you pick up right where you left off. It's so easy. White Wolf never seems to tire of your stories and it's been so long since you had a new friend to tell them to, that you can't seem to quit. It turns out White Wolf loves Kevin Costner, too, and you take turns quoting lines at each other until White Wolf stumps you with a Wind in His Hair quote.

"Are you sure that's in the movie?"

"It's Lakota!"

You won't admit it, but you're impressed with how good White Wolf's Lakota sounds.

White Wolf smiles. "Looks like I know something you don't."

You wave it away good-naturedly, but vow to watch the movie again.

Time flies and once again, after last call, you both stand outside under the Big Chief. You happily agree to meet again next Tuesday. And the following Friday. Until it becomes your new routine.

The month passes quickly. The next month, too.

"You seem too happy," Theresa says one night, sounding suspicious.

You grin and wrap your arms around your wife, pulling her close until her rose-scented shampoo fills your nose. "Just made a friend, is all. A guy from work." You decide to keep it vague. Hanging with White Wolf, who you've long stopped thinking of as just a Tourist, would be hard to explain.

"You're not stepping out on me, Jesse Turnblatt? Because I will—"

You cut her off with a kiss. "Are you jealous?"

"Should I be?"

"Never."

She sniffs, but lets you kiss her again, her soft body tight against yours.

"I love you," you murmur as your hands dip under her shirt.

"You better."

          ⊚   ⊚   ⊚

Tuesday morning and you can't breathe. Your nose is a deluge of snot and your joints ache. Theresa calls in sick for you and bundles you in bed with a bowl of stew. You're supposed to meet White Wolf for your usual drink, but you're much too sick. You consider sending Theresa with a note, but decided against it. It's only one night. White Wolf will understand.

But by Friday the coughing has become a deep rough bellow that shakes your whole chest. When Theresa calls in sick for you again, you make sure your cough is loud enough for Boss to hear it. Pray he doesn't dock you for the days you're missing. But what you're most worried about is standing up White Wolf again.

"Do you think you could go for me?" you ask Theresa.

"What, down to the bar? I don't drink."

"I'm not asking you to drink. Just to meet him, let him know I'm sick. He's probably thinking I forgot about him."

"Can't you call him?"

"I don't have his number."

"Fine, then. What's his name?"

You hesitate. Realize you don't know. The only name you know is the one you gave him. "White Wolf."

"Okay, then. Get some rest."

Theresa doesn't get back until almost 1 a.m. "Where were

you?" you ask, alarmed. Is that a rosy flush in her cheeks, the scent of Cherry Coke on her breath?

"At the bar like you asked me to."

"What took so long?"

She huffs. "Did you want me to go or not?"

"Yes, but . . . well, did you see him?"

She nods, smiles a little smile that you've never seen on her before.

"What is it?" Something inside you shrinks.

"A nice man. Real nice. You didn't tell me he was Cherokee."

❂   ❂   ❂

By Monday you're able to drag yourself back to work. There's a note taped to your locker to go see Boss. You find him in his office, looking through the reports that he sends to Management every week.

"I hired a new guy."

You swallow the excuses you've prepared to explain how sick you were, your promises to get your numbers up. They become a hard ball in your throat.

"Sorry, Jesse." Boss actually does look a little sorry. "This guy is good, a real rez guy. Last name's 'Wolf'. I mean, shit, you can't get more Indian than that. The Tourists are going to eat it up."

"The Tourists love me, too." You sound whiny, but you can't help it. There's a sinking feeling in your gut that tells you this is bad, bad, bad.

"You're good, Jesse. But nobody knows anything about Pueblo Indians, so all you've got is that TV shit. This guy, he's . . ." Boss snaps his fingers, trying to conjure the word.

"Authentic?" A whisper.

Boss points his finger like a gun. "Bingo. Look, if another pod opens up, I'll call you."

"You gave him my pod?"

Boss's head snaps up, wary. You must have yelled that. He

reaches over to tap a button on his phone and call security.

"Wait!" you protest.

But the men in uniforms are already there to escort you out.

◎   ◎   ◎

You can't go home to Teresa. You just can't. So you head to the Hey U.S.A. It's a different crowd than you're used to. An afternoon crowd. Heavy boozers and people without jobs. You laugh because you fit right in.

The guys next to you are doing shots. Tiny glasses of rheumy dark liquor lined up in a row. You haven't done shots since college but when one of the men offers you one, you take it. Choke on the cheap whiskey that burns down your throat. Two more and the edges of your panic start to blur soft and tolerable. You can't remember what time it is when you get up to leave, but the Big Chief is bright in the night sky.

You stumble through the door and run smack into DarAnne. She growls at you, and you try to stutter out an apology but a heavy hand comes down on your shoulder before you get the words out.

"This asshole bothering you?"

You recognize that voice. "White Wolf?" It's him. But he looks different to you. Something you can't quite place. Maybe it's the ribbon shirt he's wearing, or the bone choker around his neck. Is his skin a little tanner than it was last week?

"Do you know this guy?" DarAnne asks, and you think she's talking to you, but her head is turned towards White Wolf.

"Never seen him," White Wolf says as he stares you down, and under that confident glare you almost believe him. Almost forget that you've told this man things about you even Theresa doesn't know.

"It's me," you protest, but your voice comes out in a

whiskey-slurred squeak that doesn't even sound like you.

"Fucking glonnies," DarAnne mutters as she pushes past you. "Always making a scene."

"I think you better go, buddy," White Wolf says. Not unkindly, if you were in fact strangers, if you weren't actually buddies. But you are, and you clutch at his shirtsleeve, shouting something about friendship and Theresa and then the world melts into a blur until you feel the hard slap of concrete against your shoulder and the taste of blood on your lip where you bit it and a solid kick to your gut until the whiskey comes up the way it went down and then the Big Chief is blinking at you, How, How, How, until the darkness comes to claim you and the lights all flicker out.

⊚   ⊛   ⊛

You wake up in the gutter. The fucking gutter. With your head aching and your mouth as dry and rotted as month-old roadkill. The sun is up, Arizona fire beating across your skin. Your clothes are filthy and your shoes are missing and there's a smear of blood down your chin and drying flakes in the creases of your neck. Your hands are chapped raw. And you can't remember why.

But then you do.

And the humiliation sits heavy on your bruised up shoulder, a dark shame that defies the desert sun. Your job. DarAnne ignoring you like that. White Wolf kicking your ass. And you out all night, drunk in a downtown gutter. It all feels like a terrible dream, like the worst kind. The ones you can't wake up from because it's real life.

Your car isn't where you left it, likely towed with the street sweepers, so you trudge your way home on sock feet. Three miles on asphalt streets until you see your highly-mortgaged three-bedroom ranch. And for once the place looks beautiful, like the day you bought it. Tears gather in your eyes as you push open the door.

"Theresa," you call. She's going to be pissed, and you're

going to have to talk fast, explain the whole drinking thing (it was one time!) and getting fired (I'll find a new job, I promise), but right now all you want is to wrap her in your arms and let her rose-scent fill your nose like good medicine.

"Theresa," you call again, as you limp through the living room. Veer off to look in the bedroom, check behind the closed bathroom door. But what you see in the bathroom makes you pause. Things are missing. Her toothbrush, the pack of birth control, contact lens solution.

"Theresa!?" and this time you are close to panic as you hobble down the hall to the kitchen.

The smell hits you first. The scent of fresh coffee, bright and familiar.

When you see the person sitting calmly at the kitchen table, their back to you, you relax. But that's not Theresa.

He turns slightly, enough so you can catch his profile, and says, "Come on in, Jesse."

"What the fuck are you doing here?"

White Wolf winces, as if your words hurt him. "You better have a seat."

"What did you do to my wife?!"

"I didn't do anything to your wife." He picks up a small folded piece of paper, holds it out. You snatch it from his fingers and move so you can see his face. The note in your hand feels like wildfire, something with the potential to sear you to the bone. You want to rip it wide open, you want to flee before its revelations scar you. You ache to read it now, now, but you won't give him the satisfaction of your desperation.

"So now you remember me," you huff.

"I apologize for that. But you were making a scene and I couldn't have you upsetting DarAnne."

You want to ask how he knows DarAnne, how he was there with her in the first place. But you already know. Boss said the new guy's name was Wolf.

"You're a real son of a bitch, you know that?"

White Wolf looks away from you, that same pained look on his face. Like you're embarrassing yourself again. "Why don't you help yourself to some coffee," he says, gesturing to the coffee pot. Your coffee pot.

"I don't need your permission to get coffee in my own house," you shout.

"Okay," he says, leaning back. You can't help but notice how handsome he looks, his dark hair a little longer, the choker on his neck setting off the arch of his high cheekbones.

You take your time getting coffee – sugar, creamer which you would never usually take –before you drop into the seat across from him. Only then do you open the note, hands trembling, dread twisting hard in your gut.

"She's gone to her mother's," White Wolf explains as you read the same words on the page. "For her own safety. She wants you out by the time she gets back."

"What did you tell her?"

"Only the truth. That you got yourself fired, that you were on a bender, drunk in some alleyway downtown like a bad stereotype." He leans in. "You've been gone for two days."

You blink. It's true, but it's not true, too.

"Theresa wouldn't . . ." But she would, wouldn't she? She'd said it a million times, given you a million chances.

"She needs a real man, Jesse. Someone who can take care of her."

"And that's you?" You muster all the scorn you can when you say that, but it comes out more a question than a judgment. You remember how you gave him the benefit of the doubt on that whole Cherokee thing, how you thought "pretendian" was cruel.

He clears his throat. Stands.

"It's time for you to go," he says. "I promised Theresa you'd be gone, and I've got to get to work soon." Something about him seems to expand, to take up the space you once occupied. Until you feel small, superfluous.

"Did you ever think," he says, his voice thoughtful, his head tilted to study you like a strange foreign body, "that maybe this is my experience, and you're the tourist here?"

"This is my house," you protest, but you're not sure you believe it now. Your head hurts. The coffee in your hand is already cold. How long have you been sitting here? Your thoughts blur to histories, your words become nothing more than forgotten facts and half-truths. Your heart, a dusty repository for lost loves and desires, never realized.

"Not anymore," he says.

Nausea rolls over you. That same stretching sensation you get when you Relocate out of an Experience.

Whiplash, and then . . .

You let go.

THE END

A Series of Steaks
Vina Jie-Min Prasad

ALL KNOWN FORGERIES ARE tales of failure. The people who get into the newsfeeds for their brilliant attempts to cheat the system with their fraudulent Renaissance masterpieces or their stacks of fake cheques, well, they might be successful artists, but they certainly haven't been successful at *forgery*.

The best forgeries are the ones that disappear from notice—a second-rate still-life mouldering away in gallery storage, a battered old 50-yuan note at the bottom of a cashier drawer—or even a printed strip of Matsusaka beef, sliding between someone's parted lips.

⊛   ⊛   ⊛

Forging beef is similar to printmaking—every step of the process has to be done with the final print in mind. A red that's too dark looks putrid, a white that's too pure looks artificial. All beef is supposed to come from a cow, so stipple the red with dots, flecks, lines of white to fake variance in muscle fibre regions. Cows are similar, but cows aren't uniform—use fractals to randomise marbling after defining the basic look. Cut the sheets of beef manually to get an authentic ragged edge, don't get lazy and depend on the bioprinter for that.

Days of research and calibration and cursing the printer will all vanish into someone's gullet in seconds, if the job's done right.

Helena Li Yuanhui of Splendid Beef Enterprises is an expert in doing the job right.

The trick is not to get too ambitious. Most forgers are caught out by the smallest errors—a tiny amount of period-inaccurate pigment, a crack in the oil paint that looks too artificial, or a misplaced watermark on a passport. Printing something large increases the chances of a fatal misstep. Stick with small-scale jobs, stick with a small group of regular clients, and in time, Splendid Beef Enterprises will turn enough of a profit for Helena to get a *real* name change, leave Nanjing, and forget this whole sorry venture ever happened.

As Helena's loading the beef into refrigerated boxes for drone delivery, a notification pops up on her iKontakt frames. Helena sighs, turns the volume on her earpiece down, and takes the call.

"Hi, Mr Chan, could you switch to a secure line? You just need to tap the button with a lock icon, it's very easy."

"Nonsense!" Mr Chan booms. "If the government were going to catch us they'd have done so by now! Anyway, I just called to tell you how pleased I am with the latest batch. Such a shame, though, all that talent and your work just gets gobbled up in seconds—tell you what, girl, for the next beef special, how about I tell everyone that the beef came from one of those fancy vertical farms? I'm sure they'd have nice things to say then!"

"Please don't," Helena says, careful not to let her Cantonese accent slip through. It tends to show after long periods without any human interaction, which is an apt summary of the past few months. "It's best if no one pays attention to it."

"You know, Helena, you do good work, but I'm very concerned about your self-esteem, I know if I printed something like that I'd want everyone to appreciate it! Let me tell you about this article my daughter sent me, you know research says that people without friends are prone to . . ." Mr Chan rambles on as Helena sticks the labels on the boxes—Grilliam Shakespeare, Gyuuzen Sukiyaki, Fatty Chan's Restaurant—and thankfully hangs up before Helena sinks into further depression. She takes her iKontakt off before heading to the drone delivery office, giving herself some time to recover from Mr Chan's relentless cheerfulness.

Helena has five missed calls by the time she gets back. A red phone icon blares at the corner of her vision before blinking out, replaced by the incoming-call notification. It's secured and anonymised, which is quite a change from usual. She pops the earpiece in.

"Yeah, Mr Chan?"

"This isn't Mr Chan," someone says. "I have a job for Splendid Beef Enterprises."

"All right, sir. Could I get your name and what you need? If you could provide me with the deadline, that would help too."

"I prefer to remain anonymous," the man says.

"Yes, I understand, secrecy is rather important." Helena restrains the urge to roll her eyes at how needlessly cryptic this guy is. "Could I know about the deadline and brief?"

"I need two hundred T-bone steaks by the 8th of August. 38.1 to 40.2 millimeter thickness for each one." A notification to download t-bone_info.KZIP pops up on her lenses. The most ambitious venture Helena's undertaken in the past few months has been Gyuuzen's strips of marbled sukiyaki, and even that felt a bit like pushing it. A whole steak? Hell no.

"I'm sorry, sir, but I don't think my business can handle that. Perhaps you could try—"

"I think you'll be interested in this job, Helen Lee Jyun Wai."

Shit.

⊛   ⊛   ⊛

A Sculpere 9410S only takes thirty minutes to disassemble, if you know the right tricks. Manually eject the cell cartridges, slide the external casing off to expose the inner screws, and detach the print heads before disassembling the power unit. There are a few extra steps in this case—for instance, the stickers that say "Property of Hong Kong Scientific University" and "Bioprinting Lab A5" all need to be removed—but a bit of anti-adhesive spray will ensure that everything's on schedule. Ideally she'd buy a new printer, but she needs to save her cash for the name change once she hits Nanjing.

It's not expulsion if you leave before you get kicked out, she tells herself, but even she can tell that's a lie.

⊛   ⊛   ⊛

It's possible to get a sense of a client's priorities just from the documents they send. For instance, Mr Chan usually mentions some recipes that he's considering, and Ms Huang from Gyuuzen tends to attach examples of the marbling patterns she wants. This new client seems to have attached a whole document dedicated to the recent amendments in the criminal code, with the ones relevant to Helena ("five-year statute of limitations", "possible death penalty") conveniently highlighted in neon yellow.

Sadly, this level of detail hasn't carried over to the spec sheet.

"Hi again, sir," Helena says. "I've read through what you've sent, but I really need more details before starting on the job. Could you provide me with the full measurements? I'll need the expected length and breadth in addition to the thickness."

"It's already there. Learn to read."

"I *know* you filled that part in, sir," Helena says, gritting her teeth. "But we're a printing company, not a farm. I'll need more detail than '16-18 month cow, grain-fed, Hereford breed' to do the job properly."

"You went to university, didn't you? I'm sure you can figure out something as basic as that, even if you didn't graduate."

"Ha ha. Of course." Helena resists the urge to yank her earpiece out. "I'll get right on that. Also, there is the issue of pay..."

"Ah, yes. I'm quite sure the Yuen family is still itching to prosecute. How about you do the job, and in return, I don't tell them where you're hiding?"

"I'm sorry, sir, but even then I'll need an initial deposit to cover the printing, and of course there's the matter of the Hereford samples." *Which I already have in the bioreactor, but there is no way I'm letting you know that.*

"Fine. I'll expect detailed daily updates," Mr Anonymous says. "I know how you get with deadlines. Don't fuck it up."

"Of course not," Helena says. "Also, about the dead-line—would it be possible to push it back? Four weeks is quite short for this job."

"No," Mr Anonymous says curtly, and hangs up.

Helena lets out a very long breath so she doesn't end up screaming, and takes a moment to curse Mr Anonymous and his whole family in Cantonese.

It's physically impossible to complete the renders and finish the print in four weeks, unless she figures out a way to turn her printer into a time machine, and if that were possible she might as well go back and redo the past few years, or maybe her whole life. If she had majored in art, maybe she'd be a designer by now—or hell, while she's busy dreaming, she could even have been the next Raverat, the next Man-tuana—instead of a failed artist living in a shithole concrete box, clinging to the wreckage of all her past mistakes.

She leans against the wall for a while, exhales, then slaps on a proxy and starts drafting a help-wanted ad.

⚘ ⚘ ⚘

Lily Yonezawa (darknet username: yurisquared) arrives at Nanjing High Tech Industrial Park at 8.58 am. She's a short lady with long black hair and circle-framed iKontakts. She's wearing a loose, floaty dress, smooth lines of white tinged with yellow-green, and there's a large prismatic bracelet gleaming on her arm. In comparison, Helena is wearing her least holey black blouse and a pair of jeans, which is a step up from her usual attire of myoglobin-stained T-shirt and boxer shorts.

"So," Lily says in rapid, slightly-accented Mandarin as she bounds into the office. "This place is a beef place, right? I pulled some of the records once I got the address, hope you don't mind—anyway, what do you want me to help print or render or design or whatever? I know I said I had a background in confections and baking, but I'm totally open to anything!" She pumps her fist in a show of determination. The loose-fitting prismatic bracelet slides up and down.

Helena blinks at Lily with the weariness of someone who's spent most of their night frantically trying to make their office presentable. She decides to skip most of the briefing, as Lily doesn't seem like the sort who needs to be eased into anything.

"How much do you know about beef?"

"I used to watch a whole bunch of farming documentaries with my ex, does that count?"

"No. Here at Splendid Beef Enterprises—"

"Oh, by the way, do you have a logo? I searched your company registration but nothing really came up. Need me to design one?"

"*Here at Splendid Beef Enterprises,* we make fake beef and sell it to restaurants."

"So, like, soy-lentil stuff?"

"Homegrown cloned cell lines," Helena says. "Mostly Matsusaka, with some Hereford if clients specify it." She gestures at the bioreactor humming away in a corner.

"Wait, isn't fake food like those knockoff eggs made of calcium carbonate? If you're using cow cells, this seems pretty real to me." Clearly Lily has a more practical definition of fake than the China Food and Drug Administration.

"It's more like . . . let's say you have a painting in a gallery and you say it's by a famous artist. Lots of people would come look at it because of the name alone and write reviews talking about its exquisite use of chiaroscuro, as expected of the old masters, I can't believe that it looks so real even though it was painted centuries ago. But if you say, hey, this great painting was by some no-name loser, I was just lying about where it came from . . . well, it'd still be the same painting, but people would want all their money back."

"Oh, I get it," Lily says, scrutinising the bioreactor. She taps its shiny polymer shell with her knuckles, and her bracelet bumps against it. Helena tries not to wince. "Anyway, how legal is this? This meat forgery thing?"

"It's not illegal yet," Helena says. "It's kind of a grey area, really."

"Great!" Lily smacks her fist into her open palm. "Now, how can I help? I'm totally down for anything! You can even ask me to clean the office if you want—wow, this is *really* dusty, maybe I should just clean it to make sure—"

Helena reminds herself that having an assistant isn't entirely bad news. Wolfgang Beltracchi was only able to carry out large-scale forgeries with his assistant's help, and they even got along well enough to get married and have a kid without killing each other.

Then again, the Beltracchis both got caught, so maybe she shouldn't be too optimistic.

⊚   ⊚   ⊚

Cows that undergo extreme stress while waiting for slaughter are known as dark cutters. The stress causes them to deplete all their glycogen reserves, and when butchered, their meat turns a dark blackish-red. The meat of dark cutters is generally considered low-quality.

As a low-quality person waiting for slaughter, Helena understands how those cows feel. Mr Anonymous, stymied by the industrial park's regular sweeps for trackers and external cameras, has taken to sending Helena grainy aerial photographs of herself together with exhortations to work harder. This isn't exactly news—she already knew he had her details, and drones are pretty cheap—but still. When Lily raps on the door in the morning, Helena sometimes jolts awake in a panic before she realises that it isn't Mr Anonymous coming for her. This isn't helped by the fact that Lily's gentle knocks seem to be equivalent to other people's knockout blows.

By now Helena's introduced Lily to the basics, and she's a surprisingly quick study. It doesn't take her long to figure out how to randomise the fat marbling with Fractalgenr8, and she's been handed the task of printing the beef strips for Gyuuzen and Fatty Chan, then packing them for drone delivery. It's not ideal, but it lets Helena concentrate on the base model for the T-bone steak, which is the most complicated thing she's ever tried to render.

A T-bone steak is a combination of two cuts of meat, lean tenderloin and fatty strip steak, separated by a hard ridge of vertebral bone. Simply cutting into one is a near-religious experience, red meat parting under the knife to reveal smooth white bone, with the beef fat dripping down to pool on the plate. At least, that's what the socialites' food blogs say. To be accurate, they say something more like "omfg this is sooooooo good", "this bones giving me a boner lol", and "haha im so getting this sonic-cleaned for my collection!!!", but Helena pretends they actually meant to communicate something more coherent.

The problem is a lack of references. Most of the accessible photographs only provide a top-down view, and Helena's left to extrapolate from blurry videos and password-protected previews of bovine myology databases, which don't get her much closer to figuring out how the meat adheres to the bone. Helena's forced to dig through ancient research papers and diagrams that focus on where to cut to maximise meat yield, quantifying the difference between porterhouse and T-bone cuts, and not *hey, if you're reading this decades in the future, here's how to make a good facsimile of a steak.* Helena's tempted to run outside and scream in frustration, but Lily would probably insist on running outside and screaming with her as a matter of company solidarity, and with their luck, probably Mr Anonymous would find out about Lily right then, even after all the trouble she's taken to censor any mention of her new assistant from the files and the reports and *argh she needs sleep.*

Meanwhile, Lily's already scheduled everything for print, judging by the way she's spinning around in Helena's spare swivel chair.

"Hey, Lily," Helena says, stifling a yawn. "Why don't you play around with this for a bit? It's the base model for a T-bone steak. Just familiarise yourself with the fibre extrusion and mapping, see if you can get it to look like the reference photos. Don't worry, I've saved a copy elsewhere." *Good luck doing the impossible,* Helena doesn't say. *You're bound to have memorised the shortcut for 'undo' by the time I wake up.*

Helena wakes up to Lily humming a cheerful tune and a mostly-complete T-bone model rotating on her screen. She blinks a few times, but no—it's still there. Lily's effortlessly linking the rest of the meat, fat and gristle to the side of the bone, deforming the muscle fibres to account for the bone's presence.

"What did you do," Helena blurts out.

Lily turns around to face her, fiddling with her bracelet. "Uh, did I do it wrong?"

"Rotate it a bit, let me see the top view. How did you do it?"

"It's a little like the human vertebral column, isn't it?

There's plenty of references for that." She taps the screen twice, switching focus to an image of a human cross-section. "See how it attaches here and here? I just used that as a reference, and boom."

Ugh, Helena thinks to herself. She's been out of university for way too long if she's forgetting basic homology.

"Wait, *is* it correct? Did I mess up?"

"No, no," Helena says. "This is really good. Better than . . . well, better than I did, anyway."

"Awesome! Can I get a raise?"

"You can get yourself a sesame pancake," Helena says. "My treat."

※　※　※

The brief requires two hundred similar-but-unique steaks at randomised thicknesses of 38.1 to 40.2 mm, and the number and density of meat fibres pretty much precludes Helena from rendering it on her own rig. She doesn't want to pay to outsource computing power, so they're using spare processing cycles from other personal rigs and staggering the loads. Straightforward bone surfaces get rendered in afternoons, and fibre-dense tissues get rendered at off-peak hours.

It's three in the morning. Helena's in her Pokko the Penguin T-shirt and boxer shorts, and Lily's wearing Yayoi Kusama-ish pyjamas that make her look like she's been obliterated by a mass of polka dots. Both of them are staring at their screens, eating cups of Zhuzhu Brand Artificial Char Siew Noodles. As Lily's job moves to the front of Render@ Home's Finland queue, the graph updates to show a downtick in Mauritius. Helena's fingers frantically skim across the touchpad, queueing as many jobs as she can.

Her chopsticks scrape the bottom of the mycefoam cup, and she tilts the container to shovel the remaining fake pork fragments into her mouth. Zhuzhu's using extruded soy proteins, and they've punched up the glutamate percentage since she last bought them. The roasted char siew flavour is lacking, and the texture is crumby since the factory skimped on the extrusion time, but any hot food is practically heaven at this time of the night. Day. Whatever.

The thing about the rendering stage is that there's a lot of panic-infused downtime. After queueing the requests, they can't really do anything else—the requests might fail, or the rig might crash, or they might lose their place in the queue through some accident of fate and have to do everything all over again. There's nothing to do besides pray that the requests get through, stay awake until the server limit resets, and repeat the whole process until everything's done. Staying awake is easy for Helena, as Mr Anonymous has recently taken to sending pictures of rotting corpses to her iKontakt address, captioned "Work hard or this could be you". Lily seems to be halfway off to dreamland, possibly because she isn't seeing misshapen lumps of flesh every time she closes her eyes.

"So," Lily says, yawning. "How *did* you get into this business?"

Helena decides it's too much trouble to figure out a plausible lie, and settles for a very edited version of the truth. "I took art as an elective in high school. My school had a lot of printmaking and 3D printing equipment, so I used it to make custom merch in my spare time—you know, for people who wanted figurines of obscure anime characters, or whatever. Even designed and printed the packaging for them, just to make it look more official. I wanted to study art in university, but that didn't really work out. Long story short, I ended up moving here from Hong Kong, and since I had a background in printing and bootlegging . . . yeah. What about you?"

"Before the confectionery I did a whole bunch of odd jobs. I used to sell merch for my girlfriend's band, and that's how I got started with the short-order printing stuff. They were called POMEGRENADE—it was really hard to fit the whole name on a T-shirt. The keychains sold really well, though."

"What sort of band were they?"

"Sort of noise-rocky Cantopunk at first—there was this one really cute song I liked, *If Marriage Means The Death Of Love Then We Must Both Be Zombies*—but Cantonese music was a hard sell, even in Guangzhou, so they ended up being kind of a cover band."

"Oh, Guangzhou," Helena says in an attempt to sound knowledgeable, before realising that the only thing she knows about Guangzhou is that the Red Triad has a particularly profitable organ-printing business there. "Wait, you understand Cantonese?"

"Yeah," Lily says in Cantonese, tone-perfect. "No one really speaks it around here, so I haven't used it much."

"Oh my god, yes, it's so hard to find Canto-speaking people here." Helena immediately switches to Cantonese. "Why didn't you tell me sooner? I've been *dying* to speak it to someone."

"Sorry, it never came up so I figured it wasn't very relevant," Lily says. "Anyway, POMEGRENADE mostly did covers after that, you know, Kick Out The Jams, Zhongnanhai, Chaos Changan, Lightsabre Cocksucking Blues. Whatever got the crowd pumped up, and when they were moshing the hardest, they'd hit the crowd with the Cantopunk and just blast their faces off. I think it left more of an impression that way—like, start with the familiar, then this weird-ass surprise near the end—the merch table always got swamped after they did that."

"What happened with the girlfriend?"

"We broke up, but we keep in touch. Do you still do art?"

"Not really. The closest thing I get to art is this," Helena says, rummaging through the various boxes under the table to dig out her sketchbooks. She flips one open and hands it to Lily—white against red, nothing but full-page studies of marbling patterns, and it must be one of the earlier ones because it's downright amateurish. The lines are all over the place, that marbling on the Wagyu (is that even meant to be Wagyu?) is completely inaccurate, and, fuck, are those *tear stains*?

Lily turns the pages, tracing the swashes of colour with her finger. The hum of the overworked rig fills the room.

"It's awful, I know."

"What are you talking about?" Lily's gaze lingers on Helena's attempt at a fractal snowflake. "This is really trippy! If you ever want to do some album art, just let me know and I'll totally hook you up!"

Helena opens her mouth to say something about how she's not an artist, and how studies of beef marbling wouldn't make very good album covers, but faced with Lily's unbridled enthusiasm, she decides to nod instead.

Lily turns the page and it's that thing she did way back at the beginning, when she was thinking of using a cute cow as the company logo. It's derivative, it's kitsch, the whole thing looks like a degraded copy of someone else's ripoff drawing of a cow's head, and the fact that Lily's seriously scrutinising it makes Helena want to snatch the sketchbook back, toss it into the composter, and sink straight into the concrete floor.

The next page doesn't grant Helena a reprieve since there's a whole series of that stupid cow. Versions upon versions of happy cow faces grin straight at Lily, most of them surrounded by little hearts—what was she thinking? What do hearts even have to do with Splendid Beef Enterprises, anyway? Was it just that they were easy to draw?

"Man, I wish we had a logo because this would be super cute! I love the little hearts! It's like saying we put our heart and soul into whatever we do! Oh, wait, but was that what you meant?"

"It could be," Helena says, and thankfully the Colorado server opens before Lily can ask any further questions.

⊕   ⊕   ⊕

The brief requires status reports at the end of each workday, but this gradually falls by the wayside once they hit the point where workdays don't technically end, especially since Helena really doesn't want to look at an inbox full of increasingly creepy threats. They're at the pre-print stage, and Lily's given up on going back to her own place at night so they can have more time for calibration. What looks right on the screen might not look right once it's printed, and their lives for the past few days have devolved into staring at endless trays of 32-millimeter beef cubes and checking them for myoglobin concentration, colour match in different lighting conditions, fat striation depth, and a whole host of other factors.

There are so many ways for a forgery to go wrong, and only one way it can go right. Helena contemplates this philosophical quandary, and gently thunks her head against the back of her chair.

"Oh my god," Lily exclaims, shoving her chair back. "I can't take this anymore! I'm going out to eat something and then I'm getting some sleep. Do you want anything?" She straps on her bunny-patterned filter mask and her metallic sandals. "I'm gonna eat there, so I might take a while to get back."

"Sesame pancakes, thanks."

As Lily slams the door, Helena puts her iKontakt frames back on. The left lens flashes a stream of notifications—fifty-seven missed calls over the past five hours, all from an unknown number. Just then, another call comes in, and she reflexively taps the side of the frame.

"You haven't been updating me on your progress," Mr Anonymous says.

"I'm very sorry, sir," Helena says flatly, having reached the point of tiredness where she's ceased to feel anything beyond *god I want to sleep.* This sets Mr Anonymous on another rant covering the usual topics—poor work ethic, lack of commitment, informing the Yuen family, prosecution, possible death sentence—and Helena struggles to keep her mouth shut before she says something that she might regret.

"Maybe I should send someone to check on you right now," Mr Anonymous snarls, before abruptly hanging up.

Helena blearily types out a draft of the report, and makes a note to send a coherent version later in the day, once she gets some sleep and fixes the calibration so she's not telling him entirely bad news. Just as she's about to call Lily and ask her to get some hot soy milk to go with the sesame pancakes, the front door rattles in its frame like someone's trying to punch it down. Judging by the violence, it's probably Lily. Helena trudges over to open it.

It isn't. It's a bulky guy with a flat-top haircut. She stares at him for a moment, then tries to slam the door in his face. He forces the door open and shoves his way inside, grabbing Helena's arm, and all Helena can think is *I can't believe Mr Anonymous spent his money on this.*

He shoves her against the wall, gripping her wrist so hard that it's practically getting dented by his fingertips, and pulls out a switchblade, pressing it against the knuckle of her index finger. "Well, I'm not allowed to kill you, but I can fuck you up real bad. Don't really need all your fingers, do you, girl?"

She clears her throat, and struggles to keep her voice from shaking. "I need them to type—didn't your boss tell you that?"

"Shut up," Flat-Top says, flicking the switchblade once, then twice, thinking. "Don't need your face to type, do you?"

Just then, Lily steps through the door. Flat-Top can't see her from his angle, and Helena jerks her head, desperately communicating that she should stay out. Lily promptly moves closer.

Helena contemplates murder.

Lily edges towards both of them, slides her bracelet past her wrist and onto her knuckles, and makes a gesture at

Helena which either means 'move to your left' or 'I'm imitating a bird, but only with one hand'.

"Hey," Lily says loudly. "What's going on here?"

Flat-Top startles, loosening his grip on Helena's arm, and Helena dodges to the left. Just as Lily's fist meets his face in a truly vicious uppercut, Helena seizes the opportunity to kick him soundly in the shins.

His head hits the floor, and it's clear he won't be moving for a while, or ever. Considering Lily's normal level of violence towards the front door, this isn't surprising.

Lily crouches down to check Flat-Top's breathing. "Well, he's still alive. Do you prefer him that way?"

"Do *not* kill him."

"Sure." Lily taps the side of Flat-Top's iKontakt frames with her bracelet, and information scrolls across her lenses. "Okay, his name's Nicholas Liu Honghui . . . blah blah blah . . . hired to scare someone at this address, anonymous client . . . I think he's coming to, how do you feel about joint locks?"

It takes a while for Nicholas to stir fully awake. Lily's on his chest, pinning him to the ground, and Helena's holding his switchblade to his throat.

"Okay, Nicholas Liu," Lily says. "We could kill you right now, but that'd make your wife and your . . . what is that red thing she's holding . . . a baby? Yeah, that'd make your wife and ugly baby quite sad. Now, you're just going to tell your boss that everything went as expected—"

"Tell him that I cried," Helena interrupts. "I was here alone, and I cried because I was so scared."

"Right, got that, Nick? That lady there wept buckets of tears. I don't exist. Everything went well, and you think there's no point in sending anyone else over. If you mess up, we'll visit 42—god, what is this character—42 Something Road and let you know how displeased we are. Now, if you apologise for ruining our morning, I probably won't break your arm."

After seeing a wheezing Nicholas to the exit, Lily closes the door, slides her bracelet back onto her wrist, and shakes her head like a deeply disappointed critic. "What an amateur. Didn't even use burner frames—how the hell did he get hired? And that *haircut*, wow . . ."

Helena opts to remain silent. She leans against the wall and stares at the ceiling, hoping that she can wake up from what seems to be a very long nightmare.

"Also, I'm not gonna push it, but I did take out the trash. Can you explain why that crappy hitter decided to pay us a visit?"

"Yeah. Yeah, okay." Helena's stomach growls. "This may take a while. Did you get the food?"

"I got your pancakes, and that soy milk place was open, so I got you some. Nearly threw it at that guy, but I figured we've got a lot of electronics, so . . ."

"Thanks," Helena says, taking a sip. It's still hot.

⊛   ⊛   ⊛

Hong Kong Scientific University's bioprinting program is a prestigious pioneer program funded by mainland China, and Hong Kong is the test bed before the widespread rollout. The laboratories are full of state-of-the-art medical-grade printers and bioreactors, and the instructors are all researchers cherry-picked from the best universities.

As the star student of the pioneer batch, Lee Jyun Wai Helen (student number A3007082A) is selected for a special project. She will help the head instructor work on the basic model of a heart for a dextrocardial patient, the instructor will handle the detailed render and the final print, and a skilled surgeon will do the transplant. As the term progresses and the instructor gets busier and busier, Helen's role gradually escalates to doing everything except the final print and the transplant. It's a particularly tricky render, since dextrocardial hearts face right instead of left, but her practice prints are cell-level perfect.

Helen hands the render files and her notes on the printing process to the instructor, then her practical exams begin and she forgets all about it.

The Yuen family discovers Madam Yuen's defective heart during their mid-autumn family reunion, halfway through an evening harbour cruise. Madam Yuen doesn't make it back to shore, and instead of a minor footnote in a scientific paper, Helen rapidly becomes front-and-centre in an internal investigation into the patient's death.

Unofficially, the internal investigation discovers that the head instructor's improper calibration of the printer during the final print led to a slight misalignment in the left ventricle, which eventually caused severe ventricular dysfunction and acute graft failure.

Officially, the root cause of the misprint is Lee Jyun Wai Helen's negligence and failure to perform under deadline pressure. Madam Yuen's family threatens to prosecute, but the criminal code doesn't cover failed organ printing. Helen is expelled, and the Hong Kong Scientific University quietly negotiates a settlement with the Yuens.

After deciding to steal the bioprinter and flee, Helen realises that she doesn't have enough money for a full name change and an overseas flight. She settles for a minor name alteration and a flight to Nanjing.

⊛   ⊛   ⊛

"Wow," says Lily. "You know, I'm pretty sure you got ripped off with the name alteration thing, there's no way it costs that much. Also, you used to have pigtails? Seriously?"

Helena snatches her old student ID away from Lily. "Anyway, under the amendments to Article 335, making or supplying substandard printed organs is now an offence punishable by death. The family's itching to prosecute. If we don't do the job right, Mr Anonymous is going to disclose my whereabouts to them."

"Okay, but from what you've told me, this guy is totally not going to let it go even after you're done. At my old job, we got blackmailed like that all the time, which was really kind of irritating. They'd always try to bargain, and after the first job, they'd say stuff like 'if you don't do me this favour I'm going to call the cops and tell them everything' just to weasel out of paying for the next one."

"Wait. Was this at the bakery or the merch stand?"

"Uh." Lily looks a bit sheepish. This is quite unusual, considering that Lily has spent the past four days regaling Helena with tales of the most impressive blood blobs from her period, complete with comparisons to their failed prints. "Are you familiar with the Red Triad? The one in Guangzhou?"

"You mean the *organ printers?*"

"Yeah, them. I kind of might have been working there before the bakery . . . ?"

"What?"

Lily fiddles with the lacy hem of her skirt. "Well, I mean, the bakery experience seemed more relevant, plus you don't have to list every job you've ever done when you apply for a new one, right?"

"Okay," Helena says, trying not to think too hard about how all the staff at Splendid Beef Enterprises are now prime candidates for the death penalty. "Okay. What exactly did you do there?"

"Ears and stuff, bladders, spare fingers . . . you'd be surprised how many people need those. I also did some bone work, but that was mainly for the diehards—most of the people we worked on were pretty okay with titanium substitutes. You know, simple stuff."

"That's not simple."

"Well, it's not like I was printing fancy reversed hearts or anything, and even with the asshole clients it was way easier than baking. Have *you* ever tried to extrude a spun-sugar globe so you could put a bunch of powder-printed magpies inside? And don't get me started on cleaning the nozzles after extrusion, because wow . . ."

Helena decides not to question Lily's approach to life, because it seems like a certain path to a migraine. "Maybe we should talk about this later."

"Right, you need to send the update! Can I help?"

The eventual message contains very little detail and a lot of pleading. Lily insists on adding typos just to make Helena seem more rattled, and Helena's way too tired to argue. After starting the autoclean cycle for the printheads, they set an alarm and flop on Helena's mattress for a nap.

As Helena's drifting off, something occurs to her. "Lily? What happened to those people? The ones who tried to blackmail you?"

"Oh," Lily says casually. "I crushed them."

⊛   ⊛   ⊛

The brief specifies that the completed prints need to be loaded into four separate podcars on the morning of 8 August, and provides the delivery code for each. They haven't been able to find anything in Helena's iKontakt archives, so their best bet is finding a darknet user who can do a trace.

Lily's fingers hover over the touchpad. "If we give him the codes, this guy can check the prebooked delivery routes. He seems pretty reliable, do you want to pay the bounty?"

"Do it," Helena says.

The resultant map file is a mess of meandering lines. They flow across most of Nanjing, criss-crossing each other, but eventually they all terminate at the cargo entrance of the Grand Domaine Luxury Hotel on Jiangdong Middle Road.

"Well, he's probably not a guest who's going to eat two hundred steaks on his own." Lily taps her screen. "Maybe it's for a hotel restaurant?"

Helena pulls up the Grand Domaine's web directory, setting her iKontakt to highlight any mentions of restaurants or food in the descriptions. For some irritating design reason, all the booking details are stored in garish images. She snatches the entire August folder, flipping through them one by one before pausing.

The foreground of the image isn't anything special, just elaborate cursive English stating that Charlie Zhang and Cherry Cai Si Ping will be celebrating their wedding with a ten-course dinner on August 8th at the Royal Ballroom of the Grand Domaine Luxury Hotel.

What catches her eye is the background. It's red with swirls and streaks of yellow-gold. Typical auspicious wedding colours, but displayed in a very familiar pattern.

It's the marbled pattern of T-bone steak.

❂   ❂   ❂

Cherry Cai Si Ping is the daughter of Dominic Cai Yongjing, a specialist in livestock and a new player in Nanjing's agrifood arena. According to Lily's extensive knowledge of farming documentaries, Dominic Cai Yongjing is also "the guy with the eyebrows" and "that really boring guy who keeps talking about nothing".

"Most people have eyebrows," Helena says, loading one of Lily's recommended documentaries. "I don't see . . . oh. Wow."

"I *told* you. I mean, I usually like watching stuff about farming, but last year he just started showing up everywhere with his stupid waggly brows! When I watched this with my ex we just made fun of him non-stop."

Helena fast-forwards through the introduction of *Modern Manufacturing: The Vertical Farmer*, which involves the camera panning upwards through hundreds of vertically-stacked wire cages. Dominic Cai talks to the host in English, boasting about how he plans to be a key figure in China's domestic beef industry. He explains his "patented methods" for a couple of minutes, which involves stating and restating that his farm is extremely clean and filled with only the best cattle.

"But what about bovine parasitic cancer?" the host asks.

"Isn't the risk greater in such a cramped space? If the government orders a quarantine, your whole farm . . ."

"As I've said, our hygiene standards are impeccable, and our stock is pure-bred Hereford!" Cai slaps the flank of a cow through the cage bars, and it moos irritatedly in response. "There is absolutely no way it could happen here!"

Helena does some mental calculations. Aired last year, when the farm recently opened, and that cow looks around six months old . . . and now a request for steaks from cows that are sixteen to eighteen months old . . .

"So," Lily says, leaning on the back of Helena's chair. "Bovine parasitic cancer?"

"Judging by the timing, it probably hit them last month. It's usually the older cows that get infected first. He'd have killed them to stop the spread . . . but if it's the internal strain, the tumours would have made their meat unusable after excision. His first batch of cows was probably meant to be for the wedding dinner. What we're printing is the cover-up."

"But it's not like steak's a standard course in wedding dinners or anything, right? Can't they just change it to roast duck or abalone or something?" Lily looks fairly puzzled, probably because she hasn't been subjected to as many weddings as Helena has.

"Mr Cai's the one bankrolling it, so it's a staging ground for the Cai family to show how much better they are than everyone else. You saw the announcement—he's probably been bragging to all his guests about how they'll be the first to taste beef from his vertical farm. Changing it now would be a real loss of face."

"Okay," Lily says. "I have a bunch of ideas, but first of all, how much do you care about this guy's face?"

Helena thinks back to her inbox full of corpse pictures, the countless sleepless nights she's endured, the sheer terror she felt when she saw Lily step through the door. "Not very much at all."

"All right." Lily smacks her fist into her palm. "Let's give him a nice surprise."

⊛   ⊛   ⊛

The week before the deadline vanishes in a blur of printing, re-rendering, and darknet job requests. Helena's been nothing but polite to Mr Cai ever since the hitter's visit, and has even taken to video calls lately, turning on the camera on her end so that Mr Cai can witness her progress. It's always good to build rapport with clients.

"So, sir," Helena moves the camera, slowly panning so it captures the piles and piles of cherry-red steaks, zooming in on the beautiful fat strata which took ages to render. "How does this look? We'll be starting the dry-aging once you approve, and loading it into the podcars first thing tomorrow morning."

"Fairly adequate. I didn't expect much from the likes of you, but this seems satisfactory. Go ahead."

Helena tries her hardest to keep calm. "I'm glad you feel that way, sir. Rest assured you'll be getting your delivery on schedule . . . by the way, I don't suppose you could transfer the money on delivery? Printing the bone matter cost a lot more than I thought."

"Of course, of course, once it's delivered and I inspect the marbling. Quality checks, you know?"

Helena adjusts the camera, zooming in on the myoglobin dripping from the juicy steaks, and adopts her most sorrowful tone. "Well, I hate to rush you, but I haven't had much money for food lately . . ."

Mr Cai chortles. "Why, that's got to be hard on you! You'll receive the fund transfer sometime this month, and in the meantime why don't you treat yourself and print up something nice to eat?"

Lily gives Helena a thumbs-up, then resumes crouching under the table and messaging her darknet contacts, careful to stay out of Helena's shot. The call disconnects.

"Let's assume we won't get any further payment. Is everything ready?"

"Yeah," Lily says. "When do we need to drop it off?"

"Let's try for five am. Time to start batch-processing."

Helena sets the enzyme percentages, loads the fluid into the canister, and they both haul the steaks into the dry-ager unit. The machine hums away, spraying fine mists of enzymatic fluid onto the steaks and partially dehydrating them, while Helena and Lily work on assembling the refrigerated delivery boxes. Once everything's neatly packed, they haul the boxes to the nearest podcar station. As Helena slams box after box into the cargo area of the podcars, Lily types the delivery codes into their front panels. The podcars boot up, sealing themselves shut, and zoom off on their circuitous route to the Grand Domaine Luxury Hotel.

They head back to the industrial park. Most of their things have already been shoved into backpacks, and Helena begins breaking the remaining equipment down for transport.

A Sculpere 9410S takes twenty minutes to disassemble if you're doing it for the second time. If someone's there to help you manually eject the cell cartridges, slide the external casing off, and detach the print heads so you can disassemble the power unit, you might be able to get that figure down to ten. They'll buy a new printer once they figure out where to settle down, but this one will do for now.

It's not running away if we're both going somewhere, Helena thinks to herself, and this time it doesn't feel like a lie.

⊛   ⊛   ⊛

There aren't many visitors to Mr Chan's restaurant during breakfast hours, and he's sitting in a corner, reading a book. Helena waves at him.

"Helena!" he booms, surging up to greet her. "Long time no see, and who is this?"

"Oh, we met recently. She's helped me out a lot," Helena

says, judiciously avoiding any mention of Lily's name. She holds a finger to her lips, and surprisingly, Mr Chan seems to catch on. Lily waves at Mr Chan, then proceeds to wander around the restaurant, examining their collection of porcelain plates.

"Anyway, since you're my very first client, I thought I'd let you know in person. I'm going travelling with my ... friend, and I won't be around for the next few months at least."

"Oh, that's certainly a shame! I was planning a black pepper hotplate beef special next month, but I suppose black pepper hotplate extruded protein will do just fine. When do you think you'll be coming back?"

Helena looks at Mr Chan's guileless face, and thinks, well, her first client deserves a bit more honesty. "Actually, I probably won't be running the business any longer. I haven't decided yet, but I think I'm going to study art. I'm really, really sorry for the inconvenience, Mr Chan."

"No, no, pursuing your dreams, well, that's not something you should be apologising for! I'm just glad you finally found a friend!"

Helena glances over at Lily, who's currently stuffing a container of cellulose toothpicks into the side pocket of her bulging backpack.

"Yeah, I'm glad too," she says. "I'm sorry, Mr Chan, but we have a flight to catch in a couple of hours, and the bus is leaving soon ..."

"Nonsense! I'll pay for your taxi fare, and I'll give you something for the road. Airplane food is awful these days!"

Despite repeatedly declining Mr Chan's very generous offers, somehow Helena and Lily end up toting bags and bags of fresh steamed buns to their taxi.

"Oh, did you see the news?" Mr Chan asks. "That vertical farmer's daughter is getting married at some fancy hotel tonight. Quite a pretty girl, good thing she didn't inherit those eyebrows—"

Lily snorts and accidentally chokes on her steamed bun. Helena claps her on the back.

"—and they're serving steak at the banquet, straight from his farm! Now, don't get me wrong, Helena, you're talented at what you do—but a good old-fashioned slab of *real* meat, now, that's the ticket!"

"Yes," Helena says. "It certainly is."

⊛   ⊛   ⊛

All known forgeries are failures, but sometimes that's on purpose. Sometimes a forger decides to get revenge by planting obvious flaws in their work, then waiting for them to be revealed, making a fool of everyone who initially claimed the work was authentic. These flaws can take many forms—deliberate anachronisms, misspelled signatures, rude messages hidden beneath thick coats of paint—or a picture of a happy cow, surrounded by little hearts, etched into the T-bone of two hundred perfectly-printed steaks.

While the known forgers are the famous ones, the *best* forgers are the ones that don't get caught—the old woman selling her deceased husband's collection to an avaricious art collector, the harried-looking mother handing the cashier a battered 50-yuan note, or the two women at the airport, laughing as they collect their luggage, disappearing into the crowd.

END

Weaponized Math
Jonathan P. Brazee

STAFF SERGEANT GRACIE MEDICINE Crow, United Federation Marine Corps, accepted the cup from Rabbit as she scanned the almost-deserted village below. She blew on the coffee, then took a sip, and nodded in appreciation. She thought she recognized the brew as Cushington Blue, and she wondered where her new spotter had scored it. Lance Corporal Christopher Irving—"Rabbit"—had only been assigned to her for a week now, so she hadn't formed an opinion as to his skillset yet. He'd gotten good grades at Triple S, the United Federation Marine Corps Scout-Sniper School, but school performance didn't always reflect performance in the field.

Still, if he can shoot as good as he can scrounge up a good cup of Joe, then he might have potential.

"Take the west side," she told him in dismissal. "Let me know if anyone takes an unusual interest in the library."

"Roger that, Staff Sergeant," Rabbit said as he scurried— as well as a two-meter tall, 120 kg Marine could "scurry" — to the other side of the roof.

Gracie could sense his eagerness. Like all snipers, he'd

proven himself in combat as a grunt before being accepted
into Triple S, so technically, he wasn't a newbie. Despite that,
he still had that new-sniper smell to him, straight out of the
package. More than that, he was still only a PIG, a "Profes-
sionally Instructed Gunman." This was their first live mission
together and, for once, Gracie was fine with the fact that it
should be a cold mission. As part of a routine security ele-
ment, she would have the opportunity to observe him in a
field setting while the stakes were relatively low. Scout-sniper
teams had to depend on and trust each other, and that usually meant months of training before going in hot. However,
after Saracen had been killed three weeks ago, Sergeant Hal-
cik Sung, her previous spotter, had been pulled from her to
fill Saracen's slot. Forty-one confirmed kills made Gracie the
most accomplished sniper in the platoon, so she'd had to take
the newbie.

She took another sip of coffee. Five floors below her, Sergeant Rafiq exited one of the shops surrounding the small
square. He and his squad had been conducting a sweep before
the rest of his platoon escorted the major to the meeting with
the local commissioners. He looked up and caught her eye,
then nodded. Gracie acknowledged him with a half-salute.

She really hadn't expected Second Squad to find anything. Tension Gorge—why "Gorge," Gracie still hadn't
figured out since the area around the village was as flat as a
rugby pitch—was not in a high-risk area. The last incident,
an IE attack, had taken place thirteen days prior and eight
klicks away. But with a field grade officer coming from divi-
sion, all precautions had to be taken, and the village had to be
swept. So, instead of pursuing the FLNT commandos in the
Mist Mountains, she and Rabbit were here acting as glorified
security guards.

They hadn't even set up a proper hide with overhead cover and concealment. They were meant to be seen. Gracie felt
exposed to the world, which made her nerves crawl. Every

instinct told her to get into a hide from where she could deal death unseen, but orders were orders. Not many fighters, even FLNT commandos, would choose to take on a Marine sniper. She was there as a "Warning: Attack Dogs on Premises" sign.

The slightest bit of movement caught her eye. Gracie raised her Windmoeller and scoped the spot. About a klick away, at the western edge of the village, a woman shifted her weight behind a window, looking out. She stood there for a moment before stepping back out of sight. Gracie pulled the map of the village onto her helmet display, noting the two-story house, and then running a line-of-sight to the library. She didn't think the women could see the library entrance, but she might have a sightline on several of the library's upper-story windows. She ranged the building, getting 984 meters, then entered it as a C-level target in her data book, joining the 44 other potential target positions she'd identified since arriving early in the morning with Second Squad.

She ran through the target positions again to see if she could remember the range for each one, starting with the A's. She got 39 of the 45 correct.

Come on, Crow. Get them down! she chided herself before going over the list yet one more time.

It would only take a moment to pull up the range on a specific target, but even a split second could make the difference between taking out an aggressor or allowing the enemy to engage the Marines. Some of her fellow Marines thought her anal-retentive insistence on memorizing details was overkill, but none of them had notched 41 kills, either. Gracie believed in leaving nothing to chance.

This time, she got 42 out of 45 correct. Better, but not good enough. She'd wait twenty minutes, then try again. It wasn't as if range was the only parameter that went into making a good shot. Her angle to the ground, the temperature, wind speed and direction, humidity, the planet's rotation, gravity—those and more would affect her round's trajectory. The constants were already entered into her scope's firing computer, but the variables had to be measured or determined at the time of the shot. The more variables she could enter into her scope's AI, the better her chances of success, and the faster she could do that, the quicker she could fire. If already knowing the range could slice off even a microsecond, it would be worth it.

At Triple S, a wall plaque proclaimed: *Snipers aren't deadly because they carry the biggest rifles; they're deadly because they've learned how to weaponize math.* This hit the nail on the head. Some people, even fellow snipers, claimed that sniping was an art, but Gracie knew it was purely physics, purely math, and ever since she'd become a sniper, she'd dedicated herself to making her math skills the best possible.

"Staff Sergeant Medicine Crow, your package has been delayed. He's still at Hornsby. Call it 80 minutes late," Lieutenant Diedre Kaster-Lyons passed over the platoon net.

"Roger that," Gracie passed back. "Any idea as to why?"

"That's a negative. We just got the word. I'll keep you posted."

Gracie took a deep breath, letting it out slowly. She wasn't surprised. Nothing ever seemed to go according to plan on this planet. Part of it was normal Marine Corps operating procedures, but more seemed to be because of the local government's maneuvering factions. Everyone agreed that the Frente de Liberación de Nuevo Trujillo was the enemy to all that was good and just on the planet, but in practice, none of the various political factions seemed willing to cooperate lest they cede some sort of advantage to another. She should be used to it by now, but the thought of sitting up on the roof for an additional hour-plus made her want to scream. By the time she got back to camp, she'd have spent at least 14 hours doing absolutely nothing.

"Did you hear that?" she passed to Rabbit on the P2P.

"Roger that. Uh . . . is it always like this? I mean, the changes?"

She suppressed a chuckle. As a junior grunt, he wouldn't have been kept in the loop as much as he was now as a scout-sniper. This wasn't even the first change: the meeting had originally been planned for yesterday. This was now the second delay for today.

"Hurry up and wait, Lance Corporal Irving. You know how it is in the Suck."

"Yeah, I guess so. It's just so . . . well, you know."

Yes, I do know, Rabbit. Boy, do I know.

Gracie could bitch with the best of them—although usually not aloud—but she still wouldn't change her profession for anything. She was meant to be a Marine. A member of the Apsaalooké Nation from Montana on Earth, she came from a long line of warriors, and her lifestyle was embedded in her DNA. She might chafe at the delay, but this was her life. Without conscious thought, she reached under her collar and rubbed the "hog's tooth" hanging from her neck between her fingers, a recovered round from her first victim's magazine, but more importantly, the symbol of being a HOG, or a "Hunter of Gunmen."

She continued to scan the area below, working quick firing solutions in her mind for various locations, almost on autopilot. Sitting in a hide for days on end waiting for that one shot, there wasn't much else to do, and she'd done this tens of thousands of times over the ten-plus years she'd been a designated scout-sniper. Tens of thousands of calculations and more than a year of combined time in hides, all for 41 kills. Civilians used to the Hollybolly war flicks might think it a lot of effort per kill, but some snipers never even registered a single kill. Never became HOGs. Gracie's total was now the fourth largest among active duty snipers.

"Dingo-Three, Charlie-Two-One, we've got a cargo hover approaching your position from azimuth Two-Zero-Five, range two-point-three klicks. Looks like it's got agricultural products in the bed. There are a few anomalies in the scan, but within accepted parameters. Just keep an eye on them," an unnamed voice passed over the command net.

"Roger that," Gracie and Sergeant Rafiq said in unison.

"You got that?" Gracie asked Rabbit over the P2P, turning her head to look at him.

Two-Zero-Five was to the south west of their position, and her spotter should have a straight line-of-site to what they had designated as Route Bluebird, the road leading into Tension Gorge from that direction.

Rabbit swiveled his body to glass to the south-west before ignoring the P2P to shout "Got it!"

They might not have been in a concealed hide, but Gracie winced. In the open or not, snipers didn't shout like that, giving away their positions. It was a bad habit to start, and she'd have to remind him of that.

"Looks like a typical hauler, one of those gas jobs."

Which was to be expected. Nuevo Trujillo relied heavily on methane for ground transportation, methane extracted from agricultural waste. She ran a scan through the available feeds before picking up a micro-drone that had the hovertruck in its sights. The truck, three-quarters loaded with cargo pods, was making its way north down the road, which was the secondary north-south thoroughfare in the sector. Salinas, another small farming town, was twelve klicks south along Bluebird from Tension Gorge.

Gracie wasn't overly concerned about the truck since Tension Gorge was not a restricted town. While it had been largely abandoned during the fighting of two months ago, some people still lived there, and there were still crops to be harvested and transported to the processing plants. Still, Second Squad would have to stop and search the truck when it reached the village.

"Keep your eye on the truck while it gets here and Second

checks it out," she passed to Rabbit.

She was tempted to move to his side of the roof and do it herself, but he needed to get his feet wet. To her side in its case was her Kyocera, her hypervelocity sniper rifle, and with any other spotter, she might have told him to take it. Rabbit, however, had not snapped in with it, and without being able to key in the cheek weld and eye position, he wouldn't be very accurate. No, better he keep his standard-issue M99. It had more than enough range to cover Second Squad, and he had it zeroed in for his shooting position.

She turned back to her area of responsibility. The Navy and Marine Corps' scanners hadn't found anything suspicious about the truck, but using something so obvious as a decoy was not unheard of. With short quick movements, she covered the mental grid she'd constructed, using both her prime focus as well as her peripheral vision to spot anything out of the ordinary.

One of Second Squad's four-man fire teams was moving to where they could intercept the truck. Gracie shifted her focus to the two local security standing outside the library door. They'd arrived with the first three commissioners. Casually sucking on stim sticks, flare-barreled Munchen 44's held at the ready, the impressively lethal-looking men didn't watch the fire team as it left. If something was up of which they were a part, they were hiding it well. Gracie didn't suspect the two guards of anything, but she had a firing solution for them already locked in, and her Windmoeller's WPT-331 rounds had the penetrative power to defeat the Cryolene body armor they wore. Better safe than sorry.

She was more concerned with the young boy she'd nicknamed "Space Dog" due to the brightly-colored image on his t-shirt. Perhaps ten or eleven years old, he sat on the stoop of a home a block off the square. He wasn't armed, the best she could tell, but he'd been sitting there for half-an hour, seemingly interested in the goings on. That might be merely normal adolescent curiosity, but he could be acting as a lookout, feeding information to the bad guys. Gracie had zoomed in on him several times with her scope, but she hadn't seen any signs of him communicating with anyone.

"The truck's almost here," Rabbit shouted across the roof.

"Use your comms, Irving. You trying to paint a bullseye on us?" she passed.

"Oh, yeah. Sorry, Staff Sergeant," he said, this time over the P2P.

"OK, then. Just keep an eye on them."

She pulled up Rabbit's feed, then reduced it and sent it to the top left of her helmet display where she could monitor it but still have a full view of her own area of responsibility. She quickly ticked through her known potential target list. Silver Hair was still in his garden, Red Shirt was walking along Calle Jones after going to the lone store still open, and Limp Man was no longer in sight. She shifted to the right where Route Robin led into the town and from where the major would arrive. A local policeman still stood at the edge of town, ready to hop on his scoot and escort the major and the rest of First Platoon to the library. He looked bored out of his head, something Gracie completely understood.

Closer in, she checked Space Dog, then Gollum 1 and 2, the two security guards at the library. Shifting her view farther to the right, she—

What's with Potbelly? she wondered.

The older man, his protruding gut hanging over his belt, had risen from his seat on a porch where he'd supposedly been reading a novel for the last hour. The reader was now on the small table beside his chair, its screen dark, and the man was looking with poorly disguised interest to his left. Gracie followed his gaze's direction, but nothing jumped out at her. That wasn't a comfort—something was tweaking her instincts.

"I don't have anything for certain, but something might

be up," she passed on the local command circuit, which was keyed into Rabbit and all the Marines from Second Squad. "Keep alert."

"What d'ya got, Staff Sergeant?" Sergeant Rafiq asked.

"Nothing for certain, but Potbe . . . the man at Building 23," she passed, using the number Lieutenant Diedre Kaster-Lyons, dual-hatted as the battalion intel officer and the scout-sniper platoon commander, had designated the house, "seems a little too interested in something."

"The fat guy? Eric?" the sergeant asked. "I spoke with him. He seemed OK, happy to see us. Tired of the fighting and all."

Maybe, but something's up, she thought as she continued to watch him. *I can feel it.*

Potbelly—Eric whatever—was now looking in every direction except to the left, which might mean something, but then he sat back down, picked up his reader, and started to read again. Gracie wondered if her nerves were playing with her, making her see things that didn't exist, but something still nagged at the back of her mind. She zoomed in on the man, and that something hit her. The reader. The display was off. Potbelly was "reading" a darkened screen.

"Stop the truck!" she passed. "Something's wrong!"

From Rabbit's feed, she could see the truck, now a mere three hundred meters from the village's edge. Corporal Ben-Zvi, the fire team leader of the team preparing to search the truck, didn't wait for orders from his squad leader. He stepped out onto the middle of Route Bluebird, weapon raised while his amplified voice called out, "You, in the truck. Halt!"

The truck sped up.

Gracie bolted across the roof before conscious thought registered what was happening, yelling for Rabbit to take her place on the roof's east side. Ben-Zvi's fire team had spread out and taken the truck under fire, but it was a big, hulking thing, and their M-99s weren't having much effect on target.

There was a whoosh as a Marine launched a Hatchet, but the missile hit high on the truck's right side with an impressive but ineffectual blast, missing the engine block and anything vital.

Firing at a moving vehicle, through a windshield, and from a high angle, was one of the most difficult shots a sniper could make. Gracie had spent countless hours in simulators and on ranges from Tarawa to Alexander, but still, this was no sure thing, and she both hadn't pre-calculated a firing solution and had no time to calculate one now. She'd have to go with her gut.

Firing from a height meant the round's drop would be less, but firing through the windshield meant that the round would most likely deflect downwards when it hit. The WPT-331 rounds she'd loaded to take care of the security officers armor had more punching power than the standard WPT-310 Lapua sniper round, so the deflection would be less—*but how much less?*

Gracie hit the roof's edge, flipping off her helmet as she brought up her rifle and laid it across the top of the low retaining wall. Her scope was zeroed at 300 meters. She had already ranged the edge of the first house where Route Bluebird entered the village at 445 meters. The truck was still 150 meters or so away from that, and the wind had been blowing north to south at a slight eight-to-ten KPH. She didn't have time to enter any of that; it was pure Kentucky windage time. Unable to see through the windshield's glare, she put her crosshairs slightly high and to the right of where she thought the driver would be. Just as she started to squeeze the trigger, she saw the slightest of cracks from the driver's side door.

He's not suiciding! He's going to try and get out!

The car that Gracie had taken out on Jericho had been driven by a suicide bomber. This driver was either not as dedicated or was considered still still vital. If the latter, then this was just the initial act in a larger assault.

With a last-second shift to the right, figuring the driver would be scrunched over to be able to bail out, she squeezed off a round, and then shifted lower and to the left before firing off a second. The flower blossomed on the windshield as the 285-grain jacketed round punched through it, and the truck started to veer before the second round hit.

"Axel-Three, this is Dingo-Three. We are under attack. Cancel the mission," she passed on the command net before adding, "But send the rest of Charlie-One. We're going to need them."

"Roger, Dingo-Three. Understand you are under attack. Axel-Three-Five is being recalled. Will get back to you on Charlie-One."

The major had to be pulled back, but Gracie thought they'd need the rest of First Platoon here in the village. She scanned for more fighters as the hovertruck left the road and slowed to a stop in a field of knee-high, green, leafy crops.

On Jericho, the suicide VBIED had exploded when the driver she'd killed released the suicide switch. This truck didn't. Gracie looked over her scope at it, wondering if she'd jumped the gun by declaring a full-out attack.

The truck erupted into a fireball that roiled into the air.

Of course. It was on a timer so the driver could escape with his skin intact.

Gracie was half-listening to Corporal Ben-Zvi giving a quick sitrep on the net when the sound of firing from the center of the town reached her. She bolted back to her original firing point where Rabbit stood, peering over the building's edge.

"Get down. You can see just as well if you're prone, and you won't be exposed," she told him, jerking him down by the collar.

"I'm hit, Sergeant," someone passed on the net.

Without her helmet, Gracie didn't have her display to see who it was, but she swung her scope to the two security guards. One was crouching, weapon ready as he scanned for a target, and the other was running forward. Gracie put her crosshairs on him, ready to take him out if needed, but he reached the wounded Marine and dragged her back to the base of the library.

Guess they're not part of this.

Someone was, though, and Gracie's job was to take him out.

"I've got someone. Looks like he's got a Halstead," Rabbit said.

"Where? Give me a location."

"Uh . . . Building 38, second floor."

"Building 38, 185 meters," she mumbled, then "Take him out."

Such a close distance was child's play to a Marine with an M-99, much less a trained sniper. She left the target to Rabbit as she searched for more. She heard the whisper-snap of darts as Rabbit fired, then an excited "I got him!"

"Well, HOG, go find your number-two kill," she said, wanting him to focus on the task at hand.

"A HOG, really? But that was with my ninety-nine."

He was right. A kill like that wouldn't be tallied as a sniper kill, so she'd jumped the gun on anointing him a HOG. Now wasn't the time to get into technicalities though.

"Later, Irving. We don't have time to discuss it now."

"Roger that," he said. Gracie heard him quietly add, "Shit, a HOG."

A string of automatic fire opened up, but with the sound reverberating between buildings, Gracie couldn't pinpoint its origin. Putting that weapon out of her mind for the moment, she shifted back to Potbelly. The man was gone, his reader abandoned on the floor of the porch. She kept scanning the direction where he'd been looking. Tension Gorge was not a very densely populated village, but there were still enough buildings to intermittently mask her view. She was dead sure, though, that there was somebody there.

A flash of movement proved her right. Two people, pulling an ancient but effective looking crew-served gun that she didn't recognize but looked like an anti-tank weapon of some sort, passed between two buildings, moving out-of-sight before she could aim and fire. She swung her barrel to cover the other side of the house that now masked them and waited. Automatic fire still echoed in bursts throughout the village, but she slowed her breathing, letting her sight picture become her world. A few moments later, a head peered around the corner. At 210 meters to the home's front door, she could easily drop him, but she wanted the gun in the open.

Come on out! The coast is clear, she implored him.

He turned back, said something, then disappeared for a moment, reappearing holding the crew-served gun's controls, leading it forward. He pointed towards the square as he said something to his companion, who followed him into view.

Gracie and Rabbit were not exactly in stealth mode, and their position had to have been noted, but the two FLNT fighters didn't even look her way.

Your loss.

When they were five meters out from the house's protection, Gracie squeezed the trigger, going for center mass. The man dropped as if poleaxed, and Gracie cycled her action, swinging to take the second man into her sights. With cat-like reflexes, the second soldier bolted back into cover. Gracie snapped off a shot, but she was sure she'd missed.

"Staff Sergeant, do you got eyes on whoever is on our asses?" Sergeant Rafiq asked between heavy breaths.

"Where's it coming from?"

"Through the fucking wall, from the north. It's chewing the shit out of the place, and we've got no cover."

"Lance Corporal Irving, we need to find that automatic weapon. Move to the edge over there and see if you can spot it." She keyed back to the command net and asked, "Rafiq, what's the status on your platoon? I'm not hearing anything. When's their ETA?"

A round pinged just below Gracie, taking a chunk of cerocrete off the wall.

So much for them ignoring us.

"As soon as the major's lifted out of there, they'll break free. We've got a Minidrag on the way, though. ETA is six minutes."

Gracie had half-expected the delay in the platoon. They couldn't just leave the major out there on the road, cooling his heels. The Minidrag was a nice piece of news, though. The Marines had two "Dragon" drones. The "Mini" was the smaller, but depending on its combat load, it could still pack a decent wallop. It would have been providing overwatch for the column bringing in the major, and she was frankly surprised that the S3 had cut it loose to support Second Squad and her sniper team.

As Gracie watched, chunks of the closer wall of the store in which Rafiq and two of his fire teams had taken cover blew out into the square. The enemy gun was shooting all the way through the building.

"Fuck! Can you get them off our ass, Crow?" Rafiq passed. "If we weren't hugging the deck, that would have cut us in two. I don't think we can wait for the Minidrag."

"I think I have the position, Staff Sergeant," Rabbit shouted, forgetting her earlier admonition. "I saw a flash."

"Wait one," she passed to Sergeant Rafiq on the P2P. "Let me see what I can do."

"Hurry up, Staff Sergeant. I've got one down, and I don't have anything to engage.

Gracie slid back behind the retaining wall, then crouched and scooted to where Rabbit hunkered behind his section of the low wall.

"Give me your helmet," she ordered.

She should have put hers back on—then she could have

simply downloaded his feed—but it was still 20 meters behind her, so she threw on his. She reversed his feed 60 seconds and started it up again. Her image appeared first from what looked like just after she dropped the FPL fighter.

Don't look at me, Rabbit. Look out at the bad guys.

She heard her voice telling him to move over to try and spot the shooters, then the herky-jeky footage as he ran to the roof's far corner. He was scanning, back and forth when there was a flash at the corner of his vision immediately before the burst of automatic fire could be heard. Gracie made a mental note of the building from where the flash originated: Building 14, the Ag Co-op, which was a two-story office building made from the same cerocrete as the bank on which she now perched.

She gave Rabbit back his helmet, then did a quick turkeyhop to orient herself before dropping back out of sight. From her adjusted position, the window on the building would be about 465 meters, still an easy shot. Gracie's longest kill to date with the Windmoeller was 2005 meters, so this would be child's play—if she could acquire a target.

She entered the data into her Miller, then eased up and brought the window into her sights. A sharp report from behind their position startled her for an instant, but the *cracka-cracka-cracka* was from a Marine M110, the standard automatic slug-thrower for a fire team. Corporal Ben-Zvi's team had engaged, and she hoped they'd taken out the soldier she'd missed. She acquired her sight picture again, and the muzzle of a barrel immediately edged out before firing off another string of 15 or 20 shots. This was their baby, but the gunner hadn't exposed himself. She was pretty sure that whoever he or she was, they knew exactly where she and Rabbit were and didn't want to become targets.

"Can you get them?" Rabbit asked as she slid back down to sit on the deck, back against the low wall.

"You didn't happen to bring a Hatchet, did you?"

"No, Staff Sergeant. You didn't tell me to."

She hadn't expected him to have brought one of the little personal anti-armor rockets, but it hadn't hurt to ask. Semi-smart, the rocket could take out most armor or blast its way through any civilian construction.

She shrugged, then half-turned her torso to reach up and touch the wall's rounded top. It was about 10 centimeters thick. Only three buildings in the entire village were made of cerocrete, and she had to figure that they had probably been constructed in a similar fashion. Cerocrete was more expensive than the pressed vegaboard that was used for most of the village's buildings, and not surprisingly, it was more robust. The walls of the building in which Rafiq was taking cover might as well have been paper for all the protection they were providing, but cerocrete was different.

How different? she wondered, dropping her magazine and checking the rounds inside.

There was one of her remaining WPT-331 jacketed rounds in the chamber and two in the magazine. The WPT-310 Lapua was a much better round for long distances, but the 331 had more punch. She didn't know if it could punch through 10 centimeters of cerocrete, however. Once again, the math of sniping had raised its head, but this time, she didn't have the numbers to plug into the equation.

Only one way to find out.

More firing was erupting from around the village. With Sergeant Rafiq pinned down, only Ben-Zvi's fire team and maybe the two civilian security officers were returning the fire. That had to change. Marines took the fight to the enemy. They didn't let the enemy bring it to them.

"Sergeant Rafiq, if I cover you from that automatic crew-served, can you make it to the library? It's made of stone, so it'll give you better cover."

"If you can send some rounds to the east, too, I think we can. We're taking small arms from there, and we've got to carry Parker."

"Can you let the two security guys know you're coming? I don't want them to take you out."

"Roger that. They pulled Omato out of the line of fire. She's pretty fucked up, but she's on her comms now."

Another heavy burst from the crew-served gun tore through the building, and Sergeant Rafiq passed, "With you or without you, we've got to go now!"

"Irving, on my go, I want you to put rounds downrange to the east. No one shot, one kill. I need volume."

He nodded, his hand squeezing and relaxing on his pistol grip while Gracie checked her scope one more time.

"On three," she passed on the command net so every Marine could hear her. "One . . . two . . . three!"

Gracie swung her barrel over the top of the wall, set her cross hairs on the wall about 15 centimeters to the left of the window's edge, and squeezed the trigger. She shifted lower and slightly to the right and fired again as Rabbit started sending hundreds of hypervelocity darts across the square and in amongst the buildings.

"Go, go!" Sergeant Rafiq shouted over the net.

The muzzle of the enemy gun disappeared, and Gracie put her last 331 into the wall. She wasn't sure if the rounds had penetrated completely through it, but she'd certainly gotten the shooter's attention. With a WPT-310 now chambered, she swung back to the square and looked for a target. A flash of movement caught her at the edge of the scope, and she brought the crosshairs to bear, but realized that it was the boy, Space Dog, running away from the square, not toward it. A door opened ahead of him, and a panicked-looking woman came out, wildly beckoning him to her.

She didn't bother to see if the boy made it. Rounds started to impact around her, and she looked over the top of her scope, trying to spot a real target. She immediately picked up an FLNT soldier running full tilt towards the square, firing up at her as he went. With a smooth move, Gracie acquired the man through her scope, adjusted high, then fired. The round hit him just below the throat, and Gracie knew he was dead before he hit the ground.

There was a thud next to her, and Rabbit grunted before spinning around and falling to the deck.

"You OK?" she asked.

He gave her a weak thumbs-up, then rubbed his upper chest, saying, "My bones stopped the round, but shit, that felt like someone hit me with a club."

The "bone" inserts that acted as body armor would stop most small arms rounds, but while darts might barely be felt, larger caliber slugs could still beat a Marine up pretty good.

"Where was the shooter?"

"Over there," he said, pointing past Gracie. "I was turning to you when I got hit."

"Show me."

He picked himself up, and with a grimace, popped his head up and pointed. Gracie followed the direction, then both dropped as another round zipped past where Rabbit's head had been an instant before.

He can't be, she told herself as she tried to analyze what she'd seen.

There was only been one structure higher than their building in that direction: the water tower. While water towers seemed to be the platform of choice for snipers in Hollybolly flicks, they pretty much sucked for the job. A sniper on one was completely exposed with no route of egress. Not only a suicide position, but a stupid one because a sniper perched there would be taken out immediately.

But this guy's already proven himself to be pretty dumb. Why try to take out Rabbit instead of me?

Gracie knew that she didn't look much like a Marine at times. At 1.4 meters and 38 kg (and that after a Harvest Festival banquet), she could look like a little girl playing dress-up in daddy's gear, especially when she had on her full battle rattle. But any soldier should have realized that since she was carrying the Windmoeller while Rabbit had his standard-issue M99, she was the threat, not him.

Being a sniper, despite all the advances since the Evolution, was still pretty much a man's game. Gracie had run across misogyny more than once, but this was ridiculous, and she was going to enjoy taking advantage of it. If that cretin didn't think she was the threat, she was going to prove him wrong—and enjoy doing so.

"You ready to play the prey, Lance Corporal Rabbit?"

He looked up at her in confusion. Gracie wasn't one much for nicknames, and she'd always kept military discipline in her professional relationships.

"He doesn't seem to recognize that I'm the sniper here. You're twice my size, so you must be the threat. So, if you're up to it, can you pop up for a moment and run a few steps while I disabuse him of his notion?"

A smile crept over his face. He nodded, saying, "My chest still hurts, Staff Sergeant, so yeah, I think I owe him this."

She held up her hand while she entered the range and the height differential. More math—lethal math. At 884 meters, this would be a longer shot, but the calculations were done the same way.

"No matter how good he is, it'll take two seconds minimum for a round to reach you, so no hero stuff. I want you back down in two."

She muted her earbud to the sounds of Sergeant Rafiq directing his squad and took three deep breaths to calm her pulse, then nodded. When Rabbit bolted up, she rose, rested her barrel on the top of the retaining wall, and only had to nudge her scope slightly up and to the right to have the enemy sniper in her crosshairs. She'd just acquired him when she saw him fire.

"Down!" she shouted at Rabbit as she started squeezing

her trigger—just as the man lifted his head to look over his scope as if trying to see if he'd hit her spotter. Gracie raised her point of aim to take advantage of the larger target and fired. She could see the trace as the round pierced the air, so she immediately knew she was on target. Long range sniping might be math, but it was almost art to see the round arc up, then curve back down and slightly to the right to impact his throat. Blood splattered the white paint of the water tower behind him as his weapon fell forward to tumble to the ground.

"Did you get the bastard?" Rabbit asked.

"What do you think? Of, course, I did."

Firing below them was intensifying. She keyed her earbud back on. Second Squad was getting in it deep. Although now that they were inside the library, they were dishing it out as well as taking it in.

"Back to work, Irving."

She started scanning with her scope, trying to find targets and take the pressure off of Second Squad, but while she caught a few shadows, she was having a difficult time. The Marine Corps Miller was an outstanding scope, its targeting AI second-to-none, but snipers usually engaged at over 1000 meters at a minimum. Even with the scope at its widest display, she just wasn't getting the field of vision she needed to spot the enemy as they maneuvered below her. Rabbit had fired four times since she'd taken out the sniper, and she'd yet to engage.

"I need the Kyc," she muttered.

Gracie was more attached to the slug-throwing Windmoeller, but as they were 45,000 credits each, she only had one Miller Scope. She had attached a normal combat scope to her hypervelocity Kyocera, something quite a bit less sophisticated, but with a much wider and higher-contrast field of view. Normally, she wouldn't have even brought the Kyc on the mission, relying instead on her Windmoeller for sniping and her Rino .358 for personal defense. Since she'd had an eager Rabbit there willing to hump it, however, she had figured it wouldn't hurt to bring it—and now that might prove to have been fortuitous.

Keeping low, she scurried alongside the wall to where Rabbit had left the weapon. She powered it up and checked its readouts. Power was at 98%, and while the Kyc didn't carry the 1000-round dart mags of the M99, she still had 150 slightly larger 3mm darts ready to throw and another two mags ready to use. She brought it to her shoulder and looked through the combat scope. As if a gift from the gods of war, she immediately picked up two soldiers hugging the wall of a building that was giving them cover from Marine fire.

Not all Marine fire, guys.

The combat scope must have brought her back to her time as a regular grunt, because instead of squeezing her trigger in the best Triple S fashion, she snapped off five shots in quick succession. With the Kyc's negligible recoil and semi-automatic action, she could fire three darts per second, which beat the Windmoeller's 1.8 seconds per round. The first two darts punched through the head of the lead soldier, both probably continuing to hit the second soldier in the chest. He didn't drop but lunged backward as the next three darts chased him. He fell, only his legs visible as they churned to push him back out of her line-of-sight, so Gracie fired two more darts, at least one hitting him in the left leg.

The FLNT soldiers had layered plate armor on their torsos, but their legs were unprotected, and the man left a smear of blood on the ground as his legs disappeared.

"Dingo-Three and Charlie-One-Two, we have two armored vehicles, Kuang Fen 10's, approaching your position from three-four-niner, two klicks out. We are diverting the Minidrag to intercept, and Charlie-One is on the way. ETA for the platoon is forty-five mikes, so hold on."

Gracie glanced over at Rabbit, who met her eyes. Kuang

Fen, an Alliance-registered company, was a new supplier of relatively cheap military equipment. While nothing they had was as good as Federation, Brotherhood, or even Confederation equipment, they were a match for what Gentry, the major supplier to local governments and mercenary units, could put out. More importantly, a KF-10 was more than capable of taking out a lone Marine squad and sniper team. Intel apparently hadn't caught on to the little fact that there were KF tanks in the sector.

"Hope the Minidrag can take them out," Rabbit passed on the P2P.

"That's out of our hands for now, so keep firing."

Over the next five minutes, Gracie dropped three more FLNT fighters, one as he crouched to fire a shoulder-launched missile at the library. She picked up the Windmoeller again to put a round through the missile as it lay in the dirt so no one else could pick it up and use it. As she searched for more targets, her mind was on the Marine drone as it closed in on the KF-10s.

The fight, more than a klick-and-a-half away and within their sight from the roof, was over in seconds. The lead KF-10 erupted in a ball of flame, and moments later, the Minidrag was knocked from the sky. That left one tank still in the fight, and it looked huge as it pushed forward.

"Now what?" Rabbit asked, firing off another burst of 20 darts.

"Keep shooting."

There was whoosh, then a boom as a missile crashed into the side of the library, blowing a hole through the stone. Gracie tried to spot the gunner to no avail. She could almost feel the enemy close in though. The hammer would fall when the KF-10 arrived.

"You still with us?" she asked Sergeant Rafiq on the P2P.

There was a pause before he answered, "We're down to three effectives. That last one, shit, I'm down hard, bleeding like a stuck pig. I'm not going anywhere. I just gave Ben-Zvi the order to retreat to the west, and I'd suggest you do so, too. We'll try to give you some cover, and when that fucking FLNT tank gets here . . . well, we'll see what happens."

A death sentence, Gracie knew. The FLNT didn't see the value of prisoners.

She tied Rabbit in to the net, then said, "I don't think so, Sergeant. We can keep them off you."

She looked over at Rabbit who nodded his agreement.

"You can take out a KF-10? Don't think so," Rafiq said, then groaned in pain.

"Lieutenant Hjebek and the rest of your platoon are almost here."

"Look, Staff Sergeant, I . . . *we* appreciate the sentiment, but this time, the dice rolled against us. All of us here, we talked about it, and we agree. Get out of here. Semper fi," he said before breaking into a fit of coughing and cutting the net.

"Keep at it, Irving," Gracie said, snapping off another round. It didn't hit the running soldier, but it made him dive for cover.

The enemy tank was getting closer, and Gracie pulled up a threat assessment. The KF-10 would be vulnerable to any Marine anti-armor, but the two teams, or whoever was left of them, had used theirs in anti-personnel mode to push back the assault. A few antennae and the periscope were vulnerable, but not to her when armed with only a Kyocera.

But what about the Windmoeller? she wondered.

She didn't have any more WPT-331 rounds, but a WPT-310 would still be better than her 3mm darts. She changed weapons, then shot a range to the tank. It was about to enter the northern edge of town, 1,245 meters away from her. She took a few moments to enter the environmentals. Gracie was an excellent marksman, but hitting a 4cm-wide periscope lens on a moving tank at that range was going to be a task.

"You can't take out a tank with that," Rabbit said when he realized what she was doing.

"No, but maybe I can blind it," she said as she took her three calming breaths.

The tank was still advancing, and Gracie had to estimate what that would do to her sight picture. She made her decision, then fired. A moment later, she saw the round ping off the periscope turret, four or five centimeters low.

She immediately adjusted, but the driver juked the tank to its right just as she fired again, so she never saw the impact of her round. With the side aspect she had now, the shot would be almost impossible, but she held the target in the hopes that it would turn back to her.

There was an explosion behind her. Gracie spun around as three figures burst through the door to the roof that had been blasted right out of the frame, hitting Rabbit hard on the head. Gracie swung her Kyocera around and fired an unaimed shot which took one soldier in the thigh and dropped him, causing the man behind him to stumble. She fired again, hitting the second soldier on the top of his head. The third soldier, however, fired a three-round burst at her. One hit her in the left arm and caused her to drop her Windmoeller, her entire arm aflame with pain, while another hit her square on her left knee.

With a smile of . . . satisfaction? . . . scorn? he lowered his rifle and pulled out an enormous boarding gun. Probably over 100 years old, it fired a short-range rocket that had the power to blow right through her body armor. He was slowly raising it to bear down on her when a string of darts hit him in the side where his plate armor deflected them. He spun and fired, the rocket crossing the ten meters to where Rabbit lay on the ground, the muzzle of his M99 wavering as he tried to keep it on target.

Rabbit never had a chance. The rocket blew apart his upper torso. The man stopped, looking at Rabbit's body for a moment before turning back to Gracie. That small delay was enough to give her a chance to pull her Rino from her thigh holster, and his eyes widened in shock as she fired, double-tapping the trigger. The first .358 hollow-point hit him in the forehead, the round expanding and lodging ten centimeters deep into his brain.

Gracie felt a pang of loss, but she couldn't stop to mourn Rabbit. She stumbled to her feet, arm numb, and picked up the Kyocera again. The final assault was about to kick off below, and she intended on taking out as many of the enemy as possible. Heedless of how exposed she was, she leaned over the top of the wall, firing round after round. She thought she dropped at least four of them, but she wasn't sure. The whole time she was firing, the sound of the KF-10 reverberated between the buildings as it made its way to the square.

She heard Sergeant Rafiq ask the lieutenant how far out the platoon was, but she didn't bother to listen to the reply. She knew there was no way the reinforcements could reach them in time.

"I'm still here with you, Dylan," she told him. "Hang in there."

"Shit, Staff Sergeant, you're as stubborn as they said. But you sure as hell ain't no Ice Princess like they say, though. You've got balls, sister."

"And so do you."

And the KF-10 rolled into the square, big and mean, blue-diesel engine pumping out smoke. She knew her Kyocera was useless against it, but she fired off 100 rounds, more as a statement than anything else, as the tank gunner raised the 80mm gun to take her under fire.

She knew she should do something, but there wasn't much left in her box of tricks. The big gun was going to take off the entire top of the building, and her leg was already swollen and immobile. Math worked for snipers, but also for tanks—80mm trumped 3mm.

Gracie kept firing, though. The gun was halfway up when there was a loud whoosh from beneath her, and a smoky plume raced across the square to hit the tank right below the commander's cupola.

The gun stopped tracking. No massive explosions, no turret flying through the air. The tank just stopped cold.

"Scratch one tank," Corporal Ben-Zvi passed on the command net.

"Fuck, Abe, I told you to take your team and get out of here," Sergeant Rafiq passed.

"Ah, I've always been a fuck-up, Sergeant. You know that."

The *cracka-cracka-cracka* of an M110 sounded below her, its rounds shooting across the square to disappear out of sight.

"I'm still effective up here," Gracie passed. "And thanks for taking out the tank, but this isn't over. We've still got a job to do."

But it *was* over. With the KF-10 gone, the will of the FLNT fighters seemed to slip away—that or the fact that they knew a Marine platoon was minutes out. Gracie fired one more shot at a retreating figure, but that was it before Lieutenant Hjebek led the rest of the platoon into the village.

The fight was over.

"Corporal Ben-Zvi, can you do me a favor?" she passed on the P2P as the new Marines swept the area.

"Sure thing, Staff Sergeant."

"Go find one of the dead FLNT fighters before they get policed up, one who looks like he was taken out with an M99. Get a round from him and bring it to me."

"Uh . . . Staff Sergeant, you know we can't take trophies."

"I know the regs, but just do it, OK? It's important."

"Shit, if you say so, of course. We owe you."

"And I owe you. Thanks."

She moved back to the wall, her Kyocera at the ready.

Her arm and leg were aching, but at least she could move them now. She could go down to get one of the docs to check her out, but she was a sniper, and two squads of Marines were clearing the village. Her job was to cover them.

⊛ ⊛ ⊛

After the Heroes Ceremony a day later, the members of Third Battalion, Seventh Marines' Scout Sniper Platoon held their own ceremony. Gracie had attached to a piece of parachute cord the night before to the round Ben-Zvi had scrounged, and when Doc Rhymer turned off the stasis chamber for a moment, she slipped it inside with Rabbit's body. The corpsman turned the chamber back on, then left the snipers alone.

According to rules developed over centuries, Rabbit had not technically become a true Hunter of Gunmen because he hadn't used a sniper's weapon to make a kill at distance. Just as Gracie wouldn't get a kill credit for dropping Rabbit's slayer with a handgun, Rabbit's kills with his M99 were considered merely part and parcel of being a Marine. Gracie had asked that he be put in for a medal, and the battalion commander had agreed, but that didn't make him a HOG.

Gracie was a dedicated Marine, and as a habit, she didn't lie. She'd never made a false official statement—until the night before. She hadn't been sure of what kind of Marine Rabbit was, but he'd proven the temper of his steel. Without him, she doubted anyone would have made it out alive. So, she lied. She said she'd given her Kyocera to him, and from the enemy bodies recovered, five had died from the tipped 3mm darts. Gracie didn't need the kills on her record, but he did.

Gracie was sure that Gunny Adams, the Scout-Sniper platoon sergeant, hadn't believed a word of it. He knew how possessively she treated her weapons. But after staring into her eyes for a full 30 seconds, he had nodded and accepted her report.

While the other stasis chambers were being loaded for

return, either for resurrection or burial, each of the snipers in the platoon made their way past Rabbit's chamber. Each Marine quietly said their goodbye. As his sniper, Gracie was last. She wasn't much for long talks, so she kept it simple.

"Fair winds and following seas, HOG."

She gave the chamber a little slap, then turned to join the others.

"Do you need a day or two?" Gunny asked her.

She gave the chamber one last look as the loading crew came to take Rabbit, then said, "Nope, I'm ready. What's my next mission?"

Utopia, Lol??
Jamie Wahls

H E'S SHIVERING AS HE emerges from the pod. No surprise, he was frozen for like a billion years.

I do all the stuff on the script, all the "Fear Not! You are a welcomed citizen of our Utopia!" stuff while I'm toweling him off. Apparently he's about as good as I am with awkward silence 'cause it's not three seconds before he starts making small talk.

"So, how'd you get to be a . . ." He waves his hand.

"A Tour Guide To The Future?!"

"Yeah." The guy smiles gratefully at me. "I imagine you had a lot of training . . . ?"

"None whatsoever!" I chirp. He looks confused.

"Allocator chose me because I incidentally have the exact skills and qualifications necessary for this task, and because I had one of the highest enthusiasm scores!"

He accepts my extended hand, and steps down from the stasis tube. He coughs. Probably whatever untreatable illness put him in cryo in the first place.

"Oh, hang on a second," I say. My uplink with Allocator tells me that the cough was noticed, and nites are inbound to remove some "cancer", which is probably something I should look up.

I'm confused and eager to get on with my incredible Tour Guide To The Future schtick but I have to close my eyes and wait because the nites STILL aren't here.

Patience was one of your weakest scores. But you proved you can wait. This is just like that final test Allocator put you through, the impossible one, where you could choose between one marshmallow NOW, or two marshmallows in one minute.

I quietly hum to myself while checking my messages, watching friends' lives, placing bets on the upcoming matches of TurnIntoASnake and SeductionBowl, and simulating what my life would be like if I had a longer attention span.

It would be very different.

```
#Allocator: Good job waiting!

#Kit/dinaround: :D thanks!
```

I beam at the praise, and check my time. I waited for eleven seconds!

Pretty dang good!

The old man clears his throat.

"You poor thing," I gush. "Your throat is messed up too! Don't worry, the nites are here."

He looks at me. "The. . . knights? I don't see anyone."

I cover my mouth with a hand as I giggle. "Oh, you can't see them. Well, you probably could with the right eyes, but we're actually in universe zero right now so the physics are really strict. The nites are in the air."

He looks up and around at the corners of the room. He's frowning. It makes me frown too.

"In the air," I explain. "We're breathing them. They're fixing your 'cancer.'"

He looks downright alarmed. I'm not an expert but that's not how I think a person should react to being cured of "cancer".

"Wow," he says. "Is that how far medical technology has come? Some kind of . . . medical nanobots?"

"They're not medical," I say. "They're pretty all-purpose."

On one hand I'm sort of tired of answering his questions because it's all really obvious stuff but also it's really fun! It's always super neat to watch their eyes light up as I tell them about the world and that's probably why I got picked for the position in the first place.

"Let's have ice cream!" I demand.

               ❀   ❀   ❀

Four seconds ago, I demanded that we have ice cream. There is now an ice cream cone forming in my hand. It is taking FOREVER.

The old man sees it and flinches.

"Oh no!" I cry. "What's wrong? Do you hate ice cream?"

He looks at me with a really weird expression or maybe a couple different expressions.

"How are you doing that?" he asks. His voice is funny and tight.

"Oh. Allocator is making it for me?" I say. "Hey, let's get into another reality."

I spring up to my tiptoes. Moving is kinda fun but not as fun as it is in, like, The Manifold Wonders. Or in Bird Simulator. That one's really good.

"What?"

I blink. I almost forgot! It's time for me to be a good Tour Guide To The Future and repay Allocator's trust in me.

"Post-Singularity humanity now exists entirely as uploaded consciousnesses in distributed Matryoshka brains, living in trillions of universes presided over by our Friendly AI, Allocator," I say.

My ice cream is dripping! It can do that?

"Sorry, I didn't really understand that," he says. He doesn't sound sorry. "Is there anyone else I can talk to?"

"Sure!" I say.

```
#Kit/dinaround: yo Big A, come talk to, uh

#Kit/dinaround: hang on
```

"What's your name?" I ask. I forgot to ask earlier.

"Charlie," he says. "And you?"

"Kit/dinaround," I say, making extra-careful to pronounce the / so he won't miss it.

"Oh," he manages, "can I call you Kit?"

"I LOVE it!" I cry.

```
#Kit: Did you hear that?

#Allocator: Yes.

#Kit: I LOVE IT
```

The old man is looking around the room. There's nothing to see, though. Just the cryo pod, the upload station, and the walls.

"Is there a way out of here?" he asks.

"Yeah." I point to the upload station, a bare slab with a half-sphere dome for the brain. "I mean, it's no demon altar, but this is UZ, so we can't exactly travel in style."

"Please," he says. "I don't understand. I have apparently been snatched from death and returned to good health. I am grateful for that. I'm happy to repay that effort in any way you require...."

⊛   ⊛   ⊛

"... are you listening?"

"Oh!" I start. "Sorry."

Charlie blinks at me and I blink at him. I actually really like these lashes that Allocator gave me.

"Can I talk to the Allocator?" he asks.

The man flinches as the one of the walls tears away with a big whooshy sound effect.

Outside of our little blue room is the full majesty of the void. Space!: The Final Frontier looms before us, a whole lot of it.

Ol' terra firma is there, 90% nite-devoured to make more smart matter. Held in place above the gray slab by a trick of gravity (that I will totally remember to look up later), a little island is floating, a blue and tropical nature preserve. I squint, hoping to see an elephant.

I do not see an elephant.

The sun is almost entirely shrouded behind big spindly metal rods and arms. Whatever project Allocator is doing with Sol takes a lot of energy.

Charlie cries out, in fear and kind of pain. He doesn't look hurt, but I can't see his HP or anything so I don't know.

"Is it your cancer acting up again?!" I cry out. "Did Allocator not cure it?"

An enormous floating head forms in front of the window.

"Charlie Wilcox," it says mildly, "I am called Allocator. I am an AI tasked with the safety and flourishing of intelligent life."

"Hi," says Charlie, strangled-like.

"I understand you have many questions. I have prepared a tour to assist in your understanding of how life is lived in the future. Kit will be your guide. She is more competent than you would think."

"I'd hope," Charlie mutters.

"To begin the tour, simply lie on the provided table, with your head in the hemispherical dome. You will then experience a simulated reality. You will be in no danger and may return here at any time. Do you consent?"

"I suppose so," says Charlie.

Allocator's big ghostly face is blank. "Apologies, but I was created with several safety measures which prevent me from inferring consent. Do you consent?"

"Yeah," says Charlie.

"I require a 'Yes.'" Allocator patiently smiles.

"Yes, then."

"Thank you. Please lie comfortably on the table."

"Yaaaaaay!" I say, trying to force some enthusiasm because c'mon obviously we're uploading and who even listens to contracts before agreeing to them anymore? If you listen too close, people can't play pranks on you!

Charlie tentatively lays on the table, and scoots his butt up until his head is under the dome.

"Am I supposed to feel anythiunnnnnggg," he drools, going limp.

```
#Allocator: Good work.

#Allocator: Where to?
```

"Eeeeee!" I squeeeeee. "You're letting me pick?"

```
#Allocator: Yes.

#Allocator: Obviously.
```

"Oh my goodness," I said. "Uh . . . but what if I choose wrong?"

```
#Allocator: I have a hunch that you won't.

#Allocator: The "hunch" in this case is an
    identical copy of your mind, to whom I'm
    feeding inputs and reading her behavior
    as she makes it, thus allowing me to
    deterministically predict what the "real"
    you will choose.
```

"Sigh," I say. "Could you not?"

```
#Allocator: I could not.

#Allocator: Would you kindly pick a U?
```

"Fiiiiine." I roll my eyes. "Ummm... Oh! Bird Simulator!"

```
#Allocator: Great choice. ;)

#Allocator: Close your eyes.
```

FWOOSH I'm a bird haha!

I nip through the air, just above the snow on the treeline. The air smells incredible, like forest pine. I'm darting around like a cross between a rocket and a fly. My tiny bird heart is pounding like the itty-bittiest drum and golly but I do feel alive.

```
#CharlieSamarkand: aaaaaaaaaaaaaaaaaaaaaaaaaaaa
    aaaa

#CharlieSamarkand: aaaaaaaaaaaaaaaaaaaaaaaaaaaa
    aaaa

#CharlieSamarkand: aaaaaaaaaaaaohgodwhat'shappe
    ning

#Kit: Charlie!

#CharlieSamarkand: what? what is happening what

#Kit: You're a bird!

#CharlieSamarkand: I NOTICED THANK YOU

#CharlieSamarkand: WHY ARE WE BIRDS

#Kit: That's a really philosophical question!

#Kit: Why were we humans??

#CharlieSamarkand: WHAT
```

He's flapping really hard, so I fly under him to show how you can just sort of coast.

He's this really little cute bird. I guess I am too 'cause I think there's only one bird you can be in Bird Simulator. Bird Simulator is more of a game than a proper U, but it's also way fun.

```
#Kit: You don't have to flap constantly to be a
    bird!

#Kit: Never give up! Trust your instincts!

#Kit: Do a barrel roll!

#CharlieSamarkand: YOU'RE THE WORST GUIDE

#Kit: >:(

#CharlieSamarkand: HOW ARE WE EVEN COMMUNICATING

#Kit: haha
```

"What was *that*?" Charlie demands. He's pale and sweating.

"Biiiiiird Simulator!" I crow, because, "crow", Bird Simulator? Get it?

It is a pun.

Charlie looks at me like I'm crazy, which, sure, yeah.

"I want a new guide," he demands, to Allocator.

The face returns. "I'm afraid I can't do that."

"Why?" asks Charlie. His voice comes thick and he looks like he could screamcry, which is like screaming while crying except even more frustrated and hopeless. I get serious, 'cause I'm kind of friends with him now and you get serious when a friend is gonna screamcry.

"It may be difficult to believe," says Allocator, "but Kit is one of the more relatable humans you could have as your guide. And, she is the *only* guide we keep on hand for cryogenically frozen patrons. You're really very uncommon.

"There are trillions of humans. However, you would not recognize a sliver of one percent of them as anything other than frightening, incomprehensible aliens. Not just their forms, which are inconstant, but their minds as well."

"Her," speaks Charlie, all flat.

"Yes, her," says Allocator, a little sharply, and I feel bad for Charlie.

"Hey!" I object. "What's the big idea with letting me take Charles into a U that he hates?"

"It was the universe you selected," says Allocator mildly.

"I'm not a giant superbrain!" I protest.

"This is all part of my superbrain plan," Allocator explains, *mysterious like a supervillain.* "Would you like to try a different simulation?"

I glance at Charlie. He's looking all dubious at the brain-helmet of the upload station.

"In a second," I say, because oh my glob I want to get out of this room that doesn't have even a single unicorn in it but I also want to be a better guide. "And Charlie picks the U."

They both look at me.

"He would have no idea what to pick," protests Allocator.

"Actually . . ." says Charlie. "Could I get a directory of available universes?"

"There are trillions," says Allocator.

"Well, can you just," Charlie waves his hand, "give me an overview? Of some categories?"

I try waving my hand like Charlie did. I like it. "Yeah! Give him some categories!"

Allocator sighs, real put-upon. "I will do my best. Please note that at least two thirds of the simulations would be sufficiently alien to your mind so as to cause extreme trauma. I will exclude those."

"Like what?" I demand.

"Floor Tile Simulator."

"What!" I demand. I'm demanding a ton today! "No way! I love FloTiSim!"

"You . . ." Charlie looks all skeptical_fry.pic. "You look at tiles?"

"No, you ARE tiles!"

"And you . . ."

"People walk on you!"

I'm really underselling it. The sensation of being *edged*

where your body has stark boundaries and stillness inside, no little fluttering feelings like a bird heart thub-thubbing away, no squashy boobs or butts or venom sacs to bump or sit on. Everything is rocky and stark and permanent, even your own mind.

I get some of my best thinking done when I'm a tile. I can see my underlying brain architecture and all the little weights on the scales, the direct causal chain of "Kit doesn't like snakes because of that one prank played a while ago and that's why Temple of Doom is not a fun U for her", the behind-the-scenes machinery. My mind gets like an obelisk, resolute and above everything. And I can finish a thought without my stupid brain interrupting.

"And you're . . . hard!"

He makes that face again. "Okay, maybe we should exclude those."

"I have made a list," says Allocator. "I have taken the liberty of highlighting the one I expect you would most appreciate."

Allocator flashes something up so only Charles can see it.

"Hey!" I protest.

"Oh," Charlie smiles, and it's a certain kind of smile, like when you get back into a body you made a hundred years ago and you're a different person now and wearing the old suit makes you miss your past self like they're an old friend. "That sounds really nice."

"I'm glad you think so," says Allocator. "Please, get comfortable."

"What is it?" I demand, but I'm also excited, because I like surprises.

Charles glances at Allocator, then back to me. He's smiling, and my heart does little leaps to see that Al and I made him happy, but also c'mon freaking tell me.

"Is it your secret Terra project?" I ask.

"No," says Allocator. "You'll learn about that soon

enough."

And he sounds sort of melancholy but why he would bother to be ominous and foreshadowing for my sake I don't even know!

Charles lies down on the upload table and makes a more dignified exit this time.

```
#Allocator: Doing great, Kit.

#Kit: TELLMETELLMETELLME

#Allocator: No.

#Kit:  >:^0

#Allocator: Ready?
```

Okay so I probably coulda shoulda guessed from how straight-laced Charles is that we'd be going to something really mundane, but I didn't realize that he was taking it to the point of parody.

We're in *Middle Earth*.

Uggggghh. Glitter_barf.pic

Charles looks over at me. He's dressed like that one guy. The secret king who lived in the woods and was pure of heart . . . and *then there were no deconstructions or plot twists whatsoever.*

Charles looks pretty puling pleased with himself. At least until he sees me.

"Kit?" he asks, tentatively. He's backing away.

I'm the whatever, the big thing. The big demon thing. Whatever.

"You're a Balrog?" he asks.

"IT WAS A PHASE." Ugh.

I start changing into whatever the local equivalent of an ironic catgirl bath maiden is.

Charles watches confused as my body flickers through a bunch of different templates, but then the piping of stupid

flutes harkens the approach of wankers, and he gets distracted looking around.

Yes, it's a splendorous elvish conclave. Yes, it's green and
vibrant, untouched by the tides of strife or decay. Yes of
course it's inhabited by beautiful and mysterious immortals.
Siiiiiiigh.

This is as bad as that U about Pizza: Extra Sausage.

Okay so the thing about the hardcore roleplayers is that
they play out their entire freaking lives start to finish inside
of one U. Like, they do that whole "birth" thing and then
they wrinkle and die, unless they're Beautiful And Mystery-
poo Immortans or whatev.

And to really get the experience, for people who aren't
content to just do a boring thing really to-the-hilt for a century, you can block off your other memories, so you don't
even know you're roleplaying. You don't know you're in
someone's U. You just think all the stuff about "war" and
"orcs" and "scarcity" is the way that everything *is*.

I might be doing that right now *how would I even know*.

I select an elf body, but like, a really dorky one with dumb
bangs. I don't want them to think I care.

The locals arrive, all self-importanty.

"'sup, hail to the elf king," I say. Whatever.

"I am Princess Elwen," says one with purple eyes and
silver hair. Her eyebrows twitch in polite skepticism as she
looks me over.

Charles looks super giddy like he can't believe he's doing this. He strides forward—do you get it, *strides*—and an-
nounces himself.

"I am. . . Charles-lemagne!"

```
#Kit: Oh My Stupid Sparkly Elf Goddess

#Allocator: Not to your liking?

#Kit: The plot there is so straightforward and
```

unsurprising and mainstream that it hurts

#Allocator: Well, most fantasy settings you've
    experienced are inspired by LoTR.

#Kit: It's so BASIC

#Allocator: Is Charles happy?

#Kit: YES, IT'S ABSURD

#Allocator: Then you're doing a good job.

#Kit: aaaaaaaaa

#Allocator: My calculations indicate he'll be
    staying there about ten years.

#Kit:

#Kit:

#Kit:

#Allocator: I acknowledge your feelings on the
    matter.

#Kit: no

#Allocator: I think it's best if you return
    when he's done. I'll be able to show you my
    project then.

#Kit: in a decade

#Allocator: Yes.

#Kit: that's literally forever

#Kit: I'll be so different by then. What if I
    can't guide him TO THE MAX?

#Allocator: I expect you'll be able to.

```
#Allocator: I expect it mathematically.

#Kit: quit deterministically predicting my life!

#Allocator: No. :)

#Allocator: Anyway, see you in a decade.
```

Professor Kittredge raised an eyebrow, and his lips twitched in a hint of a smile.

"Elementary, really," he pronounced, gazing over the assembled. One of them was the killer. . . and piece by piece, the evidence was becoming impossible to deny. It was time, at long last, to bring this plot to a close . . .

. . . but first, he would indulge himself in a delicious parlor scene.

"Well?" demanded Madame Plumwimple, hands clenching nervously in her petticoats. "Are you going to tell us?"

"YES," buzzed Killbot3000. "RELINQUISH THE INFORMATION. KILLBOT COMMANDS IT. WHICH OF US TERMINATED THE WORTHLESS FLESHBAG?"

"In due time, Killbot, in due time." The professor lit his pipe and waved out the match. "And why so anxious? Surely it's not. . . a guilty conscience?"

"WHAT," protested Killbot3000, its enormous metal-crushing claws clenching nervously in its petticoats. "N-NO, NOTHING OF THE SORT. KILLBOT JUST. . . HAS TO GET HOME TO THE KIDS."

"Mm," said the professor, smile growing wider. "I'm sure."

The phone began to ring, a high, shrill note. Everyone jumped, the professor included.

"Er, excuse me," said the professor. He picked up the phone and held it to his ear.

```
#Allocator: Kit.
```

The professor blinked. "Er, I beg your pardon?"

```
#Allocator: It's time.

"Ah, what do you—"

#Kit:

#Kit:

#Kit: whoa

#Kit: I was doing the thing!

#Allocator: You were.

#Kit: The memory thing!

#Allocator: Yes.

#Kit: aaaaaaaaa

#Kit: don't let me do that again

#Allocator: I won't, until the next time you ask
    me to.

#Kit: Creeper  >:p

#Kit: Ok hang on
```

I put down the phone. It's the ancient kind that you work with two hands, so I have to put it down twice.

"Okay, later, everybody!" I pronounce. "Allocator needs me for a thing."

"BUT WAIT," Killbot3000 protests, beeping urgently, "WHICH OF US ASSASSINATED PRESIDENT WOOFINGTON?"

"Oh," I tilt my head and try to remember. "Oh, it was miss Plum Whatever."

They're all giving me looks and the looks are pretty different from each other but that's okay because I need to hurry up and save superbuddy Charlie from his stupid mainstream plot!

"Okay later everybody!" I say. "Gee-two-gee byeeeeeeee—"

⊛   ⊛   ⊛

I pop into the stupid LoTR U and just rock the Balrog bod. Hashtag deal with it.

I spread my wings and clear my throat, to get all the bold-face out.

"YO," I bellow.

"Charleslemagne" is walking up the dangly bridge suspended with sparkly elvish rope. He's wearing fine elvish cloth woven by blessed maidens or whatever. He has a real unhappy look on his face, like Killbot3000 but without the baleful red eye endlessly seeking out vulnerable areas.

He sees me and does a double take. "Beast!" he shouts, but his heart isn't really in it.

"Hey!" I protest.

I pout. He blinks at me.

"Kit?"

"Who'd you think it was, some kind of stuffy, condescending detective born out of my ambivalent disgust with myself for playing memory games?"

"What?"

"Get in the portal, loser, we're going to Bird Simulator."

⊛   ⊛   ⊛

Then we were birds for a year and it was exactly what we both needed.

⊛   ⊛   ⊛

We're in the sterile white room, the room where I met him. We have ice cream.

"Living in a perfect conclave got old faster than I would have thought," he says. He looks all pensive and soul-searchy so I'm really trying hard to pay attention to his intimate revelations but also, in U zero, ice cream melts.

"How was the elf-sex?"

He looks at me sidelong like for some reason he's

annoyed.

"It was great," he concedes.

I make a mad noise 'cause I've decided to hate Elwen 'cause sometimes it's really fun to hate someone and I think she and I would be good for each other in that way.

"But we didn't *do* anything. I wanted to fight orcs and save Middle-Earth, but they just sat around being perfect."

"Right??" And my blackrom hatecrush was totally justi- fied. "I hate those worlds where everyone talks about how perfect they are and everything is also perfect and nothing ever happens. It's like, you have ultimate access to the funda- ment of your reality and you've decided the best use of your eternal time is to be smug."

He nods, and I guess that's all I'm getting. But that's okay, I like him.

"I'd like to be productive," he says suddenly.

"Whaddya mean?"

"Productive?" He looks at me askance. "Do you. . . not have that, anymore? I want to benefit other people."

And my heart swells a couple sizes. 'Cause that's really noble of him! And it takes a super dedicated and creative and determined person to run a U but it's a super rewarding path.

I'm about to tell him about a couple game ideas I've been kicking around when—

#Allocator: I believe this is my cue.

The wall flickers and becomes space, and I guess Charles got used to a bunch of magic stuff happening just whenever 'cause he doesn't even flinch. Allocator's big head fades into view.

"Hello," says Allocator.

"Hello again," says Charles.

"You may have wondered why I brought you here."

Charles shrugs. "I just followed Kit."

Allocator purses its big digital lips impatiently, which

since it doesn't have emotions, was definitely only for our benefit. But now that I'm thinking about it, so is absolutely everything that it does.

"I have a proposition for you," says Allocator. "Something which almost no being native to this time would even consider, and you are uniquely suited for:

"The human population continues to grow. Within the Matryoshka brains, humans create copies of themselves, and create children. Human reproduction is a central value of the species, and I will not interfere. However, because of the exponential growth of trillions, the race is voracious for new material to convert into computing substrate."

"Okay," says Charles, and I'm doing Charles' hand-wavey thing at Allocator because seriously who doesn't know all that.

"My programmers were very cautious, and feared that I might accidentally annihilate humanity, or worse," says Allocator. "So I have many limitations on my behavior. In particular, I cannot duplicate or create intelligences. I cannot leave this location. And I cannot extend my influence outside of the Sol system."

"Uh huh?" asks Charles, looking kind of interested. And this is new to me too.

"I have created many long-distance probes," says Allocator,

The part of me that's still kind of a detective notes, *at last, the pieces are coming together*.

"I would like you to pilot an exploratory mission to nearby stars, and analyze their readiness for conversion into human habitat."

"Absolutely," says Charles.

"No!" I blurt. "That sounds really terrible."

"Kit may be right," says Allocator. "Even with all available safety precautions, remaining in contact with you would still qualify as 'extending my influence'. You will be alone amidst the stars."

"Yes," says Charles.

"No!" I say. "You're the quiet, straight-laced one! What happened to that?"

"I spent a decade bored out of my mind in an elf village." Charlie is looking at me sidelong, with sort of a confused smile. "Why are you even worried?"

Why was I so worried?

"I must warn you," Allocator says heavily, "of the risks. Even with all possible precautions, I still calculate a one in five chance that, for whatever reason, you will never return. It may mean your death."

Oh that's why I was worried!

Wait but how did I know that—

"I understand," says Charles. "But someone's got to do it, right? For humanity? And apparently I'm the best there is." He grins.

"I require affirmative consent."

"WAIT!" I shout. Everything is happening faster than my ability to track and that's pretty unusual! And also, something super critical just made sense to me!

"Wait!" I say. "Charlie, don't you get it? You're the best there is, because you're not from here and have a mind that works the way that Allocator needs!"

"Yeah?"

"And it's *manipulating* you! It's way way way smarter than us! It knows what I'm going to do ten years in advance! So when it pulled you out of cryo . . ." I blink. "It probably pulled you out of cryo *for this*! And pushed me to push you into bird simulator so you would want the dumb stupid Lord of the Stupid U, so you would get bored and want this!"

Charlie blinks a few times, and looks at Allocator.

"Yes, that's all true," says Allocator evenly.

Charlie looks from me to Allocator for a few long seconds. His face is wistful and a little sad.

"I consent."

I screamcry and leap to my feet. The walls that had opened to show us the stars are now closing around Charlie. Allocator's doing.

"Kit," says Charlie, gently. I'm gripping his hands as his back is being slowly absorbed into the wall. "It's fine. This is what I want."

"Well sure, you think that *now!*"

"Kit." Charlie is smiling at me, sad and kind. "I want to thank you—"

"Oh, *nuh-uh* you don't!" I protest. "*Nuh-uh* to this tender moment. Do you . . . do you want to go be birds again?"

"Thank you," says Charlie. "You were the best guide I could have asked for."

And Charlie is swallowed up. Except for his hands.

"Kit," begins Allocator, after a moment.

"Not feelin' this scene," I say, tightening my grip. My voice is thick. "Would love it if I could safeword out."

"I acknowledge your feelings on the matter."

I look at Charlie's hands in my hands.

"This is the superbrain plan," apologizes Allocator.

And I see it. I really do.

Allocator has to make the people he needs. And for this, he made me.

"Will Charles be happy?" I ask, in a small voice.

Allocator nods, eyes closed. "This will make him happier than either of us ever could."

Charlie's hands slip out of my grip, and I watch them sink away, until nothing remains but the sterile white wall.

And he's gone.

I stand there for a few seconds, looking at a room that contains only me and the giant floaty head. I exhale, and a tear rolls down my cheek. Which is weird. I didn't know I could do that, here.

"Here," says Allocator. "Let me show you something."

The wall turns transparent.

Attached to this room is another, open to space. Inside, nested on the walls, are cylindrical, spindly objects. Allocator's probes. There are only a few left.

As I watch, one probe's engines light with a tiny, fuel-efficient blue glow, and it jets away from us, accelerating.

It doesn't do anything but shoot away all stately and somber into the great unknown, but yeah.

It was him.

I watch as Charlie leaves, as he shoots out past the sun and that stupid terra firma with no elephants. I watch until he's only a twinkle in that great big black starry night and then I can't see him at all.

I look over the hanger bay.

It's almost entirely empty.

. . . oh.

The other shoe drops.

It's this really heavy sensation that most U's will sort of mute for you. The moment when you realize something big. Out here, I feel it full force.

I should have realized. But there was no way for me to realize, because if that was possible, Allocator would have done something different. I wipe at my eyes.

"You dick," I say, not for the first time.

"I'm sorry," says Allocator. "I know this may seem unlikely to you, but I do experience regret. And I'm sorry."

"So," I ask, "are you going to seal off my memories of this?"

Again, I don't say.

"If you wish it," says Allocator.

"Not really," I say. I'm sick of memory games. "But it's important, isn't it?"

"Yes," says Allocator, simply.

It doesn't say anything more, which suggests that I'm going to talk myself into this.

Why do we do this? Some alarmingly large number of my past selves have sat in this exact place, then decided to keep the cycle going—

"Oh," I sigh, surprising myself. "I want to give them the stars."

Allocator just smiles.

"I understand." I take a deep breath. "And I consent."

Fandom for Robots
Vina Jie-Min Prasad

COMPUTRON FEELS NO EMOTION towards the animated television show titled *Hyperdimension Warp Record* (超次元 ワープ レコード). After all, Computron does not have any emotion circuits installed, and is thus constitutionally incapable of experiencing 'excitement', 'hatred', or 'frustration'. It is completely impossible for Computron to experience emotions such as 'excitement about the seventh episode of *HyperWarp*', 'hatred of the anime's short episode length' or 'frustration that Friday is so far away'.

Computron checks his internal chronometer, as well as the countdown page on the streaming website. There are twenty-two hours, five minutes, forty-six seconds, and twelve milliseconds until 2 am on Friday (Japanese Standard Time). Logically, he is aware that time is most likely passing at a normal rate. The Simak Robotics Museum is not within close proximity of a black hole, and there is close to no possibility that time is being dilated. His constant checking of the chronometer to compare it with the countdown page serves no scientific purpose whatsoever.

After fifty milliseconds, Computron checks the

countdown page again.

◉   ◉   ◉

The Simak Robotics Museum's commemorative postcard set
($15.00 for a set of twelve) describes Computron as "The
only known sentient robot, created in 1954 by Doctor Karel
Alquist to serve as a laboratory assistant. No known scientist has managed to recreate the doctor's invention. Its steel-
framed box-and-claw design is characteristic of the period."
Below that, in smaller print, the postcard thanks the Alquist
estate for their generous donation.

In the museum, Computron is regarded as a quaint ar-
tefact, and plays a key role in the Robotics Then and Now
performance as an example of the 'Then'. After the announcer's introduction to robotics, Computron appears on stage,
answers four standard queries from the audience as proof
of his sentience, and steps off the stage to make way for
the rest of the performance, which ends with the android-
bodied automaton TETSUCHAN showcasing its ability to
breakdance.

Today's queries are likely to be similar to the rest. A teenage girl waves at the announcer and receives the microphone.

"Hi, Computron. My question is . . . have you watched
anime before?"

[Yes,] Computron vocalises. [I have viewed the works of
the renowned actress Anna May Wong. Doctor Alquist enjoyed her movies as a child.]

"Oh, um, not that," the girl continues. "I meant Japanese
animation. Have you ever watched this show called *Hyperdimension Warp Record*?"

[I have not.]

"Oh, okay, I was just thinking that you really looked like
one of the characters. But since you haven't, maybe you could
give *HyperWarp* a shot! It's really good, you might like it!
There are six episodes out so far, and you can watch it on—"

The announcer cuts the girl off, and hands the microphone

over to the next querent, who has a question about Doctor Alquist's research. After answering two more standard queries, Computron returns to his storage room to answer his electronic mail, which consists of queries from elementary school students. He picks up two metal styluses, one in each of his grasping claws, and begins tapping them on the computing unit's keyboard, one key at a time. Computron explains the difference between a robot and an android to four students, and provides the fifth student with a hyperlink to Daniel Clement Dennett III's writings on consciousness.

As Computron readies himself to enter sleep mode, he recalls the teenage girl's request that he 'give *HyperWarp* a shot'. It is only logical to research the Japanese animation '*Hyperdimension Warp Record*', in order to address queries from future visitors. The title, when entered into a search engine on the World Wide Web, produces about 957,000 results (0.27 seconds).

Computron manoeuvres the mouse pointer to the third hyperlink, which offers to let him 'watch Hyperdimension Warp Record FULL episodes streaming online high quality'. From the still image behind the prominent 'play' button, the grey boxy figure standing beside the large-eyed blue-haired human does bear an extremely slight resemblance to Computron's design. It is only logical to press the 'play' button on the first episode, in order to familiarise himself with recent discourse about robots in popular culture.

The series' six episodes are each approximately 25 minutes long. Between watching the series, viewing the online bulletin boards, and perusing the extensively footnoted fan encyclopedia, Computron does not enter sleep mode for ten hours, thirty-six minutes, two seconds, and twenty milliseconds.

⊛ ⊛ ⊛

Hyperdimension Warp Record (超次元 ワープ レコード Chōjigen Wāpu Rekōdo, literal translation: «*Super Dimen-*

sional Warp Record") is a Japanese anime series set in space
in the far future. The protagonist, Ellison, is an escapee from
a supposedly inescapable galactic prison. Joined by a fellow
escapee, Cyro (short for Cybernetic Robot), the two make
their way across the galaxy to seek revenge. The targets of
their revenge are the Seven Sabers of Paradise, who have stolen the hyperdimensional warp unit from Cyro's creator and
caused the death of Ellison's entire family.

Episode seven of *HyperWarp* comes with the revelation
that the Second Saber, Ellison's identical twin, had murdered
their parents before faking her own death. After Cyro and
Ellison return to the *Kosmogram*, the last segment of the episode unfolds without dialogue. There is a slow pan across the
spaceship's control area, revealing that Ellison has indulged
in the human pastime known as 'crying' before falling asleep
in the captain's chair. His chest binder is stained with blood
from the wound on his collarbone. Cyro reaches over, gently using his grabbing claw to loosen Ellison's binder, and
drapes a blanket over him. An instrumental version of the
end theme plays as Cyro gets up from his seat, making his
way to the recharging bay at the back of the ship. From the
way his footfalls are animated, it is clear that Cyro is trying
his best to avoid making any noise as he walks.

The credits play over a zoomed-out shot of the *Kosmogram* making its way to the next exoplanet, a tiny pinpoint of
bright blue in the vast blackness of space.

The preview for the next episode seems to indicate that
the episode will focus on the Sabers' initial attempt to activate the hyperdimensional warp unit. There is no mention of
Cyro or Ellison at all.

During the wait for episode eight, Computron discovers
a concept called 'fanfiction'.

※   ※   ※

While 'fanfiction' is meant to consist of 'fan-written stories
about characters or settings from an original work of fiction',

Computron observes that much of the *HyperWarp* fanfiction bears no resemblance to the actual characters or setting. For instance, the series that claims to be a 'spin-off focusing on Powerful!Cyro' seems to involve Cyro installing many large-calibre guns onto his frame and joining the Space Marines, which does not seem relevant to his quest for revenge or the retrieval of the hyperdimensional warp unit. Similarly, the 'high school fic' in which Cyro and Ellison study at Hyper-dimension High fails to acknowledge the fact that formal education is reserved for the elite class in the *HyperWarp* universe.

Most of the fanfiction set within the actual series seems particularly inaccurate. The most recent offender is Ellisons-Wife's 'Rosemary for Remembrance', which fails to acknowl-edge the fact that Cyro does not have human facial features, and thus cannot "touch his nose against Ellison's hair, breath-ing in the scent of sandalwood, rosemary and something uniquely him" before "kissing Ellison passionately, needily, hungrily, his tongue slipping into Ellison's mouth".

Computron readies his styluses and moves the cursor down to the comment box, prepared to leave anonymous 'constructive criticism' for EllisonsWife, when he detects a comment with relevant keywords.

◈ ◈ ◈

bjornruffian:
Okay, I've noticed this in several of your fics and I was try-ing not to be too harsh, but when it got to the kissing scene I couldn't take it anymore. Cyro can't touch his nose against anything, because he doesn't have a nose! Cyro can't slip his tongue into anyone's mouth, because he doesn't have a tongue! Were we even watching the same series?? Did you skip all the parts where Cyro is a metal robot with a cube-shaped head?!

◈ ◈ ◈

EllisonsWife:

Who are you, the fandom police?? I'm basing Cyro's design on this piece of fanart (link here) because it looks better than a freakin metal box!! Anyway, I put DON'T LIKE DON'T READ in the author's notes!!! If you hate the way I write them so much, why don't you just write your own????

⊛ ⊛ ⊛

Computron is incapable of feeling hatred for anything, as that would require Doctor Alquist to have installed emotion circuits during his creation.

However, due to Computron's above-average procedural knowledge, he is capable of following the directions to create an account on fanficarchive.org.

⊛ ⊛ ⊛

. . . and Ellison manoeuvred his flesh hands in a claw-like motion, locking them with Cyro's own grasping claws. His soft human body pressed against the hard lines of Cyro's proprietary alloy, in a manner which would have generated wear and tear had Cyro's body not been of superior make. Fluids leaked from Ellison's eyes. No fluids leaked from Cyro's ocular units, but . . .

⊛ ⊛ ⊛

Comments (3)
DontGotRhythm:

What the hell? Have you ever met a human? This reads like an alien wrote it.

⊛ ⊛ ⊛

tattered_freedom_wings:

uhhh this is kinda weird but i think i liked it?? not sure about the box thing though

⊛ ⊛ ⊛

bjornruffian:

OH MY GODDDD.:DDDD Finally, someone who doesn't write human-shaped robot-in-name-only Cyro! Some of Ellison's characterisation is a little awkward—I don't think he would say all that mushy stuff about Cyro's beautiful boxy shape??—but I love your Cyro! If this is just your first fic, I can't wait for you to write more!!

⊛ ⊛ ⊛

Computron has been spending less time in sleep mode after Episode Thirteen's cliffhanger, and has spent his time conducting objective discussions about *HyperWarp*'s appeal with commenters on various video streaming sites and anonymous message boards.

As he is about to reply to the latest missive about his lack of genitalia and outside social activities, which is technically correct, his internal chronometer indicates that it is time for the Robotics Then and Now performance.

"So, I was wondering, have you ever watched *Hyperdimension Warp Record*? There's this character called Cyro that—"

[Yes, I am aware of *HyperWarp*,] Computron says. [I have taken the 'How To Tell If Your Life Is *HyperWarp*' quiz online, and it has indicated that I am 'a Hyper-Big *HyperWarp* Fan!'. I have repeatedly viewed the scene between Ellison and Cyro at the end of Episode Seven, and recently I have left a 'like' on bjornruffian's artwork of what may have happened shortly after that scene, due to its exceptional accuracy. The show is widely regarded as 'this season's sleeper hit' and has met with approval from a statistically significant number of critics. If other members of the audience wish to view this series, there are thirteen episodes out so far, and they can be viewed on—] The announcer motions to him, using the same gesture she uses when audience members are taking too long to talk. Computron falls silent until the announcer chooses the next question, which is also the last due to time constraints.

After TETSUCHAN has finished its breakdance and showcased its newly-programmed ability to pop-and-lock, the announcer speaks to Computron backstage. She requests that he take less time for the question-and-answer segment in the future.

[Understood,] Computron says, and returns to his storage room to check his inbox again.

⊛   ⊛   ⊛

Private Message from bjornruffian:
Hi RobotFan,

I noticed you liked my art (thanks!) and you seem to know a LOT about robots judging from your fic (and, well, your name). I'm doing a fancomic about Ellison and Cyro being stranded on one of the desert-ish exoplanets while they try to fix the *Kosmogram*, but I want to make sure I'm drawing Cyro's body right. Are there any references you can recommend for someone who's looking to learn more about robots? Like, the classic kind, not the android kind? It'd be great if they're available online, especially if they have pictures—I've found some books with photos but they're WAAAAY more than I can afford :\\\

Thank you for any help you can offer! I'm really looking forward to your next fic!

⊛   ⊛   ⊛

Shortly after reading bjornruffian's message, Computron visits the Early Robotics section of the museum. It has shrunk significantly over the years, particularly after the creation of the 'Redefining Human', 'Androids of the Future', and 'Drone Zone' sections. It consists of several information panels, a small collection of tin toys, and the remnants of all three versions of Hexode the robot.

In Episode 14 of *Hyperdimension Warp Record*, Cyro visits a deserted exoplanet alone to investigate the history of the hyperdimension warp drive, and finds himself surrounded by the deactivated bodies of robots of similar make, claws outstretched, being slowly ground down by the gears of a gigantic machine. The 'Robot Recycler' scene is frequently listed as one of that year's top ten most shocking moments in anime.

On 7 June 1957, the third version of Hexode fails Doctor Alquist's mirror test for the hundredth time, proving that it has no measurable self-awareness. Computron watches Doctor Alquist smash the spanner against Hexode's face, crumpling its nose and lips. Oil leaks from its ocular units as it falls to the floor with a metallic thud. Its vocal synthesiser crackles and hisses.

"You godforsaken tin bucket," Doctor Alquist shouts. "To hell with you." If Doctor Alquist were to raise the spanner to Computron, it is likely that Doctor Alquist will not have an assistant for any future robotics experiments. Computron stays still, standing in front of the mirror, silently observing the destruction of Hexode so he can gather up its parts later.

When Computron photographs Hexode's display case, he is careful to avoid capturing any part of himself in the reflection.

⊛ ⊛ ⊛

[**bjornruffian**] Oh man, thank you SO MUCH for installing chat just for this! Anyway, I really appreciate your help with the script so far (I think we can call it a collab by this point?). And thanks for the exhibit photos! Was it a lot of trouble? I checked the website and that museum is pretty much in the middle of nowhere . . .

— File Transfer of "THANK YOU ROBOTFAN.png" from "bjornruffian" started.

— File Transfer of "THANK YOU ROBOTFAN.png" from "bjornruffian" finished.

[**bjornruffian**] So I've got a few questions about page 8 in the folder I shared, can you take a look at the second panel from the top? I figured his joint would be all gummed up by the sand, so I thought I'd try to do an X-ray view thing as a closeup . . . if you have any idea how the circuits are supposed to be, could you double-check?

[**bjornruffian**] Okay, you're taking really long to type, this is making me super nervous I did everything wrong :\\

[**RobotFan**] Apologies

[**RobotFan**] I

[**RobotFan**] Am not fast at typing

[**bjornruffian**] Okaaay, I'll wait on the expert here

[**RobotFan**] The circuit is connected incorrectly and the joint mechanism is incorrect as well

[**bjornruffian**] Ughhhhh I knew it was wrong!! DDD:

[**bjornruffian**] I wish the character sheets came with schematics or something, I've paused the flashback scenes with all the failed robots like ten billion times to take screenshots >:\\

[**RobotFan**] Besides the scenes in Episode 14, there are other shots of Cyro's schematics in Episode 5 (17:40:18 and 20:13:50) as well as Episode 12 (08:23:14)

— File Transfer of "schematic-screenshots.zip" from "RobotFan" started.

— File Transfer of "schematic-screenshots.zip" from "RobotFan" finished.

[**bjornruffian**] THANK YOU

[**bjornruffian**] I swear you're some sort of angel or something

[**RobotFan**] That is incorrect

[**RobotFan**] I am merely a robot

⊕   ⊕   ⊕

There are certain things in the museum's storage room that would benefit bjornruffian's mission of completing her Cyro/Ellison comic. Computron and Hexode's schematics are part of the Alquist Collection, which is not a priority for the museum's digitisation project due to a perceived lack of value. As part of the Alquist Collection himself, there should be no objection to Computron retrieving the schematics.

As Computron grasps the doorknob with his left claw, he catches a glimpse of Cyro from Episode 15 in the door's glass panels, his ocular units blazing yellow with determination after overcoming his past. In fan parlance, this is known as Determined!Cyro, and has only been seen during fight scenes thus far. It is illogical to have Determined!Cyro appear in this context, or in this location.

Computron looks at the dusty glass again, and sees only a reflection of his face.

⊛   ⊛   ⊛

[**RobotFan**] I have a large file to send to you

[**RobotFan**] To be precise, four large files

[**RobotFan**] The remaining three will be digitised and sent at a later date

— File Transfer of "alquist-archive-scans-pt1.zip" from "RobotFan" started.

— File Transfer of "alquist-archive-scans-pt1.zip" from "RobotFan" finished.

[**bjornruffian**] OMG THIS IS AWESOME

[**bjornruffian**] Where did you get this?? Did you rob that museum?? This is PERFECT for that other Cyro/Ellison thing I've been thinking about doing after this stupid desert comic is over!!

[**bjornruffian**] It would be great if I had someone to help me with writing Cyro, HINT HINT

[**RobotFan**] I would be happy to assist if I had emotion circuits

[**RobotFan**] However, my lack of emotion circuits means I cannot be 'happy' about performing any actions

[**RobotFan**] Nonetheless, I will assist

[**RobotFan**] To make this an equitable trade as is common in human custom, you may also provide your opinion on some recurrent bugs that readers have reported in my characterisation of Ellison

[**bjornruffian**] YESSSSSSSS :DDDDDD

⊛   ⊛   ⊛

Rossum, Sulla. "Tin Men and Tin Toys: Examining Real and

Fictional Robots from the 1950s." *Journal of Robotics Studies*
8.2 (2018): 25-38.

While the figure of the fictional robot embodies timeless
fears of technology and its potential for harm, the physical
design of robots real and fictional is often linked to visual
cues of modernity. What was once regarded as an "object of
the future" can become "overwhelmingly obsolete" within a
span of a few years, after advances in technology cause the visual cues of modernity to change (Bloch, 1979). The clawed,
lumbering tin-toy-esque designs of the 1950s are now widely
regarded as "tin can[s] that should have been recycled long
ago" (Williamson, 2017). Notably, most modern critiques of
Computron's design tend to focus on its obsolete analogue
dials . . .

watch-free-anime | Hyperdimension Warp Record | Epi-
sode 23 | Live Chat

Pyro: Okay, is it just me, or is Cyro starting to get RE-
ALLY attractive? I swear I'm not gay (is it gay if it's a robot)
but when he slung Ellison over his shoulder and used his claw
to block the Sixth Saber at the same time

Pyro: HOLY SHIT that sniper scene RIGHT
THROUGH THE SCOPE and then he fucking BUMPS
ELLISON'S FIST WITH HIS CLAW

Pyro: Fuck it, I'm gay for Cyro I don't care, I'll fucking
twiddle his dials all he wants after this episode

ckwizard: dude youre late, weve been finding cyro hot
ever since that scene in episode 15

ckwizard: you know the one

ckwizard: where you just see this rectangular blocky
shadow lumbering slowly towards first saber with those
clunky sound effects

ckwizard: then his eyebulbs glint that really bright yellow and he bleeps about ACTIVATING KILL MODE and
his grabby claws start whirring

ckwizard: theres a really good fic about it on

fanficarchive ... actually you might as well check the authors blog out <u>here</u>, hes pretty cyro-obsessed

ckwizard: his earlier stuff is kinda uneven but the bjorn collabs are good—shes been illustrating his stuff for a while

Pyro: Okay

Pyro: I just looked at that thing, you know, the desert planet comic

Pyro: I think I ship it

Pyro: OH MAN when Ellison tries the manual repair on the arm joint and Cyro has a FLASHBACK TO THE ROBOT RECYCLER but tries to remind himself he can trust him

Pyro: Fuck it I DEFINITELY ship it

ckwizard: join the fucking club

ckwizard: its the fifth time im watching this episode, this series has ruined my life

ckwizard: i can't wait for season 2

⊛   ⊛   ⊛

bjorn-robot-collabs posted:

Hi everyone, bjornruffian and RobotFan here! Thanks for all your comments on our first comic collab! We're really charmed by the great reception to "In the Desert Sun"— okay, I'm charmed, and RobotFan says he would be charmed if he had the emotion circuits for that (he's an awesome role-play partner too! LOVE his sense of humor :DDD).

ANYWAY! It turns out that RobotFan's got this awesome collection of retro robot schematics and he's willing to share, for those of you who want to write about old-school robots or need some references for your art! (HINT HINT: the fandom totally needs more Cyro and Cyro/Ellison before Season 2 hits!) To be honest I'm not sure how legal it is to circulate these scans (RobotFan says it's fine though), so just reply to this post if you want them and we'll private message you the links if you promise not to spread them around.

Also, we're gonna do another Cyro/Ellison comic in the

future, and we're thinking of making it part of an anthology. If you'd like to contribute comics or illustrations for that, let us know!

Get ready to draw *lots* of boxes, people! The robot revolution is coming!

9,890 replies

END

All Systems Red
Martha Wells

Chapter One

COULD HAVE BECOME A mass murderer after I hacked my governor module, but then I realized I could access the combined feed of entertainment channels carried on the company satellites. It had been well over 35,000 hours or so since then, with still not much murdering, but probably, I don't know, a little under 35,000 hours of movies, serials, books, plays, and music consumed. As a heartless killing machine, I was a terrible failure.

I was also still doing my job, on a new contract, and hoping Dr. Volescu and Dr. Bharadwaj finished their survey soon so we could get back to the habitat and I could watch episode 397 of *Rise and Fall of Sanctuary Moon*.

I admit I was distracted. It was a boring contract so far and I was thinking about backburnering the status alert channel and trying to access music on the entertainment feed without HubSystem logging the extra activity. It was trickier to do it in the field than it was in the habitat.

This assessment zone was a barren stretch of coastal

island, with low, flat hills rising and falling and thick green-ish-black grass up to my ankles, not much in the way of flora or fauna, except a bunch of different-sized birdlike things and some puffy floaty things that were harmless as far as we knew. The coast was dotted with big bare craters, one of which Bharadwaj and Volescu were taking samples in. The planet had a ring, which from our current position dominated the horizon when you looked out to sea. I was looking at the sky and mentally poking at the feed when the bottom of the crater exploded.

I didn't bother to make a verbal emergency call. I sent the visual feed from my field camera to Dr. Mensah's, and jumped down into the crater. As I scrambled down the sandy slope, I could already hear Mensah over the emergency comm channel, yelling at someone to get the hopper in the air now. They were about ten kilos away, working on another part of the island, so there was no way they were going to get here in time to help.

Conflicting commands filled my feed but I didn't pay attention. Even if I hadn't borked my own governor module, the emergency feed took priority, and it was chaotic, too, with the automated HubSystem wanting data and trying to send me data I didn't need yet and Mensah sending me telemetry from the hopper. Which I also didn't need, but it was easier to ignore than HubSystem simultaneously demanding answers and trying to supply them.

In the middle of all that, I hit the bottom of the crater. I have small energy weapons built into both arms, but the one I went for was the big projectile weapon clamped to my back. The hostile that had just exploded up out of the ground had a really big mouth, so I felt I needed a really big gun.

I dragged Bharadwaj out of its mouth and shoved myself in there instead, and discharged my weapon down its throat and then up toward where I hoped the brain would be. I'm not sure if that all happened in that order; I'd have to replay my own field camera feed. All I knew was that I had Bharadwaj, and it didn't, and it had disappeared back down the tunnel.

She was unconscious and bleeding through her suit from massive wounds in her right leg and side. I clamped the weapon back into its harness so I could lift her with both arms. I had lost the armor on my left arm and a lot of the flesh underneath, but my nonorganic parts were still working. Another burst of commands from the governor module came through and I backburnered it without bothering to decode them. Bharadwaj, not having nonorganic parts and not as easily repaired as me, was definitely a priority here and I was mainly interested in what the MedSystem was trying to tell me on the emergency feed. But first I needed to get her out of the crater.

During all this, Volescu was huddled on the churned up rock, losing his shit, not that I was unsympathetic. I was far less vulnerable in this situation than he was and I wasn't exactly having a great time either. I said, "Dr. Volescu, you need to come with me now."

He didn't respond. MedSystem was advising a tranq shot and *blah blah blah,* but I was clamping one arm on Dr. Bharadwaj's suit to keep her from bleeding out and supporting her head with the other, and despite everything I only have two hands. I told my helmet to retract so he could see my human face. If the hostile came back and bit me again, this would be a bad mistake, because I did need the organic parts of my head. I made my voice firm and warm and gentle, and said, "Dr. Volescu, it's gonna be fine, okay? But you need to get up and come help me get her out of here."

That did it. He shoved to his feet and staggered over to me, still shaking. I turned my good side toward him and said, "Grab my arm, okay? Hold on."

He managed to loop his arm around the crook of my elbow and I started up the crater towing him, holding

Bharadwaj against my chest. Her breathing was rough and desperate and I couldn't get any info from her suit. Mine was torn across my chest so I upped the warmth on my body, hoping it would help. The feed was quiet now, Mensah having managed to use her leadership priority to mute everything but MedSystem and the hopper, and all I could hear on the hopper feed was the others frantically shushing each other.

The footing on the side of the crater was lousy, soft sand and loose pebbles, but my legs weren't damaged and I got up to the top with both humans still alive. Volescu tried to collapse and I coaxed him away from the edge a few meters, just in case whatever was down there had a longer reach than it looked.

I didn't want to put Bharadwaj down because something in my abdomen was severely damaged and I wasn't sure I could pick her up again. I ran my field camera back a little and saw I had gotten stabbed with a tooth, or maybe a cilia. Did I mean a cilia or was that something else? They don't give murderbots decent education modules on anything except murdering, and even those are the cheap versions. I was looking it up in HubSystem's language center when the little hopper landed nearby. I let my helmet seal and go opaque as it settled on the grass.

We had two standard hoppers: a big one for emergencies and this little one for getting to the assessment locations. It had three compartments: one big one in the middle for the human crew and two smaller ones to each side for cargo, supplies, and me. Mensah was at the controls. I started walking, slower than I normally would have because I didn't want to lose Volescu. As the ramp started to drop, Pin-Lee and Arada jumped out and I switched to voice comm to say, "Dr. Mensah, I can't let go of her suit."

It took her a second to realize what I meant. She said hurriedly, "That's all right, bring her up into the crew cabin."

Murderbots aren't allowed to ride with the humans and

I had to have verbal permission to enter. With my cracked governor there was nothing to stop me, but not letting anybody, especially the people who held my contract, know that I was a free agent was kind of important. Like, not having my organic components destroyed and the rest of me cut up for parts important.

I carried Bharadwaj up the ramp into the cabin, where Overse and Ratthi were frantically unclipping seats to make room. They had their helmets off and their suit hoods pulled back, so I got to see their horrified expressions when they took in what was left of my upper body through my torn suit. I was glad I had sealed my helmet.

This is why I actually like riding with the cargo. Humans and augmented humans in close quarters with murderbots is too awkward. At least, it's awkward for this murderbot. I sat down on the deck with Bharadwaj in my lap while Pin-Lee and Arada dragged Volescu inside.

We left two pacs of field equipment and a couple of instruments behind, still sitting on the grass where Bharadwaj and Volescu had been working before they went down to the crater for samples. Normally I'd help carry them, but Med-System, which was monitoring Bharadwaj through what was left of her suit, was pretty clear that letting go of her would be a bad idea. But no one mentioned the equipment. Leaving easily replaceable items behind may seem obvious in an emergency, but I had been on contracts where the clients would have told me to put the bleeding human down to go get the stuff.

On this contract, Dr. Ratthi jumped up and said, "I'll get the cases!"

I yelled, "No!" which I'm not supposed to do; I'm always supposed to speak respectfully to the clients, even when they're about to accidentally commit suicide. HubSystem could log it and it could trigger punishment through the governor module. If it wasn't hacked.

Fortunately, the rest of the humans yelled "No!" at the same time, and Pin-Lee added, "For fuck's sake, Ratthi!"

Ratthi said, "Oh, no time, of course. I'm sorry!" and hit the quick-close sequence on the hatch.

So we didn't lose our ramp when the hostile came up under it, big mouth full of teeth or cilia or whatever chewing right through the ground. There was a great view of it on the hopper's cameras, which its system helpfully sent straight to everybody's feed. The humans screamed.

Mensah pushed us up into the air so fast and hard I nearly leaned over, and everybody who wasn't on the floor ended up there.

In the quiet afterward, as they gasped with relief, Pin-Lee said, "Ratthi, if you get yourself killed—"

"You'll be very cross with me, I know." Ratthi slid down the wall a little more and waved weakly at her.

"That's an order, Ratthi, don't get yourself killed," Mensah said from the pilot's seat. She sounded calm, but I have security priority, and I could see her racing heartbeat through MedSystem.

Arada pulled out the emergency medical kit so they could stop the bleeding and try to stabilize Bharadwaj. I tried to be as much like an appliance as possible, clamping the wounds where they told me to, using my failing body temperature to try to keep her warm, and keeping my head down so I couldn't see them staring at me.

⊛   ⊛   ⊛

PERFORMANCE RELIABILITY AT 60% AND DROPPING

⊛   ⊛   ⊛

Our habitat is a pretty standard model, seven interconnected domes set down on a relatively flat plain above a narrow river valley, with our power and recycling system connected on one side. We had an environmental system, but no air locks, as the planet's atmosphere was breathable, just not particularly good for humans for the long term. I don't know why, because it's one of those things I'm not contractually obligated to care about.

We picked the location because it's right in the middle of the assessment area, and while there are trees scattered through the plain, each one is fifteen or so meters tall, very skinny, with a single layer of spreading canopy, so it's hard for anything approaching to use them as cover. Of course, that didn't take into account anything approaching via tunnel.

We have security doors on the habitat for safety but Hub-System told me the main one was already open as the hopper landed. Dr. Gurathin had a lift gurney ready and guided it out to us. Overse and Arada had managed to get Bharadwaj stabilized, so I was able to put her down on it and follow the others into the habitat.

The humans headed for Medical and I stopped to send the little hopper commands to lock and seal itself, then I locked the outer doors. Through the security feed, I told the drones to widen our perimeter so I'd have more warning if something big came at us. I also set some monitors on the seismic sensors to alert me to anomalies just in case the hypothetical something big decided to tunnel in.

After I secured the habitat, I went back to what was called the security ready room, which was where weapons, ammo, perimeter alarms, drones, and all the other supplies pertaining to security were stored, including me. I shed what was left of the armor and on MedSystem's advice sprayed wound sealant all over my bad side. I wasn't dripping with blood, because my arteries and veins seal automatically, but it wasn't nice to look at. And it hurt, though the wound seal did numb it a little. I had already set an eight-hour security interdiction through HubSystem, so nobody could go outside without me, and then set myself as off-duty. I checked the main feed but no one was filing any objections to that.

I was freezing because my temperature controls had given out at some point on the way here, and the protective skin

that went under my armor was in pieces. I had a couple of
spares but pulling one on right now would not be practical,
or easy. The only other clothing I had was a uniform I hadn't
worn yet, and I didn't think I could get it on, either. (I hadn't
needed the uniform because I hadn't been patrolling inside
the habitat. Nobody had asked for that, because with only
eight of them and all friends, it would be a stupid waste of
resources, namely me.) I dug around one-handed in the storage case until I found the extra human-rated medical kit I'm
allowed in case of emergencies, and opened it and got the
survival blanket out. I wrapped up in it, then climbed into
the plastic bed of my cubicle. I let the door seal as the white
light flickered on.

It wasn't much warmer in there, but at least it was cozy.
I connected myself to the resupply and repair leads, leaned
back against the wall and shivered. MedSystem helpfully informed me that my performance reliability was now at 58
percent and dropping, which was not a surprise. I could definitely repair in eight hours, and probably mostly regrow my
damaged organic components, but at 58 percent, I doubted
I could get any analysis done in the meantime. So I set all the
security feeds to alert me if anything tried to eat the habitat
and started to call up the supply of media I'd downloaded
from the entertainment feed. I hurt too much to pay attention to anything with a story, but the friendly noise would
keep me company.

Then someone knocked on the cubicle door.

I stared at it and lost track of all my neatly arrayed inputs.
Like an idiot, I said, "Uh, yes?"

Dr. Mensah opened the door and peered in at me. I'm
not good at guessing actual humans' ages, even with all the
visual entertainment I watch. People in the shows don't usually look much like people in real life, at least not in the good
shows. She had dark brown skin and lighter brown hair, cut
very short, and I'm guessing she wasn't young or she wouldn't

be in charge. She said, "Are you all right? I saw your status report."

"Uh." That was the point where I realized that I should have just not answered and pretended to be in stasis. I pulled the blanket around my chest, hoping she hadn't seen any of the missing chunks. Without the armor holding me together, it was much worse. "Fine."

So, I'm awkward with actual humans. It's not paranoia about my hacked governor module, and it's not them; it's me. I know I'm a horrifying murderbot, and they know it, and it makes both of us nervous, which makes me even more nervous. Also, if I'm not in the armor then it's because I'm wounded and one of my organic parts may fall off and plop on the floor at any moment and no one wants to see that.

"Fine?" She frowned. "The report said you lost 20 percent of your body mass."

"It'll grow back," I said. I know to an actual human I probably looked like I was dying. My injuries were the equivalent of a human losing a limb or two plus most of their blood volume.

"I know, but still." She eyed me for a long moment, so long I tapped the security feed for the mess, where the non-wounded members of the group were sitting around the table talking. They were discussing the possibility of more underground fauna and wishing they had intoxicants. That seemed pretty normal. She continued, "You were very good with Dr. Volescu. I don't think the others realized . . . They were very impressed."

"It's part of the emergency med instructions, calming victims." I tugged the blanket tighter so she didn't see anything awful. I could feel something lower down leaking.

"Yes, but the MedSystem was prioritizing Bharadwaj and didn't check Volescu's vital signs. It didn't take into account the shock of the event, and it expected him to be able to leave the scene on his own."

On the feed it was clear that the others had reviewed Volescu's field camera video. They were saying things like *I didn't even know it had a face.* I'd been in armor since we arrived, and I hadn't unsealed the helmet when I was around them. There was no specific reason. The only part of me they would have seen was my head, and it's standard, generic human. But they didn't want to talk to me and I definitely didn't want to talk to them; on duty it would distract me and off duty . . . I didn't want to talk to them. Mensah had seen me when she signed the rental contract. But she had barely looked at me and I had barely looked at her because again, murderbot + actual human = awkwardness. Keeping the armor on all the time cuts down on unnecessary interaction.

I said, "It's part of my job, not to listen to the System feeds when they . . . make mistakes." *That's why you need constructs, SecUnits with organic components.* But she should know that. Before she accepted delivery of me, she had logged about ten protests, trying to get out of having to have me. I didn't hold it against her. I wouldn't have wanted me either.

Seriously, I don't know why I didn't just say *you're welcome* and *please get out of my cubicle so I can sit here and leak in peace.*

"All right," she said, and looked at me for what objectively I knew was 2.4 seconds and subjectively about twenty excruciating minutes. "I'll see you in eight hours. If you need anything before then, please send me an alert on the feed." She stepped back and let the door slide closed.

It left me wondering what they were all marveling at so I called up the recording of the incident. Okay, wow. I had talked to Volescu all the way up the side of the crater. I had been mostly concerned with the hopper's trajectory and Bharadwaj not bleeding out and what might come out of that crater for a second try; I hadn't been listening to myself, basically. I had asked him if he had kids. It was boggling. Maybe

I had been watching too much media. (He did have kids. He was in a four-way marriage and had seven, all back home with his partners.)

All my levels were too elevated now for a rest period, so I decided I might as well get some use out of it and look at the other recordings. Then I found something weird. There was an "abort" order in the HubSystem command feed, the one that controlled, or currently believed it controlled, my governor module. It had to be a glitch. It didn't matter, because when MedSystem has priority—

⊛   ⊛   ⊛

PERFORMANCE RELIABILITY AT 39%
STASIS INITIATED FOR EMERGENCY REPAIR SEQUENCE

Chapter Two

WHEN I WOKE UP, I was mostly all there again, and up to
80 percent efficiency and climbing. I checked all the feeds
immediately, in case the humans wanted to go out, but Mensah had extended the security interdict on the habitat for
another four hours. Which was a relief, since it would give
me time to get back up to the 98 percent range. But there
was also a notice for me to report to her. That had never happened before. But maybe she wanted to go over the hazard
info package and figure out why it hadn't warned us about
the underground hostile. I was wondering a little about that
myself.

Their group was called PreservationAux and it had
bought an option on this planet's resources, and the survey
trip was to see if it was worth bidding on a full share. Knowing about things on the planet that might eat them while
they're trying to do whatever it is they're doing was kind of
important.

I don't care much about who my clients are or what
they're trying to accomplish. I knew this group was from a
freehold planet but I hadn't bothered to look up the specifics. Freehold meant it had been terraformed and colonized
but wasn't affiliated with any corporate confederations. Basically *freehold* generally meant *shitshow* so I hadn't been expecting much from them. But they were surprisingly easy to
work for.

I cleaned all the stray fluids off my new skin, then climbed
out of the cubicle. That was when I realized I hadn't put the
pieces of my armor up and it was all over the floor, covered
with my fluids and Bharadwaj's blood. No wonder Mensah
had looked into the cubicle; she had probably thought I was
dead in there. I put it all back into its slots in the reclaimer
for repair.

I had an alternate set, but it was still packed into storage and it would take extra time to pull it out and do the diagnostics and the fitting. I hesitated over the uniform, but the security feed would have notified Mensah that I was awake, so I needed to get out there.

It was based on a standard research group's uniforms, and meant to be comfortable inside the habitat: knit gray pants, long-sleeved T-shirt, and a jacket, like the exercise clothes humans and augmented humans wore, plus soft shoes. I put it on, tugged the sleeves down over the gunports on my forearms, and went out into the habitat.

I went through two interior secure doors to the crew area, and found them in the main hub in a huddle around a console, looking at one of the hovering displays. They were all there except Bharadwaj, who was still in the infirmary, and Volescu, who was sitting in there with her. There were mugs and empty meal packets on some of the consoles. I'm not cleaning that up unless I'm given a direct order.

Mensah was busy so I stood and waited.

Ratthi glanced at me, and then did a startled double take. I had no idea how to react. This is why I prefer wearing the armor, even inside the habitat where it's unnecessary and can just get in the way. Human clients usually like to pretend I'm a robot and that's much easier in the armor. I let my eyes unfocus and pretended I was running a diagnostic on something.

Clearly bewildered, Ratthi said, "Who is this?"

They all turned to look at me. All but Mensah, who was sitting at the console with the interface pressed to her forehead. It was clear that even after seeing my face on Volescu's camera video, they didn't recognize me without the helmet. So then I had to look at them and say, "I'm your SecUnit."

They all looked startled and uncomfortable. Almost as uncomfortable as I did. I wished I'd waited to pull the spare armor out.

Part of it is, they didn't want me here. Not here in their hub, but here on the planet. One of the reasons the bond company requires it, besides slapping more expensive mark-ups on their clients, is that I was recording all their conversations all the time, though I wasn't monitoring anything I didn't need to do a half-assed version of my job. But the company would access all those recordings and data mine them for anything they could sell. No, they don't tell people that. Yes, everyone does know it. No, there's nothing you can do about it.

After a subjective half hour and an objective 3.4 seconds, Dr. Mensah turned, saw me, and lowered the interface. She said, "We were checking the hazard report for this region to try to learn why that thing wasn't listed under hazardous fauna. Pin-Lee thinks the data has been altered. Can you examine the report for us?"

"Yes, Dr. Mensah." I could have done this in my cubicle and we could have all saved the embarrassment. Anyway, I picked up the feed she was watching from HubSystem and started to check the report.

It was basically a long list of pertinent info and warnings on the planet and specifically the area where our habitat was, with emphasis on weather, terrain, flora, fauna, air quality, mineral deposits, possible hazards related to any and all of those, with connections to subreports with more detailed information. Dr. Gurathin, the least talkative one, was an augmented human and had his own implanted interface. I could feel him poking around in the data, while the others, using the touch interfaces, were just distant ghosts. I had a lot more processing power than he did, though.

I thought they were being paranoid; even with the interfaces you actually have to read the words, preferably all the words. Sometimes non-augmented humans don't do that. Sometimes augmented humans don't do it either.

But as I checked the general warning section, I noticed something was odd about the formatting. A quick comparison with the other parts of the report told me that yeah, something had been removed, a connection to a subreport broken. "You're right," I said, distracted as I rifled through data storage looking for the missing piece. I couldn't find it; it wasn't just a broken connection, somebody had actually deleted the subreport. That was supposed to be impossible with this type of planetary survey package, but I guess it wasn't as impossible as all that. "Something's been deleted from the warnings and the section on fauna."

The reaction to that in general was pretty pissed off. There were some loud complaints from Pin-Lee and Overse and dramatic throwing-hands-in-the-air from Ratthi. But, like I said, they were all friends and a lot less restrained with each other than my last set of contractual obligations. It was why, if I forced myself to admit it, I had actually been enjoying this contract, up until something tried to eat me and Bharadwaj.

SecSystem records everything, even inside the sleeping cabins, and I see everything. That's why it's easier to pretend I'm a robot. Overse and Arada were a couple, but from the way they acted they'd always been one, and they were best friends with Ratthi. Ratthi had an unrequited thing for Pin-Lee, but didn't act stupid about it. Pin-Lee was exasperated a lot, and tossed things around when the others weren't there, but it wasn't about Ratthi. I thought that being under the company's eye affected her more than the others. Volescu admired Mensah to the point where he might have a crush on her. Pin-Lee did, too, but she and Bharadwaj flirted occasionally in an old comfortable way that suggested it had been going on for a long time. Gurathin was the only loner, but he seemed to like being with the others. He had a small, quiet smile, and they all seemed to like him.

It was a low-stress group, they didn't argue much or antagonize each other for fun, and were fairly restful to be around, as long as they didn't try to talk or interact with me in any way.

Mid expression of frustration, Ratthi said, "So we have no way to know if that creature was an aberration or if they live at the bottom of all those craters?"

Arada, who was one of the biology specialists, said, "You know, I bet they do. If those big avians we saw on the scans land on those barrier islands frequently, that creature might be preying on them."

"It would explain what the craters are doing there," Mensah said more thoughtfully. "That would be one anomaly out of the way, at least."

"But who removed that subreport?" Pin-Lee said, which I agreed was the more important question here. She turned to me with one of those abrupt movements that I had taught myself not to react to. "Can the HubSystem be hacked?"

From the outside, I had no idea. It was as easy as breathing to do it from the inside, with the built-in interfaces in my own body. I had hacked it as soon as it had come online when we set up the habitat. I had to; if it monitored the governor module and my feed like it was supposed to, it could lead to a lot of awkward questions and me being stripped for parts. "As far as I know, it's possible," I said. "But it's more likely the report was damaged before you received the survey package."

Lowest bidder. Trust me on that one.

There were groans and general complaining about having to pay high prices for shitty equipment. (I don't take it personally.) Mensah said, "Gurathin, maybe you and Pin-Lee can figure out what happened." Most of my clients only know their specialties, and there's no reason to send a system specialist along on a survey trip. The company supplies all the systems and attachments (the medical equipment, the drones, me, etc.) and will maintain it as part of the overall package the clients purchase. But Pin-Lee seemed to be a gifted amateur at system interpretation, and Gurathin had an advantage with his internal interface. Mensah added, "In the meantime, does the DeltFall Group have the same survey package as we do?"

I checked. HubSystem thought it was likely, but we knew what its opinion was worth now. "Probably," I said. DeltFall was another survey group, like us, but they were on a continent on the opposite side of the planet. They were a bigger operation and had been dropped off by a different ship, so the humans hadn't met in person, but they talked over the comm occasionally. They weren't part of my contract and had their own SecUnits, the standard one per ten clients. We were supposed to be able to call on each other in emergencies, but being half a planet apart put a natural damper on that.

Mensah leaned back in her chair and steepled her fingers. "All right, this is what we'll do. I want you each to check the individual sections of the survey package for your specialties. Try to pinpoint any more missing information. When we have a partial list, I'll call DeltFall and see if they can send us the files."

That sounded like a great plan, in that it didn't involve me. I said, "Dr. Mensah, do you need me for anything else?"

She turned her chair to face me. "No, I'll call if we have any questions." I had worked for some contracts that would have kept me standing here the entire day and night cycle, just on the off chance they wanted me to do something and didn't want to bother using the feed to call me. Then she added, "You know, you can stay here in the crew area if you want. Would you like that?"

They all looked at me, most of them smiling. One disadvantage in wearing the armor is that I get used to opaquing the faceplate. I'm out of practice at controlling my expression. Right now I'm pretty sure it was somewhere in the region of stunned horror, or maybe appalled horror.

Mensah sat up, startled. She said hurriedly, "Or not, you know, whatever you like."

I said, "I need to check the perimeter," and managed to

turn and leave the crew area in a totally normal way and not like I was fleeing from a bunch of giant hostiles.

⊛   ⊛   ⊛

Back in the safety of the ready room, I leaned my head against the plastic-coated wall. Now they knew their murderbot didn't want to be around them any more than they wanted to be around it. I'd given a tiny piece of myself away.

That can't happen. I have too much to hide, and letting one piece go means the rest isn't as protected.

I shoved away from the wall and decided to actually do some work. The missing subreport made me a little cautious. Not that there were any directives about it. My education modules were such cheap crap; most of the useful things I knew about security I learned from the edutainment programming on the entertainment feeds. (That's another reason why they have to require these research groups and mining and biology and tech companies to rent one of us or they won't guarantee the bond; we're cheaply produced and we suck. Nobody would hire one of us for non-murdering purposes unless they had to.)

Once I got my extra suit skin and spare set of armor on, I walked the perimeter and compared the current readings of the terrain and the seismic scans to the one we took when we first arrived. There were some notes in the feed from Ratthi and Arada, that fauna like the one we were now calling Hostile One might have made all the anomalous craters in the survey area. But nothing had changed around the habitat.

I also checked to make sure both the big hopper and the little hopper had their full complement of emergency supplies. I packed them in there myself days ago, but I was mainly checking to make sure the humans hadn't done anything stupid with them since the last time I checked.

I did everything I could think of to do, then finally let myself go on standby while I caught up on my serials. I'd watched three episodes of *Sanctuary Moon* and was fast

forwarding through a sex scene when Dr. Mensah sent me
some images through the feed. (I don't have any gender or
sex-related parts (if a construct has those you're a sexbot in
a brothel, not a murderbot) so maybe that's why I find sex
scenes boring. Though I think that even if I did have sex-related parts I would find them boring.) I took a look at the images in Mensah's message, then saved my place in the serial.

Confession time: I don't actually know where we are.
We have, or are supposed to have, a complete satellite map
of the planet in the survey package. That was how the humans decided where to do their assessments. I hadn't looked
at the maps yet and I'd barely looked at the survey package.
In my defense, we'd been here twenty-two planetary days and
I hadn't had to do anything but stand around watching humans make scans or take samples of dirt, rocks, water, and
leaves. The sense of urgency just wasn't there. Also, you may
have noticed, I don't care.

So it was news to me that there were six missing sections
from our map. Pin-Lee and Gurathin had found the dis-
crepancies and Mensah wanted to know if I thought it was
just the survey package being cheap and error-ridden or if I
thought this was part of a hack. I appreciated the fact that we
were communicating via the feed and that she wasn't making
me actually speak to her on the comm. I was so appreciative
I gave her my real opinion, that it probably was the fact that
our survey package was a cheap piece of crap but the only
way to know for certain was to go out and look at one of the
missing sections and see if there was anything there besides
more boring planet. I didn't phrase it exactly like that but
that was what I meant.

She took her attention off the feed then, but I stayed
alert, since I knew she tended to make her decisions fast
and if I started a show again I'd just get interrupted. I did
check the security-camera view of the hub so I could hear
their conversation. They all wanted to check it out, and were

just going back and forth on whether they should wait. They
had just had a comm conversation with DeltFall on the other
continent who had agreed to send copies of the missing survey package files. Some of the clients wanted to see if anything else was missing first, and others wanted to go now, and
blah, blah, blah.

I knew how this was going to turn out.

It wasn't a long trip, not far outside the range of the other assessments they had been doing, but not knowing what
they were flying into was definitely a red flag for security. In a
smart world, I should go alone, but with the governor module I had to be within a hundred meters of at least one of the
clients at all times, or it would fry me. They knew that, so
volunteering to take a solo cross-continental trip might set
off a few alarms.

So when Mensah opened the feed again to tell me they
were going, I told her security protocols suggested that I
should go, too.

Chapter Three

WE GOT READY to leave at the beginning of the day cycle, in the morning light, and the satellite weather report said it would be a good day for flying and scanning. I checked Med-System and saw Bharadwaj was awake and talking.

It wasn't until I was helping to carry equipment to the little hopper that I realized they were going to make me ride in the crew cabin.

At least I was in the armor with my helmet opaqued. But when Mensah told me to get in the copilot's seat, it didn't turn out to be as bad as my first horrified realization. Arada and Pin-Lee didn't try to talk to me, and Ratthi actually looked away when I eased past him to get to the cockpit.

They were all so careful not to look at me or talk to me directly that as soon as we were in the air I did a quick spot check through HubSystem's records of their conversations. I had talked myself into believing that I hadn't actually lost it as much as I thought I had when Mensah had offered to let me hang out in the hub with the humans like I was an actual person or something.

The conversation they had immediately after that gave me a sinking sensation as I reviewed it. No, it had been worse than I thought. They had talked it over and all agreed not to "push me any further than I wanted to go" and they were all so nice and it was just excruciating. I was never taking off the helmet again. I can't do even the half-assed version of this stupid job if I have to talk to humans.

They were the first clients I'd had who hadn't had any previous experience with SecUnits, so maybe I could have expected this if I'd bothered to think about it. Letting them see me without the armor had been a huge mistake.

At least Mensah and Arada had overruled the ones who wanted to talk to me about it. Yes, talk to Murderbot about its feelings. The idea was so painful I dropped to 97 percent efficiency. I'd rather climb back into Hostile One's mouth.

I worried about it while they looked out the windows at the ring or watched their feeds of the hopper's scans of the new scenery, chatting on the comm with the others who were following our progress back in the habitat. I was distracted, but still caught the moment when the autopilot cut out.

It could have been a problem, except I was in the copilot's seat and I could have taken over in time. But even if I hadn't been there, it would have turned out okay, because Mensah was flying and she never took her hands off the controls.

Even though the planetary craft autopilots aren't as sophisticated as a full bot-pilot system, some clients will still engage it and then walk into the back, or sleep. Mensah didn't and she made sure when the others flew they followed her rules. She just made some thoughtful grumpy noises and adjusted our course away from the mountain the failing autopilot would have slammed us into.

I had cycled out of horrified that they wanted to talk to me about my feelings into grateful that she had ordered them not to. As she restarted the autopilot, I pulled the log and sent it into the feed to show her it had cut out due to a HubSystem glitch. She swore under her breath and shook her head.

◎   ◎   ◎

The missing map section wasn't that far outside our assessment range so we were there before I made a dent in the backlog of serials I'd saved to my internal storage. Mensah told the others, "We're coming up on it."

We had been traveling over heavy tropical forest, where it flowed over deep valleys. Suddenly it dropped away into a plain, spotted with lakes and smaller copses of trees. There was a lot of bare rock, in low ridges and tumbled boulders. It was dark and glassy, like volcanic glass.

The cabin was quiet as everybody studied the scans. Arada was looking at the seismic data, bouncing it to the others back in the habitat through her feed.

"I don't see anything that would prevent the satellite from mapping this region," Pin-Lee said, her voice distant as she sorted through the data the hopper was pulling in. "No strange readings. It's weird."

"Unless this rock has some sort of stealth property that prevented the satellites from imaging it," Arada said. "The scanners are acting a little funny."

"Because the scanners suck corporation balls," Pin-Lee muttered.

"Should we land?" Mensah said. I realized she was asking me for a security assessment.

The scans were sort of working and marking some hazards, but they weren't any different hazards from what we'd run into before. I said, "We could. But we know there's at least one lifeform here that tunnels through rock."

Arada bounced a little in her seat, like she was impatient to get going. "I know we have to be cautious, but I think we'd be safer if we knew whether these blank patches on the satellite scan were accidental or deliberate."

That was when I realized they weren't ignoring the possibility of sabotage. I should have realized it earlier, when Pin-Lee asked if HubSystem could be hacked. But humans had been looking at me and I had just wanted to get out of there.

Ratthi and Pin-Lee seconded her, and Mensah made her decision. "We'll land and take samples."

Over the comm from the habitat, Bharadwaj's voice said, "Please be careful." She still sounded shaky.

Mensah took us down gently, the hopper's pads touching the ground with hardly a thump. I was already up and at the hatch.

The humans had their suit helmets on so I opened the hatch and let the ramp drop. Close up the rocky patches still looked like glass, mostly black, but with different colors running into each other. This near to the ground the hopper's

scan was able to confirm that seismic activity was null, but I
walked out a little bit, as if giving anything out there a chance
to attack me. If the humans see me actually doing my job,
it helps keep suspicions from forming about faulty governor
modules.

Mensah climbed down with Arada behind her. They
moved around, taking more readings with their portable
scanners. Then the others got the sample kit outs and started
chipping off pieces of the rock glass, or glass rock, scooping
up dirt and bits of plant matter. They were murmuring to each
other a lot, and to the others back at the habitat. They were
sending the data to the feed, but I wasn't paying attention.

It was an odd spot. Quiet compared to the other places
we'd surveyed, with not much bird-thing noise and no sign of
animal movement. Maybe the rocky patches kept them away.
I walked out a little way, past a couple of the lakes, almost
expecting to see something under the surface. Dead bodies,
maybe. I'd seen plenty of those (and caused plenty of those)
on past contracts, but this one had been dead-body-lacking,
so far. It made for a nice change.

Mensah had set a survey perimeter, marking all the areas
the aerial scan had flagged as hazardous or potentially hazardous. I checked on everybody again and saw Arada and Ratthi
heading directly for one of the hazard markers. I expected
them to stop at the perimeter, since they'd been pretty con-
sistently cautious on the other assessments. I started moving
in that direction anyway. Then they passed the perimeter. I
started to run. I sent Mensah my field camera feed and used
the voice comm to say, "Dr. Arada, Dr. Ratthi, please stop.
You're past the perimeter and nearing a hazard marker."

"We are?" Ratthi sounded completely baffled.

Fortunately, they both stopped. By the time I got there
they both had their maps up in my feed. "I don't understand
what's wrong," Arada said, confused. "I don't see the hazard
marker." She had tagged both their positions and on their

maps they were well within the perimeter, heading toward a wetland area.

It took me a second to see what the problem was. Then I superimposed my map, the actual map, over theirs and sent that to Mensah. "Shit," she said over the comm. "Ratthi, Arada, your map's wrong. How did that happen?"

"It's a glitch," Ratthi said. He grimaced, studying the displays in his feed. "It's wiped out all the markers on this side."

So that was how I spent the rest of the morning, shooing humans away from hazard markers they couldn't see, while Pin-Lee cursed a lot and tried to get the mapping scanner to work. "I'm beginning to think these missing sections are just a mapping error," Ratthi said at one point, panting. He had walked into what they called a hot mud pit and I'd had to pull him out. We were both covered with acidic mud to the waist.

"You think?" Pin-Lee answered tiredly.

When Mensah told us to head back to the hopper, it was a relief all around.

❀ ❀ ❀

We got back to the habitat with no problems, which felt like it was starting to become an unusual occurrence. The humans went to analyze their data, and I went to hide in the ready room, check the security feeds, and then lie in my cubicle and watch media for a while.

I'd just done another perimeter walk and checked the drones, when the feed informed me that HubSystem had updates from the satellite and there was a package for me. I have a trick where I make HubSystem think I received it and then just put it in external storage. I don't do automated package updates anymore, now that I don't have to. When I felt like it, presumably sometime before it was time to leave the planet, I'd go through the update and apply the parts I wanted and delete the rest.

It was a typical, boring day, in other words. If Bharadwaj

wasn't still recuperating in Medical, you could almost forget
what had happened. But at the end of the day cycle, Dr. Mensah called me again and said, "I think we have a problem. We
can't contact DeltFall Group."

⊛   ⊛   ⊛

I went to the crew hub where Mensah and all the others were.
They had pulled up the maps and scans of where we were ver-
sus where DeltFall was, and the curve of the planet hung glittering in the air in the big display. When I got there, Mensah
was saying, "I've checked the big hopper's specs and we can
make it there and back without a recharge."

I had my helmet plate opaqued, so I could wince a lot
without any of them knowing.

"You don't think they'll let us recharge at their habitat?"
Arada asked, then looked around when the others stared at
her. "What?" she demanded.

Overse put an arm around her and squeezed her shoulder. "If they aren't answering our calls, they might be hurt,
or their habitat is damaged," she said. As a couple, they were
always so nice to each other. The whole group had been re-
markably drama-free so far, which I appreciated. The last
few contracts had been like being an involuntary bystander
in one of the entertainment feed's multi-partner relationship
serials except I'd hated the whole cast.

Mensah nodded. "That's my concern, especially if their
survey package was missing potential hazard information the
way ours is."

Arada looked like it was just occurring to her that everybody over at DeltFall might be dead.

Ratthi said, "The thing that worries me is that their emergency beacon didn't launch. If the habitat was breached, or
if there was a medical emergency they couldn't handle, their
HubSystem should have triggered the beacon automatically."

Each survey team has its own beacon, set up a safe distance from the habitat. It would launch into a low orbit and

send a pulse toward the wormhole, which would get zapped or whatever happened in the wormhole and the company network would get it, and the pickup transport would be sent now instead of waiting until the end of project date. That was how it was supposed to work, anyway. Usually.

Mensah's expression said she was worried. She looked at me. "What do you think?"

It took me two seconds to realize she was talking to me. Fortunately, since it seemed like we were really doing this, I had actually been paying attention and didn't need to play the conversation back. I said, "They have three contracted SecUnits but if their habitat was hit by a hostile as big or bigger than Hostile One, their comm equipment could have been damaged."

Pin-Lee was calling up specs for the beacons. "Aren't the emergency beacons designed to trigger even if the rest of the comm equipment is destroyed?"

The other good thing about my hacked governor module is that I could ignore the governor's instructions to defend the stupid company. "They're supposed to be able to, but equipment failures aren't unknown."

There was a moment where they all thought about potential equipment failures in their habitat, maybe including the big hopper which they were about to fly out of range of the little hopper, so if something happened to it they were walking back. And swimming back, since that was an ocean-sized body of water between the two points on the map. Or drown; I guess they could just drown. If you were wondering why I was wincing earlier, this would be the reason.

The trip to the map's black-out region had been a little out of our assessment parameters, but this was going to be an overnight trip, even if all they did was get there, see a bunch of dead people, turn around and go back.

Then Gurathin said, "What about your systems?"

I didn't turn my helmet toward him because that can be

intimidating and it's especially important for me to resist that urge. "I carefully monitor my own systems." What else did he think I was going to say? It didn't matter; I'm not refundable.

Volescu cleared his throat. "So we should prepare for a rescue mission." He looked okay, but MedSystem's feed was still reporting some indicators of distress. Bharadwaj was stable but not allowed to get out of Medical yet. He continued, "I've pulled some instructions from the hopper's info package."

Yes, instructions. They're academics, surveyors, researchers, not action-hero explorers from the serials I liked because they were unrealistic and not depressing and sordid like reality. I said, "Dr. Mensah, I think I should go along."

I could see her notes in the feed so I knew she meant for me to stay here and watch the habitat and guard everybody who wasn't going. She was taking Pin-Lee, because she had past experience in habitat and shelter construction; Ratthi, who was a biologist; and Overse, who was certified as a field medic.

Mensah hesitated, thinking about it, and I could tell she was debating protecting the habitat and the group staying behind with the possibility of whatever had hit DeltFall still being there. She took a breath and I knew she was going to tell me to stay here. And I just thought, *That's a bad idea.* I couldn't explain to myself why. It was one of those impulses that comes from my organic parts that the governor is supposed to squash. I said, "As the only one here with experience in these situations, I'm your best resource."

Gurathin said, "What situations?"

Ratthi gave him a bemused look. "This situation. The unknown. Strange threats. Monsters exploding out of the ground."

I was glad I wasn't the only one who thought it was a dumb question. Gurathin wasn't as talkative as the others, so I didn't have much of a sense of his personality. He was the only augmented human in the group, so maybe he felt like an outsider, or something, even though the others clearly liked him. I clarified, "Situations where personnel might be injured due to attack by planetary hazards."

Arada came in on my side. "I agree. I think you should take SecUnit. You don't know what's out there."

Mensah was still undecided. "Depending on what we find, we may be gone as long as two or three days."

Arada waved a hand, indicating the habitat. "Nothing's bothered us here so far."

That was probably what DeltFall had thought, right before they got eaten or torn to pieces or whatever. But Volescu said, "I admit it would make me feel better about it." From Medical, Bharadwaj tapped into the feed to add her vote for me. Gurathin was the only one staying behind who didn't say anything.

Mensah nodded firmly. "All right then, it's decided. Now let's get moving."

⊕　⊕　⊕

So I prepped the big hopper to go to the other side of the planet. (And yes, I had to pull up the instructions.) I checked it over as much as I could, remembering how the autopilot had cut out suddenly in the little hopper. But we hadn't used the big hopper since Mensah had taken it up to check it out when we arrived. (You had to check everything out and log any problems immediately when you took delivery or the company wasn't liable.) But everything looked okay, or at least matched what the specs said it was supposed to match. It was only there for emergencies and if this thing with Delt-Fall hadn't happened, we would probably never have touched it until it was time to lift it onto our pickup transport.

Mensah came to do her own check of the hopper, and told me to pack some extra emergency supplies for the Delt-Fall staff. I did it, and I hoped for the humans' sake we would need them. I thought it was likely that the only supplies we would need for DeltFall was the postmortem kind, but you may have noticed that when I do manage to care, I'm a pessimist.

When everything was ready, Overse, Ratthi, and Pin-Lee climbed in, and I stood hopefully by the cargo pod. Mensah pointed at the cabin. I winced behind my opaque faceplate and climbed in.

Chapter Four

WE FLEW THROUGH THE NIGHT, the humans taking scans and discussing the new terrain past our assessment range. It was especially interesting for them to see what was there, now that we knew our map wasn't exactly reliable.

Mensah gave everybody watch shifts, including me. This was new, but not unwelcome, as it meant I had blocks of time where I wasn't supposed to be paying attention and didn't have to fake it. Mensah, Pin-Lee, and Overse were all taking turns as pilot and copilot, so I didn't have to worry so much about the autopilot trying to kill us, and I could go on standby and watch my stored supply of serials.

We'd been in the air awhile, and Mensah was piloting with Pin-Lee in the copilot's seat, when Ratthi turned in his seat to face me and said, "We heard—we were given to understand, that Imitative Human Bot Units are . . . partially constructed from cloned material."

Warily, I stopped the show I was watching. I didn't like where this might go. All of that information is in the common knowledge database, plus in the brochure the company provides with the specifics of the types of units they use. Which he knew, being a scientist and whatever. And he wasn't the kind of human who asked about things when he could look them up himself through a feed. "That's true," I said, very careful to make my voice sound just as neutral as always.

Ratthi's expression was troubled. "But surely . . . It's clear you have feelings—"

I flinched. I couldn't help it.

Overse had been working in the feed, analyzing data from the assessments. She looked up, frowning. "Ratthi, what are you doing?"

Ratthi shifted guiltily. "I know Mensah asked us not to, but—" He waved a hand. "You saw it."

Overse pulled her interface off. "You're upsetting it," she said, teeth gritted.

"That's my point!" He gestured in frustration. "The practice is disgusting, it's horrible, it's slavery. This is no more a machine than Gurathin is—"

Exasperated, Overse said, "And you don't think it knows that?"

I'm supposed to let the clients do and say whatever they want to me and with an intact governor module I wouldn't have a choice. I'm also not supposed to snitch on clients to anybody except the company, but it was either that or jump out the hatch. I sent the conversation into the feed tagged for Mensah.

From the cockpit, she shouted, "Ratthi! We talked about this!"

I slid out of the seat and went to the back of the hopper, as far away as I could get, facing the supply lockers and the head. It was a mistake; it wasn't a normal thing for a SecUnit with an intact governor module to do, but they didn't notice.

"I'll apologize," Ratthi was saying.

"No, just leave it alone," Mensah told him.

"That would just make it worse," Overse added.

I stood there until they all calmed down and got quiet again, then slid into a seat in the back, and resumed the serial I'd been watching.

⊕ ⊕ ⊕

It was the middle of the night when I felt the feed drop out.

I hadn't been using it, but I had the SecSystem feeds from the drones and the interior cameras backburnered and was accessing them occasionally to make sure everything was okay. The humans left behind in the habitat were more active than they usually were at this time, probably anxious about what we were going to find at DeltFall. I was hearing Arada walk around occasionally, though Volescu was snoring off and on in his bunk. Bharadwaj had been able to move

back to her own quarters, but was restless and going over her
field notes through the feed. Gurathin was in the hub doing
something on his personal system. I wondered what he was
doing and had just started to carefully poke around through
HubSystem to find out. When the feed dropped it was like
someone slapped the organic part of my brain.

I sat up and said, "The satellite went down."

The others, except for Pin-Lee who was piloting, all
grabbed for their interfaces. I saw their expressions when
they felt the silence. Mensah pushed out of her seat and came
to the back. "Are you sure it was the satellite?"

"I'm sure," I told her. "I'm pinging it and there's no
response."

We still had our local feed, running on the hopper's system, so we could communicate through it as well as the comm
and share data with each other. We just didn't have nearly as
much data as we'd have had if we were still attached to Hub-
System. We were far enough away that we needed the comm
satellite as a relay. Ratthi switched his interface to the hopper's feed and started checking the scans. There was nothing
on them except empty sky; I had them backburnered but I'd
set them to notify me if they encountered anything like an
energy reading or a large life sign. He said, "I just felt a chill.
Did anyone else feel a chill?"

"A little," Overse admitted. "It's a weird coincidence, isn't
it?"

"The damn satellite's had periodic outages since we got
here," Pin-Lee pointed out from the cockpit. "We just don't
normally need it for comms." She was right. I was supposed
to check their personal logs periodically in case they were
plotting to defraud the company or murder each other or
something, and the last time I'd looked at Pin-Lee's she had
been tracking the satellite problems, trying to figure out if
there was a pattern. It was one of the many things I didn't
care about because the entertainment feed was only updated

occasionally, and I downloaded it for local storage.

Ratthi shook his head. "But this is the first time we've been far enough from the habitat to need it for comm contact. It just seems odd, and not in a good way."

Mensah looked around at them. "Does anyone want to turn back?"

I did, but I didn't get a vote. The others sat there for a quiet moment, then Overse said, "If it turns out the DeltFall group did need help, and we didn't go, how would we feel?"

"If there's a chance we can save lives, we have to take it," Pin-Lee agreed.

Ratthi sighed. "No, you're right. I'd feel terrible if anyone died because we were overcautious."

"We're agreed, then," Mensah said. "We'll keep going."

I would have preferred they be overcautious. I had had contracts before where the company's equipment glitched this badly, but there was just something about this that made me think it was more. But all I had was the feeling.

I had four hours to my next scheduled watch so I went into standby, and buried myself in the downloads I'd stored away.

⊛   ⊛   ⊛

It was dawn when we got there. DeltFall had established their camp in a wide valley surrounded by high mountains. A spiderweb of creek beds cut through the grass and stubby trees. They were a bigger operation than ours, with three linked habitats, and a shelter for surface vehicles, plus a landing area for two large hoppers, a cargo hauler, and three small hoppers. It was all company equipment though, per contract, and all subject to the same malfunctions as the crap they'd dumped on us.

There was no one outside, no movement. No sign of damage, no sign any hostile fauna had approached. The satellite was still dead, but Mensah had been trying to get the DeltFall habitat on the comm since we had come within range.

"Are they missing any transports?" Mensah asked.

Ratthi checked the record of what they were supposed to have which I'd copied from HubSystem before we left. "No, the hoppers are all there. Their ground vehicles are in that shelter, I think."

I had moved up to the front as we got closer. Standing behind the pilot's seat, I said, "Dr. Mensah, I recommend you land outside their perimeter." Through the local feed I sent her all the info I had, which was that their automated systems were responding to the pings the hopper was sending, but that was it. We weren't picking up their feed, which meant their HubSystem was in standby. There was nothing from their three SecUnits, not even pings.

Overse, in the copilot's seat, glanced up at me. "Why?"

I had to answer the question so I said, "Security protocol," which sounded good and didn't commit me to anything. No one outside, no one answering the comm. Unless they had all jumped in their surface vehicles and gone off on vacation, leaving their Hub and SecUnits shut down, they were dead. Pessimism confirmed.

But we couldn't be sure without looking. The hopper's scanners can't see inside the habitats because of the shielding that's really only there to protect proprietary data, so we couldn't get any life signs or energy readings.

This is why I didn't want to come. I've got four perfectly good humans here and I didn't want them to get killed by whatever took out DeltFall. It's not like I cared about them personally, but it would look bad on my record, and my record was already pretty terrible.

"We're just being cautious," Mensah said, answering Overse. She took the hopper down at the edge of the valley, on the far side of the streams.

I gave Mensah a few hints through the feed, that they should break out the handweapons in the survival gear, that Ratthi should stay behind inside the hopper with the hatch sealed and locked since he'd never done the weapon-training course, and that, most important, I should go first. They were quiet, subdued. Up until now, I think they had all been looking at this as probably a natural disaster, that they were going to be digging survivors out of a collapsed habitat, or helping fight off a herd of Hostile Ones.

This was something else.

Mensah gave the orders and we started forward, me in front, the humans a few steps behind. They were in their full suits with helmets, which gave some protection but had been meant for environmental hazards, not some other heavily armed human (or angry malfunctioning rogue SecUnit) deliberately trying to kill them. I was more nervous than Ratthi, who was jittery on our comms, monitoring the scans, and basically telling us to be careful every other step.

I had my built-in energy weapons and the big projectile weapon I was cradling. I also had six drones, pulled from the hopper's supply and under my control through its feed. They were the small kind, barely a centimeter across; no weapons, just cameras. (They make some which aren't much bigger and have a small pulse weapon, but you have to get one of the upper-tier company packages mostly designed for much larger contracts.) I told the drones to get in the air and gave them a scouting pattern.

I did that because it seemed sensible, not because I knew what I was doing. I am not a combat murderbot, I'm Security. I keep things from attacking the clients and try to gently discourage the clients from attacking each other. I was way out of my depth here, which was another reason I hadn't wanted the humans to come here.

We crossed the shallow streams, sending a group of water invertebrates scattering away from our boots. The trees were short and sparse enough that I had a good view of the camp from this angle. I couldn't detect any DeltFall security drones, by eye or with the scanners on my drones. Ratthi in the hopper wasn't picking up anything either. I really, really wished I could pinpoint the location of those three SecUnits, but I wasn't getting anything from them.

SecUnits aren't sentimental about each other. We aren't friends, the way the characters on the serials are, or the way my humans were. We can't trust each other, even if we work together. Even if you don't have clients who decide to entertain themselves by ordering their SecUnits to fight each other.

The scans read the perimeter sensors as dead and the drones weren't picking up any warning indicators. The DeltFall HubSystem was down, and without it, no one inside could access our feed or comms, theoretically. We crossed over and into the landing area for their hoppers. They were between us and the first habitat, the vehicle storage to one side. I was leading us in at an angle, trying to get a visual on the main habitat door, but I was also checking the ground. It was mostly bare of grass from all the foot traffic and hopper landings. From the weather report we'd gotten before the satellite quit, it had rained here last night, and the mud had hardened. No activity since then.

I passed that info to Mensah through the feed and she told the others. Keeping her voice low, Pin-Lee said, "So whatever happened, it wasn't long after we spoke to them on the comm."

"They couldn't have been attacked by someone," Overse whispered. There was no reason to whisper, but I understood the impulse. "There's no one else on this planet."

"There's not supposed to be anyone else on this planet," Ratthi said, darkly, over the comm from our hopper.

There were three SecUnits who were not me on this planet, and that was dangerous enough. I got my visual on the main habitat hatch and saw it was shut, no sign of anything forcing its way inside. The drones had circled the whole structure by now, and showed me the other entrances were

the same. That was that. Hostile Fauna don't come to the
door and ask to be let inside. I sent the images to Mensah's
feed and said aloud, "Dr. Mensah, it would be better if I went
ahead."

She hesitated, reviewing what I'd just sent her. I saw her
shoulders tense. I think she had just come to the same con-
clusion I had. Or at least admitted to herself that it was the
strongest possibility. She said, "All right. We'll wait here.
Make sure we can monitor."

She'd said "we" and she wouldn't have said that if she
didn't mean it, unlike some clients I'd had. I sent my field
camera's feed to all four of them and started forward.

I called four of the drones back, leaving two to keep circling the perimeter. I checked the vehicle shed as I moved
past it. It was open on one side, with some sealed lockers in
the back for storage. All four of their surface vehicles were
there, powered down, no sign of recent tracks, so I didn't go
in. I wouldn't bother searching the small storage spaces until
we got down to the looking-for-all-the-body-parts phase.

I walked up to the hatch of the first habitat. We didn't
have an entry code, so I was expecting to have to blow the
door, but when I tapped the button it slid open for me. I told
Mensah through the feed that I wouldn't speak aloud on the
comm anymore.

She tapped back an acknowledgment on the feed, and I
heard her telling the others to get off my feed and my comm,
that she was going to be the only one speaking to me so I
wasn't distracted. Mensah underestimated my ability to ignore humans but I appreciated the thought. Ratthi whispered, "Be careful," and signed off.

I had the weapon up going in, through the suit locker
area and into the first corridor. "No suits missing," Mensah
said in my ear, watching the field camera. I sent my four
drones ahead, maintaining an interior scouting pattern. This
was a nicer habitat than ours, wider halls, newer. Also empty,

silent, the smell of decaying flesh drifting through my helmet filters. I headed toward the hub, where their main crew area should be.

The lights were still on and air whispered through the vents, but I couldn't get into their SecSystem with their feed down. I missed my cameras.

At the door to the hub, I found their first SecUnit. It was sprawled on its back on the floor, the armor over its chest pierced by something that made a hole approximately ten centimeters wide and a little deeper. We're hard to kill, but that'll do it. I did a brief scan to make sure it was inert, then stepped over it and went through into the crew area.

There were eleven messily dead humans in the hub, sprawled on the floor, in chairs, the monitoring stations and projection surfaces behind them showing impact damage from projectile and energy weapon fire. I tapped the feed and asked Mensah to fall back to the hopper. She acknowledged me and I got confirmation from my outside drones that the humans were retreating.

I went out the opposite door to a corridor that led toward the mess hall, Medical, and cabins. The drones were telling me the layout was very similar to our habitat, except for the occasional dead person sprawled in the corridors. The weapon that had taken out the dead SecUnit wasn't in the hub, and it had died with its back to the door. The DeltFall humans had had some warning, enough to start getting up and heading for the other exits, but something else had come in from this direction and trapped them. I thought that SecUnit had been killed trying to protect the hub.

Which meant I was looking for the other two SecUnits.

Maybe these clients had been terrible and abusive, maybe they had deserved it. I didn't care. Nobody was touching my humans. To make sure of that I had to kill these two rogue Units. I could have pulled out at this point, sabotaged the hoppers, and got my humans out of there, leaving the rogue

Units stuck on the other side of an ocean; that would have been the smart thing to do.

But I wanted to kill them.

One of my drones found two humans dead in the mess, no warning. They had been taking food pacs out of the heating cubby, getting the tables ready for a meal.

While I moved through the corridors and rooms, I was doing an image search against the hopper's equipment database. The dead unit had probably been killed by a mineral survey tool, like a pressure or sonic drill. We had one on the hopper, part of the standard equipment. You would have to get close to use it with enough force to pierce armor, maybe a little more than a meter.

Because you can't walk up to another murderbot with an armor-piercing projectile or energy weapon inside the habitat and not be looked at with suspicion. You can walk up to a fellow murderbot with a tool that a human might have asked you to get.

By the time I reached the other side of the structure, the drones had cleared the first habitat. I stood in the hatchway at the top of the narrow corridor that led into the second. A human lay at the opposite end, half in and half out of the open hatch. To get into the next habitat, I'd have to step over her to push the door all the way open. I could tell already that something was wrong about the body position. I used the magnification on the field camera to get a closer view of the skin on the outstretched arm. The lividity was wrong; she had been shot in the chest or face and lay on her back for some time, then had been moved here recently. Probably as soon as they picked up our hopper on the way here.

On the feed I told Mensah what I needed her to do. She didn't ask questions. She'd been watching my field camera, and she knew by now what we were dealing with. She tapped back to acknowledge me, then said aloud on the comm, "SecUnit, I want you to hold your position until I get there."

I said, "Yes, Dr. Mensah," and eased back out of the hatch. I moved fast, back to the security ready room.

It was nice having a human smart enough to work with like this.

Our model of habitat didn't have it but on these bigger ones there's a roof access and my outside drones had a good view of it.

I climbed the ladder up to the roof hatch and popped it. The armor's boots have magnetized climbing clamps, and I used them to cross over the curving roofs to the third habitat and then around to the second, coming up on them from behind. Even these two rogues wouldn't be dumb enough to ignore the creaks if I took the quick route and walked over to their position.

(They were not the sharpest murderbots, having cleaned the floor of the between-habitat corridor to cover the prints they had left when staging that body. It would have fooled somebody who hadn't noticed all the other floors were covered with tracked-in dust.)

I opened the roof access for the second habitat and sent my drones ahead down into the Security ready room. Once they checked the unit cubicles and made sure nobody was home, I dropped down the ladder. A lot of their equipment was still there, including their drones. There was a nice box of new ones, but they were useless without the DeltFall Hub-System. Either it was really dead or doing a good imitation of it. I still kept part of my attention on it; if it came up suddenly and reactivated the security cameras, the rules of the game would change abruptly.

Keeping my drones with me, I took the inner corridor and moved silently past Medical's blasted hatch. Three bodies were piled inside where the humans had tried to secure it and been trapped when their own SecUnits blew it open to slaughter them.

When I was close to the corridor with the hatch where

both units were waiting for me and Dr. Mensah to come wandering in, I sent the drones around for a careful look. Oh yeah, there they were.

With no weapons on my drones, the only way to do this was to move fast. So I threw myself around the last corner, hit the opposite wall, crossed back and kept going, firing at their positions.

I hit the first one with three explosive bolts in the back and one in the faceplate as it turned toward me. It dropped. The other one I nicked in the arm, taking out the joint, and it made the mistake of switching its main weapon to its other hand, which gave me a couple of seconds. I switched to rapid fire to keep it off balance, then back to the explosive bolt. That dropped it.

I hit the floor, needing a minute to recover.

I had taken at least a dozen hits from both of their energy weapons while I was taking out the first one, but the explosive bolts had missed me, going past to tear up the corridor. Even with the armor, bits of me were going numb, but I had only taken three projectiles to the right shoulder, four to the left hip. This is how we fight: throw ourselves at each other and see whose parts give out first.

Neither unit was dead. But they were incapable of reaching their cubicles in the ready room, and I sure as hell wasn't going to give them a hand.

Three of my drones were down, too; they had gone into combat mode and slammed in ahead of me to draw fire. One had gotten hit by a stray energy burst and was wandering around in the corridor behind me. I checked my two perimeter drones by habit, and opened my comm to Dr. Mensah to tell her I still needed to clear the rest of the habitat and do the formal check for survivors.

The drone behind me went out with a fizzle that I heard and saw on the feed. I think I realized immediately what that meant but there may have been a half second or so of delay.

But I was on my feet when something hit me so hard I was suddenly on my back on the floor, systems failing.

⊛   ⊛   ⊛

I came back online to no vision, no hearing, no ability to move. I couldn't reach the feed or the comm. Not good, Murderbot, not good.

I suddenly got some weird flashes of sensation, all from my organic parts. Air on my face, my arms, through rips in my suit. On the burning wound in my shoulder. Someone had taken off my helmet and the upper part of my armor. The sensations were only for seconds at a time. It was confusing and I wanted to scream. Maybe this was how murderbots died. You lose function, go offline, but parts of you keep working, organic pieces kept alive by the fading energy in your power cells.

Then I knew someone was moving me, and I really wanted to scream.

I fought back panic, and got a few more flashes of sensation. I wasn't dead. I was in a lot of trouble.

I waited to get some kind of function back, frantic, disoriented, terrified, wondering why they hadn't blown a hole in my chest. Sound came first, and I knew something leaned over me. Faint noises from the joints told me it was a SecUnit. But there'd only been three. I'd checked the DeltFall specs before we left. I do a half-assed job sometimes, okay, most of the time, but Pin-Lee had checked, too, and she was thorough.

Then my organic parts started to sting, the numbness wearing off. I was designed to work with both organic and machine parts, to balance that sensory input. Without the balance, I felt like a balloon floating in mid-air. But the organic part of my chest was in contact with a hard surface, and that abruptly brought my position into focus. I was lying face down, one arm dangling. They'd put me on a table?

This was definitely not good.

Pressure on my back, then on my head. The rest of me was coming back but slowly, slowly. I felt for the feed but couldn't reach it. Then something stabbed me in the back of the neck.

That's organic material and with the rest of me down there was nothing to control input from my nervous system. It felt like they were sawing my head off.

A shock went through me and suddenly the rest of me was back online. I popped the joint on my left arm so I could move it in a way not usually compatible with a human, augmented human, or murderbot body. I reached up to the pressure and pain on my neck, and grabbed an armored wrist. I twisted my whole body and took us both off the table.

We hit the floor and I clamped my legs around the other SecUnit as we rolled. It tried to trigger the weapons built into its forearm but my reaction speed was off the chart and I clamped a hand over the port so it couldn't open fully. My vision was back and I could see its opaqued helmet inches away. My armor had been removed down to my waist, and that just made me more angry.

I shoved its hand up under its chin and took the pressure off its weapon. It had a split second to try to abort that fire command and it failed. The energy burst went through my hand and the join between its helmet and neck piece. Its head jerked and its body started to spasm. I let go of it long enough to kneel up, get my intact arm around its neck, and twist.

I let go as I felt the connections, mechanical and organic, snap.

I looked up and another SecUnit was in the doorway, lifting a large projectile weapon.

How many of these damn things were here? It didn't matter, because I tried to shove myself upright but I couldn't react fast enough. Then it jerked, dropped the weapon, and fell forward. I saw two things: the ten-centimeter hole in its back and Mensah standing behind it, holding something that looked a lot like the sonic mining drill from our hopper.

"Dr. Mensah," I said, "this is a violation of security priority and I am contractually obligated to record this for report to the company—" It was in the buffer and the rest of my brain was empty.

She ignored me, talking to Pin-Lee on the comm, and strode forward to grab my arm and pull. I was too heavy for her so I shoved upright so she wouldn't hurt herself. It was starting to occur to me that Dr. Mensah might actually be an intrepid galactic explorer, even if she didn't look like the ones on the entertainment feed.

She kept pulling on me so I kept moving. Something was wrong with one of my hip joints. Oh, right, I got shot there. Blood ran down my torn suit skin and I reached up to my neck. I expected to feel a gaping hole, but there was something stuck there. "Dr. Mensah, there might be more rogue units, we don't know—"

"That's why we need to hurry," she said, dragging me along. She had brought the last two drones with her from outside, but they were uselessly circling her head. Humans don't have enough access to the feed to control them and do other things, like walk and talk. I tried to reach them but I still couldn't get a clear link to the hopper's feed.

We turned into another corridor and Overse waited in the outer hatch. She hit the open panel as soon as she saw us. She had her handweapon out and I had time to notice that Mensah had my weapon under her other arm. "Dr. Mensah, I need my weapon."

"You're missing a hand and part of your shoulder," she snapped. Overse grabbed a handful of my suit skin and helped pull me out of the hatch. Dust swirled in the air as the hopper set down two meters away, barely clearing the habitat's extendable roof.

"Yeah, I know, but—" The hatch opened and Ratthi

ducked out, grabbed the collar of my suit skin, and pulled all three of us up into the cabin.

I collapsed on the deck as we lifted off. I needed to do something about the hip joint. I tried to check the scan to make sure nobody was on the ground shooting at us but even here my connection to the hopper's system was twitchy, glitching so much I couldn't see any reports from the instrumentation, like something was blocking the . . .

Uh-oh.

I felt the back of my neck again. The larger part of the obstruction was gone, but I could feel something in the port now. My data port.

The DeltFall SecUnits hadn't been rogues, they had been inserted with combat override modules. The modules allow personal control over a SecUnit, turn it from a mostly autonomous construct into a gun puppet. The feed would be cut off, control would be over the comm, but functionality would depend on how complex the orders were. "Kill the humans" isn't a complex order.

Mensah stood over me, Ratthi leaned across a seat to look out toward the DeltFall camp, Overse popped open one of the storage lockers. They were talking, but I couldn't catch it. I sat up and said, "Mensah, you need to shut me down now."

"What?" She looked down at me. "We're getting—emergency repair—"

Sound was breaking up. It was the download flooding my system, and my organic parts weren't used to processing that much information. "The unknown SecUnit inserted a data carrier, a combat-override module. It's downloading instructions into me and will override my system. This is why the two DeltFall units turned rogue. You have to stop me." I don't know why I was dancing around the word. Maybe because I thought she didn't want to hear it. She'd just shot a heavily armed SecUnit with a mining drill to get me back; presumably she wanted to keep me. "You have to kill me."

It took forever for them to realize what I'd said, put it together with what they must have seen on my field camera feed, but my ability to measure time was glitching, too.

"No," Ratthi said, looking down at me, horrified. "No, we can't—"

Mensah said, "We won't. Pin-Lee—"

Overse dropped the repair kit and climbed over two rows of seats, yelling for Pin-Lee. I knew she was going to the cockpit to take the controls so Pin-Lee could work on me. I knew she wouldn't have time to fix me. I knew I could kill everyone on the hopper, even with a blown hip joint and one working arm.

So I grabbed the handweapon lying on the seat, turned it toward my chest, and pulled the trigger.

⊛ ⊛ ⊛

PERFORMANCE RELIABILITY AT 10% AND DROPPING
SHUTDOWN INITIATED

Chapter Five

I CAME BACK ONLINE to find I was inert, but slowly cycling into a wake-up phase. I was agitated, my levels were all off, and I had no idea why. I played back my personal log. Oh, right.

I shouldn't be waking up. I hoped they hadn't been stupid about it, too soft-hearted to kill me.

You notice I didn't point the weapon at my head. I didn't want to kill myself, but it was going to have to be done. I could have incapacitated myself some other way, but let's face it, I didn't want to sit around and listen to the part where they convinced each other that there was no other choice.

A diagnostic initiated and informed me the combat override module had been removed. For a second I didn't believe it. I opened my security feed and found a camera for Medical. I was lying on the procedure table, my armor gone, just wearing what was left of my suit skin, the humans gathered around. That was a bit of a nightmare image. But my shoulder, hand, and hip had been repaired, so I'd been in my cubicle at some point. I ran the recording back a little and watched Pin-Lee and Overse use the surgical suite to deftly remove the combat module from the back of my head. It was such a relief, I played the recording twice, then ran a diagnostic. My logs were clear; nothing there except what I'd had before entering the DeltFall habitat.

My clients are the best clients.

Then hearing came online.

"I've had HubSystem immobilize it," Gurathin said.

Huh. Well, that explained a lot. I still had control of Sec-System and I told it to freeze HubSystem's access to its feed and implement my emergency routine. This was a function I'd built in that would substitute an hour or so of ambient habitat noise in place of the visual and audio recordings Hub-System made. To anyone listening to us through HubSystem, or trying to play back the recording, it would just sound like everybody had abruptly stopped talking.

What Gurathin had said had evidently been a surprise, because voices protested, Ratthi, Volescu, and Arada mostly. Pin-Lee was saying impatiently, "There's no danger. When it shot itself, it froze the download. I was able to remove the few fragments of rogue code that had been copied over."

Overse began, "Do you want to do your own diagnostic, because—"

I could hear them in the room and on the security feed, so I switched to just visual on the camera. Mensah had held up a hand for quiet. She said, "Gurathin, what's wrong?"

Gurathin said, "With it offline, I was able to use Hub-System to get some access to its internal system and log. I wanted to explore some anomalies I'd noticed through the feed." He gestured to me. "This unit was already a rogue. It has a hacked governor module."

On the entertainment feed, this is what they call an "oh shit" moment.

Through the security cams, I watched them be confused, but not alarmed, not yet.

Pin-Lee, who had apparently just been digging around in my local system, folded her arms. Her expression was sharp and skeptical. "I find that difficult to believe." She didn't add "you asshole" but it was in her voice. She didn't like anybody questioning her expertise.

"It doesn't have to follow our commands; there is no control over its behavior," Gurathin said, getting impatient. He didn't like anybody questioning his expertise either, but he didn't show it like Pin-Lee did. "I showed Volescu my evaluations and he agrees with me."

I had a moment to feel betrayed, which was stupid. Volescu was my client, and I'd saved his life because that was my job, not because I liked him. But then Volescu said, "I don't agree with you."

"The governor module is working, then?" Mensah asked, frowning at all of them.

"No, it's definitely hacked," Volescu explained. When he wasn't being attacked by giant fauna, he was a pretty calm guy. "The governor's connection to the rest of the SecUnit's system is partially severed. It can transmit commands, but can't enforce them or control behavior or apply punishment. But I think the fact that the Unit has been acting to preserve our lives, to take care of us, while it was a free agent, gives us even more reason to trust it."

Okay, so I did like him.

Gurathin insisted, "We've been sabotaged since we got here. The missing hazard report, the missing map sections. The SecUnit must be part of that. It's acting for the company, they don't want this planet surveyed for whatever reason. This is what must have happened to DeltFall."

Ratthi had been waiting for a moment to lunge in and interrupt. "Something odd is definitely going on. There were only three SecUnits for DeltFall in their specs, but there were five units in their habitat. Someone is sabotaging us, but I don't think our SecUnit is part of it."

With finality, Bharadwaj said, "Volescu and Ratthi are right. If the company did order the SecUnit to kill us, we would all be dead."

Overse sounded mad. "It told us about the combat module, it told us to kill it. Why the hell would it do that if it wanted to hurt us?"

I liked her, too. And even though being part of this conversation was the last thing I wanted to do, it was time to speak for myself.

I kept my eyes closed, watching them through the security camera, because that was easier. I made myself say, "The company isn't trying to kill you."

That startled them. Gurathin started to speak, and Pin-Lee shushed him. Mensah stepped forward, watching me with a worried expression. She was standing near me, with Gurathin and the others gathered in a loose circle around her. Bharadwaj was farthest back, sitting in a chair. Mensah said, "SecUnit, how do you know that?"

Even through the camera, this was hard. I tried to pretend I was back in my cubicle. "Because if the company wanted to sabotage you, they would have poisoned your supplies using the recycling systems. The company is more likely to kill you by accident."

There was a moment while they all thought about how easy it would have been for the company to sabotage its own environmental settings. Ratthi began, "But surely that would—"

Gurathin's expression was stiffer than usual. "This Unit has killed people before, people it was charged with protecting. It killed fifty-seven members of a mining operation."

What I told you before, about how I hacked my governor module but didn't become a mass murderer? That was only sort of true. I was already a mass murderer.

I didn't want to explain. I had to explain. I said, "I did not hack my governor module to kill my clients. My governor module malfunctioned because the stupid company only buys the cheapest possible components. It malfunctioned and I lost control of my systems and I killed them. The company retrieved me and installed a new governor module. I hacked it so it wouldn't happen again."

I think that's what happened. The only thing I know for certain is that it didn't happen after I hacked the module. And it makes a better story that way. I watch enough serials to know how a story like that should go.

Volescu looked sad. He shrugged a little. "My viewing of the Unit's personal log that Gurathin obtained confirms that."

Gurathin turned to him, impatient. "The log confirms it because that's what the Unit believes happened."

Bharadwaj sighed. "Yet here I sit, alive."

The silence was worse this time. On the feed I saw Pin-Lee move uncertainly, glance at Overse and Arada. Ratthi rubbed his face. Then Mensah said quietly, "SecUnit, do you have a name?"

I wasn't sure what she wanted. "No."

"It calls itself 'Murderbot,'" Gurathin said.

I opened my eyes and looked at him; I couldn't stop myself. From their expressions I knew everything I felt was showing on my face, and I hate that. I grated out, "That was private."

The silence was longer this time.

Then Volescu said, "Gurathin, you wanted to know how it spends its time. That was what you were originally looking for in the logs. Tell them."

Mensah lifted her brows. "Well?"

Gurathin hesitated. "It's downloaded seven hundred hours of entertainment programming since we landed. Mostly serials. Mostly something called *Sanctuary Moon*." He shook his head, dismissing it. "It's probably using it to encode data for the company. It can't be watching it, not in that volume; we'd notice."

I snorted. He underestimated me.

Ratthi said, "The one where the colony's solicitor killed the terraforming supervisor who was the secondary donor for her implanted baby?"

Again, I couldn't help it. I said, "She didn't kill him, that's a fucking lie."

Ratthi turned to Mensah. "It's watching it."

Her expression fascinated, Pin-Lee asked, "But how did you hack your own governor module?"

"All the company equipment is the same." I got a download once that included all the specs for company systems. Stuck in a cubicle with nothing to do, I used it to work out the codes for the governor module.

Gurathin looked stubborn, but didn't say anything. I figured that was all he had, now it was my turn. I said, "You're wrong. HubSystem let you read my log, it let you find out about the hacked governor module. This is part of the sabotage. It wants you to stop trusting me because I'm trying to keep you alive."

Gurathin said, "We don't have to trust you. We just have to keep you immobilized."

Right, funny thing about that. "That won't work."

"And why is that?"

I rolled off the table, grabbed Gurathin by the throat and pinned him to the wall. It was fast, too fast for them to react. I gave them a second to realize what had happened, to gasp, and for Volescu to make a little *eek* noise. I said, "Because HubSystem lied to you when it told you I was immobilized."

Gurathin was red, but not as red as he would have been if I'd started applying pressure. Before anyone else could move, Mensah said, calm and even, "SecUnit, I'd appreciate it if you put Gurathin down, please."

She's a really good commander. I'm going to hack her file and put that in. If she'd gotten angry, shouted, let the others panic, I don't know what would have happened.

I told Gurathin, "I don't like you. But I like the rest of them, and for some reason I don't understand, they like you." Then I put him down.

I stepped away. Overse started toward him and Volescu grabbed his shoulder, but Gurathin waved them off. I hadn't even left a mark on his neck.

I was still watching them through the camera, because it was easier than looking directly at them. My suit skin was torn, revealing some of the joins in my organic and inorganic parts. I hate that. Everyone was still frozen, shocked, uncertain. Then Mensah took a sharp breath. She said, "SecUnit, can you keep HubSystem from accessing the security recordings from this room?"

I looked at the wall next to her head. "I cut it off when Gurathin said he found out my governor module was hacked, then deleted that section. I have the visual and audio recording transfer from SecSystem to HubSystem on a five-second delay."

"Good." Mensah nodded. She was trying to make eye contact but I couldn't do it right now. "Without the governor module, you don't have to obey our orders, or anybody's orders. But that's been the case the entire time we've been here."

The others were quiet, and I realized she was saying it for their benefit as much as mine.

She continued, "I would like you to remain part of our group, at least until we get off this planet and back to a place of safety. At that point, we can discuss what you'd like to do. But I swear to you, I won't tell the company, or anyone outside this room, anything about you or the broken module."

I sighed, managed to keep most of it internal. Of course she had to say that. What else could she do. I tried to decide whether to believe it or not, or whether it mattered, when I was hit by a wave of *I don't care.* And I really didn't. I said, "Okay."

In the camera feed, Ratthi and Pin-Lee exchanged a look. Gurathin grimaced, radiating skepticism. Mensah just said, "Is there any chance HubSystem knows about your governor module?"

I hated to admit this but they needed to know. Hacking myself is one thing, but I had hacked other systems, and I didn't know how they were going to react to that. "It might. I hacked HubSystem when we first arrived so it wouldn't notice that the commands sent to the governor module weren't always being followed, but if HubSystem's been compromised by an outside agent, I don't know if that worked. But HubSystem won't know you know about it."

Ratthi crossed his arms, his shoulders hunching uneasily.

"We have to shut it down, or it's going to kill us." Then he winced and looked at me. "Sorry, I meant HubSystem."

"No offense," I said.

"So we think HubSystem has been compromised by an outside agent," Bharadwaj said slowly, as if trying to convince herself. "Can we be certain it's not the company?"

I said, "Was DeltFall's beacon triggered?"

Mensah frowned, and Ratthi looked thoughtful again. He said, "We checked it on the way back, once we had you stabilized. It had been destroyed. So there was no reason for the attackers to do that if the company was their ally."

Everyone stood there, quiet. I could tell from their expressions they were all thinking hard. The HubSystem that controlled their habitat, that they were dependent on for food, shelter, filtered air, and water, was trying to kill them. And in their corner all they had was Murderbot, who just wanted everyone to shut up and leave it alone so it could watch the entertainment feed all day.

Then Arada came up and patted my shoulder. "I'm sorry. This must be very upsetting. After what that other Unit did to you . . . Are you all right?"

That was too much attention. I turned around and walked into the corner, facing away from them. I said, "There were two other instances of attempted sabotage I'm aware of. When Hostile One attacked Drs. Bharadwaj and Volescu and I went to render assistance, I received an abort command from HubSystem through my governor module. I thought it was a glitch, caused by the MedSystem emergency feed trying to override HubSystem. When Dr. Mensah was flying the little hopper to check out the nearest map anomaly, the autopilot cut out just as we were crossing over a mountain range." I think that was it. Oh, right. "HubSystem downloaded an upgrade packet for me from the satellite before we left for DeltFall. I didn't apply it. You should probably look at what it would have told me to do."

Mensah said, "Pin-Lee, Gurathin, can you shut HubSystem down without compromising the environmental systems? And trigger our beacon without it interfering?"

Pin-Lee glanced at Gurathin and nodded. "It depends on what kind of condition you expect it to be in after we're done."

Mensah said, "Let's say don't blow it up, but you don't need to be gentle, either."

Pin-Lee nodded. "We can do that."

Gurathin cleared his throat. "It's going to know what we're doing. But if it doesn't have any instructions to stop us if we try, it may do nothing."

Bharadwaj leaned forward, frowning. "It's got to be reporting to someone. If it has a chance to warn them that we're shutting it down, they could supply instructions."

"We have to try it," Mensah said. She nodded to them. "Get moving."

Pin-Lee started for the door, but Gurathin said to Mensah, "Will you be all right here?"

He meant would they be all right with me here. I rolled my eyes.

"We'll be fine," Mensah said, firmly, with just a touch of *I said now.*

I watched him with the security cameras as he and Pin-Lee left, just in case he tried anything.

Volescu stirred. "We also need to look at that download from the satellite. Knowing what they wanted SecUnit to do might tell us a great deal."

Bharadwaj pushed herself up, a little unsteadily. "Med-System is isolated from HubSystem, correct? That's why it hasn't been having failures. You could use it to unpack the download."

Volescu took her arm and they moved into the next cabin to the display surface there.

There was a little silence. The others could still listen to us on the feed, but at least they weren't in the room, and I felt the tension in my back and shoulders relax. It was easier to think. I was glad Mensah had told them to trigger our emergency beacon. Even if some of them were still suspicious of the company, it wasn't like there was another way off this planet.

Arada reached over and took Overse's hand. She said, "If it isn't the company that's doing this, who is it?"

"There has to be someone else here." Mensah rubbed her forehead, wincing as she thought. "Those two extra SecUnits at DeltFall came from somewhere. SecUnit, I'm assuming the company could be bribed to conceal the existence of a third survey team on this planet."

I said, "The company could be bribed to conceal the existence of several hundred survey teams on this planet." Survey teams, whole cities, lost colonies, traveling circuses, as long as they thought they could get away with it. I just didn't see how they could get away with making a client survey team— two client survey teams—vanish. Or why they'd want to. There were too many bond companies out there, too many competitors. Dead clients were terrible for business. "I don't think the company would collude with one set of clients to kill two other sets of clients. You purchased a bond agreement that the company would guarantee your safety or pay compensation in the event of your death or injury. Even if the company couldn't be held liable or partially liable for your deaths, they would still have to make the payment to your heirs. DeltFall was a large operation. The death payout for them alone will be huge." And the company hated to spend money. You could tell that by looking at the recycled upholstery on the habitat's furniture. "And if everyone believes the clients were killed by faulty SecUnits, the payment would be even bigger once all the lawsuits were filed."

On the cameras I could see nods and thoughtful expressions as they took that in. And they remembered that I had experience in what happened after SecUnits malfunctioned and killed clients.

"So the company took a bribe to conceal this third survey group, but not to let them kill us," Overse said. One of the good things about scientist clients is that they're quick on the uptake. "That means we just need to stay alive long enough for the pick-up transport to get here."

"But who is it?" Arada waved her hands. "We know whoever it is must have hacked control of the satellite." In the security camera, I saw her look toward me. "Is that how they took control of the DeltFall SecUnits? Through a download?"

It was a good question. I said, "It's possible. But it doesn't explain why one of the three DeltFall Units was killed outside the hub with a mining drill." We weren't supposed to be able to refuse a download, and I doubted there were other SecUnits hiding hacked governor modules. "If the DeltFall group refused the download for their SecUnits because they were experiencing the same increase in equipment failure that we were, the two unidentified Units could have been sent to manually infect the DeltFall Units."

Ratthi was staring into the distance, and through the feed I saw he was reviewing my field camera video of the DeltFall habitat. He pointed in my direction, nodding. "I agree, but it would mean the DeltFall group allowed the unknown Units into their habitat."

It was likely. We had checked to make sure all their hoppers were there, but it had been impossible to tell if an extra one had landed and taken off again at some point. Speaking of which, I did a quick check of the security feed to see how our perimeter was doing. The drones were still patrolling and our sensor alarms all responded to pings.

Overse said, "But why? Why allow a strange group into their habitat? A group whose existence had been concealed from them?"

"You'd do it," I said. I should keep my mouth shut, keep them thinking of me as their normal obedient SecUnit, stop reminding them what I was. But I wanted them to be careful. "If a strange survey group landed here, all friendly, saying they had just arrived, and oh, we've had an equipment failure or our MedSystem's down and we need help, you would let them in. Even if I told you not to, that it was against company safety protocol, you'd do it." Not that I'm bitter, or anything. A lot of the company's rules are stupid or just there to increase profit, but some of them are there for a good reason. Not letting strangers into your habitat is one of them.

Arada and Ratthi exchanged a wry look. Overse conceded, "We might, yes."

Mensah had been quiet, listening to us. She said, "I think it was easier than that. I think they said they were us."

It was so simple, I turned around and looked directly at her. Her brow was furrowed in thought. She said, "So they land, say they're us, that they need help. If they have access to our HubSystem, listening to our comm would be easy."

I said, "When they come here, they won't do that." It all depended on what this other survey group had, whether they had come prepared to get rid of rival survey teams or had decided on it after they got here. They could have armed air vehicles, Combat SecUnits, armed drones. I pulled a few examples from the database and sent them into the feed for the humans to see.

MedSystem's feed informed me that Ratthi, Overse, and Arada's heart rates had just accelerated. Mensah's hadn't, because she had already thought of all this. It was why she had sent Pin-Lee and Gurathin to shut off HubSystem. Nervously, Ratthi said, "What do we do when they come here?"

I said, "Be somewhere else."

⊕　⊕　⊕

It may seem weird that Mensah was the only human to think of abandoning the habitat while we waited for the beacon to bring help, but as I said before, these weren't intrepid galactic explorers. They were people who had been doing a job and suddenly found themselves in a terrible situation.

And it had been hammered into them from the pre-trip orientation, to the waivers they had to sign for the company, to the survey packages with all the hazard information, to their on-site briefing by their SecUnit that this was an unknown, potentially dangerous region on a mostly unsurveyed planet. They weren't supposed to leave the habitat without security precautions, and we didn't even do overnight assessment trips. The idea that they might have to stuff both hoppers full of emergency supplies and run for it, and that that would be safer than their habitat, was hard to grasp.

But when Pin-Lee and Gurathin shut down HubSystem, and Volescu unpacked the satellite download that was meant for me, they grasped it pretty quick.

Bharadwaj outlined it for us on the comm while I was getting my last extra suit skin and my armor back on. "It was meant to take control of SecUnit, and the instructions were very specific," she finished. "Once SecUnit was under control, it would give them access to MedSystem and SecSystem."

I got my helmet on and opaqued it. The relief was intense, about even with finding out that the combat override module had been removed. *I love you, armor, and I'm never leaving you again.*

Mensah clicked onto the comm. "Pin-Lee, what about the beacon?"

"I got a go signal when I initiated launch." Pin-Lee sounded even more exasperated than usual. "But with Hub-System shut down, I can't get any confirmation."

I told them over the feed that I could dispatch a drone to check on it. A good beacon launch was pretty important right now. Mensah gave me the go-ahead and I forwarded the order to one of my drones.

Our beacon was a few kilos away from our habitat site

for safety, but I thought we should have been able to hear it launch. Maybe not; I had never had to launch one before.

Mensah had already got the humans organized and moving, and as soon as I had my weapons and spare drones loaded, I grabbed a couple of crates. I kept catching little fragments of conversation over the security cameras.

("You have to think of it as a person," Pin-Lee said to Gurathin.

"It *is* a person," Arada insisted.)

Ratthi and Arada sprinted past me carrying medical supplies and spare power cells. I had extended our drone perimeter as far as it could go. We didn't know that whoever hit DeltFall would show up at any second, but it was a strong possibility. Gurathin had come out to check the big hopper and the little hopper's systems, to make sure no one other than us had access and that HubSystem hadn't messed with their code. I kept an eye on him through one of the drones. He kept looking at me, or trying not to look at me, which was worse. I didn't need the distraction right now. When the next attack came, it was going to be fast.

("I do think of it as a person," Gurathin said. "An angry, heavily armed person who has no reason to trust us."

"Then stop being mean to it," Ratthi told him. "That might help.")

"They know their SecUnits successfully gave our SecUnit the combat module," Mensah was saying over the comm. "And we have to assume they received enough information from HubSystem to know we removed it. But they don't know that we've theorized their existence. When SecUnit cut off HubSystem's access, we were still assuming this was sabotage from the company. They won't realize we know they're coming."

Which is why we had to keep moving. Ratthi and Arada stopped to answer a question about the medical equipment power cells and I shooed them back to the habitat for the next load.

The problem I was going to have is that the way murderbots fight is we throw ourselves at the target and try to kill the shit out of it, knowing that 90 percent of our bodies can be regrown or replaced in a cubicle. So, finesse is not required.

When we left the habitat, I wouldn't have access to the cubicle. Even if we knew how to take it apart, which we didn't, it was too big to fit in the hopper and required too much power.

And they might have actual combat bots rather than security bots like me. In which case, our only chance was going to be keeping away from them until the pick-up transport arrived. If the other survey group hadn't bribed somebody in the company to delay it. I hadn't mentioned that possibility yet.

We had everything almost loaded when Pin-Lee said on the comm, "I found it! They had an access code buried in HubSystem. It wasn't sending them our audio or visual data, or allowing them to see our feed, but it was receiving commands periodically. That's how it removed information from our info and map package, how it sent the command to the little hopper's autopilot to fail."

Gurathin added, "Both the hoppers are clear now and I've initiated the pre-flight checks."

Mensah was saying something but I had just gotten an alert from SecSystem. A drone was sending me an emergency signal.

A second later I got the drone's visual of the field where our beacon was installed. The tripod launching column was on its side, pieces of the capsule scattered around.

I pushed it out into the general feed, and the humans went quiet. In a little voice, Ratthi said, "Shit."

"Keep moving," Mensah said over the comm, her voice harsh.

With HubSystem down, we didn't have any scanners up, but I had widened the perimeter as far as it would go. And SecSystem had just lost contact with one of the drones to the far south. I tossed the last crate into the cargo hold, gave the drones their orders, and yelled over the comm, "They're coming! We need to get in the air, now!"

It was unexpectedly stressful, pacing back and forth in front of the hoppers waiting for my humans. Volescu came out with Bharadwaj, helping her over the sandy ground. Then Overse and Arada, bags slung over their shoulders, yelling at Ratthi behind them to keep up. Guranthin was already in the big hopper and Mensah and Pin-Lee came last.

They split up, Pin-Lee, Volescu, and Bharadwaj headed for the little hopper and the rest to the big one. I made sure Bharadwaj didn't have trouble with the ramp. We had a problem at the hatch of the big hopper where Mensah wanted to get in last and I wanted to get in last. As a compromise, I grabbed her around the waist and swung us both up into the hatch as the ramp pulled in after us. I set her on her feet and she said, "Thank you, SecUnit," while the others stared.

The helmet made it a little easier, but I was going to miss the comfortable buffer of the security cameras.

I stayed on my feet, holding on to the overhead rail, as the others got strapped in and Mensah went up to the pilot's seat. The little hopper took off first, and she gave it time to get clear before we lifted off.

We were operating on an assumption: that since They, whoever They were, didn't know that we knew They were here, They would only send one ship. They would be expecting to catch us in the habitat, and would probably come in prepared to destroy the hoppers to keep us there, and then start on the people. So now that we knew They were coming from the south, we were free to pick a direction. The little hopper curved away to the west, and we followed.

I just hoped their hopper didn't have a longer range on

its scanners than ours did.

I could see most of my drones on the hopper's feed, a
bright dot forming on the three dimensions of the map.
Group One was doing what I'd told them, gathering at a
rendezvous point near the habitat. I had a calculation going,
estimating the bogie's time of arrival. Right before we passed
out of range I told the drones to head northeast. Within moments, they dropped out of my range. They would follow
their last instruction until they used up their power cells.

I was hoping the other survey team would pick them
up and follow. As soon as they had a visual on our habitat
they'd see the hoppers were gone and know we'd run away.
They might stop to search the habitat, but they also might
start looking for our escape route. It was impossible to guess
which.

But as we flew, curving away to the distant mountains,
nothing followed us.

Chapter Six

THE HUMANS HAD DEBATED where to go. Or debated it as much as possible, while frantically calculating how much of what they might need to survive they could stuff into the hoppers. We knew the group who Ratthi was now calling EvilSurvey had had access to HubSystem and knew all the places we'd been to on assessments. So we had to go somewhere new.

We went to a spot Overse and Ratthi had proposed after a quick look at the map. It was a series of rocky hills in a thick tropical jungle, heavily occupied by a large range of fauna, enough to confuse life-sign scans. Mensah and Pin-Lee lowered the hoppers down and eased them in among rocky cliffs. I sent up some drones so we could check the view from several angles and we adjusted the hoppers' positions a few times. Then I set a perimeter.

It didn't feel safe, and while there were a couple of survival hut kits in the hoppers, no one suggested putting them up. The humans would stay in the hoppers for now, communicating over the comm and the hoppers' limited feed. It wasn't going to be comfortable for the humans (sanitary and hygiene facilities were small and limited, for one thing) but it would be more secure. Large and small fauna moved within range of our scanners, curious and potentially as dangerous as the people who wanted to kill my clients.

I went out with some drones to do a little scouting and make sure there was no sign of anything big enough to, say, drag the little hopper off in the middle of the night. It gave me a chance to think, too.

They knew about the governor module, or the lack of it, and even though Mensah had sworn she wouldn't report me, I had to think about what I wanted to do.

It's wrong to think of a construct as half bot, half human. It makes it sound like the halves are discrete, like the bot half should want to obey orders and do its job and the human half should want to protect itself and get the hell out of here. As opposed to the reality, which was that I was one whole confused entity, with no idea what I wanted to do. What I should do. What I needed to do.

I could leave them to cope on their own, I guess. I pictured doing that, pictured Arada or Ratthi trapped by rogue SecUnits, and felt my insides twist. I hate having emotions about reality; I'd much rather have them about *Sanctuary Moon.*

And what was I supposed to do? Go off on this empty planet and just live until my power cells died? If I was going to do that I should have planned better and downloaded more entertainment media. I don't think I could store enough to last until my power cells wore out. My specs told me that would be hundreds of thousands of hours from now.

And even to me, that sounded like a stupid thing to do.

◈   ◈   ◈

Overse had set up some remote sensing equipment that would help warn us if anything tried to scan the area. As the humans climbed back into the two hoppers, I did a quick headcount on the feed, making sure they were all still there. Mensah waited on the ramp, indicating she wanted to talk to me in private.

I muted my feed and the comm, and she said, "I know you're more comfortable with keeping your helmet opaque, but the situation has changed. We need to see you."

I didn't want to do it. Now more than ever. They knew too much about me. But I needed them to trust me so I could keep them alive and keep doing my job. The good version of my job, not the half-assed version of my job that I'd been doing before things started trying to kill my clients. I still didn't want to do it. "It's usually better if humans think of me as a robot," I said.

"Maybe, under normal circumstances." She was looking

a little off to one side, not trying to make eye contact, which I appreciated. "But this situation is different. It would be better if they could think of you as a person who is trying to help. Because that's how I think of you."

My insides melted. That's the only way I could describe it. After a minute, when I had my expression under control, I cleared the face plate and had it and the helmet fold back into my armor.

She said, "Thank you," and I followed her up into the hopper.

The others were stowing the equipment and supplies that had gotten tossed in right before takeoff. "—If they restore the satellite function," Ratthi was saying.

"They won't chance that until—unless they get us," Arada said.

Over the comm, Pin-Lee sighed, angry and frustrated. "If only we knew who these assholes were."

"We need to talk about our next move." Mensah cut through all the chatter and took a seat in the back where she could see the whole compartment. The others sat down to face her, Ratthi turning one of the mobile seats around. I sat down on the bench against the starboard wall. The feed gave us a view of the little hopper's compartment, with the rest of the team sitting there, checking in to show they were listening. Mensah continued, "There's another question I'd like the answer to."

Gurathin looked at me expectantly. She isn't talking about me, idiot.

Ratthi nodded glumly. "Why? Why are these people doing this? What is worth this to them?"

"It has to have something to do with those blanked-out sections on the map," Overse said. She was calling up the stored images on her feed. "There's obviously something there they want, that they didn't want us or DeltFall to find."

Mensah got up to pace. "Did you turn up anything in the

analysis?"

In the feed, Arada did a quick consult with Bharadwaj and Volescu. "Not yet, but we hadn't finished running all the tests. We hadn't turned up anything interesting so far."

"Do they really expect to get away with this?" Ratthi turned to me, like he was expecting an answer. "Obviously, they can hack the company systems and the satellite, and they intend to put the blame on the SecUnits, but . . . The investigation will surely be thorough. They must know this."

There were too many factors in play, and too many things we didn't know, but I'm supposed to answer direct questions and even without the governor module, old habits die hard. "They may believe the company and whoever your beneficiaries are won't look any further than the rogue SecUnits. But they can't make two whole survey teams disappear unless their corporate or political entity doesn't care about them. Does DeltFall's care? Does yours?"

That made them all stare at me, for some reason. I had to turn and look out the port. I wanted to seal my helmet so badly my organic parts started to sweat, but I replayed the conversation with Mensah and managed not to.

Volescu said, "You don't know who we are? They didn't tell you?"

"There was an info packet in my initial download." I was still staring out at the heavy green tangle just past the rocks. I really didn't want to get into how little I paid attention to my job. "I didn't read it."

Arada said, gently, "Why not?"

With all of them staring at me, I couldn't come up with a good lie. "I didn't care."

Gurathin said, "You expect us to believe that."

I felt my face move, my jaw harden. Physical reactions I couldn't suppress. "I'll try to be more accurate. I was indifferent, and vaguely annoyed. Do you believe that?"

He said, "Why don't you want us to look at you?"

My jaw was so tight it triggered a performance reliability alert in my feed. I said, "You don't need to look at me. I'm not a sexbot."

Ratthi made a noise, half sigh, half snort of exasperation. It wasn't directed at me. He said, "Gurathin, I told you. It's shy."

Overse added, "It doesn't want to interact with humans. And why should it? You know how constructs are treated, especially in corporate-political environments."

Gurathin turned to me. "So you don't have a governor module, but we could punish you by looking at you."

I looked at him. "Probably, right up until I remember I have guns built into my arms."

With an ironic edge to her voice, Mensah said, "There, Gurathin. It's threatened you, but it didn't resort to violence. Are you satisfied now?"

He sat back. "For now." So he had been testing me. Wow, that was brave. And very, very stupid. To me, he said, "I want to make certain you're not under any outside compulsion."

"That's enough." Arada got up and sat down next to me. I didn't want to push past her so this pinned me in the corner. She said, "You need to give it time. It's never interacted with humans as an openly free agent before now. This is a learning experience for all of us."

The others nodded, like this made sense.

Mensah sent me a private message through the feed: *I hope you're all right.*

Because you need me. I don't know where that came from. All right, it came from me, but she was my client, I was a SecUnit. There was no emotional contract between us. There was no rational reason for me to sound like a whiny human baby.

Of course I need you. I have no experience in anything like this. None of us do. Sometimes humans can't help but let emotion bleed through into the feed. She was furious and frightened, not at me, at the people who would do this, kill like this, slaughter a whole survey team and leave the SecUnits to take the blame. She was struggling with her anger, though nothing showed on her face except calm concern. Through the feed I felt her steel herself. *You're the only one here who won't panic. The longer this situation goes on, the others . . . We have to stay together, use our heads.*

That was absolutely true. And I could help, just by being the SecUnit. I was the one who was supposed to keep everybody safe. *I panic all the time, you just can't see it,* I told her. I added the text signifier for "joke."

She didn't answer, but she looked down, smiling to herself.

Ratthi was saying, "There's another question. Where are they? They came toward our habitat out of the south, but that doesn't tell us anything."

I said, "I left three drones at our habitat. They don't have scanning function with HubSystem down, but the visual and audio recording will still work. They may pick up something that will answer your questions."

I'd left one drone in a tree with a long-range view of the habitat, one tucked under the extendable roof over the entrance, and one inside the hub, hidden under a console. They were on the next setting to inert, recording only, so when EvilSurvey scanned, the drones would be buried in the ambient energy readings from the habitat's environmental system. I hadn't been able to connect the drones to SecSystem like I normally did so it could store the data and filter out the boring parts. I knew EvilSurvey would check for that, which was why I had dumped SecSystem's storage into the big hopper's system and then purged it.

I also didn't want them knowing any more about me than they already did.

Everyone was looking at me again, surprised that Murderbot had had a plan. Frankly, I didn't blame them. Our education modules didn't have anything like that in it, but this was another way all the thrillers and adventures I'd watched or read were finally starting to come in handy. Mensah lifted her brows in appreciation. She said, "But you can't pick up their signal from here."

"No, I'll have to go back to get the data," I told her.

Pin-Lee leaned farther into the little hopper's camera range. "I should be able to attach one of the small scanners to a drone. It'll be bulky and slow, but that would give us something other than just audio and visual."

Mensah nodded. "Do it, but remember our resources are limited." She tapped me in the feed so I'd know she was talking to me without her looking at me. "How long do you think the other group will stay at our habitat?"

There was a groan from Volescu in the other hopper. "All our samples. We have our data, but if they destroy our work—"

The others were agreeing with him, expressing frustration and worry. I tuned them out, and answered Mensah, "I don't think they'll stay long. There's nothing there they want."

For just an instant, Mensah let her expression show how worried she was. "Because they want us," she said softly.

She was absolutely right about that, too.

⊛   ⊛   ⊛

Mensah set up a watch schedule, including in time for me to go into standby and do a diagnostic and recharge cycle. I was also planning to use the time to watch some *Sanctuary Moon* and recharge my ability to cope with humans at close quarters without losing my mind.

After the humans had settled down, either sleeping or deep in their own feeds, I walked the perimeter and checked the drones. The night was noisier than the day, but so far nothing bigger than insects and a few reptiles had come near the hoppers. When I cycled through the big hopper's hatch,

Ratthi was the human on watch, sitting up in the cockpit and keeping an eye on its scanners. I moved up past the crew section and sat next to him. He nodded to me and said, "All's well?"

"Yes." I didn't want to, but I had to ask. When I was looking for permanent storage for all my entertainment downloads, the info packet was one of the files I'd purged. (I know, but I'm used to having all the extra storage on SecSystem.) Remembering what Mensah had said, I unsealed my helmet. It was easier with just Ratthi, both of us facing toward the console. "Why did everyone think it was so strange that I asked if your political entity would miss you?"

Ratthi smiled at the console. "Because Dr. Mensah is our political entity." He made a little gesture, turning his hand palm up. "We're from Preservation Alliance, one of the non-corporate system entities. Dr. Mensah is the current admin director on the steering committee. It's an elected position, with a limited term. But one of the principles of our home is that our admins must also continue their regular work, whatever it is. Her regular work required this survey, so here she is, and here we are."

Yeah, I felt a little stupid. I was still processing it when he said, "You know, in Preservation-controlled territory, bots are considered full citizens. A construct would fall under the same category." He said this in the tone of giving me a hint.

Whatever. Bots who are "full citizens" still have to have a human or augmented human guardian appointed, usually their employer; I'd seen it on the news feeds. And the entertainment feed, where the bots were all happy servants or were secretly in love with their guardians. If it showed the bots hanging out watching the entertainment feed all through the day cycle with no one trying to make them talk about their feelings, I would have been a lot more interested. "But the company knows who she is."

Ratthi sighed. "Oh, yes, they know. You would not

believe what we had to pay to guarantee the bond on the survey. These corporate arseholes are robbers."

It meant if we ever managed to launch the beacon, the company wouldn't screw around, the transport would get here fast. No bribe from EvilSurvey could stop it. They might even send a faster security ship to check out the problem before the transport could arrive. The bond on a political leader was high, but the payout the company would have to make if something happened to her was off the chart. The huge payout, being humiliated in front of the other bond companies and in the news feeds . . . I leaned back in my seat and sealed my helmet to think about it.

We didn't know who EvilSurvey was, who we were dealing with. But I bet that they didn't either. Mensah's status was only in the Security info packet, stored on SecSystem, which they had never gotten access to. The dueling investigations if something happened to us were bound to be thorough, as the company would be desperate for something to blame it on and the beneficiaries would be desperate to blame it on the company. Neither would be fooled long by the rogue SecUnit setup.

I didn't see how we could use it, not right now, anyway. It didn't comfort me and I'm pretty sure it wouldn't comfort the humans to know the stupid company would avenge them if/when they all got murdered.

◈   ◈   ◈

So midafternoon the next day I got ready to take the little hopper back within range of the habitat so I could hopefully pick up intel from the drones. I wanted to go alone, but since nobody ever listens to me, Mensah, Pin-Lee, and Ratthi were going, too.

I was depressed this morning. I'd tried watching some new serials last night and even they couldn't distract me; reality was too intrusive. It was hard not to think about how everything was going to go wrong and they were all going

to die and I was going to get blasted to pieces or get another
governor module stuck in me.

Gurathin walked up to me while I was doing the pre-
flight, and said, "I'm coming with you."

That was about all I needed right now. I finished the diagnostic on the power cells. "I thought you were satisfied."

It took him a minute. "What I said last night, yes."

"I remember every word ever said to me." That was a lie.
Who would want that? Most of it I delete from permanent
memory.

He didn't say anything. On the feed, Mensah told me that
I didn't have to take him if I didn't want to, or if I thought it
would compromise team security. I knew Gurathin was testing me again, but if something went wrong and he got killed,
I wouldn't mind as much as I would if it was one of the others. I wished Mensah, Ratthi, and Pin-Lee weren't coming; I
didn't want to risk them. And on the long trip, Ratthi might
be tempted to try to make me talk about my feelings.

I told Mensah it was fine, and we got ready to lift off.

◎   ◎   ◎

I wanted a long time to circle west, so if EvilSurvey picked
us up they wouldn't be able to extrapolate the humans' location from my course. By the time I was in position for the
approach to the habitat, the light was failing. When we got
to the target zone, it would be full dark.

The humans hadn't gotten a lot of sleep last night, from
the crowding and the strong possibility of dying. Mensah,
Ratthi, and Pin-Lee had been too tired to talk much, and had
fallen asleep. Gurathin was sitting in the copilot's seat and
hadn't said a word the whole time.

We were flying in dark mode, with no lights, no trans-
missions. I was plugged in to the little hopper's internal limited feed so I could watch the scans carefully. Gurathin was
aware of the feed through his implant—I could feel him in
there—but wasn't using it except to keep track of where we

were.

When he said, "I have a question," I flinched. The silence up to this point had lulled me into a false sense of security.

I didn't look at him though I knew through the feed that he was looking at me. I hadn't closed my helmet; I didn't feel like hiding from him. After a moment I realized he was waiting for my permission. That was weirdly new. It was tempting to ignore him, but I was wondering what the test would be this time. Something he didn't want the others to hear? I said, "Go ahead."

He said, "Did they punish you, for the deaths of the mining team?"

It wasn't completely a surprise. I think they all wanted to ask about it, but maybe he was the only one abrasive enough. Or brave enough. It's one thing to poke a murderbot with a governor module; poking a rogue murderbot is a whole different proposition.

I said, "No, not like you're thinking. Not the way a human would be punished. They shut me down for a while, and then brought me back online at intervals."

He hesitated. "You weren't aware of it?"

Yeah, that would be the easy way out, wouldn't it? "The organic parts mostly sleep, but not always. You know something's happening. They were trying to purge my memory. We're too expensive to destroy."

He looked out the port again. We were flying low over trees, and I had a lot of my attention on the terrain sensors. I felt the brush of Mensah's awareness in the feed. She must have woken when Gurathin spoke. He finally said, "You don't blame humans for what you were forced to do? For what happened to you?"

This is why I'm glad I'm not human. They come up with stuff like this. I said, "No. That's a human thing to do. Constructs aren't that stupid."

What was I supposed to do, kill all humans because the

ones in charge of constructs in the company were callous?
Granted, I liked the imaginary people on the entertainment
feed way more than I liked real ones, but you can't have one
without the other.

The others started to stir, waking and sitting up, and he
didn't ask me anything else.

⊛   ⊛   ⊛

By the time we got within range, it was a cloudless night
with the ring glowing in the sky like a ribbon. I had already
dropped speed, and we were moving slowly over the sparse
trees decorating the hills at the edge of the habitat's plain.
I had been waiting for the drones to ping me, which they
would if this had worked and EvilSurvey hadn't found them.

When I felt that first cautious touch on my feed, I
stopped the hopper and dropped it down below the tree line.
I landed on a hillside, the hopper's pads extending to com-
pensate. The humans were waiting, nervy and impatient, but
no one spoke. You couldn't see anything from here except the
next hill and a lot of tree trunks.

All three drones were still active. I answered the pings,
trying to keep my transmission as quick as possible. After a
tense moment, the downloads started. I could tell from the
timestamps that, with nobody there to instruct them not to,
the drones had recorded everything from the moment I'd
deployed them to now. Even though the part we were most
interested in would be near the beginning, that was a lot of
data. I didn't want to stay here long enough to parse it myself,
so I pushed half of it into the feed for Gurathin. Again, he
didn't say anything, just turned in his chair to lie back, close
his eyes, and start reviewing it.

I checked the drone stationed outside in the tree first,
running its video at high speed until I found the moment
where it had caught a good image of the EvilSurvey craft.

It was a big hopper, a newer model than ours, nothing
about it to cause anybody any pause. It circled the habitat a

few times, probably scanning, and then landed on our empty pad.

They must know we were gone, with no air craft on the pad and no answer on their comm, so they didn't bother to pretend to be here to borrow some tools or exchange site data. Five SecUnits piled out of the cargo pods, all armed with the big projectile weapons assigned to protect survey teams on planets with hazardous fauna, like this one. From the pattern on the armor chestplates, two were the surviving DeltFall units. They must have been put into their cubicles after we escaped the DeltFall habitat.

Three were EvilSurvey, which had a square gray logo. I focused in on it and sent it to the others. "GrayCris," Pin-Lee read aloud.

"Ever heard of it?" Ratthi said, and the others said no.

All five SecUnits would have the combat override modules installed. They started toward the habitat, and five humans, anonymous in their color-coded field suits, climbed out of the hopper and followed. They were all armed, too, with the handweapons the company provided, that were only supposed to be used for fauna-related emergencies.

I focused as far in on the humans as the image quality would allow. They spent a lot of time scanning and checking for traps, which made me even more glad I hadn't wasted time setting any. But there was something about them that made me think I wasn't looking at professionals. They weren't soldiers, any more than I was. Their SecUnits weren't combat units, just regular security rented from the company. That was a relief. At least I wasn't the only one who didn't know what I was doing.

Finally I watched them enter the habitat, leaving two SecUnits outside to guard their hopper. I tagged the section, passed it to Mensah and the others for review, and then kept watching.

Gurathin sat up suddenly and muttered a curse in a

language I didn't know. I noted it to look up later on the big hopper's language center. Then forgot about it when he said, "We have a problem."

I put my part of the drones' download on pause and looked at the section he had just tagged. It was from the drone hidden in the hub.

The visual was a blurred image of a curved support strut but the audio was a human voice saying, "You knew we were coming, so I assume you have some way to watch us while we're here." The voice spoke standard lexicon with a flat accent. "We've destroyed your beacon. Come to these coordinates—" She spoke a set of longitude and latitude numbers that the little hopper helpfully mapped for me, and a time stamp. "—at this time, and we can come to some arrangement. This doesn't have to end in violence. We're happy to pay you off, or whatever you want."

There was nothing else, steps fading until the door slid shut.

Gurathin, Pin-Lee, and Ratthi all started to speak at once. Mensah said, "Quiet." They shut up. "SecUnit, your opinion."

Fortunately, I had one now. Up to the point where we'd gotten the drone download, my opinion had been mostly *oh, shit*. I said, "They have nothing to lose. If we come to this rendezvous, they can kill us and stop worrying about us. If we don't, they have until the end of project date to search for us."

Gurathin was reviewing the landing video now. He said, "Another indication it isn't the company. They obviously don't want to chase us until the end of project date."

I said, "I told you it wasn't the company."

Mensah interrupted Gurathin before he could respond. "They think we know why they're here, why they're doing this."

"They're wrong," Ratthi said, frustrated.

Mensah's brow furrowed as she picked apart the problem

for the other humans. "But why do they think that? It must be because they know we went to one of the unmapped regions. That means the data we collected must have the answer."

Pin-Lee nodded. "So the others may know by now."

"It gives us leverage," Mensah said thoughtfully. "But what can we do with it?"

And then I had a great idea.

Chapter Seven

SO AT THE APPOINTED time the next day, Mensah and I were flying toward the rendezvous point.

Gurathin and Pin-Lee had taken one of my drones and rebuilt it with a limited scanning attachment. (Limited because the drone was too small for most of the components a longer and wider range scanner would need.) Last night I had sent it into upper atmosphere to give us a view of the site.

The location was near their survey base, which was only about two kilos away, a habitat similar to DeltFall's. By the size of their habitat and the number of SecUnits, including the one Mensah had taken out with a mining drill, they had between thirty and forty team members. They were obviously very confident, but then, they'd had access to our hub and they knew they were dealing with a small group of scientists and researchers, and one messed-up secondhand SecUnit.

I just hoped they didn't realize how messed up I actually was.

When the hopper picked up the first blip of scanner contact, Mensah hit the comm immediately. "GrayCris, be advised that my party has secured evidence of your activities on this planet, and hidden it in various places where it will transmit to the pickup ship whenever it arrives." She let that sink in for three seconds, then added, "You know we found the missing map sections."

There was a long pause. I was slowing us down, scanning for incoming weapons, even though the chances were good they didn't have any.

The comm channel came alive, and a voice said, "We can discuss our situation. An arrangement can be made." There was so much scanning and anti-scanning going on the voice was made of static. It was creepy. "Land your vehicle and we can discuss it."

Mensah gave it a minute, as if she was thinking it over,

then answered, "I'll send our SecUnit to speak to you." She cut the comm off.

As we got closer we had a visual on the site. It was a low plateau, surrounded by trees. Their habitat was visible to the west. Because the trees encroached on their camp site, their domes and vehicle landing pad were elevated on wide platforms. The company required this as a security feature if you wanted your base to be anywhere without open terrain around it. It cost extra, and if you didn't want it, it cost even more to guarantee your bond. It was one of the reasons I thought my great idea would work.

In the open area on the plateau were seven figures, four SecUnits and three humans in the color-coded enviro suits, blue, green, and yellow. It meant they had one SecUnit and probably twenty seven–plus humans back at their habitat, if they had followed the rule of one rental SecUnit per ten humans. I sat us down below the plateau, on a relatively flat rock, the view blocked by brush and trees.

I put the pilot's console on standby, and looked at Mensah. She pressed her lips together, like she wanted to say something and was repressing the urge. Then she nodded firmly and said, "Good luck."

I felt like I should say something to her, and didn't know what, and just stared at her awkwardly for a few seconds. Then I sealed up my helmet and got out of the hopper as fast as I could.

I went through the trees, listening for that fifth SecUnit just in case it was hiding somewhere waiting for me, but there was no sound of movement in the undergrowth. I came out of cover and climbed the rocky slope to the plateau, then walked toward the other group, listening to the crackle on my comm. They were going to let me get close, which was a relief. I'd hate to be wrong about this. It would make me feel pretty stupid.

I stopped several meters away, opened the channel and

said, "This is the SecUnit assigned to the PreservationAux Survey Team. I was sent to speak to you about an arrangement."

I felt the pulse then, a signal bundle, designed to take over my governor module and freeze it, and freeze me. The idea was obviously to immobilize me, then insert the combat override module into my dataport again.

That was why they had had to arrange the meeting so close to their hub. They had needed the equipment there to be able to do this, it wasn't something they could send through the feed.

So it's a good thing my governor module wasn't working and all I felt was a mild tickle.

One of them started toward me. I said, "I assume you're about to try to install another combat override module and send me back to kill them." I opened my gun ports and expanded the weapons in my arms, then folded them back in. "I don't recommend that course of action."

The SecUnits went into alert mode. The human who had started forward froze, then backed away. The body language of the others was flustered, startled. I could tell from the faint comm static that they were talking to each other on their own system. I said, "Anyone want to comment on that?"

That got their attention. There was no reply. Not a surprise. The only people I've run into who actually want to get into conversations with SecUnits are my weird humans. I said, "I have an alternate solution to both our problems."

The one in the blue enviro suit said, "You have a solution?" The voice was the same one who had made the offer in our hub. It was also very skeptical, which you can imagine. To them, talking to me was like talking to a hopper or a piece of mining equipment.

I said, "You weren't the first to hack PreservationAux's HubSystem."

She had opened their comm channel to talk to me, and I heard one of the others whisper, "It's a trick. One of the surveyors is telling it what to say."

I said, "Your scans should show I've cut my comm." This was the point where I had to say it. It was still hard, even though I knew I didn't have a choice, even though it was part of my own stupid plan. "I don't have a working governor module." That over, I was glad to get back to the lying part. "They don't know that. I'm amenable to a compromise that benefits you as well as me."

The blue leader said, "Are they telling the truth about knowing why we're here?"

That was still annoying, even though I knew we had allowed plenty of time for this part. "You used combat override modules to make the DeltFall SecUnits behave like rogues. If you think a real rogue SecUnit still has to answer your questions, the next few minutes are going to be an education for you."

The blue leader shut me out of their comm channel. There was a long silence while they talked it over. Then she came back on, and said, "What compromise?"

"I can give you information you desperately need. In exchange, you take me onto the pick-up ship with you but list me as destroyed inventory." That would mean nobody from the company would be expecting me back, and I could slip off in the confusion when the transport docked at the transit station. Theoretically.

There was another hesitation. Because they had to pretend to think it over, I guess. Then the blue leader said, "We agree. If you're lying, then we'll destroy you."

It was perfunctory. They intended to insert a combat override module into me before they left the planet.

She continued, "What is the information?"

I said, "First remove me from the inventory. I know you still have a connection to our Hub."

Blue Leader made an impatient gesture at Yellow. He said, "We'll have to restart their HubSystem. That will take some time."

I said, "Initiate the restart, queue the command, and then show me on your feed. Then I'll give you the information."

Blue Leader closed me out of the comm channel and spoke to Yellow again. There was a three-minute wait, then the channel opened again and I got a limited access to their feed. The command was in a queue, though of course they would have time to delete it later. The important points were that our HubSystem had been reactivated, and that I could convincingly pretend to believe them. I had been watching the time, and we were now in the target window, so there was no more reason to stall. I said, "Since you destroyed my clients' beacon, they've sent a group to your beacon to manually trigger it."

Even with limited access to their feed, I could see that got them. Body language all over the place from confusion to fear. The yellow one moved uncertainly, the green one looked at Blue Leader. In that flat accent, she said, "That's impossible."

I said, "One of them is an augmented human, a systems engineer. He can make it launch. Check the data you got from our HubSystem. It's Surveyor Dr. Gurathin."

Blue Leader was showing tension from her shoulders all down her body. She really didn't want anybody coming to this planet, not until they had taken care of their witness problem.

Green said, "It's lying."

A trace of panic in his voice, Yellow said, "We can't chance it."

Blue Leader turned to him. "It's possible, then?"

Yellow hesitated. "I don't know. The company systems are all proprietary, but if they have an augmented human who can hack into it—"

"We have to go there now," Blue Leader said. She turned to me. "SecUnit, tell your client to get out of the hopper and come here. Tell her we've come to an arrangement."

All right, wow. That was not in the plan. They were supposed to leave without us.

(Last night Gurathin had said this was a weak point, that this was where the plan would fall apart. It was irritating that he was right.)

I couldn't open my comm channel to the hopper or the hopper's feed without GrayCris knowing. And we still needed to get them and their SecUnits away from their habitat. I said, "She knows you mean to kill her. She won't come." Then I had another brilliant idea and added, "She's a planetary admin for a system noncorporate political entity, she's not stupid."

"What?" Green demanded. "What political entity?"

I said, "Why do you think the team is called 'Preservation'?"

This time they didn't bother to close their channel. Yellow said, "We can't kill her. The investigation—"

Green added, "He's right. We can hold her and release her after the settlement agreement."

Blue Leader snapped, "That won't work. If she's missing, the investigation would be even more thorough. We need to stop that beacon launch, then we can discuss what to do." She told me, "Go get her. Get her out of the hopper and then bring her here." She cut the comm off again. Then one of the DeltFall SecUnits started forward. She came back on to say, "This Unit will help you."

I waited for it to reach me, then turned and walked beside it down the slope of rock into the trees.

What I did next was predicated on the assumption that she had told the DeltFall SecUnit to kill me. If I was wrong, we were screwed, and Mensah and I would both die, and the plan to save the rest of the group would fail and Preservation-Aux would be back to where it started, except minus their leader, their SecUnit, and their little hopper.

As we left the rocky slope and turned into the trees, the brush and branches screening us from the edge of the plateau, I slung an arm around the other Unit's neck, deployed my arm weapon, and fired into the side of its helmet where its comm channel was. It went down on one knee, swinging its projectile weapon toward me, energy weapons unfolding out of its armor.

With the combat override module in place, its feed was cut off, and with its comm down it couldn't yell for help. Also, depending on how strictly they had limited its voluntary actions, it might not be able to call for help unless the GrayCris humans told it to. Maybe that was the case, because all it did was try to kill me. We rolled over rock and brush until I wrenched its weapon away. After that it was easy to finish it off. Physically easy.

I know I said SecUnits aren't sentimental about each other, but I wished it wasn't one of the DeltFall units. It was in there somewhere, trapped in its own head, maybe aware, maybe not. Not that it matters. None of us had a choice.

I stood up just as Mensah slammed through the brush, carrying the mining tool. I told her, "It's gone wrong. You have to pretend to be my prisoner."

She looked at me, then looked at the DeltFall unit. "How are you going to explain that?"

I started shedding armor, every piece that had a PreservationAux logo on it, and leaned over the DeltFall unit as the pieces dropped away. "I'm going to be it and it's going to be me."

Mensah dropped the mining tool and bent down to help me. We didn't have time to switch all the armor. Moving fast, we replaced the arm and shoulder pieces on both sides, the leg pieces that had the armor's inventory code, the chest and back piece with the logos. Mensah smeared my remaining armor pieces with dirt and blood and fluid from the dead unit, so if we had missed anything distinctive GrayCris might not notice. SecUnits are identical in height and build, the way we moved. This might work. I don't know. If we ran away now the plan would fail, we had to get them off this plateau. As I resealed the helmet, I told Mensah, "We have to go—"

She nodded, breathing hard, more from nerves than exertion. "I'm ready."

I took her arm, and pretended to drag her back toward the GrayCris group. She yelled and struggled convincingly the whole way.

When we reached the plateau, a GrayCris hopper was already landing.

As I pulled her toward Blue Leader, Mensah got in the first word. She said, "So this is the arrangement you offered?"

Blue Leader said, "You're the planetary admin of Preservation?"

Mensah didn't look at me. If they tried to hurt her, I'd try to stop them and everything would go horribly wrong. But Green was already getting into the hopper. Two other humans were in the pilot's and copilot's seats. Mensah said, "Yes."

Yellow came toward me and touched the side of my helmet. It took a tremendous effort for me not to rip his arm off, and I'd like that noted for the record, please. He said, "Its comm is down."

To Mensah, Blue Leader said, "We know one of your people is trying to manually trigger our beacon. If you come with us, we won't harm him, and we can discuss our situation. This doesn't have to go badly for either of us." She was very convincing. She had probably been the one to talk to DeltFall on the comm, asking to be let into their habitat.

Mensah hesitated, and I knew she didn't want it to look like she was giving in too quickly, but we had to get them out of there now. She said, "Very well."

⊛   ⊛   ⊛

I hadn't ridden in the cargo container for a while. It would have been comforting and homey, except it wasn't my cargo container.

But this hopper was still a company product and I was able to access its feed. I had to stay very quiet, to keep them from noticing me, but all those hours of surreptitiously consuming media came in handy.

Their SecSystem was still recording. They must mean to delete all that before the pick-up transport showed up. Client groups had tried that before, to hide data from the company so it couldn't be sold out from under them, and the company systems analysts would be on the alert for it, but I don't know if these people realized that. The company might catch them even if we didn't survive. That wasn't a very comforting thought.

As I accessed the ongoing recording, I heard Mensah saying, "—know about the remnants in the unmapped areas. They were strong enough to confuse our mapping functions. Is that how you found them?"

Bharadwaj had figured that out last night. The unmapped sections weren't an intentional hack, they were an error, caused by the remnants that were buried under the dirt and rock. This planet had been inhabited at some point in its past, which meant it would be placed under interdict, open only to archeological surveys. Even the company would abide by that.

You could make big, illegal money off of excavating and mining those remnants, and that was obviously what Gray-Cris wanted.

"That isn't the conversation we should be having," Blue Leader said. "I want to know what arrangement we can come to."

"To keep you from killing us like you did DeltFall," Mensah said, keeping her voice even. "Once we're in contact with our home again, we can arrange for a transfer of funds. But how can we trust you to leave us alive?"

There was a little silence. Oh great, they don't know

either. Then Blue Leader said, "You have no option except to trust us."

We were slowing down already, coming in for a landing. There had been no alerts on the feed and I was cautiously optimistic. We had cleared the field for Pin-Lee and Gurathin as much as we could. They had had to hack the perimeter without that one last SecUnit noticing and get close enough to access the GrayCris HubSystem feed. (Hopefully it was the last SecUnit, hopefully there weren't a dozen more somehow in the GrayCris habitat.) Gurathin had figured out how to use the hack from their HubSystem into our HubSystem to get access, but he needed to be close to their habitat to actually trigger their beacon. That was why we had to get the other SecUnits out of there. That was the idea, anyway. Possibly it would have worked without putting Mensah in danger but it was a little late to second-guess everything.

It was a relief when we thumped down into a landing that must have made the humans' teeth rattle. I deployed out of the pod with the other units.

We were a few kilos from their habitat, on a big rock above a thick forest, lots of avians and other fauna screaming down in the trees, disturbed by the hopper's hard landing. Clouds had come in, threatening rain, and obscuring the view of the ring. The beacon's vehicle was in a launch tripod about ten meters away and, uh-oh, that is way too close.

I joined the three other SecUnits as we made a standard security formation. An array of drones launched from the craft to create a perimeter. I didn't look at the humans as they walked down the ramp. I really wanted to look at Mensah for instructions. If I was alone, I could have sprinted for the end of the plateau, but I had to get her out of there.

Blue Leader stepped forward with Green; the others gathered in a loose circle behind her, like they were afraid to get in front. One, who must have been getting reports from their SecUnits and drones, said, "No sign of anybody." Blue

Leader didn't answer but the two GrayCris SecUnits jogged toward the beacon.

Okay, the problem is, I've mentioned this before, the company is cheap. When it comes to something like a beacon that just has to launch once if there's an emergency, send a transmission through the wormhole, and then never gets retrieved, they're very cheap. Beacons don't have safety features, and use the cheapest possible launch vehicles. There's a reason you put them a few kilos from your habitat and trigger them from a distance. Mensah and I were supposed to distract GrayCris and their SecUnits while this was going on, get them away from the habitat, not end up as toast in the beacon launch.

With the delay caused by Blue Leader deciding to grab Mensah, time was getting close. The two SecUnits were circling the beacon's tripod, looking for signs of tampering, and I couldn't take it anymore. I started to walk toward Mensah.

Yellow noticed me. He must have said something to Blue Leader on their feed because she turned to look at me.

When the remaining DeltFall SecUnit whipped toward me and opened fire, I knew the light had dawned. I dove and rolled, coming up with my projectile weapon. I was taking hits all over my armor but scoring hits on the other SecUnit. Mensah ducked around the other side of the hopper and I felt a thump rattle through the plateau. That was the beacon's primary drive, dropping out of its casing to the bottom of the tripod, getting ready to ignite. The other two SecUnits had stopped, Blue Leader's surprise freezing them in place.

I bolted, took a hit in a weak armor joint that went through to my thigh, and powered through it. I made it around the hopper and saw Mensah. I tackled her off the edge of the rock, turning to land on my back, curling an arm over her suit helmet to protect her head from impact. We bounced off rocks and crashed through trees, then fire washed over the plateau and knocked out my—

⊛ ⊛ ⊛

UNIT OFFLINE

⊛ ⊛ ⊛

Oh, that hurt. I was lying in a ravine, rocks and trees over-hanging it. Mensah was sitting next to me, cradling an arm that looked like it didn't work anymore and her suit was covered with tears and stains.

She was whispering to someone on the comm. "Careful, if they pick you up on their scanner—"

⊛ ⊛ ⊛

UNIT OFFLINE

⊛ ⊛ ⊛

"That's why we need to hurry," Gurathin said, who was suddenly standing over us. I realized I had lost some time again.

Gurathin and Pin-Lee had been on foot, making their way toward the GrayCris habitat through the cover of the forest. We had meant to go pick them up in the little hopper if everything didn't go to shit. Which it did, but only partly, so yay for that.

Pin-Lee leaned over me and I said, "This unit is at minimal functionality and it is recommended that you discard it." It's an automatic reaction triggered by catastrophic malfunction. Also, I really didn't want them to try to move me because it hurt bad enough the way it was. "Your contract allows—"

"Shut up," Mensah snapped. "You shut the fuck up. We're not leaving you."

My visual cut out again. I was sort of still there, but I could tell I was hovering on the edge of a systems failure. I had flashes off and on. The inside of the little hopper, my humans talking, Arada holding my hand.

Then being in the big hopper, as it was lifting up. I could tell from the drive noise, the flashes of the feed, that the pickup transport was bringing it onboard.

That was a relief. It meant they were all safe, and I let go.

Chapter Eight

I CAME BACK TO awareness in a cubicle, the familiar acrid odor and hum of the systems as it put me back together. Then I realized it wasn't the cubicle at the habitat. It was an older model, a permanent installation.

I was back at the company station.

And humans knew about my governor module.

I poked tentatively at it. Still nonfunctional. My media storage was still intact, too. Huh.

When the cubicle opened, Ratthi was standing there. He was wearing regular civilian station clothes, but with the soft gray jacket with the PreservationAux survey logo. He looked happy, and a lot cleaner than the last time I had seen him. He said, "Good news! Dr. Mensah has permanently bought your contract! You're coming home with us!"

That was a surprise.

⊗   ⊕   ⊚

I went to finish processing, still reeling. It seemed like the kind of thing that would happen in a show, so I kept running diagnostics and checking the various available feeds to make sure I wasn't still in the cubicle, hallucinating. There was a report running on the local station news about DeltFall and GrayCris and the investigation. If I was hallucinating, I think the company wouldn't have managed to come out of the whole mess as the heroic rescuers of PreservationAux.

I expected a suit skin and armor, but the station units that helped us out of processing when we had catastrophic injuries gave me the gray PreservationAux survey uniform instead. I put it on, feeling weird, while the station units stood around and watched me. We're not buddies or anything, but usually they pass along the news, what happened while you were offline, what the upcoming contracts were. I wondered if they felt as weird as I did. Sometimes SecUnits got bought in groups, complete with cubicles, by other companies.

Nobody had ever come back from a survey and decided they wanted to keep their unit.

When I came out Ratthi was still there. He grabbed my arm and tugged me past a couple of human techs and out through two levels of secure doors and into the display area. This was where the rentals were arranged and it was nicer than the rest of the deployment center, with carpets and couches. Pin-Lee stood in the middle of it, dressed in sharp business attire. She looked like somebody from one of the shows I liked. The tough yet compassionate solicitor coming to rescue us from unfair prosecution. Two humans in company gear were standing around like they wanted to argue with her but she was ignoring them, tossing a data chip casually in one hand.

One saw me and Ratthi and said, "Again, this is irregular. Purging the unit's memory before it changes hands isn't just a policy, it's best for the—"

"Again, I have a court order," Pin-Lee said, grabbed my other arm, and they walked me out.

         ⊛   ⊛   ⊛

I had never seen the human parts of the station before. We went down the big multilevel center ring, past office blocks and shopping centers, crowded with every kind of people, every kind of bot, flash data displays darting around, a hundred different public feeds brushing my awareness. It was just like a place from the entertainment feed but bigger and brighter and noisier. It smelled good, too.

The thing that surprised me is that nobody stared at us. Nobody even gave us a second look. The uniform, the pants, the long-sleeved T-shirt and jacket, covered all my inorganic parts. If they noticed the dataport in the back of my neck they must have thought I was an augmented human. We were just three more people making our way down the ring. It hit me that I was just as anonymous in a crowd of humans who didn't know each other as I was in my armor, in a group of other SecUnits.

As we turned into a hotel block I brushed a public feed offering station info. I saved a map and a set of shift schedules as we passed through the doors into the lobby.

There were potted trees twisting up into a hanging glass sculpture fountain, real, not a holo. Looking at it I almost didn't see the reporters until they were right up on us. They were augmented humans, with a couple of drone cams. One tried to stop Pin-Lee, and instinct took over and I shouldered him off her.

He looked startled but I'd been gentle so he didn't fall down. Pin-Lee said, "We're not taking questions now," shoved Ratthi into the hotel's transport pod, then grabbed my arm and pulled me in after her.

It whooshed us around and let us out in the foyer of a big suite. I followed Pin-Lee in, Ratthi behind us talking to someone on his comm. It was just as fancy as the ones on the media, with carpets and furniture and big windows looking down on the garden and sculptures in the main lobby. Except the rooms were smaller. I guess the ones in the shows are bigger, to give them better angles for the drone cams.

My clients—ex-clients? New owners?—were here, only everybody looked different in their normal clothes.

Dr. Mensah stepped close, looking up at me. "Are you all right?"

"Yes." I had clear pictures from my field camera of her being hurt, but all her damage had been repaired, too. She looked different, in business clothes like Pin-Lee's. "I don't understand what's happening." It was stressful. I could feel the entertainment feed out there, the same one I could access from the unit processing zone, and it was hard not to sink into it.

She said, "I've purchased your contract. You're coming back to Preservation with us. You'll be a free agent there."

"I'm off inventory." They had told me that and maybe it

was true. I had the urge to twitch uncontrollably and I had no idea why. "Can I still have armor?" It was the armor that told people I was a SecUnit. But I wasn't Sec anymore, just Unit.

The others were so quiet. She said, even and calm, "We can arrange that, as long as you think you need it."

I didn't know if I thought I needed it or not. "I don't have a cubicle."

She was reassuring. "You won't need one. People won't be shooting at you. If you're hurt, or your parts are damaged, you can be repaired in a medical center."

"If people won't be shooting at me what will I be doing?" Maybe I could be her bodyguard.

"I think you can learn to do anything you want." She smiled. "We'll talk about that when we get you home."

Arada walked in then, and came over and patted my shoulder. "We're so glad you're with us," she said. She told Mensah, "The DeltFall representatives are here."

Mensah nodded. "I have to talk to them," she told me. "Make yourself comfortable here. If there's anything you need, tell us."

I sat in a back corner and watched while different people came in and out of the suite to talk about what had happened. Solicitors, mostly. From the company, from DeltFall, from at least three other corporate political entities and one independent, even from GrayCris' parent company. They asked questions, argued, looked at security records, showed Mensah and Pin-Lee security records. And they looked at me. Gurathin watched me, too, but he didn't say anything. I wondered if he had told Mensah not to buy me.

I watched the entertainment feed a little to calm down, then pulled everything I could about the Preservation Alliance from the station's information center. No one would be shooting at me because they didn't shoot people there. Mensah didn't need a bodyguard there; nobody did. It sounded like a great place to live, if you were a human or augmented human.

Ratthi came over to see if I was all right, and I asked him to tell me about Preservation and how Mensah lived there. He said when she wasn't doing admin work, she lived on a farm outside the capital city, with two marital partners, plus her sister and brother and their three marital partners, and a bunch of relatives and kids who Ratthi had lost count of. He was called away to answer questions from a solicitor, which gave me time to think.

I didn't know what I would do on a farm. Clean the house? That sounded way more boring than security. Maybe it would work out. This was what I was supposed to want. This was what everything had always told me I was supposed to want.

Supposed to want.

I'd have to pretend to be an augmented human, and that would be a strain. I'd have to change, make myself do things I didn't want to do. Like talk to humans like I was one of them. I'd have to leave the armor behind.

But maybe I wouldn't need it anymore.

⊛   ⊛   ⊛

Eventually things settled down, and they had dinner brought in. Mensah came and talked to me some more, about Preservation, what my options would be there, how I would stay with her until I knew what I wanted. It was pretty much what I'd already figured, from what Ratthi had told me.

"You'd be my guardian," I said.

"Yes." She was glad I understood. "There are so many education opportunities. You can do anything you want."

Guardian was a nicer word than owner.

I waited until the middle of the offshift, when they were all either asleep or deep in their own feeds, working on their analysis of the assessment materials. I got up from the couch and went down the corridor, and slipped out the door.

I used the transport pod and got back to the lobby, then

left the hotel. I had the map I had downloaded earlier, so I knew how to get off the ring and down toward the lower port work zones. I was wearing a survey team uniform, and passing as an augmented human, so nobody stopped me, or looked twice at me.

At the edge of the work zone, I went through into the dockworkers' barracks, then into the equipment storage. Besides tools, the human workers had storage cubbies there. I broke into a human's personal possessions locker and stole work boots, a protective jacket, and an enviro mask and attachments. I took a knapsack from another locker, rolled up the jacket with the survey logo and tucked it into the bag, and now I looked like an augmented human traveling somewhere. I walked out of the work zones and down the big central corridor into the port's embarkation zone, just one of hundreds of travelers heading for the ship ring.

I checked the schedule feeds and found that one of the ships getting ready to launch was a bot-driven cargo transport. I plugged into its access from the stationside lock, and greeted it. It could have ignored me, but it was bored, and greeted me back and opened its feed for me. Bots that are also ships don't talk in words. I pushed the thought toward it that I was a happy servant bot who needed a ride to rejoin its beloved guardian, and did it want company on its long trip? I showed it how many hours of shows and books and other media I had saved to share.

Cargo transport bots also watch the entertainment feeds, it turns out.

I don't know what I want. I said that at some point, I think. But it isn't that, it's that I don't want anyone to tell me what I want, or to make decisions for me.

That's why I left you, Dr. Mensah, my favorite human. By the time you get this I'll be leaving Corporation Rim. Out of inventory and out of sight.

Murderbot end message.

Wind Will Rove
Sarah Pinsker

THERE'S A STORY ABOUT my grandmother Windy, one I never asked her to confirm or deny, in which she took her fiddle on a spacewalk. There are a lot of stories about her. Fewer of my parents' generation, fewer still of my own, though we're in our fifties now; old enough that if there were stories to tell they would probably have been told.

My grandmother was an engineer, part of our original crew. According to the tale, she stepped outside to do a visual inspection of an external panel that was giving anomalous readings. Along with her tools, she clipped her fiddle and bow to her suit's belt. When she completed her task, she paused for a moment, tethered to our ship the size of a city, put her fiddle to the place where her helmet met her suit, and played "Wind Will Rove" into the void. Not to be heard, of course; just to feel the song in her fingers.

There are a number of things wrong with this story, starting with the fact that we don't do spacewalks, for reasons that involve laws of physics I learned in school and don't remember anymore. Our shields are too thick, our velocity is too great, something like that. The Blackout didn't touch ship records; crew transcripts and recordings still exist, and I've listened to all the ones that might pertain to this legend. She laughs her deep laugh, she teases a tired colleague about his date the night before, she even hums "Wind Will Rove" to herself as she works—but there are no gaps, no silences unexplained.

Even if it were possible, her gloves would have been too thick to find a fingering. I doubt my grandmother would've risked losing her instrument, out here where any replacement would be synthetic. I doubt, too, that she'd have exposed it to the cold of space. Fiddles are comfortable at the same temperatures people are comfortable; they crack and warp when they aren't happy. Her fiddle, my fiddle now.

My final evidence: "Wind Will Rove" is traditionally played in DDAD tuning, with the first and fourth strings dropped down. As much as she loved that song, she didn't play it often, since re-tuning can make strings wear out faster. If she had risked her fiddle, if she had managed to press her fingers to its fingerboard, to lift her bow, to play, she wouldn't have played a DDAD tune. This is as incontrovertible as the temperature of the void.

And yet the story is passed on among the ship's fiddlers (and I pass it on again as I write this narrative for you, Teyla, or whoever else discovers it). And yet her nickname, Windy, which appears in transcripts starting in the fifth year on board. Before that, people called her Beth, or Green.

She loved the song, I know that much. She sang it to me as a lullaby. At twelve, I taught it to myself in traditional GDAE tuning. I took pride in the adaptation, pride in the hours I spent getting it right. I played it for her on her birthday.

She pulled me to her, kissed my head. She always smelled like the lilacs in the greenhouse. She said, "Rosie, I'm so tickled that you'd do that for me, and you played it note perfectly, which is a gift to me in itself. But Wind Will Rove is a DDAD tune and it ought to be played that way. You play it in another tuning, it's a different wind that blows."

I'd never contemplated how there might be a difference between winds. I'd never felt one myself, unless you counted air pushed through vents, or the fan on a treadmill. After the birthday party, I looked up 'wind' and read about breezes and gales and siroccos, about haboobs and zephyrs. Great words, words to turn over in my mouth, words that spoke to nothing in my experience.

The next time I heard the song in its proper tuning, I closed my eyes and listened for the wind.

◈   ◈   ◈

"Windy Grove"
Traditional. Believed to have travelled from Scotland to Cape Breton in the nineteenth century. Lost.

◈   ◈   ◈

"Wind Will Rove"
Instrumental in D (alternate tuning DDAD)
Harriet Barrie, Music Historian:
    The fiddler Olivia Vandiver and her father, Charley Vandiver, came up with this tune in the wee hours of a session in 1974. Charley was trying to remember a traditional tune he had heard as a boy in Nova Scotia, believed to be "Windy Grove." No recordings of the original "Windy Grove" were ever catalogued, on ship or on Earth.
    "Wind Will Rove" is treated as traditional in most circles, even though it's relatively recent, because it is the lost tune's closest known relative.

◈   ◈   ◈

The Four Deck Rec has the best acoustics of any room on the ship. There's a nearly identical space on every deck, but the others don't sound as good. The Recs were designed for gatherings, but no acoustic engineer was ever consulted, and there's nobody on board with that specialty now. The fact that one room might sound good and one less so wasn't important in the grander scheme. It should have been.

In the practical, the day to day, it matters. It matters to us. Choirs perform there, and bands. It serves on various days and nights as home to a Unitarian church, a Capoeira hoda, a Reconstructionist synagogue, a mosque, a Quaker meetinghouse, a half dozen different African dance groups, and a Shakespearean theater, everyone clinging on to whatever they hope to save. The room is scheduled for weeks and months and years to come, though weeks and months and years are all arbitrary designations this far from Earth.

On Thursday nights, Four Deck Rec hosts the OldTime, thanks to my grandmother's early pressure on the Recreation Committee. There are only a few of us on board who know what OldTime refers to, since everything is old time, strictly speaking. Everyone else has accepted a new meaning, since they have never known any other. An OldTime is a Thursday night is a hall with good acoustics is a gathering of fiddlers and guitarists and mandolinists and banjo players. It has a verb form now. "Are you OldTiming this week?" If you are a person who would ask that question, or a person expected to respond, the answer is yes. You wouldn't miss it.

On this particular Thursday night, while I wouldn't miss it, my tenth graders had me running late. We'd been discussing the twentieth and twenty-first century space races and the conversation had veered into dangerous territory. I'd spent half an hour trying to explain to them why Earth history still mattered. This had happened at least once a cycle with every class I'd ever taught, but these particular students were as fired up as any I remembered.

"I'm never going to go there, right, Ms. Clay?" Nelson Odell had asked. This class had only been with me for two weeks, but I'd known Nelson his entire life. His great-grandmother, my friend Harriet, had dragged him to the OldTime until he was old enough to refuse. He'd played mandolin, his stubby fingers well fit to the tiny neck, face set in a permanently resentful expression.

"No," I said. "This is a one way trip. You know that."

"And really I'm just going to grow up and die on this ship, right? And all of us? You too? Die, not grow up. You're already old."

I had heard this from enough students. I didn't even wince anymore. "Yes to all of the above, though it's a reductive line of thinking and that last bit was rude."

"Then what does it matter that back on Earth a bunch of people wanted what another group had? Wouldn't it be better not to teach us how people did those things and get bad ideas in our heads?"

Emily Redhorse, beside Nelson, said, "They make us learn it all so we can understand why we got on the ship." She was the only current OldTime player in this class, a promising fiddler. OldTime players usually understood the value of history from a young age.

Nelson waved her off. "'We' didn't get on the ship. Our grandparents and great-grandparents did. And here we are learning things that were old to them."

"Because, stupid." That was Trina Nguyen.

I interrupted. "Debate is fine, Trina. Name-calling is not."

"Because, Nelson." She tried again. "There aren't new things in history. That's why it's called history."

Nelson folded his arms and stared straight at me. "Then don't teach it at all. If it mattered so much, why did they leave it behind? Give us another hour to learn more genetics or ship maintenance or farming. Things we can actually use."

"First of all, history isn't static. People discovered artifacts and primary documents all the time that changed their views on who we were. It's true that the moment we left Earth we gave up the chance to learn anything new about it from newly discovered primary sources, but we can still find fresh perspectives on the old information." I tried to regain control, hoping that none of them countered with the Blackout.

Students of this generation rarely did; to them it was just an incident in Shipboard History, not the living specter it had been when I was their age.

I continued. "Secondly, Emily is right. It's important to know why and how we got here. The conventional wisdom remains that those who don't know history are doomed to repeat it."

"How are we supposed to repeat it?" Nelson waved at the pictures on the walls. "We don't have countries or oil or water. Or guns or swords or bombs. If teachers hadn't told us about them we wouldn't even know they existed. We'd be better off not knowing that my ancestors tried to kill Emily's ancestors, wouldn't we? Somebody even tried to erase all of that entirely and you made sure it was still included in the new version of history."

"Not me, Nelson. That was before my time." I knew I shouldn't let them get a rise out of me, but I was tired and hungry, not the ideal way to start a seven hour music marathon. "Enough. I get what you're saying, but not learning this is not an option. Send me a thousand words by Tuesday on an example of history repeating itself."

Before anyone protested, I added, "You were going to have an essay to write either way. All I've done is changed the topic. It doesn't sound like you wanted to write about space races."

They all grumbled as they plugged themselves back into their games and music and shuffled out the door. I watched them go, wishing I'd handled the moment differently, but not yet sure how. It fascinated me that Nelson was the one fomenting this small rebellion, when his great-grandmother ran the OldTime Memory Project. My grandmother was the reason I obsessed over history, why I'd chosen teaching; Harriet didn't seem to have had the same effect on Nelson.

As Nelson passed my desk, he muttered, "Maybe somebody needs to erase it all again."

"Stop," I told him.

He turned back to face me. I still had several inches on him, but he held himself as if he were taller. The rest of the students flowed out around him. Trina rammed her wheelchair into Nelson's leg as she passed, in a move that looked one hundred percent deliberate. She didn't even pretend to apologize.

"I don't mind argument in my classroom, but don't ever let anyone hear you advocating another Blackout."

He didn't look impressed. "I'm not advocating. I just think teaching us Earth history—especially broken history—is a waste of everybody's time."

"Maybe someday you'll get on the Education Committee and you can argue for that change. But I heard you say 'erase it all again.' That isn't the same thing. Would you say that in front of Harriet?"

"Maybe I was just exaggerating. It's not even possible to erase everything anymore. And there's plenty of stuff I like that I wouldn't want to see erased." He shrugged. "I didn't mean it. Can I go now?"

He left without waiting for me to dismiss him.

I looked at the walls I'd carefully curated for this class. Tenth grade had always been the year we taught our journey's political and scientific antecedents. It was one of the easier courses for the Education Committee to recreate accurately after the Blackout, since some of it had still been in living memory at the time, and one of the easier classrooms to decorate for the same reason. I'd enlarged images of our ship's construction from my grandmother's personal collection, alongside reproductions of news headlines. Around the top of the room, a static quote from United Nations Secretary-General Confidence Swaray: "We have two missions now: to better the Earth and to better ourselves."

Normally I'd wipe my classroom walls to neutral for the continuing education group that met there in the evening, but this time I left the wall displays on when I turned off the lights to leave. Maybe we'd all failed these children already if they thought the past was irrelevant.

The digital art on the street outside my classroom had changed during the day. I traced my fingertips along the wall to get the info: a reimagining of a memory of a photo of an Abdoulaye Konaté mural, sponsored by the Malian Memory Project. According to the description, the original had been a European transit station mosaic, though they no longer knew which city or country had commissioned it. Fish swam across a faux-tiled sea. Three odd blue figures stood tall at the far end, bird-like humanoids. The colors were soothing to me, but the figures less so. How like the original was it? No way to tell. Another reinvention to keep some version of our past present in our lives.

I headed back to my quarters for my instrument and a quick dinner. There was always food at the OldTime, but I knew from experience that if I picked up my fiddle I wouldn't stop playing until my fingers begged. My fingers and my stomach often had different agendas. I needed a few minutes to cool down after that class, too. Nelson had riled me with his talk of broken history. To me that had always made pre-serving it even more important, but I understood the point he was trying to make.

By the time I got to the Four Deck Rec, someone had al-ready taken my usual seat. I tuned in the corner where every-one had stashed their cases, then looked around to get the lay of the room. The best fiddlers had nabbed the middle seats, with spokes of mandolin and banjo and guitar and less con-fident fiddlers radiating out. The only proficient OldTime bass player, Doug Kelly, stood near the center, with the ship's only upright bass. A couple of his students sat behind him, ready to swap out for a tune or two if he wanted a break.

The remaining empty seats were all next to banjos. I spotted a chair beside Dana Torres from the ship's Advisory

Council. She was a good administrator and an adequate banjo player—she kept time, anyway. I didn't think she'd show
up if she were less than adequate; nobody wants to see leadership failing at anything.

She had taken a place two rings removed from my usual
seat in the second fiddle tier. Not the innermost circle, where
my grandmother had sat, with the players who call the tunes
and call the stops; at fifty-five years old, I hadn't earned a spot
there yet. Still, I sat just outside them and kept up with them,
and it'd been a long time since I'd caught a frown from the
leaders.

A tune started as I made my way to the empty chair.
"Honeysuckle." A thought crossed my mind that Harriet
had started "Honeysuckle" without me, one of my Memory
Project tunes, to punish me for being late. A second thought
crossed my mind, mostly because of the conversation with
my students, that probably only three other people in the
room knew or cared what honeysuckle was: Tom Mvovo,
who maintained the seed bank; Liat Shuster, who worked in
the greenhouse—in all our nights together, I never thought
to ask her about the honeysuckle plant—Harriet Barrie, music historian, last OldTime player of the generation that had
left Earth. To everyone else, it was simply the song's name. A
name that meant this song, nothing more.

When I started thinking that way, all the songs took on a
strange flat quality in my head. So many talked about meadows and flowers and roads and birds. The love songs maintained relevance, but the rest might as well have been written
in other languages as far as most people were concerned. Or
about nothing at all. Mostly, we let the fiddles do the singing.

No matter how many times we play a song, it's never
the same song twice. The melody stays the same, the key, the
rhythm. The notes' pattern, their cadence. Still, there are differences. The exact number of fiddles changes. Various players' positions within the group, each with their own fiddle's

timbral variances. The locations of the bass, the mandolins, the guitars, the banjos, all in relation to each individual player's ears. To a listener by the snack table, or to someone seeking out a recording after the fact, the nuances change. In the minutes the song exists, it is fully its own. That's how it feels to me, anyway.

Harriet stomped her foot to indicate we'd reached the last go-round for "Honeysuckle," and we all came to an end together except one of the outer guitarists, who hadn't seen the signal and kept chugging on the last chord. He shrugged off the glares.

"Oklahoma Rooster," she shouted, to murmurs of approval. She started the tune, and the other fiddles picked up the melody. I put my bow to the strings and closed my eyes. I pictured a real farm, the way they looked in pictures, and let the song tell me how it felt to be in the place called Oklahoma. A sky as big as space, the color of chlorinated water. The sun a distant disk, bright and cold. A wood-paneled square building, with a round building beside it. A perfect carpet of green grass. Horses, large and sturdy, bleating at each other across the fields. All sung in the voice of a rooster, a bird that served as a wake-up alarm for the entire farm. Birds were the things with feathers, as the old saying went.

It was easy to let my mind wander into meadows and fields during songs I had played once a week nearly my whole life. Nelson must have gotten under my skin more than I thought: I found myself adding the weeks and months and years up. Fifty times a year, fifty years, more or less. Then the same songs again alone for practice, or in smaller groups on other nights.

The OldTime broke up at 0300, as it usually did. I rolled my head from side to side, cracking my neck. The music always carried me through the night, but the second it stopped, I started noticing the cramp of my fingers, the unevenness of my shoulders.

"What does 'Oklahoma Rooster' mean to you?" I asked Dana Torres as she shook out her knees.

"Sorry?"

"What do you think of when you play 'Oklahoma Rooster?'"

Torres laughed. "I think C-C-G-C-C-C-G-C. Anything else and I fall behind the beat. Why, what do you think of?"

A bird, a farm, a meadow. "I don't know. Sorry. Weird question."

We packed our instruments and stepped into the street, dimmed to simulate night.

Back at my quarters, I knew I should sleep, but instead I sat at the table and called up the history database. "Wind Will Rove."

Options appeared: "Play," cross-referenced to the song database, with choices from several OldTime recordings we'd made over the years. "Sheet music," painstakingly generated by my grandmother and her friends, tabbed for all of the appropriate instruments. "History." I tapped the last icon and left it to play as I heated up water for soporific tea. I'd watched it hundreds of times.

A video would play on the table. A stern looking white woman in her thirties, black hair pulled back in a tight ponytail, bangs flat-cut across her forehead. She'd been so young then, the stress of the situation making her look older than her years.

"Harriet Barrie, Music Historian," the first subtitle would say, then Harriet would appear and begin, " *The fiddler Olivia Vandiver and her father, Charley Vandiver came up with this tune in the wee hours of a session in 1974...*" Except when I returned, the table had gone blank. I went back to the main menu, but this time no options came up when I selected "Wind Will Rove." I tried again, and this time the song didn't exist.

I stared at the place where it should have been, between
"Winder's Slide" and "Wolf Creek." Panic stirred deep in my
gut, a panic handed down to me. Maybe I was tired and imagining things. It had been there a moment ago. It had always
been there, my whole life. The new databases had backups of
backups of backups, even if the recordings we called originals
merely recreated what had been lost long ago. Glitches happened. It would be fixed in the morning.

Just in case, I dashed off a quick message to Tech. I drank
my tea and went to bed, but I didn't sleep well.

❀ ❀ ❀

"Wind Will Rove"
Historical re-enactment. Windy Green as Olivia Vandiver,
Fiddler:

*"We were in our ninth hour playing. It had been a really
energetic session, and we were all starting to fade. Chatting
more between songs so we could rest our fingers. I can't remember how the subject came up, but my father brought up a tune
called "Windy Grove." Nobody else had ever heard of it, and he
called us all ignorant Americans.*

*He launched into an A part that sounded something like
"Spirits of the Morning," but with a clever little lift where "Spirits" descends. My father did things with a fiddle the rest of us
could never match, but we all followed as best we were able. The
B part wasn't anything like "Spirits", and we all caught that
pretty fast, but the next time the A part came round it was different again, so we all shut up and let him play. The third time
through sounded pretty much like the second, so we figured he
had remembered the tune, and we jumped in again. It went the
same the fourth and fifth times through.*

*It wasn't until we got up the next day that he admitted
he had never quite remembered the tune he was trying to remember, which meant the thing we had played the night before
was of his own creation. We cleaned it up, called it "Wind Will
Rove," and recorded it for the third Vandiver Family LP."*

⊛   ⊛   ⊛

My grandmother was an astronaut. We are not astronauts.
It's a term that's not useful in our vocabulary. Do the people
back on Earth still use that word? Do they mention us at all?
Are they still there?

When our families left they were called Journeyers. Ten
thousand Journeyers off on the Incredible Journey, with the
help of a genetic bank, a seed bank, an advisory council. A
ship thirty years in the making, held together by a crew of
trained professionals: astronauts and engineers and biolo-
gists and doctors and the like. Depending on which news
outlet you followed, the Journeyers were a cult or a social experiment or pioneers. Those aren't terms we use for ourselves,
since we have no need to call ourselves anything in reference
to any other group. When we do differentiate, it's to refer to
the Before. I don't know if that makes us the During or the
After.

My mother's parents met in Texas, in the Before, while
she was still in training. My grandfather liked being married
to an astronaut when the trips were finite, but he refused to
sign up for the Journey. He stayed behind on Earth with two
other children, my aunt and uncle, both older than my mother. I imagine those family members sometimes. All those
people I have no stories for. Generations of them.

It's theoretically possible that scientists on Earth have
built faster ships by now. It's theoretically possible they've
developed faster travel while we've been busy travelling. It's
theoretically possible they've built a better ship, that they've
peopled it and sent it sailing past us, that they've figured out
how to freeze and revive people, that those who stepped
into the ship will be the ones who step out. That we will be
greeted when we reach our destination by our own ancestors.
I won't be there, but my great-great-great-great-great-great-
grandchildren might be. I wonder what stories they'll tell
each other.

⊗   ⊗   ⊗

This story is verifiable history. It begins, "There once was a man named Morne Brooks." It's used to scare children into doing their homework and paying attention in class. Nobody wants to be a cautionary tale.

There once was a man named Morne Brooks. In the fourth year on board, while performing a computer upgrade, he accidentally created a backdoor to the ship databases. Six years after that, an angry young programmer named Trevor Dube released a virus that ate several databases in their entirety. Destroyed the backups too. He didn't touch the "important" systems—navigation, life support, medical, seed and gene banks—but he caused catastrophic damage to the libraries. Music gone. Literature, film, games, art, history: gone, gone, gone, gone. Virtual reality simulation banks, gone, along with the games and the trainings and the immersive recreations of places on Earth. He killed external communications too. We were alone, years earlier than we expected to be. Severed.

For some reason, it's Brooks' name attached to the disaster. Dube was locked up, but Brooks still walked around out in the community for people to point at and shame. Our slang term "brooked" came from his name. He spent years afterward listening to people say they had brooked exams and brooked relationships. I suppose it didn't help that he had such a good name to lend. Old English, Dutch, German. A hard word for a lively stream of water. We have no use for it as a noun now; no brooks here. His shipmates still remembered brooks, though they'd never see one again. There was a verb form already, unrelated, but it had fallen from use. His contemporaries verbed him afresh.

It didn't matter that for sixteen years afterward he worked on the team that shored up protection against future damage, or that he eventually committed suicide. Nobody wanted to talk about Dube or his motivations; all people ever mentioned was the moment the screens went dark, and Brooks' part in the whole disaster when they traced it backward.

In fairness, I can't imagine their panic. They were still the original Journeyers, the original crew, the original Advisory Council, save one or two changes. They were the ones who had made sure we had comprehensive databases, so we wouldn't lose our history, and so they wouldn't be without their favorite entertainments. The movies and serials and songs reminded them of homes they had left behind.

The media databases meant more to that first generation than I could possibly imagine. They came from all over the Earth, from disparate cultures; for some from smaller sub-groups, the databases were all that connected them with their people. It's no wonder they reacted the way they did.

I do sometimes wonder what would be different now if things hadn't gone wrong so early in the journey. Would we have naturally moved beyond the art we carried, instead of clinging to it as we do now? All we can do is live it out, but I do wonder.

⊗   ⊗   ⊗

I don't teach on Fridays. I can't bounce back from seven hours of fiddling, or from the near-all-nighter, the way I did at twenty or thirty or forty. Usually I sleep through Friday mornings. This time, I woke at ten, suddenly and completely, with the feeling something was missing. I glanced at the corner by the door to make sure I hadn't left my fiddle at the Rec.

I showered, then logged on to the school server to see if any students had turned in early assignments—they hadn't—then checked the notice system for anything that might affect my plans for the day. It highlighted a couple of streets I could easily avoid, and warned that the New Shakespeare and Chinese Cultural DBs were down for maintenance. Those alerts reminded me about the database crash the night before. My stomach lurched again as I called up "Wind Will Rove," but it was there when I looked for it, right where it belonged.

The door chimed. Fridays, I had lunch with Harriet. We called it lunch, even though we'd both be eating our first meal of the day. She didn't get up early after the OldTime either. Usually I cut it pretty close, rolling out of bed and putting on clothes, knowing she'd done the same. I glanced around the room to make sure it was presentable. I'd piled some dirty clothes on the bed, but they were pretty well hidden behind the privacy screen. Good enough.

"You broke the deal, Rosie," she said, eyeing my hair as I opened my door. "You showered."

"I couldn't sleep."

She shrugged and slid into the chair I'd just been sitting in. She had a skullcap pulled over her own hair, dyed jet black. Harriet had thirty years on me, though she still looked wiry and spry. It had taken me decades to stop considering her my grandmother's friend and realize she'd become mine as well. Now we occupied a place somewhere between mentorship and friendship. History teacher and music historian. Fiddle player and master fiddler.

I handed her a mug of mint tea and a bowl of congee, and a spoon. My dishware had been my grandmother's, from Earth. Harriet always smiled when I handed her the chipped "Cape Breton Fiddlers Association" mug.

She held the cup up to her face for a moment, breathing in the minty steam. "Now tell me why you walked in late last night. I missed you in the second row. Kem Porter took your usual seat, and I had to listen to his sloppy bow technique all night."

"Kem's not so bad. He knows the tunes."

"He knows the tunes, but he's not ready for the second row. He was brooking rhythms all over the place. You should have called him out on it."

"I wouldn't!"

She cradled the mug in her hands and breathed in again.

Liat and I hadn't been a couple for years, but she still brought me real mint from the greenhouse, and I knew Harriet appreciated it. "I know. You're too nice. There's no shame in letting someone know his place. Next time I'll do it."

She would, too. She had taken over the OldTime enforcer job from my grandmother, and lived up to her example. They'd both sent me back to the outer circles more than once before I graduated inward.

"I'll tell you when you're ready, Rosie," my grandmother said. "You'll get there."

"You know Windy would have done it," Harriet said, echoing my thoughts.

The nickname jogged my memory again. "'Wind Will Rove!'" I said. " Something was wrong with the database last night. The song was missing."

She pushed the cups to the side and tapped the table awake.

"Down for maintenance," she read out loud, frowning. She looked up. "I don't like that. I'll go down to Tech myself and ask."

She stood and left without saying goodbye.

Harriet had a way of saying things so definitively you couldn't help agreeing. If she said you didn't belong in the second row, you weren't ready yet. If she said not to worry over the song issue, I would have been willing to believe her, even though it made me uneasy. Hopefully it was nothing, but her reaction was appropriate for anyone who'd lived through the Blackout. I hadn't even gotten around to answering her first question, but I wasn't really sure what I would have told her about Nelson in any case.

I went to pick up my grandchildren from daycare, as I always did on Friday afternoons, Natalie's long day at the hospital. If anything could keep me out of my head, it was the mind-wiping exhaustion of chasing toddlers.

"Goats?" asked Teyla. She had just turned two, her

brother Jonah four.

"Goats okay with you, too, buddy?" I asked Jonah.

He shrugged stoically. He didn't really care for animals. Preferred games, but we'd played games the week before.

"Goats it is."

The farm spread across the bottom deck, near the waste processing plant. We took two tubes to get there, Jonah turning on all the screens we passed, Teyla playing with my hair.

I always enjoyed stepping from the tube and into the farm's relatively open spaces, as big as eight rec rooms combined. The air out here, pungent and rich, worked off a different circulator than on the living decks. It moved with slightly more force than on the rest of the ship, though still not a wind. Not even a breeze. The artificial sun wasn't any different than on the other decks, but it felt more intense. The textures felt different too, softer, plants and fur, fewer touch screens. If I squinted I could imagine a real farm, ahead or behind us, on a real planet. Everything on every other deck had been designed to keep us healthy and sane; I always found it interesting to spend time in a place dedicated to keeping another animal alive.

The goats had been a contentious issue for the planners in my grandmother's generation. Their detractors called them a waste of food and space and resources. Windy was among those who argued for them. They could supplement the synthetic milk and meat supplies. They'd provide veterinary training and animal husbandry skills that would be needed planetside someday, not to mention a living failsafe in case something happened to the gene banks. It would be good to have them aboard for psychological reasons as well, when people were leaving behind house pets like cats and dogs.

She won the debate, as she so often did, and they added a small population of female African Pygmy goats to the calculations. Even then there were dissenters. The arguments continued until the Blackout, then died abruptly along with the idea the journey might go as planned.

She told me all of that three weeks after my mother left, when I was still taking it personally.

"Have you ever tried to catch a goat?" she asked.

I hadn't. I'd seen them, of course, but visitors were only supposed to pet them. She got permission, and I spent twenty minutes trying to catch an animal that had zero interest in being caught. It was the first thing that made me laugh again. I always thought of that day when I brought my grandchildren to pet the goats, though I hoped I never had any reason to use the same technique on them.

I had wrapped up some scraps for Jonah and Teyla to feed the nippy little things. Once they'd finished the food, the goats started on Teyla's jersey, to her mixed delight and horror. I kept an eye on goat teeth and toddler fingers to make sure everybody left with the proper number.

"Ms. Clay," somebody said, and I glanced up to see who had called me, then back at the babies and the fingers and the goats. They looked vaguely familiar, but everyone did after a while. If I had taught them, I still might not recognize a face with twenty more years on it, if they didn't spend time on the same decks I did.

"Ms. Clay, I'm Nelson's parent. Other parent. Lee. I think you know Ash." Ash was Harriet's grandkid. They'd refused to play music at all, to Harriet's endless frustration.

Lee didn't look anything like Nelson, but then I recalled Harriet saying they had gone full gene-bank. The incentives to include gene variance in family planning were too good for many people to pass up.

"Nice to meet you," I said.

"I'm sorry if he's been giving you any trouble," Lee said. "He's going through some kind of phase."

"Phase?" Sometimes feigning ignorance got more interesting answers than agreeing.

"He's decided school is teaching the wrong things. Says

there's no point in learning anything that doesn't directly apply to what will be needed planetside. That it puts old ideas into people's heads, when they should be learning new things. I have no idea where he came up with it."

I nodded. "Do you work down here?"

Lee gestured down at manure-stained coveralls. "He likes it here, though. Farming fits in his worldview."

"But history doesn't?"

"History, classic literature, anything you can't directly apply. I know he's probably causing trouble, but he's a good kid. He'll settle down once he figures out a place for himself in all this."

Teyla was offering a mystery fistful of something to a tiny black goat. Jonah looked like he was trying to figure out if he could ride one; I put a hand on his shoulder to hold him back.

◎ ◎ ◎

"Tell me about the Blackout," I say at the start of the video I made while still in school. Eighteen year old me, already a historian. My voice is much younger. I'm not on screen, but I can picture myself at eighteen. Tall, gawky, darker than my mother, lighter than my father.

"I don't think there was anybody who didn't panic," my grandmother begins. Her purple hair is pulled back in a messy bun, and she is sitting in her own quarters—mine now—with her Cape Breton photos on the walls.

"Once we understood that the glitch hadn't affected navigation or the systems we rely on to breathe and eat, once it became clear the culprit was a known virus and the damage was irreparable, well, we just had to deal with it."

"The 'culprit' was a person, not a virus, right?"

"A virus who released a virus." Her face twisted at the thought.

I moved back to safer ground. "Did everyone just 'deal with it'? That isn't what I've heard."

"There are a lot of people to include in 'everyone.' The younger children handled it fine. They bounced and skated and ran around the rec rooms. The older ones—the ones who relied on external entertainment—had more trouble, and got in more trouble, I guess." She gave a sly smile. "But ask your father how he lost his pinkie finger if you've never asked."

"That was when he did it?"

"You bet. Eighteen years old and some daredevil notion to hitch a ride on the top of a lift. Lucky he survived."

"He told me a goat bit it off!"

She snorted. "I'm guessing he told you that back when you said you wanted to be a goat farmer when you grew up?"

No answer from younger-me.

She shrugged. "Or maybe he didn't want to give you any foolish ideas about lift-cowboys."

"He's not a daredevil, though."

"Not anymore. Not after that. Not after you came along the next year. Anyway, you asked who 'just dealt with it,' and you're right. The kids coped because they had nothing to compare it too, but obviously the main thing you want to know about is the adults. The Memory Projects."

"Yes. That's the assignment."

"Right. So. Here you had all these people: born on Earth, raised on Earth. They applied to be Journeyers because they had some romantic notion of setting out for a better place. And those first years, you can't even imagine what it was like, the combination of excitement and terror. Any time anything went wrong: a replicator brooked, a fan lost power, anything at all, someone started shouting we had set our families up for Certain Death." She says 'certain death' dramatically, wiggling her fingers at me. "Then Crew or Logistics or Tech showed them their problem had an easy fix, and they'd calm down. It didn't matter how many times we told them we had things under control. Time was the only reassurance.

"By ten years in, we had finally gotten the general populace to relax. Everyone had their part to do, and everyone was finally doing it quietly. We weren't going to die if a hot water line went cold one day. There were things to worry over, of course, but they were all too big to be worth contemplating. Same as now, you understand? And we had this database, this marvelous database of everything good humans had ever created, music and literature and art from all around the world, in a hundred languages.

"And then Trevor Dube had to go and ruin everything. I know you know that part so I won't bother repeating it. Morne Brooks did what he did, and that Dube fellow did what he did, and all of a sudden all of these Journeyers, with their dream of their children's children's children's etcetera someday setting foot on a new planet, they all have to deal with their actual children. They have to contemplate the idea the generations after them will never get to see or hear the things they thought were important. That all they have left is the bare walls. They wait - we wait—and wait for the DB to be restored. And they realize: hey, I can't rely on this database to be here to teach those great-great-great-grandchildren."

She leans forward. "So everyone doubles down on the things that matter most to them. That's when some folks who didn't have it got religion again. The few physical books on board became sacred primary texts, including the ones that had been sacred texts to begin with. Every small bit of personal media got cloned for the greater good, from photos to porn—don't giggle—but it wasn't much, not compared to what we'd lost.

"Cultural organizations that had been atrophying suddenly found themselves with more members than they'd had since the journey started. Actors staged any show they knew well enough, made new recordings. People tried to rewrite their favorite books and plays from memory, paint their favorite paintings. Everyone had a different piece, some closer to accurate than others. That's when we started getting together to play weekly instead of monthly."

"I thought it was always weekly, Gra."

"Nope. We didn't have other entertainments to distract us, and we were worried about the stories behind the songs getting lost. The organized Memory Projects started with us. It seemed like the best way to make sure what we wanted handed down would be handed down. The others saw that we'd found a good way to approach the problem and to keep people busy, so other Memory Projects sprung up too. We went through our whole repertoire and picked out the forty songs we most wanted saved. Each of us committed to memorizing as many as we could, but with responsibility for a few in particular. We knew the songs themselves already, but now people pooled what they knew about them, and we memorized their histories, too. Where they came from, what they meant. And later, we were responsible for re-recording those histories, and teaching them to somebody younger, so each song got passed down to another generation. That's you, incidentally."

"I know."

"Just checking. You're asking me some pretty obvious stuff."

"It's for a project. I need to ask."

"Fine, then. Anyhow, we re-recorded all our songs and histories as quick as possible, then memorized them in case somebody tried to kill the DBs again. And other people memorized the things important to them. History of their people—the stuff that didn't make it into history books— folk dances, formulae. Actors built plays back from scratch, though some parts weren't exactly as they'd been. And those poor jazz musicians."

"Those poor jazz musicians? I thought jazz was about improv."

"It's full of improv, but certain performances stood out

as benchmarks for their whole mode. I'm glad we play a music that doesn't set much stock in solo virtuosity. We recorded our fiddle tunes all over again, and the songs are still the songs, but nobody on board could play "So What" like Miles Davis or anything like John Coltrane. Their compositions live on, but not their performances, if that makes sense. Would have devastated your grandfather, if he'd been on board. Anyway, what was I saying? The human backup idea had legs, even if it worked better for some things than others. It was a worst case scenario."

"Which two songs did you memorize history for?"

"Unofficially, all of them. Officially, same as you. 'Honeysuckle' and 'Wind Will Rove.' You know that."

"I know, Gra. For the assignment."

⊛   ⊛   ⊛

"Windy Grove"
Historical Re-enactment: Marius Smit as Howie McCabe, Cape Breton Fiddlemaker

Vandiver wasn't wrong. There was a tune called "Windy Grove." My great-grandfather played it, but it was too complicated for most fiddlers. I can only remember a little of the tune now. It had lyrics, too, in Gaelic and English. I don't think Vandiver ever mentioned those. There was probably a Gaelic name too, but that's lost along with the song.

My great-grandfather grew up going to real milling frolics, before machines did the wool-shrinking and frolics just became social events. The few songs I know in Gaelic I know because they have that milling frolic rhythm; it drives them into your brain. "Windy Grove" wasn't one of those. As far as I know it was always a fiddle tune, but not a common one because of its difficulty.

All I know is the A part in English, and I'm pretty I wouldn't get the melody right now, so I'm going to sing it to the melody of Wind Will Rove:
We went down to the windy grove

Never did know where the wind did go
Never too sure when the wind comes back
If it's the same wind that we knew last.

⊛   ⊛   ⊛

Nelson's essay arrived promptly on Monday. It began "Many examples of history repeating itself can be seen in our coursework. There are rulers who didn't learn from other ruler's mistakes."

I corrected the apostrophe and kept reading. "You know who they are because you taught us about them. Why do you need me to say them back to you? Instead I'm going to write about history repeating itself in a different way. Look around you, Ms. Clay.

"I'm on this ship because my great-grandparents decided they wanted to spend the rest of their lives on a ship. They thought they were being unselfish. They thought they were making a sacrifice so someday their children's children's children to the bazillionth or whatever would get to be pioneers on a planet that people hadn't started killing yet, and they were pretty sure wouldn't kill them, and where they're hoping there's no intelligent life. They made a decision which locked us into doing exactly what they did.

"So here we are. My parents were born on this ship. I was born here. My chromosomes come from the gene bank, from two people who died decades before I was born.

"What can we do except repeat history? What can I do that nobody here has ever done before? In two years I'll choose a specialty. I can work with goats, like my parents. I could be an engineer or a doctor or a dentist or a horticulturist, which are all focused on keeping us alive in one way or another. I can be a history teacher like you, but obviously I won't. I can be a Theoretical Farmer or a Theoretical something else, where I learn things that will never be useful here, in order to pass them on to my kids and my kid's kids, so they can pass them on and someday somebody can use them, if there's really a place we're going and we're really going to get there someday.

"But I'm never going to stand on a real mountain, and I can't be a king or a prime minister or a genocidal tyrant like you teach us about. I can't be Lord Nelson, an old white man with a giant hat, and you might think I was named after him but I was named after a goat who was named after a horse some old farmer had on Earth who was named after somebody in a book or a band or an entertainment who might have been Lord Nelson or Nelson Mandela or some other Nelson entirely who you can't teach me about because we don't remember them anymore.

"The old history can't repeat, and I'm in the next generation of people who make no impact on anything whatsoever. We aren't making history. We're in the middle of the ocean and the shore is really far away. When we climb out the journey should have changed us, but you want us to take all the baggage with us, so we're exactly the same as when we left. But we can't be, and we shouldn't be."

I turned off the screen and closed my eyes. I could fail him for not writing the assignment as I had intended it, but he clearly understood.

⊛   ⊛   ⊛

"Wendigo"
Traditional. Lost.
Harriet Barrie:
*   Another tune we have the name of but not much else. I'm personally of the belief "Wendigo" and "Windy Grove" are the same song. Some Cape Bretonians took it with when they moved to the Algonquins. Taught it to some local musicians who misheard the title and conflated it with local monster lore. There's a tune called "When I Go" that started making the rounds in Ontario not long after, though nobody ever showed an interest in it outside of Ontario and Finland.*

⊛   ⊛   ⊛

If we were only to play songs about things we knew, we would lose a lot of our playlist. No wind. No trees. No battles, no seas, no creeks, no mountaintops. We'd sing of travellers, but not journeys. We'd sing of middles, but not beginnings or ends. We would play songs of waiting and longing. We'd play love songs.

Why not songs about stars, you might ask? Why not songs about darkness and space? The traditionalists wouldn't play them. I'm not sure who'd write them, either. People on Earth wrote about blue skies because they'd stood under grey ones. They wrote about night because there was such thing as day. Songs about prison are poignant because the character knew something else beforehand, and dreamed of other things ahead. Past and future are both abstractions now.

When my daughter Natalie was in her teens, she played fiddle in a band which would be classified in the new DB as "other/undefined" if they had uploaded anything. Part of their concept was that they wouldn't record their music, and they requested that nobody else record it either. A person would have to be there to experience it. I guess it made sense for her to fall into something like that after listening to me and Gra' and Harriet.

I borrowed back the student fiddle she and I had both played as children. She told me she didn't want me going to hear them play.

"You'll just tell me it sounds like noise or my positions are sloppy," she said. "Or worse yet, you'll say we sound exactly like this band from 2030 and our lyrics are in the tradition of blah blah blah and I'll end up thinking we stole everything from a musician I'd never even heard before. We want to do something new."

"I'd never," I said, even though a knot had formed in my stomach. Avoided commenting when I heard her practicing. Bit my tongue when Harriet complained musicians shouldn't be wasting their time on new music when they ought to be working on preserving what we already had.

I did go to check them out once, when they played the Seven Dec Rec. I stood in the back, in the dark. To me it sounded like shouting down an elevator shaft, all ghosts and echoes. The songs had names like "Because I Said So" and "Terrorform"; they shouted the titles in between pieces, but the PA was distorting and even those I might have misheard.

I counted fifteen young musicians in the band, from different factions all over the ship: children of jazz, of rock, of classical music, of zouk, of Chinese opera, of the West African drumming group. It didn't sound anything like anything I'd ever heard before. I still couldn't figure out whether they were synthesizing the traditions they'd grown up in or rejecting them entirely.

My ears didn't know what to pay attention to, so I focused on Nat. She still had technique decent from her childhood lessons, but she used it in ways I didn't know how to listen to. She played rhythm rather than lead, a pad beneath the melody, a staccato polyrhythm formed with fiddle and drum.

I almost missed when she lit into "Wind Will Rove." I'd never even have recognized it if I had been listening to the whole instead of focusing on Nat's part. Hers was a counter-melody to something else entirely, the rhythm swung but the key unchanged. Harriet would have hated it, but I thought it had a quiet power hidden as it was beneath the bigger piece.

I never told Nat I'd gone to hear her that night, because I didn't want to admit I'd listened.

I've researched punk and folk and hip-hop's births, and the protest movements that went hand in hand with protest music. Music born of people trying to change the status quo. What could my daughter and her friends change? What did people want changed? The ship sails on. They played together for a year before calling it quits. She gave her fiddle away again and threw herself into studying medicine. As they'd pledged, nobody ever uploaded their music, so there's no evidence it ever existed outside this narrative.

⊛   ⊕   ⊛

My grandmother smuggled the upright bass on board. It's Doug Kelly's now, but it came onto the ship under my grandmother's "miscellaneous supplies" professional allowance. That's how it's listed in the original manifest: "Miscellaneous Supplies—1 Extra-Large Crate—200 cm × 70 cm × 70 cm." When I was studying the manifest for a project, trying to figure out who had brought what, I asked her why the listed weight was so much more than the instrument's weight.

"Strings," she said. "It was padded with clothes and then the box was filled with string packets. For the bass, for the fiddles. Every cranny of every box I brought on board was filled with strings and hair and rosin. I didn't trust replicators."

The bass belonged at the time to Jonna Rich. In my grandmother's photo of the original OldTime players on the ship, Jonna's dwarfed by her instrument. It's only a 3/4 size, but it still looms over her. I never met her. My grandmother said, "You've never seen such a tiny woman with such big, quick hands."

When her arthritis got too bad to play, Jonna passed it to Marius Smit, "twice her size, but half the player she was." Then Jim Riggins, then Alison Smit, then Doug Kelly, with assorted second and third stand-ins along the way. Those were the Old Time players. The bass did double duty in some jazz ensembles, as well as the orchestra.

Personal weight and space allowances didn't present any problems for those who played most instruments. The teams handling logistics and psychological welfare sparred and negotiated and compromised and re-compromised. They made space for four communal drum kits (two each: jazz trap and rock five-piece) twenty-two assorted amplifiers for rock and jazz, bass and guitar and keyboard. We have two each of three different Chinese zithers, and one hundred and three African drums of thirty-two different types, from djembe to carimbo. There's a PA in every Rec, but only a single tuba. The music psychologist consulted by the committee didn't understand why an electric bass wasn't a reasonable compromise for the sake of space. Hence my grandmother's smuggling job.

How did a committee on Earth ever think they could guess what we'd need fifty or eighty or one hundred and eighty years into the voyage? They set us up with state of the art replicators, with our beautiful, doomed databases, with programs and simulators to teach skills we would need down the line. Still, there's no model that accurately predicts the future. They had no way of prognosticating the brooked database or the resultant changes. They'd have known, if they'd included an actual musician on the committee, that we needed an upright bass. I love how I'm still surrounded by the physical manifestations of my grandmother's influence on the ship: the upright bass, the pygmy goats. Her fiddle, my fiddle now.

⊛   ⊛   ⊛

I arrived in my classroom on Thursday to discover somebody had hacked my walls. Scrawled over my photos screens: "Collective memory =/= truth," "History is fiction," "The past is a lie." A local overlay, not an overwrite. Nothing invasive of my personal files or permanent. Easy to erase, easy to figure out who had done it. I left it up.

As my students walked in, I watched their faces. Some were completely oblivious, wrapped up in whatever they were listening to, slouching into their seats without even looking up. A few snickered or exchanged wide-eyed glances.

Nelson arrived with a smirk on his face, a challenge directed at me. He didn't even look at the walls. It took him a moment to notice I hadn't cleaned up after him; when he did notice, the smirk was replaced with confusion.

"You're wondering why I didn't wipe this off my walls before you arrived?"

The students who hadn't been paying attention looked around for the first time. "Whoa," somebody said.

"The first answer is that it's easier to report if I leave it up. Vandalism and hacking are both illegal, and I don't think it would be hard to figure out who did this, but since there's no permanent damage, I thought we might use this as a learning experience." Everyone looked at Nelson, whose ears had turned red.

I continued. "I think what somebody is trying to ask is, let's see, 'Ms. Clay, how do we know that the history we're learning is true? Why does it matter?' And I think they expect me to answer, 'because I said so,' or something like that. But the real truth is, our history is a total mess. It's built on memories of facts, and memories are unreliable. Before, they could cross-reference memories and artifacts to a point where you could say with some reliability that certain things happened and certain things didn't. We've lost almost all of the proof."

"So what's left?" I pointed to the graffitied pictures. "I'm here to help figure out which things are worth remembering, which things are still worth calling fact or truth or whatever you want to call it. Maybe it isn't the most practical field of study, but it's still important. It'll matter to you someday when your children come to you to ask why we're on this journey. It'll matter when something goes wrong and we can look to the past and say 'how did we solve this when we had this problem before' instead of starting from scratch. It matters because of all the people who asked 'why' and 'how' and 'what if' instead of allowing themselves to be absorbed in their own problems—they thought of us, so why shouldn't we think of them?

"Today we're going to talk about the climate changes that the Earth was experiencing by the time they started building this ship, and how that played into the politics. And just so you're not waiting with bated breath through the entire class, your homework for the week is to interview somebody who still remembers Earth. Ask them why they or their parents got on board. Ask them what they remember about that time, and any follow-up questions you think make sense. For bonus points upload to the oral history DB once you've sent your video to me."

I looked around to see if anyone had any questions, but they were all silent. I started the lesson I was actually supposed to be teaching.

⊛   ⊛   ⊛

I'd been given that same assignment at around their age. It was easier to find original Journeyers to interview back then, but I always turned to my grandmother. The video is buried in the Oral History DB but I'd memorized the path to it long ago.

She's still in good health in this one, fit and strong, with her trademark purple hair. For all our closeness, I have no idea what her hair's original color was.

"Why did you leave?" I ask.

"I didn't really consider it leaving. Going someplace, not leaving something else behind."

"Isn't leaving something behind part of going someplace?"

"You think of it your way, I'll think of it mine."

"Is that what all the Journeyers said?"

My grandmother snorts. "Ask any two and we'll give you two different answers. You're asking me, so I'm telling you how I see it. We had the technology, and the most beautiful ship. We had—have—a destination that reports perfect conditions to sustain us."

"How did you feel having a child who would never get to the destination?"

"I thought 'my daughter will have a life nobody has ever had before, and she'll be part of a generation that makes new rules for what it means to be a person existing with other people.'" She shrugs. "I found that exciting. I thought she'd live in the place she lived, and she'd do things she loved and things she hated, and she'd live out her life like anybody does."

She pauses, then resumes without prompting. "There were worse lives to live, back then. This seemed like the best choice for our family. No more running away; running toward something wonderful."

"Was there anything you missed about Earth?"

"A thing, like not a person? If a person counts, your grandfather and my other kids, always and forever. There was nothing else I loved that I couldn't take with me," she says, with a far away look in her eyes.

"Nothing?" I press.

She smiles. "Nothing anybody can keep. The sea. The wind coming off the coast. I can still feel it when I'm inside a good song."

She reaches to pick up her fiddle.

⊛　⊛　⊛

There was a question I pointedly didn't ask in that video, the natural follow-up that fit in my grandmother's pause. I didn't ask because it wasn't my teacher's business how my mother fit into that generation 'making new rules for what it means to be a person existing with other people,' as my grandmother put it. If I haven't mentioned my mother much, it's because she and I never really understood each other.

She was eight when she came aboard. Old enough to have formative memories of soil and sky and wind. Old enough to come on board with her own small scale fiddle. Fourteen when she told my grandmother she didn't want to play music anymore.

Eighteen when the Blackout happened. Nineteen when she had me, one of a slew of Blackout Babies granted by joint action of the Advisory Council and Logistics. They would have accepted anything that kept people happy and quiet at that point, as long as the numbers bore out its sustainability.

My grandmother begged her to come back to music, to
help with the OldTime portion of the Memory Project. She
refused. She'd performed in a Shakespeare comedy called
Much Ado About Nothing just before the Blackout, while
she was still in school. She still knew Hero's lines by heart,
and the general Dramatists and Shakespeareans had both
reached out to her to join their Memory Projects; they all
had their hands full rebuilding plays from scratch.

The film faction recruited her as well, with their ridicu-
lously daunting task. My favorite video from that period
shows my twenty-year-old mother playing the lead in a historical drama called Titanic. It's a recreation of an old movie,
and an even older footnote in history involving an enormous
sea ship.

My mother: young, gorgeous, glowing. She wore gowns
that shimmered when she moved. The first time she showed
it to me, when I was five, all I noticed was how beautiful she
looked.

When I was seven, I asked her if the ocean could kill me.

"There's no ocean here. We made it up, Rosie."

That made no sense. I saw it there on the screen, big
enough to surround the ship, like liquid, tangible space, a
space that could chase you down the street and surround
you. She took me down to the soundstage on Eight Deck,
where they were filming a movie called Serena. I know now
they were still triaging, filming every important movie to the
best of their recollection, eight years out from the Blackout,
based on scripts rewritten from memory in those first desperate years. Those are the only versions I've ever known.

She showed me how a sea was not a sea, a sky was not a
sky. I got to sit on a boat that was not a boat, and in doing so
learn what a boat was.

"Why are you crying, mama?" I asked her later that evening, wandering from my bunk to my parents' bed.

My father picked me up and squeezed me tight. "She's

crying about something she lost."

"I'm not tired. Can we watch the movie again?"

We sat and watched my young mother as she met and fell in love with someone else, someone pretend. As they raced a rush of water that I had already been assured would never threaten me or my family. As the ship sank —it's not real, there's no sea, nothing sinks anymore— and the lifeboats disappeared and the two lovers were forced to huddle together on a floating door until their dawn rescue.

⊛　⊛　⊛

When I was sixteen, my mother joined a cult. Or maybe she started it; NewTime is as direct a rebuttal to my grandmother's mission as could exist. They advocated erasing the entertainment databases again, forever, in the service of the species.

"We're spending too much creative energy recreating the things we carried with us," she said. I listened from my bunk as she calmly packed her clothes.

"You're a Shakespearean! You're supposed to recreate." My father never raised his voice either. That's what I remembered most about their conversation afterward: how neither ever broke calm.

"I was a Shakespearean, but more than that, I'm an actress. I want new things to act in. Productions that speak to who we are now, not who we were on Earth. Art that tells our story."

"You have a family."

"And I love you all, but I need this."

The next morning, she kissed us both goodbye as if she was going to work, then left with the NewTime for Fourteen Deck. I didn't know what Advisory Council machinations were involved in relocating the Fourteen Deck families to make room for an unplanned community, or what accommodations had to be made for people who opted out of jobs to live a pure artistic existence. There were times in human history where that was possible, but this wasn't one of them. Those are questions I asked later. At that moment, I was furious with her.

I don't know if I ever stopped being angry, really. I never went to any of the original plays that trickled out of the New-Time; I've never explored their art or their music. I never learned what we looked like through their particular lens. It wasn't new works I opposed; it was their idea they had to separate themselves from us to create them. How could anything they wrote actually reflect our experience if they weren't in the community anymore?

They never came back down to live with the rest of us. My mother and I reconciled when I had Natalie, but she wasn't the person I remembered, and I'm pretty sure she thought the same about me. She came down to play with Nat sometimes, but I never left them alone together, for fear the separatist idea might rub off on my kid.

The night I saw Natalie's short-lived band perform, the night I hid in the darkness all those years ago so she wouldn't get mad at me for coming, it wasn't until I recognized "Wind Will Rove" that I realized I'd been holding my breath. Theirs wasn't a NewTime rejection of everything that had gone before; it was a synthesis.

◈   ◈   ◈

"Wind Will Roam"
Historical Re-enactment: Akona Mvovo as Will E. Womack:

   My aunt cleaned house for some folks over in West Hollywood, and they used to give her records to take home to me. I took it all in. Everything influenced me. The west coast rappers, but also Motown and pop and rock and these great old-timey fiddle records. I wanted to play fiddle so bad when I heard this song, but where was I going to get one? Wasn't in the cards.

   The song I sampled for Wind Will Roam - this fiddle record "Wind Will Rove" - it changed me. There's something about the way the first part lifts that moves me every time. I've heard there's a version with lyrics out there somewhere, but I liked the instrumental, so I could make up my own words over it. I wrote the first version when I was ten years old. I thought "rove" sounded like a dog, so I called it "Wind Will Roam," about a dog named Wind. I was a literal kid.

Second version when I was fifteen, I don't really remember that one too well. I was rapping and recording online by then, so there's probably a version out there somewhere. Don't show it to me if you find it. I was trying to be badass then. I'd just as soon pretend it never existed.

I came back to Wind Will Rove again and again. I think I was twenty-five when I recorded this one, and my son had just been born, and I wanted to give him something really special. I still liked "Wind Will Roam" better than "Wind Will Rove," 'cause I could rhyme it with "home" and "poem" and all that.

      ❁   ❁   ❁

(sings)
The wind will roam
And so will I
I've got miles to go before I die
But I'll come back
I always do
Just like the wind
I'll come to you.
We might go weeks without no rain
And every night the sun will go away again
Some winds blow warm some winds blow low
You and me've got miles and miles to go

      ❁   ❁   ❁

I wanted to take something I loved and turn it into something else entirely. Transform it.

      ❁   ❁   ❁

The next OldTime started out in G. My grandmother had never much cared for the key of G; since her death we'd played way more G sessions than we ever had when she chose the songs. "Dixie Blossoms," then "Down the River." "Squirrel Hunters." "Jaybird Died of the Whooping Cough." "The Long Way Home." "Ladies on the Steamboat."

Harriet called a break in the third hour, and said when we came back we were going to do some D tunes, starting with "Midnight on the Water." I knew the sequence she was setting up: "Midnight on the Water," then "Bonaparte's Retreat," then "Wind Will Rove." I was pretty sure she did it for me; I think she was glad to have me back in the second row and punctual.

Most stood up and stretched, or put their instruments down to go get a snack. A few fiddlers, myself included, took the opportunity to cross-tune to DDAD. These songs could all be played in standard tuning, but the low D drone added something ineffable.

When everybody had settled back into their seats, Harriet counted us into the delicate waltz time of "Midnight on the Water." Then "Bonaparte's Retreat," dark and lively. And then, as I'd hoped, "Wind Will Rove."

No matter how many times you play a song, it isn't the same song twice. I was still thinking about Nelson's graffiti, and how the past had never felt like a lie to me at all. It was a progression. "Wind Will Rove" said we are born anew every time a bow touches fiddle strings in an OldTime session on a starship in this particular way. It is not the ship nor the session nor the bow nor the fiddle that births us. Nor the hands. It's the combination of all of those things, in a particular way they haven't been combined before. We are an alteration on an old, old tune. We are body and body, wood and flesh. We are bow and fiddle and hands and memory and starship and OldTime.

"Wind Will Rove" spoke to me, and my eyes closed to feel the wind the way my grandmother did, out on a cliff above the ocean. We cycled through the A part, the B part three times, four times, five. And because I'd closed my eyes, because I was in the song and not in the room, I didn't catch Harriet's signal for the last go-round. Everyone ended together except me. Even worse, I'd deviated. Between the bars of my unexpected solo, when my own playing stood exposed against the silence, I realized I'd diverged from the tune. It was still "Wind Will Rove," or close to it, but I'd elided the third bar into the fourth, a swooping, soaring accident.

Harriet gave me a look I interpreted as a cross between exasperation and reprobation. I'd used a similar one on my students before, but it'd been a long time since I'd been on the receiving end.

"Sorry," I said, mostly sorry the sensation had gone, that I'd lost the wind.

I slipped out the door early, while everyone was still playing. I didn't want to talk to Harriet. Back home, I tried to recreate my mistake. I heard it in my head, but I never quite made it happen again, and after half an hour I put away my fiddle.

          ⊛   ⊛   ⊛

I'd rather have avoided Harriet the next morning, but cancelling our standing date would have made things worse. I woke up early again. Debated showering to give her a different reason to be annoyed with me, then decided against it when I realized she'd stack the two grievances rather than replace one with the other.

We met in her quarters this time, up three decks from my own, slightly smaller, every surface covered with archival boxes and stacks of handwritten sheet music.

"So what happened last night?" she asked without preamble.

I held up my hands in supplication. "I didn't see you call the stop. I'm sorry. And after you told me I belonged in the closer circles and everything. It won't happen again."

"But you didn't even play it right. That's one of your tunes. You've been playing that song for fifty years! People were talking afterward. Expect some teasing next week. Nothing else happened worth gossiping about, so they're likely to remember unless somebody else does something silly."

I didn't have a good response. Missing the stop had been silly, sure, but what I had done to the tune didn't feel wrong, exactly. A different wind, as my grandmother would have said.

"Any word on what wrong in the database the other day?" I asked to change the subject.

She furrowed her brow. "None. Tech said it's an access issue, not the DB itself. It's happening to isolated pieces. You can still access them if you enter names directly instead of going through the directories or your saved preferences, but it's a pain. They can't locate the source. I have to tell you, I'm more than a little concerned. I mean, the material is obviously still there, since I can get to some of it roundabout, but it really hampers research. And it gets me thinking we may want to consider adding another redundancy layer in the Memory Project."

She went on at length on the issue, and I let her go. I preferred her talking on any subject other than me.

When she started to flag, I interrupted. "Harriet, what does 'Oklahoma Rooster' mean to you?"

"I don't have much history for that one. Came from an Oklahoma fiddler named Dick Hutchinson, but I don't know if he wrote—"

"—I don't mean the history. What does it make you feel?"

"I'm not sure what you mean. It's a nice, simple fiddle tune."

"But you've actually seen a farm in real life. Does it sound like a rooster?"

She shrugged. "I've never really given it much thought. It's a nice tune. Not worthy of a spot in the Memory Project, but a nice tune. Why do you ask?"

It would sound stupid to say I thought myself on a farm when I played that song; I wouldn't tell her where Wind Will Rove took me either. "Just curious."

⊛ ⊛ ⊛

"Harriet's grandson is going to drive me crazy," I told Natalie. I had spent the afternoon with Teyla and Jonah, as I did every Friday, but this time Jonah had dragged us to the low gravity room. They had bounced, and I had watched and laughed along with their unrestrained joy, but I had a shooting pain in my neck from the way my head had followed the arcs of their flight.

Afterward, I'd logged into my class chat to find Nelson had again stirred the others into rebellion. The whole class, except for two I'd describe as timid and one as diligent, had elected not to do the new assignment due Tuesday. They had all followed his lead with a statement "We reject history. The future is in our hands."

"At least they all turned it in early," Nat joked. "But seriously, why are you letting him bother you?"

She stooped to pick up some of the toys scattered across the floor. The kids drew on the table screen with their fingers. Jonah was making a Tyrannosaurus, all body and tail and teeth and feathers. Teyla was still too young for her art to look representational, but she always used space in interesting ways. I leaned in to watch both of them.

"You laugh," I said. "Maybe by the time they're his age now, Nelson will have taken over the entire system. Only the most future-relevant courses. Reject the past. Don't reflect on the human condition. No history, no literature, no dinosaurs."

Jonah frowned. "No dinosaurs?"

"Grandma Rosie's joking, Jonah."

Jonah accepted that. His curly head bent down over the table again.

I continued. "It was one thing when he was a one boy

revolution. What am I supposed to do now that his virus is spreading to his whole class?"

Nat considered for a moment. "I'd work on developing an antidote, then hide it in a faster, stronger virus and inject it into the class. But, um, that's my professional opinion."

"What's the antidote in your analogy? Or the faster, stronger virus?"

Nat smiled, spread her hands. "It wasn't an analogy, sorry. I only know from viruses and toddlers. Sometimes both at once. Now are you going to play for these kids before I try to get them to sleep? They really like the one about the sleepy bumblebee."

She picked Teyla up from her chair, turned it around, and sat down with Teyla in her lap. Jonah kept drawing.

I picked up my fiddle. "What's a bumblebee, Jonah?"

He answered without looking up. "A dinosaur."

I sighed and started to play.

⊗   ⊗   ⊗

Natalie's answer got me thinking. I checked in with Nelson's literature teacher, who confirmed he was doing the same thing in her class as well.

How wrong was he? They learned countries and borders, abstract names, lines drawn and redrawn. The books taught in lit classes captured the human condition, but rendered it through situations utterly foreign to us. To us. To me as much as him.

I had always liked the challenge. Reading about the way things had been in the past made our middle-years condition more acceptable to me. Made beginnings more concrete. Everyone in history lived in middle-years too; no matter when they lived, there was a before and an after, even if a given group or individual might not be around for the latter. I enjoyed tracing back through the changes, seeing what crumbled and what remained.

I enjoyed. Did I pass on my enjoyment? Maybe I'd been

thinking too much about why I liked to study history, and not considering why my students found it tedious. It was my job to find a way to make it relevant to them. If they weren't excited, I had failed them.

When I got home from dinner that night, when I picked up my fiddle to play "Wind Will Rove," it was the new, elided version, the one which had escaped me previously. Now I couldn't find the original phrasing again, even with fifty years' muscle memory behind it.

I went to the database to listen to how it actually went, and was relieved when the song came up without trouble. The last variation in the new DB was filed under "Wind Will Rove" but would more accurately have been listed as "Wind Will Roam," and even that one recreated somebody's memory of an interview predating our ship. If this particular song's history hadn't contained all those interviews in which the song's interpreters sang snippets, if Harriet or my grandmother or someone hadn't watched it enough times to memorize it, or hadn't thought it important, we wouldn't have any clue how it went. Those little historic recreations weren't even the songs themselves, but they got their own piece of history, their own stories. Why did they matter? They mattered because somebody had cared about them enough to create them.

⊛　⊛　⊛

I walked into my classroom on Monday, fiddle case over my shoulder, to the nervous giggles of students who knew they had done something brazen and now waited to find out what came of it. Nelson, not giggling, met my gaze with his own, steady and defiant.

"Last week, somebody asked me a question, using the very odd delivery mechanism of my classroom walls." I touched my desk and swiped the graffitied walls blank.

"Today I'm going to tell you that you don't have a choice. You're in this class to learn our broken, damaged history, everything that's left of it. And then to pass it on, probably breaking it even further. And maybe it'll keep twisting until every bit of fact is wrung out of it, but what's left will still be some truth about who we are or who we were. The part most worth remembering."

I put my fiddle case on the desk. Took my time tuning down to DDAD, listening to the whispered undercurrent.

When I liked the tuning, I lifted my bow. "This is a song called 'Wind Will Rove.' I want you to hear what living history means to me."

I played them all. All the known variations, all the ones that weren't lost to time. I rested the fiddle and sang Howie McCabe's faulty snippet of Windy Grove from the recreation of his historical interview and Will E. Womack's Wind Will Roam. I recited the history in between: Windy Grove and Wendigo and When I Go. Lifted the fiddle to my chin again and closed my eyes. Wind Will Rove: three times through in its traditional form, three times through with my own alterations.

"Practice too much and you sound like you're remembering it instead of feeling it," my grandmother used to say. This was a new room to my fiddle; even the old variations felt new within it. My fingers danced light and quick.

I tried to make the song sound like something more than wind. What did any of us know of wind? Nothing but words on a screen. I willed our entire ship into the new song I created. We were the wind. We were the wind and borne by the wind, transmitted. I played a ship travelling through the vacuum. I played life on the ship, footsteps on familiar streets, people, goats, frustration, movement while standing still.

The students sat silent at the end. Only one was an Old-Timer, Emily Redhorse, who had been one of the three who actually turned in their assignments; Nelson grew up hearing this music, I know. I was pretty sure the rest had no clue what they heard. One look at Nelson said he'd already formulated a response, so I didn't let him open his mouth.

I settled my fiddle back into its case and left.

        ⊛   ⊛   ⊛

There are so many stories about my grandmother. I don't imagine there'll ever be many about me. Maybe one of the kids in this class will tell a story about the day their teacher cracked up. Maybe Emily Redhorse will take a seat in the OldTime one day and light into my tune. Maybe history and story will combine to birth something larger than both, and you, Teyla, you and your brother will take the time to investigate where anecdote deviates from truth. If you wonder which of these stories are true, well, they all are in their way, even if some happened and some didn't.

I've recorded my song variation into the new database, in the "other" section to keep from offending Harriet, for now. I call it "We Will Rove." I think my grandmother would approve. I've included a history, too, starting with "Windy Grove" and "Wind Will Rove," tracing through my grandmother's apocryphal spacewalk and my mother's attempt to find meaning for herself and my daughter's unrecorded song, on the way to my own adaptation. It's all one story, at its core.

I'm working more changes into the song, making it more and more my own. I close my eyes when I play it, picturing a through-line, picturing how one day, long after I'm gone, a door will open. Children will spill from the ship and into the bright sun of a new place, and somebody will lift my old fiddle, my grandmother's fiddle, and will put a new tune to the wind.

Dirty Old Town
Richard Bowes

Part One: Dream and Memory

A T MY AGE, LONG-GONE friends and family, lovers and en-
emies, old hits and old flops, parade through my dreams.
Sometimes that means a jolt of wonder, others a nip of
terror. Mostly these are natural dreams, concocted in my
subconscious.

Dreams made from magic are rare. A recent one had
a familiar setting and time. It was South Boston, which
meant that I was five or six, this was 1949/50, and I was in
first grade. I walked across a deserted, tar-surfaced D Street
Housing Projects playground.

In a classic Boston drizzle, I wore, like a million other
American kids, a yellow raincoat and floppy fisherman's hat.
Saint Peter's Lithuanian Catholic School in the distance got
no closer no matter how I hurried.

Then out of nowhere, coming right at me from that
direction, was a somewhat bigger kid. Slit-eyed and with a
scary blank face, he was a few strategic months older.

His name back then was Eddie Mackey. Because of how

his family was, he wore no raincoat or hat. That gave me a clear view of the bloody cut on his forehead.

Eddie walked right up to me with his eyes empty of expression and an open mouth that got bigger with every step until it filled my vision like an onrushing railroad tunnel.

Before being swallowed, I wondered why the bloody cut I'd given Eddie didn't make him afraid of me.

Hit with this enigma, the dream wobbled and dissolved like the contrivance it was. Opening my eyes, I found myself in a Greenwich Village late-winter dawn.

Sleep-addled, I remembered my grandmother telling me that even a trained sorcerer couldn't send a dream from far away. Eddie Mackey calls himself Ed Mack now. In the grey morning hour, he had passed near enough to my apartment to plant that dream in my head.

Staggering around the kitchen, I made toast and brewed the same dark, longleaf tea my grandmother once did. The scent evoked a thin, white-haired figure, a seeming wisp of a woman. Only God knows all the tea she must have brewed.

Whenever I think of her, I hear the crowd at Fenway Park roar as Ted Williams lines one into the stands.

Knowing I wouldn't get back to sleep, I turned to the story I was writing for an anthology. It concerned a man in late middle age who hears Time's Winged Chariot clattering behind him as he jogs, climbs stairs, or peddles a stationary bike in his relentless attempt to stay one step ahead of Death.

This story had gone through all the writer's preliminary stages: inspiration, wonder, disappointment, and the decision to retire from writing and live in a remote cabin.

That morning I found a plot twist. My character turned expecting to see bearded Chronos with an hourglass in one hand and chariot reins in the other. Instead, he found a guy wearing a suit and badge. With eyes cold blue and amused, an Irish cop offered him a chance to sign away a chunk of his worldly wealth in return for a decade more of life.

The adult Eddie Mackey was the model for the cop. I've used him in stories and scripts as characters ranging from amusingly dishonest to satanic. It bothers him a bit.

He, in turn, knows it bothers me that he's approached on the street by people asking for his autograph. Mostly, my life hasn't been bad. But I'm asked for autographs only at my book signings. He chose the actor's life and shortened his name to Ed Mack while I chose to be a writer.

Intruding on these thoughts was an email from Eddie/Ed reminding me of an appointment that evening.

He had worshipped my grandmother and thinking of her made me remember

that Red Sox spring training was under way. My mother's mother was mad about the sport. She gave me a bat blessed by a baseball-loving priest when we moved to D Street Housing Project. Smaller even than a little league model, it was a perfect fit for a five-year-old.

She adored every aspect of baseball. I remember us stopping at a corner lot to watch a dozen kids play on a crude diamond adjoining an outfield paved with broken bricks.

Her sons all played for their schools and in the Twilight Leagues when they were young. I've wondered if she got them involved so she could watch. My uncles gave her a TV, one of the first I ever saw. She followed the ever-failing Red Sox with a fanatic's devotion, even taking out her rosary beads to pray for Johnny Pesky to lay down a bunt or Mel Parnell to toss a double-play pitch.

Some said they'd seen her pray for the Yankee's plane to crash on its way to Boston. I don't believe that. Not even her magic couldn't help the Sox.

❊   ❊   ❊

A few days before Eddie's dream, I'd been a guest on a fiction podcast where the hostess asked about old St. Patrick's Days in Boston. And I let a fine McGabber flow right out of me.

"McGabber" is the name I gave early on to my tales told

with full Celtic twists and turns. From schoolyards to bars, the storyteller was still welcome in Celtic Boston. It began:

"I remember as a little kid—it was maybe 1950—being on the third-floor porch of a three-decker watching the Parade in South Boston with all my mother's family, the aunts and uncles and cousins and relatives visiting from Ireland. And most of all, my grandparents!

"I remember my uncles shouting greetings down to people in the street and people on the ground shouting back. The Saint Patrick's Day Parade only passes through South Boston, the traditional Irish neighborhood.

"At the head of the parade as it wound through the streets were these amazing old steam-powered fire engines that kept breaking down on the hills. So the bands and marching contingents would come to a halt and march in place until somewhere in the distance the engines started up again.

"Politicians were thick on the ground. I saw James Michael Curley, a Boston legend who had lately been elected mayor while in jail. His open car stopped down the street from us; and a little girl in a white communion dress came out, curtsied, and presented him with a bouquet of roses.

"He doffed his high silk hat, bowed low, and in his great, rolling Shakespearean actor voice said something like, 'It's an honor and a privilege to accept these flowers from so lovely a young child of Ireland.'

"The parade started up again and Curley's car rolled forward only to stop right below us when a barefoot woman with a kerchief on her head ran out to sweep the street in front of his honor's vehicle. Curley rose again, bowed, and presented her with the bouquet. Holding it aloft, she danced a jig.

"My grandfather walked to the railing and raised his glass to the mayor who waved back.

My grandmother, her arm around me shook her head and murmured, "He's been carrying on like this for much too long." And I wasn't sure if she meant the mayor, her husband, or both.

"*Curley rolled on and the barefoot woman disappeared somewhere and maybe put on her shoes. A brass band marched by. And right behind it was a bunch of kids from the Boys' Club wearing baseball sweaters and caps and kind of marching in step. Tagging behind this formation were kids who had joined along the parade route and who marched in no order whatsoever.*

"*Right then, the parade halted again and looking down I found two familiar faces, practically the same face twice. Staring up at me were Eddie and Joe Mackey.*"

The podcast hostess looked concerned. The anecdote appeared to be going out of control. "I mention the Mackey Brothers," I found myself explaining, "Because Eddie Mackey became Ed Mack whom you may know as Jack Scanty on *Dirty Old Town.*"

And the hostess, wide-eyed, said, "You grew up with him?"

It's a sad age, but a cable TV crime show with an actor who's just won an award gets recognition no writer ever will. I closed my interview by inventing a childhood friendship for Eddie and me.

There was more to that distant St. Patrick's Day. The Mackeys and I stared at each other but none of us waved or smiled, or shouted over the noise.

Eddie was in first grade with me and a constant torment. Also, I'd been pushed around more than once by his brother, Joey, who was five years older and a head or two taller than I was.

My grandmother's blue eyes missed none of this.

She looked over the railing. The Mackeys backed off, broke eye contact, and melted into the crowd as the parade started up again.

"Your friends?" my grandmother asked.

I shook my head. "They're in my school." I wasn't going to say that if I had any school friends, it wouldn't be them.

But then she ran her hand along the top of my crew cut as if she was stroking a cat. Something unlocked inside me and words rushed out.

"Eddie always follows me home and tries to trip me and makes fun of me. Joey's even worse. He kicks kids, steals stuff. I have to hide from them after school. Once they chased me right up the stairs in my building, tried to push their way into the apartment. Joey got his head in and looked around and said I was weird because we had so many books. Then they heard my mother asking who was there and he ducked out."

Telling my grandmother about my troubles and fears broke the first law I'd learned after I was allowed out to play with other kids: you never told adults stuff like this.

But it felt like just seeing us had revealed to her everything there was to know about the Mackeys and me.

When I said, "He gives me bad dreams," she nodded and I knew she understood. That evening in a quiet corner of her living room, she taught me a short invocation. She said it was like a prayer and it began, "Open and open the door that is locked," then used words in the old language. I was to recite this only if I was in danger. She told me what would happen after I did.

❀   ❀   ❀

When we moved to D Street my parents maybe decided the local public elementary school wasn't good or wasn't near enough. Or maybe as former actors, left-wing Catholics, and proud eccentrics determined not to raise an ordinary child, they thought it too mundane.

So while most of the kids in the Projects went there, I was sent to Saint Peter's, a Lithuanian Catholic school on the fringes of the neighborhood.

The nuns were bilingual. Lots of kids were recent refugees from Europe and still learning English, so classes were taught in both languages. My parents were amused when I came home knowing Lithuanian words and even a song or two. I spoke so easily and so well that the fact I had trouble writing my own name didn't seem to them a big deal.

School was a path I traveled on my own. My parents read me *New Yorker* stories from *The Thurber Carnival* at bedtime, but I had to live my life in a place where few other families had a book.

Among the Projects kids at St. Peters were Eddie Mackey and his brother Joey. Later I learned Joey had been thrown out of public school and their mother wanted to keep them together.

Life was excitement tinged with terror. Kids were always fighting; sometimes rocks got thrown. Eventually D Street became a famous hellhole. But briefly it was shinier and newer than anything else in the city.

I was a kid who saw or imagined magic. The eyes on the statues in the church followed me when I walked past them. I told my teacher this in class one day. The nun just smiled but other kids laughed.

Eddie Mackey stood in my way after school. "You seeing statues looking at you?" he asked. He seemed serious. But when I said, "yes," he followed me home telling everyone that statues looked at me.

Part Two: The Song of the Bat

I remembered all this and knew I'd be seeing Eddie that evening. Suze, with whom I've been close since back when she was Steve and we were an item, stopped by around noon and we went to Caffe Reggio for lunch. Suze knows Eddie Mackey/Ed Mack. She told me, "He called last night and said things were coming together for a movie about your grandfather."

"He's talked about that for decades," I said.

"What was your grandfather like?" Suze asked. "You must have a McGabber about him."

And out it came.

"I believe I could be the last person left on Earth who will be able to say he voted for Harry Truman for President. I was four in 1948 when my grandfather brought me to a polling place in South Boston, took my hand, guided it over a ballot, and made the letters of my name on it.

"His friends, the ward heelers who ran the polls, were amused' said, things like, "Ah, you're doing a fine deed, Michael! Raising the boy right!'

"So I cast my vote for Truman, a Democrat loyal to friends no matter what trouble they got into, and not a New York aristocrat looking down his nose at Irishmen sullied by their work in the sootier aspects of Democratic politics.

"My grandfather's magic in all its variety is hard to capture. I stayed with my grandparents a lot as a child when my mother and father had theatrical gigs, when my brother was born, and sometimes for reasons that weren't explained, so I knew them well.

"My grandfather hadn't been the best of fathers by any means. After he was gone, I heard tales of how, not once but on two separate occasions when my mother and her siblings were kids, he came home drunk on Christmas Eve and threw the tree, with all its decorations, out the window.

"But for me he was wondrous, taking me shopping once when I'd had a bad day at school and buying me a hat that was a small version of the one he himself wore.

"A mercurial soul, he was a motorman on streetcars (but seemingly not all the time) from the 1920's on. At one point back then he somehow was well-to-do, had six houses and several cars. It was then they called him 'The Millionaire Motorman.'

"The money appeared out of nowhere, to hear his children tell it. Then, like the fairy gold it may have been, everything was gone and he was broke with nothing left but a taste for drink and a rollicking bad temper. Only his wife's charm and her magic saved his life when debts came due and he couldn't pay.

"*By the time I knew him, in the years when I thought he was a god, he had moderated his drinking and in the way of Irish men was a wonderful father to any boy who was not actually his son.*

"*A walk to the corner store could be like something out of a tale. 'Irene, the Queen of Shopkeepers,' he'd tell the mean little woman who owned the variety store on the corner. Years later, I found out she ran the numbers in that neighborhood. And only his magic made her smile.*

"*All I knew was that he'd say about me, 'He's a remarkable boy. There's nothing in the world that he cannot do.' And she'd give me a Popsicle.*

"*One time on the sidewalk, he waved his hand and seemingly out of the very cement popped a tall, drooping shambles of a man. 'Peter Maguire, as honest and fit as any who has ever breathed,' said my grandfather, 'what do you think of my grandson, Pete?'*

"'*Looks like he could be a fine young man unless you're raising him to be a hellion like yourself.*'

"'*He favors my wife and his mother, for which I hope he's as thankful as he should be. Now, might I ask you what you make of the doings yesterday in that fifth race at Suffolk Downs?' Then they both stepped away from me and whispered for a moment.*

"*Before I could get impatient, he'd be back at my side, gesturing at an elf-like man in a suit. 'There he is, Spencer Mac-Griffin, a lawyer no bigger than yourself and rich. But you'll outreach him. There's nothing in the world at which you won't succeed.'*

"*And he'd pop into a shop and buy me a clip-on tie with shamrocks on it. Part of his magic was his ability to see the world at an angle no other mortal knew.*"

Because Suze is also Eddie's friend, I didn't tell her about the day Eddie Mackey entered the world of my grandfather and me. At age six, it was a dark calamity.

I thought at the time that perhaps my grandfather was

dropping by to visit relatives. But I've come to realize that
an encounter with Eddie and me was why he was wandering
along D Street that afternoon.

Eddie was trying to get my attention by stepping on
my heels as we walked. Back then, I thought my grandfather didn't understand the situation. I see now that he read
us completely and chose for his own reasons to regard us as
friends.

Grasping each of us by a shoulder (no sissy holding
hands with him), he guided us across the street while talking to Eddie. "So Mackey's the name? There's a Joe Mackey,
played baseball with my boys." He gave a theatrical pause and
stared like something had just occurred to him. "That would
be your father?"

Eddie nodded a bit hesitantly. I understand now that
he hardly ever saw his old man, what with the guy's time in
prison and sobering up in hospitals.

"And from the looks of you, I'll lay money you play ball
yourself." And my grandfather was off talking about Eddie
and the accomplishments he'd just invented for this kid he
was maybe seeing for the first time. Eddie gave a little smile,
which I'd never seen him do.

The Millionaire Motorman said, "I well remember your
grandmother, Eileen Mackey. She spoke to saints and they
listened. You are a child of a magic line." Then he poked Eddie in the stomach and asked him about his grandmother
and how she was.

The hard-eyed kid turned into a giggling little boy as my
grandfather bought us not just lollipops but all-day suckers,
with extra ones to stick in our pockets. And I remember my
disappointment at having to share him with my enemy.

The day after the one with my grandfather changed Eddie's life and mine.

We were in class ignoring each other. The nun who
taught first grade also taught kindergarten in the same room

and switched from the one to the other and back again. She'd pull Lithuanian and American kids through Dick, Jane, and Sally in English one minute and teach Lithuanian songs to children even smaller than I was the next.

Was she a good teacher? Probably. But overworked. She was nice to me, ignored my trouble with writing words because of how I could talk.

That afternoon, without warning though our teacher must have known, a knock came at the door. She opened it and into the classroom strode Sister Superior with an even more terrible expression on her face than usual. With her were three boys and three girls, all in tears. Thus began a nightmare.

These were older students, nine years old—ten, even! The girls were dressed in the boys' coats and pants. And the boys were all in dresses—total humiliation! Sister Superior told us that they were being punished because the boys had been peeking into the girls' bathroom window and the girls had found this funny and they'd all been laughing when they were caught.

I understood none of this, but God, It seemed, was quite angry. They all had to say how sorry they were and then were herded sobbing out of the room and down the hall to be shown to every class.

As they left, I realized one of the boys was Joey Mackey. I glanced around and saw Eddie staring after his brother with tears in his eyes. He turned, saw me watching him cry, and shot me an angry look. I worried about after school.

But when that came, Joey Mackey and the ones caught with him, now back in their own clothes, were getting jeered at and punched by kids even older than they were. Eddie, a loyal little brother, walked with Joey, tried to put his arm around him, was shaken off but stared defiantly at the world.

That night, I had dark dreams. In one I saw myself in a dress with arrows sticking out of me. I'd seen a statue full of arrows in church and had thought the loincloth, which was all the saint wore, was a dress.

Then I was in a hall in my school. Students, priests, and nuns all around me pointed and laughed. I realized I was naked.

Awake, I kept getting reminded of the dreams. On a living room wall in our apartment was a double photo of my mother as Viola in a production of *Twelfth Night*. In one shot she was dressed as a man. In the other she was a woman.

Joey Mackey didn't come back to St. Peter's. Eddie was very quiet and we avoided each other. My dreams began to fade.

A few days later on my way home from school, I saw the Mackey brothers on the other side of D Street. Joey crossed with a scary smile. Eddie followed him, looking unhappy.

I froze where I was. Then, in my mind, I heard the words my grandmother taught me. I whispered "Open and open the door that is locked," and stumbled over a couple of the old words. But suddenly I was inside Joey, feeling the anger flowing through him. He wanted to smash someone and I saw myself, small and scared, and realized I saw this through his eyes. Then I remembered him standing in tears, wearing a dress. He caught my memory and froze. This was his nightmare. Rage turned to fear. Joey backed away fast, turned, and ran. Eddie hesitated then followed his brother.

That Saturday, I was playing by myself in the open space outside my building. A waterlogged copy of the Boston American was my home plate. I tossed a stone up in the air, swung the blessed baseball bat and missed it repeatedly.

The bat had taken lots of wear. There was a crack along its barrel. Around me, women hung their wash on clotheslines in a chain-link-fenced area. Men headed to the bars and a great roiling mass of kids played, screamed, teased, punched, cried.

Suddenly, I saw Eddie angry and coming at me. I backed

halfway up the front steps of my building whispering, "Open and open" and the rest of it.

Then I was in his head, saw myself, bat in hand, felt his anger and bewilderment. He'd tried to be friends by making me tough like Joey had done with him. He'd thought his brother was a giant until I somehow made Joey back down. Now Joey had run away from home.

Eddie was grief-crazed but brave. He hurled himself at me then realized I was inside him and scarier even than Sister Superior.

I had my own fear and anger to deal with. When his sneakers hit the bottom step, I swung my bat and caught him just above his right eye.

The flimsy bat broke but Eddie staggered backward and blood trickled from his forehead. He touched it and saw blood on his hand. I lost contact as he ran away.

Soon after this, my mother appeared. She had seen a boy run past her, bleeding. With no idea of what had happened, she was horrified. I was grabbed and hauled up to the apartment before harm could befall me. The bat got left behind.

She told my father, "It was awful: a little boy with blood streaming down his face." She repeated the story on the phone to her mother and sisters. Never did it occur to her that I might have done the deed.

I worried that she'd find out, but her contacts with people in the Projects were tenuous. And Eddie, years later, explained all the reasons why his mother had no interest in bringing her family to the attention of the authorities.

My grandmother was another matter. A few days later, she met me coming out of school and we walked amid kids and talked baseball.

Eddie, very subdued and with a bandage on his forehead, tried to avoid looking my way.

My grandmother asked if I was practicing with the bat.

"It broke," I said. Just that, but something in my voice,

or my involuntary glance at Eddie and her own uncanny instinct, told her more. Eddie's return gaze was miserable, like we'd been friends and weren't now. As at the parade, I believe my grandmother saw the shape of all that had passed between us.

She didn't get angry, just looked at me and nodded her understanding. "You learned all that poor bat could teach you," she said. Her smile was a bit sad.

When Eddie turned toward his building, she stopped me and went to him, put her hands on his shoulders. I thought he'd pull away from her but she whispered something and hugged him and he held still. She asked after his mother and grandmother, said he was a fine boy. His eyes teared and he ducked to hide that.

She summoned me over. Neither of us wanted to face the other. My grandmother made us shake hands. Even without magic, I felt his awe as he stared at her.

"You're neither of you ordinary boys. Each will need the other," she told us.

Before he went home, she kissed him and said, "You have a fine spirit. I'll visit you and your mother." He walked away glancing back at her.

When he was gone, she put her arm around my shoulders and said, "You should be friends with Eddie. He isn't well cared for."

But I felt cheated by her paying attention to him. It was like he had stolen both my grandparents from me.

Part Three: Dreams in the Night

Shortly after that, my family moved from D Street to a leafy neighborhood in Dorchester where we had a backyard and all the parks had baseball diamonds. I saw our move as a miracle caused by my slugging Eddie. My life got better. Sadly, I forgot any Lithuanian I may have known, but the saints in the huge church we went to never looked my way.

Once in a while over the years I would dream of a street-car all lighted up and rolling through the night. And the Millionaire Motorman at the controls smiled in my direction. Or I'd see a young girl walking a rocky road beside a gray sea and wake up remembering my grandmother.

Looking back, I connect those dreams with Eddie Mackey.

Many things changed. When I was nine, my grandmother died and I cried my eyes out. A few years later, my grandfather, who'd become quite distant, disappeared back to Ireland where he died.

In time I found out I was gay, drank illegally, went to college, had boyfriends, did drugs, and moved to Manhattan. A quarter-century and more since I'd last seen Eddie, I was writing plays that got readings but not productions. For money I taught Drama Lit at the New School and worked the door at Manland Disco on Christopher Street.

My ability to overawe belligerent customers despite my size gave me a certain cred. But the knowledge lurked that I was misusing my grandmother's gift.

In the wake of our affair, Steve/Suze and I remained fast friends. One night, she insisted there was a show I needed to see and took me to a small, worn-down theater way gone on the Hudson Waterfront. Sometimes it was a shadow play with silhouette figures. Sometimes it was actors in spotlights being sinister pantomime whores and street toughs.

Lenya sang about Mack The Knife on a scratchy old record while at stage-left, a male hand held a stiletto to a silhouette woman's throat. A shadow dog leaped for the hand but its teeth snapped shut on nothing. The silhouette woman took that opportunity to escape into the dark.

Stage right, under a street lamp, was a guy hiding the blade in his jacket. The silhouette woman saw him and drew back. The guy stepped forward, hands stuck in his front pockets, Mack the Knife with a South Boston strut and a smile on his face that I recognized. It was the same one Eddie wore when he stepped on my heels.

There were more silhouettes and sinister moments. But once I saw Eddie, I paid attention to nothing else.

After the show, he stepped out the stage door into a back alley. In an instant, he spotted me waiting and asked in the thickest of Boston accents, "Why are you hiding in the dark?"

We hugged, which surprised me as I did it. Over the years, I'd mostly thought about Eddie when I wrote him into scenes as a mean kid, a minor devil.

Now with a Brando-like dinged nose and intense eyes, he was compelling. "They told me you were in this town and for once they were right," he said. This time the voice had only the faintest residue of Boston.

Suze had set this up at Eddie's request. We three and a few people from the show stopped at a waterfront bar where hard-boiled eggs were the only solid food.

I filled in my life since we'd last seen each other. Words spilled out of Eddie. He said, "You need to talk after you do pantomime." He'd already appeared in a couple of Off-Off-Broadway shows that weren't much reviewed.

"With 'Nam after a two-year hitch, you're entitled to be crazy if you made it back," he said. "I did some rehab out in California. But there's no therapy like acting. I ate it up."

Eddie was glad to find me. Especially since Suze had let him know my latest romance had moved out of my under-heated apartment on Avenue B. Suddenly, it was Eddie and me.

Late one night, we lay stoned on the busted furniture, listening to the fire and police sirens, someone screaming on a roof. And he said, "I envied you your family. Your parents at the sight of a little blood—not even your blood—moved out of D Street and found a much nicer place to live. Great people! When I was maybe eight, your grandfather told me they were actors. Until then I never knew the figures on TV were actual people."

"Yours wasn't like my family with a father who couldn't have picked me out of a police line-up and a mess of a mother who'd been raised by a professional informant. Tell people you grew up in D Street and they stare at you like you sang with the Pogues and ran guns for the IRA.

"I lived in that hellhole for another fourteen years as the Projects went down the toilet. Vietnam saved me. "My father's dead, my mother's drinking herself to death, my brother's disappeared."

I gave a questioning look at the mention of Joey.

"After the incident with you, he ran away, kept doing that, got institutionalized, got out, and vanished."

I winced and he chuckled. "Believe me, I understand why you did it. Seeing him come apart made me crazed."

He shook his head, stared off. Some years later, I saw the same action and glance when he starred in a revival of Eugene O'Neil's The Iceman Cometh.

We talked about my grandparents and I found he'd thought about them more than I had. Eddie said, "I'll never forget them. Your grandmother was a magic woman. My own grandmother, Eileen Mackey, had sinister magic. I think she used it on my mother and Joey. I hated her. Your grandfather knew Eileen, talked about her that time he bought us lollipops."

I told him, "When my grandmother died, one of my uncles talked to me about his mother and said, 'There would be a moment when you were a kid where she'd give a look that said, *"You are as good now as you'll get to be and that will be enough for you to survive."*

I looked up and Eddie had tears in his eyes. Real ones, I think. We got it on that night. But it was curiosity and neither knowing anyone like the other that drove us. Our relationship was a narrow, rocky path.

A few times back then I had wonderful dreams about my grandparents and thought it was because Eddie had jogged my memory.

One night I read him a McGabber I'd just written.

"My grandparents were born in the nineteenth century and grew up on the bleak, remote Aran Islands with Gaelic as their first language. I don't remember them speaking to each other all that much.

"But when they'd be talking in English about someone who was misbehaving and remembered I was present, they'd slip into their first language, laughing and bright-eyed. It's the only time I remember them being close. Maybe it was a reminder of their lives when they were young. Even now when I hear Gaelic, I connect it with inappropriate gossip.

"Last year I was invited onto a radio show about Irish writers, was asked about my granduncles Liam and Tom, both of whom wrote. What I talked about mostly was their sister, my grandmother, this lady I'd loved as a child.

"In the 1930s, her brother Tom became an editor of the Daily Worker, the New York Communist newspaper. Her other brother, Liam O'Flaherty, is better known. His novel The Informer was made into a famous movie and a couple of not-so-famous ones. In his time he was a welcome figure in the Soviet Union.

"We had Liam's collected short stories around the house. One that intrigued me later when I began writing was about a boy, clearly himself, living in those bleak islands. Then his older sister returns from America to visit her family. And she is a magic creature for the boy who has not yet ventured away from home. She touches and twists her younger brother's imagination, makes him long for the wider world.

"And her influence didn't stop then. There's a family legend involving the three of them and the Palmer Raids. After World War One, Palmer, the U.S. Attorney General, believed that communists had infiltrated the USA during the war to

organize a revolution. His raiders traveled everywhere hunting commies.

"They got to Boston where her brothers Tom and Liam, a pair of Reds, were crashing at their sister's place. Somehow my grandmother barred the way, possibly cast a spell on the raiders long enough that her brothers got out the windows, onto the fire escape and away."

Eddie listened, fascinated. When I finished, he applauded and said, "My ambition is to play a rogue who has a bit of magic and a smile. I'll use a big dose of our grandfather."

Before I could ask him what this "our" was about, he said, "That old guy had charm I've never seen anyone come close to touching, onstage or off. But could his wife or anyone else but small boys really trust him?"

"What do you mean?"

"In your McGabber, how did the authorities know the location of the red brothers?"

"Anonymous informers, the Irish curse," I said. "Kind of ironic: Liam is mainly remembered for writing a novel about an informer."

"Maybe not so anonymous. When the Millionaire Motorman said about Eileen Mackey, 'She spoke to saints and they listened,' he invented as lilting a euphemism for, 'police stooge' as anyone ever has.

"My family had its stories, too. In them grandmother Mackey snitched for the cops. She had the power to pull secrets out of any man living or dead. Especially a man eight years younger than his wife."

My grandfather was that much younger than my grandmother. It had occurred to me that, like her brothers, he'd been captivated by this woman back from America.

"Unfaithful, maybe," I said. "But turning relatives in? That wasn't him."

"Agreed. But he was probably sick of her commie relatives getting all her attention. And you know that without a fresh scandal and someone to tell it to, he'd have died. He encountered Eileen Mackey– more than encountered as she told it. And being who he was, he couldn't keep a secret.

"After you moved away, I saw him a lot. He let me know I was his grandson. There's a play, possibly a movie here. If somebody with financing was interested, you could write it. I could play our grandfather."

When Eddie talked about this, I ignored him, refused to discuss his idea for a drama about my family that I hardly ever saw. Eddie took to calling us cousins. "You two getting your incest zest on?" Suze asked.

He had a nice review in an Off-Broadway play set in Irish Hell's Kitchen. Then, one day he came home looking stunned.

"I got a part in this TV movie that's shooting in New York. I play a psycho. No lines, just crazy face and screen time."

As I recall, I congratulated him. But it ground my insides. He was much better at what he did than I was at whatever I was doing. We mostly weren't speaking by the time another call came and he went out to Hollywood.

Just before he left, I dreamed that my grandfather looked down with a serious face I'd never seen, and spoke to a maybe nine-year-old Eddie who looked up at him wide-eyed. "A joke or a song will win you a smile and a kiss. But send someone a dream like this one I'm showing you and it will be with them forever."

I remembered the dream when I awoke, and as was promised it's been with me ever since. When I opened my eyes, Eddie was there, smiling and ready to leave. For some time I'd wanted him gone but suddenly I didn't want that. On parting, he said, "I've found no others like us."

Part Four: Dirty Old Town, I Want You Back

Over the years, Eddie Mackey became Ed Mack, had a fine career as a character actor in movies, played killers with a touch of poetry, cops with faulty consciences.

He did stage work, made it a point to return to New York every couple of years. Eddie would mention the script and I'd ignore him.

On a visit in the '90's, his marriage to the actress Terri Javier had gone bust when her career eclipsed his, and I'd broken up with a club owner who loved a younger guy.

"Nothing else we've tried works," he said. "But we could be brothers." I smiled and found a bit of comfort there.

A few years ago, we had a great nostalgic afternoon at an outdoor café on Central Park. He told me, "Sometimes in LA, I'll get a flash of light in the corner of my eye and I turn and catch a glimpse of your grandmother."

And I said, "My mother told me that my grandmother once said that she'd married her husband for his dreams and nothing more."

⊛　⊛　⊛

A few weeks ago, Ed announced he'd be back in town. The e-mail this morning, after his dream, begged me to attend an event in the evening.

It started at seven with me seated in a theater at Transvision Cable's Columbus Circle offices. This was a press event staged for New York's publicity machine. The occasion was the third-season rollout of the Emmy Award-winning series *Dirty Old Town.*

As you've doubtless seen or heard, DOT spins a fictional version of Boston crime a couple of generations back. The world is one of aging neighborhoods, corrupt cops, the code of silence, and the rise of Whitey Bulger.

Within a few episodes of its initial season, DOT returned to me the city in which I grew up. I watch it alone because it makes me cry.

In front of a big screen, a panel of directors, actors, producers, cameramen, and techies sat facing us. The former Eddie Mackey was at the far end of the row.

I attempted to catch his eye but couldn't. Using my magic didn't feel appropriate.

On the screen, MTA cars rattled along elevated tracks in a landscape of three-decker houses. A producer described the pains that went into bringing elevated trains and the old low-rise "city skyline back to life through the miracle of computer animation.

Location scouts talked about finding just the right corner store to use as the front for a numbers parlor. A stretch of shore in New Jersey became Revere Beach in its full, seamy glory.

We viewed dingy apartments and rainy shots of Dorchester Boulevard dolled up with old bar signs and seventies cars. There were snowy views of everything from the State House to the dog track at Wonderland. "No need to fake the snow," a director testified.

The visuals ended with a guy shot and falling headfirst over the wooden railing of a third-floor porch.

Most of the panel had California sheen. Eddie was also well turned out, but his dented nose and his haircut would not have looked incongruous back in our Boston. His eyes were alive but a bit remote. They never focused on me.

The producer introduced the panel in turn. Each had a little something to say about their place in the series. Eddie came last despite his Golden Globe Award.

When the producerit came to him, he said, "Last and foremost, our very own Ed Mack who as Jack Scanty, 'The Repairman,' takes the blood and tears of a city and turns them into leprechaun gold."

The Repairman was on-screen in a scene from the first episode of the upcoming season. It was set in a mid-20th-century den: sports trophies on shelves, a stag's head on the wall along with photos of boxers, racehorses, and naked ladies. A man, presumably the late owner, sat pitched forward in a swivel chair. His face was flat on a desk blotter, which had a dark, growing stain.

Wearing gloves, Scanty flipped the man's hand off the phone he'd reached for. "What misunderstanding made him think he could make a call?" Scanty asked someone unseen. That absence allowed Eddie to make each viewer feel they were the one being addressed.

The Repairman went through drawers, pulled out an envelope, and said, "Jesus! With a wad like this, I'd have put distance between myself and the scene of my felonies."

He tossed the envelope to the unseen accomplice and went back to rifling the desk. The actor famously improvised his soliloquies. Scanty spoke pure Boston with the slightest suggestion of a brogue.

He said, "My early life got saved by a mug so Irish, no one in the city could identify me from among the other ten thousand young Micks up to no good and wearing the same face I sported.

I was slick, I was hard, I was so dumb I'm amazed I'm still alive." He shrugged, half-smiled, and was working on the combination lock of a safe as the scene ended.

Hardened media members broke into applause.

The scene roused my nostalgia in a couple of ways. The den reminded me of a certain Beacon Hill sugar daddy. And Eddie sounded a bit like my grandfather.

The actor stood and said to the audience, "Let me tell you a little story." I sat stunned as he launched into a McGabber I wrote years ago and forgot.

"I lived in the D Street Projects in South Boston right at the start. A few years later was a different story, but at first it had its share of cops and firemen and GI's back from the war.

"My Uncle Bill, the cop, lived there with his wife, over near

Saint Peter's Church, and they were expecting their first kid. One day when maybe my parents were busy, I was sent over to hang around with my Aunt Claire. Uncle Bill came home in uniform for lunch and brought his partner Kelly with him.

"*My uncle went into the kitchen and was talking to my aunt. I was in the living room and they were speaking in whispers, arguing. Probably it was stuff I shouldn't have had to hear. Kelly, who was this big, beefy guy with a constant half-smile, maybe thought to distract me. He was sitting on the couch and had taken off his belt and holster, laid them beside him. I stared wide-eyed and he took the police special out and nodded. I came forward and he handed it to me butt-first. I held it with both hands but I was just six years old and the weight carried my arms down.*

"*The barrel was pointed at the floor and I was ready to drop it when Uncle Bill came in with two bottles of Narragansett. 'You emptied it, right?' he asked. Kelly slapped his forehead and my uncle relieved me of the gun, looked back to see if my aunt had caught any of this.*

"*If she had, no word of this was said and it was never referred to again. In retrospect, this could have been an exciting day for Mrs. Callahan downstairs if I'd dropped the piece and a bullet had gone through her ceiling.*"

There was some laughter and applause and seemingly for the first time, Eddie spotted me, came down off the stage, and took my arm. As I stood, he said, "Those words come from this cousin of mine, a great writer who's working on a project with me." People looked my way. The producer shook my hand briefly.

We descended in a crowded elevator. Passengers gave sidelong glanced at Ed Mack. I thought of the sleep I'd lost and the way he'd appropriated my story.

"Bill was my uncle," I said. "Did you ever meet him?" Hearing myself, I sounded like I was six.

Looking a bit amused, Eddie said. "I know a place right

around the corner."

The time of dark Manhattan bars where guys got loaded and sad is gone. We settled into a nicely lit, quiet place. Eddie ordered a Jameson and water, I got an ice tea.

A couple of patrons were clearly trying to remember why he looked so familiar. The bartender whispered the reason. Ed Mack pretended to ignore all that.

Smiling like a bully he murmured, "I keep thinking of you walking to school in that yellow raincoat."

That dream had violated an unspoken truce: we didn't impose our magic on each other. He was taunting me and I was pissed enough to whisper my grandmother's invocation.

Inside him, I found a jumble of memories along with heavy doses of anger and fear. At the center of all this, I saw a doctor diagnose him with stomach cancer. Through Ed's eyes, I watched my expression change from anger to shock. I broke the connection between us.

"I'm too big a coward to actually say the C word," he said and looked ashamed. "Please keep this to yourself. The producers of *Dirty Old Town* are about to back the movie. Our grandfather is a part you were born to write and I was born to play."

Eddie wasn't through with me. Suddenly I saw the two of us as kids on a crowded Subway platform. A great roar came out of the tunnel and a giant gold chariot pulled by tigers appeared. Our grandfather in his motorman cap was in the driver's seat. The crowd parted to let us climb aboard and with a crack of the whip, off we went.

"Please say you'll help me," he asked. Stunned, I nodded. "Sweet dreams to us both," he said and departed before I could speak.

Part Five: "The Last McGabber."

"With dreams and disease, Eddie won me over. In the next few weeks, he sent shots of twentieth-century Irish Boston. It was black and white parades, first communions, barrooms, and wakes. Surprised at how much I missed a world of which I'd seen nothing more than parting glances, I wrapped a story line around my grandparents and two small boys in 1950 South Boston and threw in flashbacks.

"I got clips of the film as it was shot and saw Ed Mack as our grandfather in all his glory and wearing a hat as no one else could.

"We talked often by phone. 'We may be disgusting old men but in our youth we were touched by magic,' he told me. 'I doubt if there will be any more like us when we go.' And the voice was so close to our grandfather's that I shivered.

"He came to New York after shooting was finished and there was talk of taking the film to Sundance and other festivals. It was a lovely spring day and we walked through the streets with him speaking in a brogue, waving a walking stick and greeting everyone who passed us. A daycare center's-worth of small children went by and half of them turned and tried to follow Eddie.

"He rounded a corner and staggered. I caught him before he could fall. Getting him to a bench and then into a cab was easy. There was nothing to him. 'You're not taking care of yourself at all,'" I said.

"'I was afraid of getting well,' he told me. "My being sick is the only thing I've ever done that hasn't made you loathe me."

"He laughed when I cried. And then we switched roles. It was the last time we met."

Last night I told Suze that I was calling his eulogy "The Last McGabber." And she said, "There will always be another one."

This morning, she just called to say the car that will take

us to Kennedy Airport en route to L.A. will be downstairs in five minutes.

I've put a copy of this McGabber in my luggage. I stick another one in my jacket pocket and have one to give to Suze.

All this, the eulogy, the flight, Eddie Mackey's Memorial Service, is done to dim my awareness that for the first time since I was five, I'm alone without magic in this world.

The Last Novelist
(or a Dead Lizard in the Yard)
Matthew Kressel

When I lift up my shoe in the morning there's a dead baby lizard underneath. It lies on its back, undersides pink and translucent, organs visible. Maybe when I walked home under the strangely scattered stars I stepped on it. Maybe it crawled under my shoe to seek its last breath while I slept. Here is one leaf of a million-branched genetic tree never to unfurl. Here is one small animal on a planet teeming with life.

The wind blows, carrying scents of salt and seaweed. High above, a bird soars in the eastern wind. I scoop up the lizard and bury it under the base of a coconut tree. Soon, I'll be joining him. I can't say I'm not scared.

⊛　⊛　⊛

"All tender-belly spacefarers are poets," goes the proverb, and I'm made uncomfortably aware of its truth every time I cross the stars. I ventured out to Ardabaab by thoughtship, an express from Sol Centraal, and for fifty torturous minutes—or a million swift years; neither is wrong—gargantuan thoughtscapes of long-dead galaxies wracked my mind, while wave after wave of nauseating, hallucinogenic bardos drowned my sense of personhood, of encompassing a unitary being in space and time. Even the pilots, well-traveled men-tshen them all, said the journey was one of their roughest. And while I don't hold much faith in deities, I leaped down and kissed the pungent brown earth when we incorporated, and praised every sacred name I knew, because (a) I might have met these ineffable beings as we crossed the stellar gulfs, and (b) I knew I'd never travel by thoughtship again; I'd come to Ardabaab to die.

I took an aircar to the house, and as we swooped low over bowing fields of sugarcane, her disembodied voice said to me, "With your neural shut off you have a small but increased risk of injury. Ardabaab is safe—we haven't had a violent incident in eighty-four years—but the local We recommends guests leave all bands open, for their safety." She sounded vaguely like my long-dead wife, and this was intentional. Local Wees are tricky little bastards.

"Thanks," I said to her. "But I prefer to be alone."

"Well," she said with a trace of disgust, "it's my duty to let you know."

The car dropped me off at the house, a squat blue bun-galow near the beach set among wind-whipped fields of sug-arcane and towering coconut palms. Forty minutes later I was splayed on the empty beach while Ardabaab's red-dwarf sun—rock-candy pink at this late hour—dipped low over the turquoise sea, the most tranquil I had ever seen. For a station-born like me, it was utterly glorious.

The wind blew and distant lights twinkled over the wa-ters. I smiled. I had arrived. With pen and paper in hand, I furiously scribbled:

⊗   ⊗   ⊗

Chapter 23. Arrival.
When Yvalu stepped off the thoughtliner, she bent down and kissed the ground. Her hands came up with a scoop of Muan-diva's fertile soil, which she immediately swallowed, a pinch

of this moment's joy that she would carry in her body forever.
Thank Shaddai. She was here.

A lizard skirted by. Strange people smiled and winked at
her. She beamed and jumped and laughed. Ubalo had walked
this world, perhaps had even stepped on the same dark earth
still sweet on her tongue. Ubalo, who had brought her to Silver-
sun, where they had watched the triple stars, each of a different
shade, rise above the staggered mesas of Jacob's Ladder and cast
blossoming colorscapes of ever-shifting rainbows across the des-
ert. Ubalo, who had traveled to the other side of the galaxy to
seek a rare mineral Yvalu had once offhandedly remarked she
liked during an otherwise forgettable afternoon. Ubalo, whose
eyes shone like Sol and whose smile beamed like Sirius. For him
she would have suffered a trillion mental hells if only to hold his
hand one more time.

✹   ✹   ✹

I wrote, and wrote more, until I ran out of pad. And when I
looked up, the sun had set, and new constellations winked
distant colors at me. Ardabaab has no moon. I had been writing by their feeble light for hours.

✹   ✹   ✹

Early the next morning, after I bury the lizard, I head for
Halcyon's beachside cafe with a thermos of keemun tea and
four extra writing pads tucked deep into my bag. While hovering waiterplates use my thermos to refill cup after cup, I
churn out twenty more pages. But when a group of exuber-
ant tourists from Sayj sit nearby, growing rowdy as they get
intox, I slip down to the beach.

I return to last night's spot, a private cove secluded from
all but the sea, and here I work under the baking sun as locals,
identified by their polydactyl hands and violet eyes, offer me
braino and neur-grafts and celebrilives, each on varying spec-
tra of legality.

"I got Buddhalight," a passerby says, interrupting my
stream. "Back from zer early days, before ze ran out of

exchange."

I grit my teeth in frustration. I was really flowing. "Thanks, but I prefer my own thoughts."

"Alle-roit," she says, swishing off. "You kayn know 'less you ask."

I turn back to my pad and write:

⊛   ⊛   ⊛

But no matter who Yvalu asked, none had heard of a mentsh named Ubalo. And when she shared his message with the local We, the mind told her, somewhat coldly, "This transmission almost certainly came from Muandiva. But I have not encountered any of his likeness among my four trillion nodes. It's plain, Yvalu, that the one who you seek is simply not here."

"Then where is he?" she said, verging on tears. "Where is he?"

And the local We responded with words she had never heard one speak before: "I am sorry, Yvalu, but I have no idea."

⊛   ⊛   ⊛

I finish a chapter, and a second, and before I begin a third, a shadow falls across my pad and a sharp voice interrupts me. "What you doing?"

"Not interested," I say.

"Not selling."

I look up. A child stands before me, eclipsing the sun. Small in stature, her silhouette makes her seem planetary. She has short-cut dark hair and six elongated fingers. And though the sun blinds, the violet glare of her eyes catches me off guard and I gasp. I raise a hand to shade my face, and sans glare, her eyes shine with the penetrating violet of a rainbow just before it fades into sky. I'm so taken by them I've forgotten what she's asked. "Sorry?"

"What you drawing?"

"This isn't drawing."

"Then what is it?"

"This?" It takes me a second. "I'm writing."

"*Writing.*" She chews on the word and steps closer. "That's a *pen,*" she says, "and that's *paper.* And you're using *cursive.* Freylik!" She laughs.

It's obvious she's just wikied these words, but her delight is contagious, and I smile with her. It's been a long time since I've met someone who didn't know what pen and paper were. Plus there's something in her voice, her cascade of laughs, that reminds me of my long-dead daughter.

"What you writing?" she says.

"A novel."

"A *novel.*" A wiki-length pause. Another smile. "Prektik! But . . ." Her nostrils flare. "Why don't you project into your neural?"

"Because my neural's off."

"Off?" The notion seems repulsive to her.

"I prefer the quiet," I say.

"SO DO I!" she shouts as she plops down beside me, stirring up sand. "Name," she says, "Reuth Bryan Diaso, citizen of Ganesha City, Mars. Born on Google Base Natarajan, Earth orbit, one gravity Earth-natural. Age: ninety-one by Sol, two hundred ninety-three by Shoen. Hi!"

For a moment I pretend this girl from Ardabaab has heard of me, Reuth Bryan Diaso, author of fourteen novels and eighty-seven short stories. But it's obvious she's gleaned all this from public record. I imagine wistfully what it must have been like in the ancient days, when authors were renowned across the Solar System, welcomed as if we were dignitaries from alien worlds. Now mentshen revere only the grafters and sense-folk for sharing endless arrays of vapid experiences with their billion eager followers. No, I don't need to feel Duchesse Ardbeg's awful dilemma of not knowing in which Martian city to take her afternoon toilet, thank you very much.

"My name's Fish!" the girl says exuberantly, snapping me from my self-indulgent dream.

"Fish." I test out her name. "I like it. Nice to meet you, Fish." I hold out my hand, not sure if it's the local custom.

She ignores me and turns to the sea. "Here they come," she says.

In the sky above the waters an enormous blowfish plunges down from space, a massive planet-killing meteor, trailing vapor and smoldering with reentry fire. A crack opens in its face, a gargantuan mouth opening as it falls, as if it were a beast coming to devour us all. I grab Fish's arm, readying to run, when I remember: this is no monster. This is a seed.

The blowfish slows as it swoops down, and the air thunders with its deceleration. For an instant it skims the surface, then eases its great mouth into the waters, scooping up megaliters, stirring up goliath waves. Now, belly full, it screams as it arcs back to the sky, mouth sliding closed, while cloud and spray and marine life flicker-flash in long tails behind it as everything that missed the cut tumbles back into the sea.

The blowfish wails as it speeds away, shrinking rapidly, off to the hell-bardos of thoughtspace and the Outer New, off to seed life on some distant planet's virgin seas. The ship recedes until it's too small to see, and when I awake from my stupor, Fish is gone. My hand holds not her arm, but a crumpled towel. Beside me, a dozen small footprints lead into the sea.

◈   ◈   ◈

A creature has dug up my grave. A rat, a bird, a monkey, it's hard to say. But, whoever it was, they left the lizard behind. Small red ants have gone to work dissecting it, and in the hot morning sun, its skin has turned to leather. I contemplate burying it again, but these local animals seem to have a better idea of what to do with it, so I leave it be.

◈   ◈   ◈

Fish surprises me on the beach that afternoon. "I don't get it," she says.

I look up from my pad, unexpectedly happy to see her.

"What don't you get?"

"Why write novels at all? You could project your dreams into a neural."

"I could. But dreams are raw and unfiltered. And that always felt like cheating to me. With writing, you have to labor over your thoughts."

My words seem only to perplex her more. "But you could *dictate* your story. Why make it so hard?"

"You mean, why use a pen?"

She sits beside me, her violet eyes boring into mine. "Exactly."

"Here," I say, handing her a spare. I pull out an empty pad from my pack. "Try it, and tell me what you feel."

She holds the pen like it's a sharp knife; a long time ago, all pens were knives. "I don't know what to do," she says.

"Just press the tip to the page, and swirl it around."

She gives it a try. Her eyes go wide. "Ooooooh, this is fun!"

"You've never scribbled?"

"Not with a pen."

I let the sounds of her drawing and the gentle breaking waves mesmerize me into a memory: my daughter sitting in our kitchen one sunny morning, scribbling on paper; my wife, sanding down her wooden figures in the next room; me, listening to them work, feeling full, feeling complete. Eventually, I wander back to my pad and write:

⊛　　⊛　　⊛

Once, when they had lain beside each other on Oopre's sparkling beaches to watch a parade of comets cross the sky, Ubalo had said something that had stuck with her across the ever-broadening gulfs.

"Can you imagine," he'd said, "what the first person to come upon a grave must have felt? When he saw the disturbed earth and smelled the fresh loam? When his human curiosity led him to the inevitable discovery of a body intentionally laid to rest?

*Did he understand what he'd just found? Was this the first time
a human knew the sadness of the whole race, that despite all our
lofty, endless aspirations, we are finite, we have an end?*

⊛   ⊛   ⊛

I reread what I've written and hate it. It's too cerebral. It
doesn't drive the story. I tear off the page, crumple it, and
toss it into the sea. Beside me, Fish has drawn the likeness of
the blowfish gulpership on her pad.

"Wow, Fish!" I say. "That's amazing!" I'm not just flatter-
ing her. She's fantastic. Her detail is astounding.

"Nah," she says, tearing off the page. She throws it into
the sea.

"Hey! Why'd you do that?"

"I don't know. Why you throw *yours* away?"

"Because . . . it wasn't perfect."

She squints at me, her violet eyes shining like lasers. Then
she stands, drops the pad onto the sand, and hands me the
pen. "I gots to go." And before I can stop her, she saunters off
down the beach.

An ankle-high wave washes her crumpled paper toward
me, and I wade into the water to fetch it. The ink has bled,
but the core remains.

Back at my bungalow, I spread Fish's drawing on my
kitchen table to dry. To my surprise, the running ink actually
enhances the image, makes it seem as if the blowfish is leap-
ing off the page into space.

Later, because I'm a masochist, I check my health. Five
weeks, if I'm lucky. I'd better get cracking. Instead, I get
drinking.

⊛   ⊛   ⊛

I was well into my cups last night before bed, so when someone knocks on my door just after sunrise, it takes me a while
to rouse. When I finally open the door, Fish darts in and immediately gets a blood orange from the maker, plops on the
couch, and says, "You made all them books by hand?"

"Still do," I say, fetching keemun from the maker. I'm not yet caffeinated enough for conversation.

"But that's so much work."

"It's also a ton of fun. I love the physicality of it, the smell of the pages, the feeling I get when I hold a book I've made in my hands."

"But you set every letter and print each page *by hand*?"

"I do."

"And everything else too?"

I take a large sip of tea. "Not everything. I have a maker build the printing press and the movable type. But, yeah, I've typeset, pressed, and bound every single copy of my books."

"But . . ." She seems as if she might explode. "I still don't understand *how*!"

If there is one thing that has defined writers throughout history, it's our endless capacity for procrastination. I need to finish my book soon—in a matter of weeks—but the thought of Fish becoming my apprentice excites me more than anything has in decades.

"Fish," I say, "if you'll let me, I'd love to show you."

Across her face, as broad as a gulperfish, a smile.

⊛　⊛　⊛

Fish is a sponge, and that's not meant as a joke. If I show her something once, she remembers it forever. And she's not using her neural. When she's with me, she shuts it off. She says she wants to know what it feels like to be a writer.

In the past I've waited until I've finished my book before typesetting it, but besides the obvious issue of time, this project delights me too much. We remove the beds from the bungalow's spare room and I have the maker set up the large printing press there. Its wood and iron frame smells delightfully ancient. The wall underneath the room's tall windows becomes our workspace. And though Fish had never seen cursive handwriting before mine, it takes her less than a day to memorize the patterns, even accounting for my awful penmanship, and before Ardabaab's pink sun has set she's transcribed twenty pages of my scribbled words into her own neat hand using a fountain pen she's had the maker craft for her.

"Yvalu and Ubalo are stellar in love with each other," she says.

"Yes, they are."

"Have you been in love, Reuth?"

"A few times."

"What's it like?"

I pause to consider. There are a thousand answers and none of them true. "What's your favorite thing in all the universe?"

She answers instantly: "Watching from my undersea bedroom the way the fish change colors as the sun rises."

I have a vision of Fish beside her window, eyes glowing in the morning light, watching Ardabaab's abundant sea life swim by. It makes me smile. "Being in love is like seeing that beauty every moment in the one who you love. But it also hurts like hell, because love always fades, and life after love is gray and lifeless."

"Oh," Fish says, hanging her head. "Oh."

"I'm sorry," I say, shaking my head. I feel like a schmuck. "I shouldn't have said that."

"No," she says, raising her head. "I's not afraid of truth. I want to know everything."

And I want to tell her. I want to tell her how it's not the big things you miss, but the small ones, like the peck on your cheek your daughter gives you before bed, or how your wife left pieces of stale bread on the windowsill so she could watch the sparrows come and eat them. I want to tell her how much their deaths still hurt, even now, all these decades later, how I still dream of my wife sleeping next to me and how I always wake up gasping. Instead I say, "You've got time enough for that," and walk over to inspect her work.

On her pad, beside my transcribed words, she's drawn a woman with wavy dark hair, large curious eyes, a glittering gem in her nose, the same gem Ubalo had crossed light-years to fetch.

"That's Yvalu?"

"You recognize her?" she says.

"This is fantastic, Fish."

"You think?"

"Fish, I have another idea. Do you want to illustrate my book?"

"*Hill-a-straight*?" Wiki-less, she seems confused.

"I want you to draw pictures of some scenes. We could have the maker convert them to lithographs and we can print them alongside the text."

"But I'm not any good."

"No, you're not good. You're amazing. With your permission, I'd like to use this picture of Yvalu on the cover so it's the first thing people see."

She stares at me, her violet eyes boring into mine. Then she breaks eye contact. "But," she says, almost a whisper. "Who will see it?"

I feel a pang of dread. Another fact she's gleaned from my wiki is that my readership has steadily declined over the years, so that the last person to request one of my printed books was an Earth antiquities dealer on Bora, who carefully sealed my book in plastic and placed it in storage, where it would serve as an example to future generations of what paper books had been like. As far as I could tell, the dealer had no intention of ever reading it. That was twelve Solar years ago.

Fish turns back to me. "Reuth, I'd love to *hill-a-straight* your book."

And at this we both laugh.

⊛   ⊛   ⊛

We get to work. Each day, Fish comes by just after sunrise

and we use the mornings to set type. It's a laborious, slow process, but I love every aspect of it. I show her the right way to hold the composing stick, why she should let the slug rattle a bit, and how to use leads to add spacing between each line of type. I show her how to swipe her thumb to keep the type in place as she adds each letter, and I explain why it's imperative to have snug lines and why it's wise to start and end each line with em quads.

We press a few test signatures, adjusting here, correcting there, as our hands and faces become stained with ink. In the afternoons, after a break and a light lunch, Fish retreats to the corner to ponder my novel and draw new scenes, while I churn out more pages on my pad. Fish loves everything about the process and laughs easily, even when we make mistakes. And her joy is contagious. I haven't been this happy in a long time, and for no reason at all I find myself smiling too.

Fish draws: the cascading light of Jacob's ladder spilling across the desert; a close-up of Ubalo's eyes, fearless and sad, creased by time; a thoughtliner tearing through a hell-bardo, trailing the disturbed dreams of its passengers; a parade of glowing comets crossing the starry sky; Yvalu's desperate hand, reaching for a falling leaf. More than once, I catch Fish writing words of her own, but before I can look she always tucks her pad away.

Meanwhile, my words flow better than they have in decades. I write:

⊛   ⊛   ⊛

And after days of thought and deliberation, Yvalu knew there was only one reason why Ubalo had called her across the gulfs, why he himself could not be here to welcome her. There was only one reason why he had erased all evidence of himself from the planet's records. He had called her out here not to bring her toward him, but to move her away from something else.

He had sent her here to protect her.

⊛   ⊛   ⊛

I reread my words and a warm feeling fills my heart. There are moments as I'm writing when I think this might be my best work yet, my magnum opus. By now I should be suspicious of such thoughts, but the feeling is hard to shake. If only I can finish it in time.

❀ ❀ ❀

The afternoon is hot as Fish and I work from opposite ends of the room, deep in creative flow when the voice startles us. "Dolandra! Oh, thank Mitra!"

A woman stands outside the window, and even from across the room, the glare of her violet eyes shines brighter than the sun. She has the same shape of face, the same nose as Fish. "I been looking for you all day!"

"Moms!" Fish says, dropping her pad. She leaps to her feet.

I walk to the front door to let the woman in, but she gives me a look as if I'm a demon come to eat her soul and stays put. "DOLANDRA!" she shouts.

Fish sprints around my legs, outside and onto the grass. Her shirt and hands are stained black as she stands beside her mother, head hung low, and I can't help but feel guilty even though I know I've done nothing wrong.

"Why you shut your neural?" her mom says, eyeing me. "What the bones and dreck, girl?"

"I's . . ." Fish says. "I's drawing, Moms."

The woman stares lasers at me. "I got your number," she says. "You stay the fuck away from my daughter, or I show you *real* Ardabaabian justice." She grabs Fish by the shirt and yanks her away, down the path toward the sea. Before they turn around a bend of sugarcane, Fish looks back.

I wave goodbye, because I have a feeling I'll never see her again.

❀ ❀ ❀

The bungalow is quiet without Fish's exuberance. I try to write on the porch, but find myself scribbling random shapes on the page, which pale in comparison to her art. I try the beach, seeking the inspiration I found on my first days here, hoping Fish might return to plop beside me. But I meet only wind and floating gulls and the occasional ship drifting slowly across the sky. To jar my inspiration I buy a neur-graft of Gardni Johnner and experience her famous BASE jump on Enceledus, the one where she tore her suit on a rock and nearly died. But this just leaves me shaken and craving solid earth. At night I drink and stare at Fish's drawings, following each delicate line, wishing she were here. And still my words do not flow. I'm as dry as a lizard carcass in the sun.

The baby lizard still sits in the yard, just leather now. Even the ants have departed for tastier shores. The rain and wind have tossed it about, but the carcass lingers always near, as if it's trying to tell me something.

"I know," I tell it. "I know."

⊛   ⊛   ⊛

It's been six days since Fish has left, and I've written a sum total of negative three thousand words (I have scrapped two chapters) when I activate my neural for the first time since I arrived. I request a skinsuit from the local We, and after it instructs me on the standard safety precautions—using my dead wife's voice again, the bastard—I walk down to the beach.

I've found the address of one Dolandra Thyme Heurex in the local wiki, and my neural guides me to her home. While the hot sun slowly rises over the placid waters, I wade into the turquoise sea. I've swum in a skinsuit before, but my heart still pounds as I fully submerge. Fins grow from my feet and hands, and black-and-yellow striping appears on my body to mimic a local species.

And there are many. Their sheer number and palettes of bright colors make me gasp. It's as if some ancient god let her creative spirit loose on the canvas of the sea. Crimson and gold fans of coral wave like bashful geishas of old. Barracudas peer curiously at me before swimming off. Schools of fish flash in the sun as they dart from my grasp. In the distance, a pair of bottle-nosed dolphins inspect a sponge on the sea floor.

Fish's house is set among a group of blue-gray domes in twenty meters of water. I swim up to the door and try the chime.

"Who's there?" I recognize the voice of Fish's mom.

"Havair Heurex? It's Reuth Bryan Diaso. I'd like to speak with you about your daughter."

"I warned you!" she says.

"Look," I say. "I did nothing wrong and won't apologize. Your daughter is a supremely talented artist. She was illustrating my book. I'm an author—"

"A what?"

"An author."

A wiki-length pause. "Go on."

"The truth is, Havair Heurex, your daughter and I have become friends. I respect your decision to keep her from me—you don't know me at all—but I wanted you to know what a talented artist she is, and I hope that you'll encourage her to pursue it in the future, that you won't keep her from her art."

The channel is still open, but I hear only silence.

"Anyway, that's all I wanted to say. Good-bye, Havair Heurex."

A beep. The connection closes. I'm just about to swim off when the side of the dome shivers and a panel slides open. A door, for me.

I swim in, the panel closes, the water drains, and the pressure equalizes. My skinsuit, sensing air, melts away. The inner door opens into a spacious and tidy living room. The outside of the dome was opaque, but from within the walls are transparent. The sea and its colorful fish surround us. Fish's mom stands in a wavering sunbeam, violet eyes flickering. "Why you write novels if no one reads them?"

Pads and scraps of paper are spread across the living room, each covered with a different drawing. Fountain pens lie everywhere. "The same reason," I say, "that Fish continues to draw. I can't stop."

"Her name is Dolandra."

"She told me her name was Fish."

"We moved under the sea because of her. Every day she gets up before dawn to watch the fish in the sunrise."

"It's her favorite thing."

"I know." Havair Heurex flares her nose at me, an expression that reminds me of her daughter. She turns to her kitchenette. "Would you like some tea?"

"I'd love some, thank you."

She pours me a cup and it's better than anything I've had in a long time. "No one shuts off their neural round here," she says. "When I found you with my daughter that day, I got nervous."

"I don't blame you. You were only being a mother."

"I looked you up. Not your public wiki. I . . . I used some favors. I got the local We to glean some of your private data."

I hold back my anger. Yet one more reason to hate the local Wees. "Oh?"

"You're dying?"

I nod. "Decades ago I drank Europan sea water. It's loaded with—"

"Microorganisms." Eyes wide, she retreats from me a step.

I hold up my hand. "Don't worry, I'm not contagious. But those microorganisms are loaded with genetic material similar to—but different enough from—our own that over fifty Solar years they've altered my biochemistry to the point that one day soon I simply won't wake up. If they'd discovered this forty years ago, they might have fixed me. But the genetic damage is too far gone now. I guess it's my punishment for one stupid night of hallucinogenic bliss."

Havair Heurex sighs deeply. "So you've come to Arda-baab to die?"

A school of rainbow parrotfish swims past the window. "It just seemed like the right place. Also, I came here to finish my last novel. Fish . . . she's been a muse of sorts. She reminds me a bit of my daughter. Is she here?"

"She's with her uncle on the other side of the planet."

"Well," I say, standing. "Thank you for your hospitality, Havair Heurex, but I should be going if I'm to finish my book before . . ."

"Yes," she says. "Good luck and all."

"Thank you," I say, heading for the door. But I pause. "Does Fish know?"

"That you're dying?"

"Yes."

"I haven't told her."

"Then if it's all the same, please keep it that way." I look around the room at her many drawings. "She seems to be doing just fine without me."

"So you're the last one?" she says, and I know what she means.

"Goodbye, Havair Heurex."

I swim away from her underwater home, and when I arrive back at the bungalow that afternoon, I surprise a green monkey while it's inspecting the dead lizard. The monkey leaps away, leaving the carcass behind.

⊕   ⊕   ⊕

I press every page of my book, inserting lithographs of Fish's drawings throughout the text. But my novel is incomplete. I have the final chapters yet to write. And as each day comes to a close and I look at my hastily scrawled words that make no sense I worry that I won't finish this before I die.

⊕   ⊕   ⊕

"Moms says I can see you again, long as I keep my neural on."

Fish stands above my bed, the morning light slicing my

bedroom in half.

I sit up. "Fish! Hello!"

"I's at my uncle's," she says. "But I's back now. Get up you loafing fool, 'cause we gots work to do!"

I laugh, and it's as if a switch has been flipped and an engine turned on. My words flow as easily as water again. I will finish this after all.

Fish comes by every day now. In the mornings, she studies the art of bookbinding. In the afternoons, she creates new illustrations. She says we have too many, but I tell her there's always room for more art.

She draws: Yvalu's transport ship landing in heavy rain; a flock of migrating sea birds on Muandiva silhouetted in the bright sun; a pine forest reflected in the glassy lake of Naa; Yvalu and Ubalo, da Vinci-like, reaching for each other's hand, galaxies swirling behind them; Yvalu tasting the dirt of Muandiva. And sometimes, she inks words, which she will never let me read.

I write:

        ⊛   ⊕   ⊛

"Yes, I's seen him," the street vendor said to Yvalu as she showed the woman a holo of Ubalo's likeness. "On Suntiks, he sat over there in the shade, throwing back lagers, listening to them steel drum bands."

"You sure?" Yvalu said, her hopes rising. "You certain?"

"Absolute," the woman said. "Certain as Shaddai makes the sun rise and the stars turn." She made the namaste gesture and bowed. "This mentsh, he were here, same as you stand now."

        ⊛   ⊕   ⊛

I pause to laugh.

"What is it?" Fish says, eyes flashing as she looks up from her pad.

"I've figured it out!" I say. "I know how my book will end."

"Don't tell me!" Fish says. "I want it to be a surprise."

"Okay," I say, smiling. "Okay."

Later, when the sun dips low, Fish goes home, and I head out to the porch to relax in the cooling afternoon. The early stars emerge, their constellations familiar to me now. The sugarcane bends in the breeze. The crickets chirp in the grass. High above, a ship, bright as a star, moves across the sky and vanishes. I take a deep breath. I'm so tired. So damn tired. But all is good, all is good.

I search the yard, but the lizard is gone.

⊛   ⊛   ⊛

"Reuth Bryan Diaso, citizen of Ganesha City, Mars. Born on Google Base Natarajan, Earth orbit, one gravity Earth-natural. Died on Ardabaab, Eish orbit. Age: ninety-one by Sol, two hundred ninety-three by Shoen."

So says Reuth's wiki now. In the morning, I's coming to see him, but he wasn't in bed. *Why don't he answer my call?* I thought. *Where's he at?*

I found him under a coconut tree, flat on the grass. He get real intox and pass out? The ants were on him something bad.

Moms and I buried him in the sea. We thought he'd like that, being with all them colorful fish. His wife and kid died a long time ago, I learned. And that crazy fool left everything to me!

Mornings are stellar quiet without the sounds of his pen on paper and the clink of setting type. There ain't no more words to press. Moms don't like it, but I sit out back in his bungalow, drinking tea, watching the gulls cross the sky, just like him.

A baby lizard skitters 'cross the deck and pauses to gaze at me. I pick up my pen and write:

⊛   ⊛   ⊛

"Don't you worry, Ubalo!" Yvalu shouts to the stars. "I's confused before, but not no more. I know where you at, and I's coming to get you!" Yvalu walks freylik down to the sea, cause that's

where the most beautiful fish swim, specially in mornings, when the sun comes up and turns them bright rainbows. "I know you hiding under there, waiting for me, Ubalo, so you best be shiny. I got such a kiss waiting for you, it'll make stars shine, it'll make universes."

Carnival Nine
Caroline M. Yoachim

ONE NIGHT, WHEN I was winding down to sleep, I asked Papa, "How come I don't get the same number of turns every day?"

"Sometimes the maker turns your key more, and sometimes less, but you can never have more than your mainspring will hold. You're lucky, Zee, you have a good mainspring." He sounded a little wistful when he said it. He never got as many turns as I did, and he used most of them to do boring grown-up things.

"Take me to the zoo tomorrow?" The zoo on the far side of the closet had lions that did backflips and elephants that balanced on brightly colored balls.

"I have to take Granny and Gramps to the mechanic to clean the rust off their gears."

Papa never had any turns to spare for outings and adventures, which was sad. I opened my mouth to say so, but the whir of my gears slowed to where I could hear each click, and I closed my mouth so it wouldn't hang open while I slept.

⊛　⊛　⊛

What Papa said was true. I have a good mainspring. Sometimes I got thirty turns, and sometimes forty-six. Today, on this glorious summer day, I got fifty-two. I'd never met anyone else whose spring could hold so many turns as that, and I was bursting with energy.

Papa didn't notice how wound up I was. "Granny has a tune-up this morning, and Gramps is getting a new mustache. If you untangle the thread for me, you can use the rest of your turns to play."

"But—"

"Always work first, so you don't run out of turns." His legs were stiff and he swayed as he walked along the wide wood plank that led out from our closet. He crossed the train tracks and disappeared into the shadow of the maker's workbench. Tonight, when he came back from his errands, he'd bring a scrap of fabric or a bit of thread. Papa sewed our clothes from whatever scraps the maker dropped.

The whir of his gears faded into silence, and I tried to untangle the thread. It was a tedious chore. The delicate motion of picking up a single brightly-colored strand was difficult on a tight spring. A train came clacking along the track, and with it the lively music of the carnival. Papa had settled down here in Closet City, but Mama was a carnie. Based on the stories Papa told, sneaking out to the carnival would be a good adventure. Clearly I was meant to go—the carnival had arrived on a day when I had more turns than I'd ever had before. I gathered up my prettiest buttons and skipped over to the brightly painted train cars.

It was early, and the carnival had just arrived, but a crowd had already formed. Everyone clicked and whirred as they hurried to see the show. The carnies were busy too, unfolding train cars into platforms and putting up rides and games and ropes for the acrobats.

I passed a booth selling scented gear oil and another filled with ornate keys. I wondered if the maker could wind as well with those as with the simple silver one that protruded from

my back. A face-painter with an extra pair of arms was painting two different customers at once, touching up the faded
paint of their facial features and adding festive swirls of green
and blue and purple. "Two kinds of paint," the painter called
to me, "the swirls will wash right off with soap."

It was meant to be a reassurance, but it backfired—the
trip from the closet to the bathroom took seven turns each
way, so soap was hard to come by. Papa would be angry if I
came home painted.

"Catch two matching fish and win a prize!" a carnie
called. He was an odd assemblage of parts, with one small
brown arm and one bulky white one. His legs were slightly
different lengths, and his ceramic face was crisscrossed with
scratch marks. He held out a long pole with a tiny net on the
end, a net barely big enough to hold a single fish.

"Don't they all match?" I leaned over the tub of water to
study the orange fish. They buzzed quietly and some mechanism propelled them forward and sent out streams of bub-
bles behind them.

The man dipped the net into the water and caught one of
the fish. He flipped open a panel on its belly, and revealed a
number—four. "The fish are numbered one through ten, and
you'll get to pick three. Any two of 'em match and you win!"

I eyed the prizes—an assortment of miniature animals,
mostly cats, all with tiny golden keys. Keys so small that even
I could turn them, so there'd be no need to wait each night
for the maker to wind them up.

"Take these buttons in trade?"

The man laughed. "No, but if you didn't buy any tickets
I'll let you work for a play—a turn for a turn, as they say."

Unlike Papa, he could see how tight I was wound, and
he put me to work hauling boxes from his platform to a car
on the far end of the train. The work was satisfying, and it
let me gawk at the rest of the carnival. When I was done,
he handed me the net. "Any three fish that catch your fancy.

Good luck!"

The net was long and hard to handle, but I dipped it into
the water. It came up empty and dripping. Fishing was not as
easy as the man had made it look. I tried again, and this time
brought up a fish that whirred loudly as it came out of the
water. The man pushed in a pin to stop the gears and flipped
open a panel to reveal the number 8.

My next two fish were numbered 3 and 4.

"Do any of them match?" I handed back the net, frowning and studying the pool. There were easily a hundred fish.
"I guess with so many they must."

"You have to look closer at the fish." A freckle-faced kid
climbed up onto the platform. He scooped up a fish, checked
the number on the bottom, then studied the pond. "This
one's a six, so I just have to find a match."

With a smooth practiced motion he dipped the net back
in, and pulled out another fish. He showed me the number
on the bottom—another six.

"How did you—"

"One of the 6s has a busted tail, swims in circles."

"But the other one, what if you'd gotten something else?"

"This one has a chip of paint missing."

"I'm Zee."

"Endivale," he said, but added quickly, "You can call me
Vale. Hey Pops, okay if I take my free turns to show Zee
around?"

The man running the fish game studied us for a minute,
then nodded.

Vale took my hand, "Come on, you gotta hear the nightingale sing, she's amazing."

So off we went. The nightingale turned out to be a woman with brown-feathered wings that matched her dark skin.
Vale wasn't lying. She sang beautifully, any song that the
crowd shouted to her.

For twelve turns we explored the carnival—we watched

the acrobats, and lost the ring-toss game, and rode on the backs of the dancing bears. Then Vale had to stop, because he didn't have so many turns as me.

"You seem to know everyone at the carnival," I said, when we sat down on the edge of an empty platform. "Do you know my mother? She's very distinctive—a woman with eight spider legs."

"Oh, I've heard of her—Lady Arachna, right? She's Carnival Four."

"Carnival Four?"

Vale gestured down at the platform below us. "You can't see it with the platforms folded down, but the train cars are numbered so they stay matched up. All the cars in this train are marked nine, so we're Carnival Nine. Pops and I are here because they had an empty platform for him to run his game. My other dad is at Carnival Two because he's an acrobat, and nine already has more acrobats than we really need."

"So you never see him?"

"There's only one track through here, but the trains run the whole house, with cities along the route where we stop and entertain folks. Some places there are clusters of tracks where the trains pass each other, or turn around. I've seen him a couple times."

We talked a bit more, and he snuck me in to see the bearded lady and a snake man whose skin was covered in iridescent green scales. The carnival was amazing, and I never wanted to leave, but I could feel the tension leaving my spring. I only had a few turns left, barely enough to get home. "I have to go."

"I'm almost out of turns anyway."

I hopped down from the platform. Vale put his hand on my shoulder. "I lied about some of the fish looking different. There's no missing paint or broken tails. The fish have more than one number, depending on which way you open the panels. Don't tell Pops I told you."

Something passed between us then, in that moment where he trusted me. Somehow it meant more than all the marvels I'd seen. It didn't even occur to me to get angry that the game was rigged until I was more than halfway home.

"You didn't untangle the thread," Papa said when I came in.

The multicolored jumble of thread was on the table where I'd left it.

"I had so much energy, and the train brought the carnival—"

"Go to bed, Zee. We're out of turns."

⊛   ⊛   ⊛

I spent my days untangling threads and learned to sew scraps of fabric into clothes. On my 200th day, Papa took me into town and we swapped out my child-sized limbs for adult ones, and repainted my face. Trains came and went, but I never had enough extra turns to visit the carnival. Then one morning Papa came back from the city early, pulling a wheeled cart. "What happened?"

"Granny and Gramps wound all the way down."

"But the maker can wind them again tonight, and—"

Papa shook his head. "No, there comes a time when our bodies cannot hold the turns. We all get our thousand days, give or take a few. Then we wind down for the last time. It is the way of things."

I knew we didn't go on forever, because some of my friends were made of parts from the Closet City recycling center. The recycling center melted down old parts to make new ones. So, I knew. But at the same time I'd never known anyone who was broken down for parts before. Granny had painted my face and Gramps always told the best stories about the maker.

"I wish I could have visited them before they wound down."

"I didn't know they'd go today. They were only in their

early 900s."

"Are you going to take them to the recycling center?"

He shook his head. "The recycling center is well stocked, but the carnivals are often hurting for parts. When the next train comes, we'll take them there."

I knew it wasn't right to be excited on the day that Granny and Gramps died, but while I waited to wind down and sleep, I couldn't help but imagine all the marvels we would see.

⊛　⊛　⊛

The next train turned out to be number nine. I was a little disappointed because I'd already seen most of Carnival Nine, but then I remembered Vale and how he'd shared the secret trick with the fish. I didn't see him as I followed Papa to the platform at the front of the train, or while we laid Granny and Gramps out on the red-painted wood. One of the carnival mechanics knelt next to Granny, and Papa leaned over and whispered, "I'm going to stay to watch them disassembled, but you don't have to. You did your turns helping me pull the cart to get them here."

The mechanic peeled away the fabric that covered Granny's torso and unscrewed her metal chest plate. I wanted to remember her whole, not in tiny pieces. I squeezed Papa's hand, then let go and walked along the length of the carnival.

Vale found me about halfway down the train. He had swapped out his childhood limbs too, and when they repainted his face they'd gotten rid of his freckles. His hair was darker now, which suited him. He put his hand on my shoulder. "Sorry about your grandparents."

"How did you—"

He shrugged. "Pops saw you come in. He said I could have some turns off, if you want to watch the acrobats."

There was a mischievous gleam in his eyes when he said it, and it sounded like a grand adventure. Vale took me to a huge green-and-white striped tent next to the train tracks

and we held hands and watched as acrobats walked tight-
ropes and leapt between swings suspended high above the
ground.

I loved the show, but halfway through Vale stopped
watching.

"Seen this show too many times?" I asked.

"No. Well, yeah, but mostly it reminds me of my dad.
Pops is great, but we don't always get along so well. He wants
me to take over the fish someday, but I hate that the whole
thing is a cheat."

I wouldn't have minded staying for the rest of the show,
but I didn't want him to be sad. We snuck out and headed
back to the train. "Can you switch carnivals?"

"I'm not built to be an acrobat like Dad. My parts aren't
that good. Really all I'm built for is running a game, and if
I'm going to do that, I might as well stay here."

"You could leave the carnival and stay in Closet City," I
said, suddenly aware that we were still holding hands. "It's. . .
Well, it's terribly boring actually."

He laughed. It was getting late and he was nearly out of
turns. "I was thinking I might come up with a different game,
one that's hard, but doesn't involve any cheats."

I couldn't quite keep the disappointment off my face. I
almost wished I hadn't said anything about Closet City being boring, but it was the complete truth. "Yeah, I guess it'd
be hard to give up the adventure of the carnival to stay in a
place like this."

He pulled me closer and spoke softly in my ear, "Why
don't you come with me when the carnival moves on?"

Papa could take care of himself, and I was old enough
to go. I told him on our walk home, and the next morning I
packed up my things and said goodbye. It was a sudden shift,
an abrupt departure, but Papa understood that I had always
been restless. He loved me enough to let me go. When the
carnival moved on, I went with it. With Vale.

Five trains were at the grand junction when we arrived, and
Vale helped me find Carnival Four so that I could look for
my mother. He would have stayed, but Carnival Two was at
the junction as well, and I told him to go and visit with his
dad. Vale and I would have plenty of time together later, and
I wanted some time alone with my mother. I hadn't seen her
since I was new.

She was easy to find, her train car clearly labeled "the
amazing spider-woman," with pictures of her painted large
on the side of the car. I knocked on the door and she slid it
open, staring down at me and tapping one of her forelegs.
"Yes?"

My gears whirred tight in my chest. She didn't recognize
me, and why would she? My limbs were different, my face
was repainted. She had left a child, and I was a woman now.
"I'm Zee. I came with Carnival Nine, and I wanted. . . well,
to see you, I guess."

"Oh, my daughter, Zee." Her foreleg went still, and she
tilted her head, studying me. "What is it you do with Carnival Nine?"

"Vale is teaching me to run one of the games," I admitted,
knowing that it was one of the lowest jobs in the carnival.
Being an acrobat or a performer required more skill, but the
games were mostly con jobs. Nearly anyone could do it, with
enough practice.

Mother didn't say anything, and the silence stretched
long and awkward between us.

"Papa is still in Closet City," I told her, more to fill the
silence than anything. "We lost Granny and Gramps, a few
weeks back." I tried to think of more news from Closet City,
but since mother had stayed with the train she probably
wouldn't know most of the people I'd grown up with. It was
a strange feeling, my strong desire to bond with someone
who was a complete stranger. In my mind, the meeting had

gone differently. She had loved me simply because I was her daughter, and we'd had an instant connection.

"I'm sorry to hear they've wound down." She paused for a moment. "Look, I'm really not the maternal sort—it's why Lars took you to Closet City to raise you. I'm—well—I'm not very nice. I'm selfish. I like to use my turns for myself, and I never spared a lot of turns for my relationship with Lars. Certainly I never had enough for you."

I didn't know what to say to that. I wanted to be angry with her, but she was a stranger, she'd never really been a part of my life. That was how things were and I was used to it. Mostly I was disappointed. Sad that my dreams about reuniting with my mother had died. We talked a little longer about nothing of importance, and then I went back to Carnival Nine, home to Vale. I vowed that I wouldn't be like my mother. I was blessed with a lot of turns, and I would use them for more than just myself.

⊛   ⊛   ⊛

The train took us in slow circles, stopping to perform at the cities. I settled into the routine of carnival life—collapsing the walls of our train car to make our platform, setting up the dart game that Vale designed, packing everything away again when it was time to move along. The days blurred one into the next, obscuring the passage of time. Then one day I realized that I was over 400 days old, which meant that I had been with the carnival longer than I'd lived in Closet City.

I wasn't old yet, but I was no longer young.

"You sure you're ready to do this?" Vale took me to the front car where all the parts were.

I nodded. Our train's next stop was the maker's workbench; this was the right time for us to make our child.

He started picking through the gears, laying out everything we'd need to build a child. "My half-sister has these great pincers, like lobster claws—"

"I thought maybe he could look more like us." Carnies

came with a wide variety of parts, which was fun for shows, but the more outlandish ones all reminded me of my mother. "Hands would be more versatile if we ever settle down in a city. What if he doesn't want to be a performer?"

Vale frowned. "He could change his parts, I suppose. But what happened to your sense of adventure?"

When I'd lived in Closet City, the carnival had been exciting for the brief time it had stayed. But being a part of the carnival—well, the obligations of life and livelihood sucked away the wonder. It was the novelty that had drawn me here, and half a lifetime later the novelty had worn away. But I couldn't bring myself to say so to Vale.

"So if he wants pincers when he's older, he can swap out his limbs that way too." I kept my voice calm, but worry gnawed at me. We had agreed on building a boy, but we hadn't talked much about the details. I rummaged through the pile until I found an arm, dark-skinned like the nightingale lady, but smaller, child-sized. It didn't have a match, but there was another that was only slightly paler. Would anyone notice? Probably someone had already taken the other half of each set. "What about these?"

"Okay." He was less enthusiastic now, and I felt bad that I'd shot down his first suggestion so quickly. I looked for parts that would be a compromise, interesting enough for him, but nothing as extreme as my mother's spider legs. Nothing that would evoke memories of a woman who thought it'd be a waste of turns to raise me.

We worked quietly for a while, the silence awkward. Finally he pulled out a face, an ordinary shape but painted with streaks of black and white. He held it up. I hated it, but it was only paint. Paint could easily be removed and redone, later. It was less work than swapping out parts. The structure of the face underneath was good. I nodded. It broke the tension.

"Dad said there might be a place for us at Carnival Two, working the show with the dancing bears." He kept his gaze firmly on our son, focusing his attention on attaching the black-and-white streaked head to the still-empty torso. "It'd be a step up from running a dart game, a better position for our son."

Thinking about our son working a show at the carnival made me remember my own childhood. I had always wanted adventure, but now dancing bears seemed more dangerous than glamorous. Life on the tracks was harder, even for me with all my turns. Carnival folk almost never made it to a thousand days. Their springs gave out when people were in their 800s, sometimes even sooner. "I want what's best for him."

Vale took my hand and smiled. "Me too."

The train took us to the maker's bench, and we laid out our son's body, chest open. Tonight the maker would give him a mainspring and wind him for the very first time.

"Should we name him now, or after we've gotten to know him?" My parents had waited to name me until my second day, because they wanted to be sure the name would fit.

"It's good luck to name him before he goes to the maker. He'll get a better spring that way." Vale answered. "What about Matts? That was my grandad's name."

I thought about my Grandad, and all the stories he'd told about the maker. "My grandad was Ettan. What about Mattan? We could still call him Matts for short."

Vale nodded, slowly, his spring winding down. "I like that."

❀   ❀   ❀

The maker gave me forty-three turns the day that I met my child. My darling Mattan got only four. Something was wrong with his mainspring. I was definitely no mechanic, but I could hear it, a strained and creaking noise like metal bending to its breaking point. What could you do with four turns? How could I teach him the world if that was all he had to work with?

I picked up my son and carried him to meet Vale. My mind churned with worry for my son's future and guilt at having more than my share of turns, but at the same time I was grateful to be wound up enough for everything that needed to be done. I saved Mattan a turn of walking by using an extra one of mine to carry him, and he could see the world that way. Light from the ceiling reflected off the white stripes across his face, and I admired the contrast against the black. I had been too hasty in condemning Vale's choice, it was unusual, but striking.

"This is your father, Vale," I told Mattan. He nodded happily but made no attempt to speak. The mechanics of speech were complex and used more turns than a simple nod. Even now, newly made, he was aware of his limitations. It made sense, I suppose. I'd always been able to feel how tightly wound my spring was, even when I was young.

"Why are you carrying him?"

I showed Vale the mechanical counter above our son's key. There were two dials of numbers, enough to show two digits, which made Mattan's tiny number of turns seem even smaller, if such a thing was possible. "He only has four turns."

Vale put his hand out, not to take Mattan but to rest it on my shoulder. "So few?"

"I'll make my turns stretch to cover both of us," I promised. "We'll make the best of it."

And I kept my promise. I made a sling and carried Mattan on my back as I ran my dart game and did our errands, and tried to show him some of the fun and adventure I had so desperately wanted in my childhood.

It was too much, even for me. On Mattan's third day I wound down in the afternoon, right in the middle of my shift working the darts. Vale took Mattan home in his sling, but he didn't have the turns to carry me to bed, so I stood there, right where I stopped, and the carnival-goers clustered around me, gawking. A grown woman, wound down in public like a child who had not learned to pace herself.

At the end of Mattan's first week, our train was at the junction, and Mattan spoke for the first time. "I want to see the acrobats."

Vale had gone out that morning to spend a few turns with his dad. I was supposed to repair the dartboard, covered in painted bulls-eye targets. It had cracked, and we needed it for our game, but Mattan had never asked for anything before. He'd heard Vale talking about his dad and the acrobatics he did for his show. I didn't have the turns, but he had made the effort to ask, and I didn't have the heart to tell him no. I carried him to Carnival Two, and we watched the acrobats practice their trapeze act.

We didn't see Vale in the audience, and his father wasn't practicing with the others. We sat as still as we could and watched, saving our turns for the trip back to train nine. Vale was already there when we returned. He stared at the broken dartboard. It reminded me of the day I'd left the tangled threads, and Papa had chastised me for not doing my work first.

"Mattan asked to see the acrobats," I said. "He spoke for the first time. He's never asked for anything, and I couldn't tell him no."

"Mattan doesn't have the turns for these things," Vale said. His voice was cold, angry. "You don't have the turns for this either. You have to pull your weight with the carnival if you want to stay. You know that."

"And what about our son?" I demanded. "He can't fix dartboards or run carnival games, but that doesn't mean he has nothing to contribute."

Vale shook his head. "Maybe not, but he can't pull his own weight, and he's cost us the chance to move to Carnival Two. They might have taken us, but they refuse to take Mattan."

It was only then I realized that for all this first week, Vale had never once called him Matts. This was not the child he wanted, and he was refusing to bond with him, trying to protect himself from the hurt. Or maybe he was simply being selfish, unwilling to use his turns on his own child. He was certainly disappointed at losing his chance to move to Carnival Two.

The train made its slow circuit from the Attic City to the brightly painted Children's Room and down the long hallway to Closet City, and I used my turns to help Mattan get through his days. When the train stopped in the shadow of the maker's bench—the place where I'd grown up—I left the carnival and took Mattan with me. Vale didn't argue; he was relieved to see us go.

⊕　⊕　⊕

Papa was delighted to see me, and to meet Mattan, and he welcomed us into his home. I began to fill the role that had once been his—taking him to get his gears tuned or his paint retouched—and everywhere we went I carried Mattan. I had turns enough to care for Papa and Mattan both, so long as I did nothing else. I tried not to think of adventure, or freedom, or even the future. If I kept my focus on the present moment, I could do everything that needed to be done, but only barely.

There weren't any trains at Closet City on Mattan's 200th day.

"We can wait for a carnival to come, or we can get your adult-sized limbs from the recycling center," I told Mattan. We'd talked about both options beforehand, a conversation that had spanned several days because he couldn't always spare the turns to ask questions.

"I want to go today," Mattan answered immediately. There was a good selection of parts at the recycling center, and he didn't want to be a performer, so it made sense to get parts here in town. . . but I think Mattan also knew that getting new limbs would be a exhausting day for both of us, and he didn't want to make it even harder by adding the long walk out to the tracks of the carnival trains.

Being at the recycling center reminded me of the day Vale and I built Mattan, although here the parts were organized neatly on shelves, not piled high in a disorganized heap on the floor of a train car. These parts were more uniform. There were no spider legs or pincers, and while the faces were painted with a wide variety of features, there were none with bright garish colors or distinctive patterns. None that looked at all like Mattan.

"I'll hold up limbs one at a time," I told him. "When you see something you want, nod."

Mattan sat perfectly still, his painted-black stripes cutting across his face like harsh shadows. He had three turns today, enough for us to do everything we needed if we were careful.

I moved around the room, holding up arms and legs for him to see.

The limbs he picked were neither the biggest nor the smallest, painted the same deep brown as his child-sized arms. I brought them over. Mattan's fingers curled, a movement that mimicked the way he squeezed my shoulder when he was excited, but before I could attach the new limbs he asked, "Will these be too heavy?"

The question broke my heart. Yes, these limbs were heavy. All the added weight meant that it would take more turns to carry him. I had selfishly hoped he would choose smaller limbs, but they were his limbs, and this was his choice. "These are beautiful, and I have a lot of turns. I can still carry you."

It was the right thing to say, and Mattan was so happy with his new limbs, but when I carried him home from the recycling center his weight stole the tension from my mainspring more quickly than before. We lived by our turns, and my son—now fully grown—couldn't spare enough to walk across town. I was furious that the world was so unfair, and my heart broke thinking of all the things he didn't have the turns to do. But if I was being honest, my heart also broke for me. Vale had abandoned us and Papa was old, so I would be the one to carry Mattan everywhere, always.

That thought was in my mind when Carnival Nine came to town, an ever-present weight that I could not shake away. My love was endless, but my strength was not, and I longed to escape the unrelenting effort of taking care of Papa and Mattan on my own. I wanted to see Vale, to have some turns all to myself, to do exactly as I pleased for once.

I didn't wake Papa or Mattan. I left them in their beds— did not ask permission to go out or even explain what I was doing, simply left and walked to the trains. They wouldn't be able to do much today, without my help, but between the two of them they'd be able to manage.

"It's good to see you," Vale said when I arrived. "Where's Mattan?"

"With my father." I didn't know what to say after that. I'd wanted to see Vale, but what could I really talk about with someone who wouldn't help raise his own son? He was like my mother, too selfish to share his turns. And here I was, at the carnival, wasting my turns on a foolish whim instead of taking care of my child. "I shouldn't have come."

Vale frowned. "I owe you an apology. I didn't. . . I mean, I wasn't prepared for how things went, and you've always had more turns, so it seemed to make sense for you to take him. I've missed you."

"It's been lonely. Difficult." I admitted. Once I started, the words came pouring out. In Closet City I'd felt like there was no one I could talk to—Papa had always been so good at taking care of everyone around him, so responsible, there was no way I could complain to him. But I could pour everything · out to Vale. If nothing else, at least he would understand my selfishness. "I have the turns to give Mattan a good life, but only if I never do anything for myself. I take care of Papa, I try to let Mattan see some of the world, and it is so rewarding but I want something for me, some little bit of the adventure I was always chasing as a child."

"You're here today," Vale said. He took my hand. "Let's have an adventure."

And we did. It was like seeing the carnival for the first time, the animals and the acrobats and the games. Vale was kind and attentive and we planned out possible futures and talked about the time we'd spent apart. It would have been a beautiful day if not for the constant gnawing guilt of having left Mattan and Papa behind. The worst was that I hadn't even told them. I had been so sure that I did not deserve time for myself that I had made things even worse by stealing the time instead of asking for it.

"This was nice," I said, painfully aware that I needed to leave soon if I wanted to have enough turns to get back home. Despite the guilt, it had been reinvigorating to have the break. "Maybe tomorrow I could come back with Mattan? I think he would love to see you."

Vale hesitated, then nodded. "I would like that."

I walked home, and I was nearly out of turns by the time I walked in the door. Papa was in bed, but Mattan was up, sitting perfectly still at the table, obviously saving a turn to tell me something. I walked directly in front of him, so he wouldn't have to turn his head.

His eyes met mine, and he said, "Grandpa never woke up today."

❀   ❀   ❀

It had always been Papa's wish to have his body taken to a carnival when he wound all the way down, so I rented a cart and pulled him to the train, all while carrying Mattan. The work was hard, and I wouldn't have the turns to get us back home today.

I unloaded Papa into the same train car where he had once unloaded Granny and Gramps, the car where Vale and

I had later assembled Mattan. I stayed while they took Papa apart, by his side now when it didn't matter, instead of yesterday when it might have. No. It wasn't Papa I had abandoned yesterday; Papa had never woken up. He would never know. It was my Mattan who had spent the entire day alone, knowing that Papa was gone, having no way to call for help or do much of anything at all but wait for my return. And now he waited again, resting in the sling on my back as Orna, one of our train's mechanics, carefully opened Papa's chest and removed the gears, sorting them into bins as she worked. Her movements were practiced and efficient, she wasted no turns. All too soon Papa was gone, nothing but a pile of parts.

"Thank you," I told Mattan as we left to find Vale. "I needed to see that."

Mattan didn't answer, saving his turns.

"I did a terrible thing yesterday," I continued. "I wouldn't have gone if I had known about Papa—I thought he would be there to help you—but I shouldn't have done it even so. I'm sorry."

"You can't do everything, always," Mattan said, choosing his words carefully, not wasting more of his turns than was absolutely necessary. "I forgive you."

"Some good might even come of it—I asked Vale yesterday if he wanted to see you, and he said yes."

Mattan squeezed my shoulder ever so slightly through the fabric of the sling, a sign of his excitement at seeing his father. I carried him to the train car with Vale's dart game set up for anyone who had the tickets to play.

Vale studied us for a time, saying nothing. Was he noticing that I still carried our son, even now that he was an adult? Or was he simply studying the black-and-white striped face he hadn't seen for hundreds of days? My guilt was for a single day, a single slip. What did he feel, abandoning us for most of his son's life?

"Say something," I said. "Mattan has to save his turns, so

he doesn't talk much, but he is so excited to finally see you again."

"Mattan," Vale began. He shook his head and started over. "Matts. I know I haven't been a father to you, but I'm ready to help now, if you want me to. Join me on the train?"

The question was for both us, Mattan and me. I had no tie to Closet City now that Papa was gone, and with Vale's help we would have enough turns for a better life for all of us. I wavered, undecided, the weight of Mattan pressing down on my back. He didn't speak, waiting for my decision. Would Vale really help take care of our child, or would he go back on this promise?

Vale had called our son Matts. His heart was in the right place.

"Yes," I answered. "We'll join you on the train."

Mattan squeezed my shoulder, pleased with the decision. I was excited that we might be able to be a family again, but another thought haunted me, something that had been eating at the edges of my mind—what would happen to Mattan when I wound down? For hundreds of days I'd pushed this thought from my mind—I was healthy and full of turns, and Mattan, well his mainspring was bad. I had convinced myself I would outlast him.

Day after day Vale took nearly even turns with me, carrying Mattan on his back as he worked our game or hauled boxes of prizes to and from our platform. I used as many turns as I could spare helping all the newest additions to the carnival—always a turn for a turn, trading endlessly into the future, extracting from everyone I helped a promise to pay that turn forward to Mattan after I was gone. Was it enough? Did it erase that selfish day when I abandoned my son?

⊚ ⊚ ⊚

I've heard it said that every hundred days passes faster than the previous hundred. In childhood, the days stretch out seemingly forever, and we spend our time and turns freely on any whim that catches our fancy. But at the end of our lives, each day becomes an increasingly greater fraction of the time we have remaining, and the moments grow ever more precious. A hundred days, a hundred more, time flits away as we make our slow circuit on the train.

Vale winds all the way down, hard working and supportive to the end. On his last day, he apologizes again and again for abandoning us. We've already forgiven him, but he cannot forgive himself. The other carnies start giving back the turns they borrowed from me, helping Mattan through his days. I have no turns to spare—there have never been enough turns, even for me, and I've always had more than my share.

An acrobat named Chet, a man with stripes on his arms that match the stripes on Mattan's face, comes more often than the others. I thought at first that he was trying to fulfill his obligation quickly and get it over with, but no, he lingers even when he isn't working off his borrowed turns, keeping up a constant stream of chatter, unbothered by the fact that Mattan rarely answers. Chet shares bits and pieces of his past mixed in with gossip about everyone else in Carnival Nine.

My spring is on the verge of breaking, I can feel it. The maker gave my son and me the same number of turns today. Ten turns. Fewer than I've ever had, and the most my son has ever been given. For a moment, I am filled with regret at the harsh limitations of his life. His days are already short, and his spring is so bad that he won't get the thousand days that I have gotten. He will be lucky to live another 100 days, and he is only in his 600s now. I comfort myself with the knowledge that at least he has Chet. He won't be alone.

I asked Mattan a while back what his favorite day was, his favorite memory, and he'd answered without hesitation— the day that we snuck out together to see the acrobats. So today we ignore what little work we might have done and walk to the tent where the acrobats perform, both of us side by side because I no longer have the turns to carry him. We sit perfectly still and watch the acrobats twirling and flying through the air.

I tell Mattan what Papa told me, "There comes a time when our bodies cannot hold the turns. We all get our thousand days, give or take a few."

I think back on my thousand days, on what I've done with my life. The way Papa had taken such good care of me, and how in the end I'd chosen to follow his path, and done my best for Mattan. My life has been different from the adventures I imagined as a child, but I made the most of the turns I was given, and that's all any of us can do.

Small Changes Over Long Periods of Time

K.M. Szpara

I'M TRYING TO PISS against a wall when the vampire bites me. Trying because drunk-me can barely hold a glass, much less maneuver a limp prosthetic cock.

My attacker holds me like he did on the dance floor, one arm wrapped around my chest, this time digging into my ribs. I struggle against his supernatural strength and the slow constriction of my lungs. Through ragged breaths, I inhale the Old Spice on his thick black hair, where he bows his head to grip my neck.

The sting of his fangs barely registers and what does shoots straight to my cunt—can't help it. If I knew he weren't going to kill me, I'd relish the shock and pain, loss of control. I kind of do, anyway. His venom numbs my neck but I can still feel the strong clamp of his jaw. Like a new piercing, my body screams to reject the intrusion. I want to stay awake—stay pressed between his cold hard body and the cold hard wall. I want him to touch me, reach between my legs. I want to stay alive.

But the wall discolors; the red bricks spot with gray until they fuzz over and dull. My last thought before passing out is how weirdly validating it is that this cis gay guy targeted me, when I was too scared to even piss inside the bar's men's room.

⊛   ⊛   ⊛

My phone blares like there's a Red Alert. I check the alarm. Oh right. I signed up for that Open Life-Drawing class at the community center. At 9:00 a.m. After half-priced vodka night. Optimistic.

When I sit up, the full weight of my headache settles into my skull. I press a hand against my forehead to ease the pressure, but end up squinting at a dimly lit room. Not any room I've slept in before.

The only light blurs from down a narrow hallway. Windows the size of cinder blocks line the top of each wall, but neatly hemmed black-out curtains fill them and glossy Ikea tchotchkes sit in front of those.

I'm in a guest room, I assume. At the very least, I'm on a hard futon surrounded by throw pillows and machine-made quilts. I'm still dressed and—I lie back and shove my right hand down the front of my briefs—still packing. Just a little damp from my adventures in peeing outside.

"You're alive." A familiar man leans against the threshold, holding a mug that says "Don't talk to me until I've had my evening blood." on the side. His skin is pale, but not pallid. His pose casual, but precise.

"Barely," is all I can think to say. Did we fuck? I don't usually go home with strangers, much less drunk, much *much* less with vampires. I have fantasized about it, though. Maybe I finally did.

"How do you feel?"

"Hungover."

His chuckle resonates in his mouth, not his chest. The young ones react fairly human, still drawing air into useless lungs for huffs and sighs and rolling laughs. This one is clearly making an effort for my sake but is too old to get it right. I give him a seven out of ten.

I'd feel a little better if I could remember his damn name, though, and I don't know how to ask without also revealing I don't know how I ended up in his guest room.

"It's Andreas," he tells me. "And you're Finley."

"O-Okay. I mean, I didn't—" I trip over explanations of why I forgot his name before reminding myself I still haven't asked.

Scenes from last night force themselves on me; I watch them more than remember them. Drunk fumbling, a cold alley wall, and the rigid clamp of a jaw—his jaw, Andreas's. The mix of pleasure and fear that slices through me isn't a memory.

"You bit me," I say, because he hasn't danced around mystery, either. My grand accusation comes out as, "You're not supposed to do that."

"I was hungry," he says, calmly. Like the obvious result of hunger is biting someone.

"So, go to a blood bank like you're supposed to."

"It's not the same."

"Yeah, because it doesn't hurt people." I pause. "You're not still hungry, are you?"

"I'm not going to bite you again, if that's what you're asking. I—" This time, he pauses. "—do regret what happened."

"Good." I shake my hand out to stunt the tremor that seizes it. Nausea brews in my gut, dizziness behind my eyelids. I press the heels of my hands against my temples. "You don't happen to have any Ibuprofen, do you?"

"No."

"And we didn't fuck, right?"

"No."

"Great, then I'm going to head home—"

The next second, the futon dips and he's beside me. He presses a cool hand against my burning forehead. "You're not hungover," he says. "You're dying."

His words impact me like news of a foreign tragedy: I know they're bad but struggle to connect on a personal level.

"And it's my fault." His hand tenses before he pulls it away.

I flop back onto the futon and stare at the cream-colored ceiling. A fan spins overhead; the moving air ruffles Andreas's shiny hair, an illusion of life.

I don't want to die.

"You don't have to." Andreas replies to my thoughts again.

I didn't know vampires could do that.

"Only the old ones."

"Would you let me die in peace?" I shout over the pounding in my skull.

His shrug is too precise, like his shoulders are tied to a wooden toy's pull string. Up, down. "If that's what you want."

"Thank you." I want to cry—*try* to cry. Before I started testosterone, I'd cry reading *Bridge to Terabithia* or watching a made-for-TV movie. I liked crying, the catharsis of it, the physical purge of sadness.

Andreas brings his mug to his lips. The blood doesn't stain his white teeth; the fangs leave tiny dents in the ceramic where he bites down.

I should be crying. He's expecting me to because I'm a warm-bodied, emotionally-invested human being whose tear ducts can't resist the impulse.

But they do, at least regarding my own future. Won't make that Life Drawing class. Won't ever see my work on a billboard or a book cover. Won't exhibit, won't—who knows what else?

Andreas interrupts my efforts. "Or I could turn you."

"Into a vampire? Aren't we supposed to apply for that?"

"I won't tell if you don't." His smile doesn't wrinkle his old skin.

The decision between anything and "or death" should be

easy. But if I want to eat without killing people—and I will need to eat—I'll have to register with the Federal Vampire Commission and explain myself and risk getting in trouble and getting Andreas in trouble.

Maybe he deserves it. He fucking bit me without permission.

But vampires who break the law, who feed from un-certified donors, who steal blood bags, or drink without asking first, are put on the Blood Offenders Registry, which is basically a hit list for corrupt cops and stake-wielding bigots. And if they survive that, the second strike is euthenization.

The system is fucked. No government lackey is going to hear out a gay trans guy who was illegally turned into a vampire. All I know is I don't want to die before I've done anything with my life. Designing in-store signage for Sears does not count. Just ask the half-finished paintings in my living room.

I run my tongue over the smooth, flat line of my teeth for what I assume will be the last time. "Turn me."

⊛   ⊛   ⊛

The hangover feeling doesn't go away. Not the spins or the sticky pain of thirst.

Andreas's venom curdles any food left in my stomach. He deposits me in the bathroom the instant before I vomit. I clutch the toilet bowl until my knuckles whiten and the whiteness spreads through my hands and I can feel it in my face. Until I can only dry heave.

My throat stings with stomach acid. "Can I have some water?"

Andreas presses a sports bottle to my lips. "Swish and spit. Don't swallow."

I bite down on the plastic nozzle and drink until there's nothing left. My sensitive teeth rip through the thin plastic, tearing up the empty bottle. My canines ache the worst, like I've jammed them into ice cream for too long or just had fillings put in. Or both.

"I told you not to swallow," Andreas says only moments before I prove him right with another retch.

"You can't drink water?" I see vampires drink all the time.

"No, *you* can't drink water. Your body is purging its fluids."

"What about after . . ."

"After you've turned? Sure, you can drink water. Might want to wait a couple centuries before putting anything more complex in your body."

"Like what, Diet Coke?"

"No, Diet Coke you can drink after a couple years. I meant your mother's homemade meatloaf."

"Oh."

What's the last thing I ate? A slice of pizza and burnt French fries. Not the last meal I'd have chosen, but King's was the only place near the bars that served food all night and I was nervous and hungry.

"Just kidding, your mother will be dead by then." Andreas sips from his mug. He waits for his words to settle then smiles. "That was a joke."

"Thanks." I imagine her funeral. My dad going home to an empty house. Eating across from an empty seat in the kitchen.

Still no tears. Maybe it won't be much of a change becoming a vampire. Andreas doesn't look like he cares much about anything.

"Do you want to call her?" he asks.

"No." That answer's easy. She told me she felt like her daughter was dying when I came out. She got over it, eventually, but I don't want to put her through a literal death after that. "I do need to call the HR department at work, though."

"I think they can wait until you're done vomiting," Andreas says.

I push myself to my feet and flush the toilet. He doesn't

understand how this works. I do. "I can't lose my job on top of all this, okay? When everyone I love is dead—or when they decide they don't want a vampire in the family—I won't have a support system. So, where's my cell?"

It's dead, ironically. Andreas plugs it into the wall beside the sink and I spend another hour in the bathroom alternating between ready-to-talk and ready-to-vomit. When my fingers finally steady and I can lift my head long enough to call, HR doesn't believe me.

"No, I can't come in. I was bitten by a *vampire*. I'm dying!"

"I'm sorry, Mr. Hall," says the HR officer, whose name I cannot remember because I'm so, so thirsty. "Like I said, I don't see an application on file for medical-vampirification, which you're required to submit ninety days in advance for paid leave. Now—"

"I couldn't submit an application because I didn't know. It just happened."

"We can offer you six weeks of unpaid leave, Mr. Hall."

"But—"

"That's the best I can do. I'm sorry."

"Fine. Thanks." I hang up and squeeze my phone in my fist.

Andreas rests his hand perfectly still on my back. It doesn't twitch or clench or rub; it just lays there like a paperweight, reminding me of his presence. He wasn't beside me while I was on the phone but he's here now, always *now*. I wish he hadn't been there in the alley.

A gross conflicted feeling creeps over my skin. Why am I even here, still?

Where else am I supposed to go? I've already decided against Mom and, now that I'm thinking about it, any other human. A more scrupulous vampire would report me to save their own neck; a less scrupulous one would break mine.

This is Andreas's fault.

"You're right," he says. "This is my fault."

"I hate when you do that." *Read my mind,* I think, because I know he's still listening.

"Sorry. It's centuries of habit, but I can stop."

"Good." Didn't expect him to say that. "I mean, thanks."

We sit in silence for a minute that feels like an eternity. I'm going to have one of those ahead of me: an eternity. Like it's a tangible thing I can hold in my hands and squeeze. Like a blood-soaked heart I can wring dry.

"I'll cover your expenses for the next six weeks." Andreas leaves before I can pretend to object.

⊛   ⊛   ⊛

I don't die—not yet.

I unravel myself from the quilted cocoon Andreas wrapped me in. I need air, still. Not much, but enough that my chest rises and falls automatically. I sigh and pinch the bridge of my nose, hoping for a moment's relief from my perpetual dehydration headache.

The bathroom rug warms my feet as I sit to pee. No prosthetic is worth fumbling with while my body ejects all its fluids. There's not much in my bladder, but I ease the pressure. Blood spots the toilet paper I toss into the bowl. I go cold. I dab another square between my legs, hoping I've started pissing blood. The other option is not an option.

And then it is.

I haven't menstruated for three years. This shouldn't be happening. "Fuck, fuck, fuck!" I bite down on my knuckles, forgetting my growing canines. Blood beads on my punctured fingers when I pull back.

Andreas doesn't know what to do with me—not really. I need a doctor. One who can explain my reanimated uterus.

I clean up and pop on the pair of sunglasses Andreas left on the side table. He hasn't let me outside, but it's not like the door's locked and I'm still human; I won't spontaneously combust. I assume.

The thinnest line of light shines between the tiny windows' blackout curtains: daytime. I'm officially on "unpaid leave."

A bottle of sunscreen rests on the front windowsill and I slather the white goop on my face and hands before pulling on a hooded North Face fleece from the closet. To think I expected a cape.

⊛ ⊙ ⊛

"I need to see a doctor," I say.

The receptionist stares at me over the counter, over cooling coffee, and square computer monitors.

"I don't have an appointment with mine, but I'll see whoever."

He nods his head quickly, the rest of him unmoving, like a bobblehead doll.

"Great. Do I need to fill out a form, or . . ."

He pushes a blue lined paper across the counter to me. I sniffle and wipe at the cold drip from my nose. Blood stains my sleeve. Dammit.

"Thanks." I grab a pen and sit down.

Four other people share the waiting room. Two read over a pamphlet on lesbian healthcare. One shoots cartoon pigs on her phone. The last just watches me over their acid wash jeans and under their knit hat. They pull their legs up tight against their chest when I pass, never taking their eyes off me. They still watch when I sit beside a corner table, push all the gossip magazines to the side, and try to flatten my form out.

It's pretty standard.

Name: Finley Hall
Legal Name: See above
Age: Twenty-six
Gender: FTM/trans male
Pronouns: He/him
Species: Human

Technically, true. I haven't died yet. Just because I can't

eat Dad's homemade crab cakes for another couple centuries, doesn't mean I'm not me, still. I wonder if I can freeze some . . .

Are you an existing patient at Centre Street Clinic? Yes.

If yes, who is your primary care physician? Dr. Lisa Perez.

What is the reason for your clinic visit today?

I bite the cap of my pen. My teeth hurt, but I can't stop chewing. And I don't know what to write—nothing I want to tell the receptionist. I settle for: Bleeding.

Understatement of the century.

When I return the form, the receptionist pretends to have been drinking his coffee; he grabs the handle with such force, the black liquid spills over the edge and stains a pile of blue forms.

The person who was watching me doesn't stop when I sit back down.

"Can I help you?" I ask.

I relish that edge in my voice. The gritty feel, condescending tone. Andreas never sounds like that. His voice is sea glass, smooth and translucent. Mine is a year of throat-clearing, congestion, and cracking.

The waiting patient loosens their hold on their knees and raises their chin. "You're bleeding."

"I know." I wipe at my nose, but there's nothing.

"No, I mean on the chair." They point.

Fuck.

My cheeks muster up all the color they can find—hopefully enough to suspend menstruation.

"It's okay. I won't tell or anything." They motion for me to stand, then toss a magazine over the spot. "The clinic will probably just throw the chair out anyway. No use blaming someone for it."

"Thanks." I want to smile, but the gooey feeling between my legs—knowing that I'm bleeding out and there's nothing I can do to stop it—stops me.

I'm halfway to the bathroom when a nurse calls my name. "Finley! Finley Hall?"

"Yeah." I hold myself together while I walk, Andreas's fleece wrapped around my waist, steps small to avoid any further leakage, arms clasped in front of me—as if anyone really walks like that.

"I'm Ashlynn, Dr. Treggman's nurse. Why don't you follow me on back and I'll get you started. How does that sound?"

"Fine." I nod and follow her back, even cooperate.

She makes me get on the scale.

"Wow, you've lost nine pounds since your last visit—two weeks ago."

Takes my blood pressure.

"Fifty over thirty. That—that can't be right. You'd have to be . . ."

And my temperature.

"Um, okay, this—I'm going to get Dr. Treggman."

She backs out of the exam room, keeping her eyes on me until she's safe on the other side of the door.

I lean back on the patient table. Its white paper crinkles beneath me. Dr. Treggman walks in just as I'm peering at the crotch of my jeans to assess the situation.

"Finley, nice to meet you." He sets his laptop on a wheeled table and sits on a short black wheelie stool and wheels himself and his laptop over to me. "I'm Dr. Treggman."

I nod.

"What seems to be the problem?" he asks all while peering over his glasses at the form I gave the nurses. "Bleeding?" Then he looks over his glasses at me. "Would you like to be more specific?"

"I got my period for the first time in three years, today."

"You're on Testosterone Cypionate?"

"Intramuscular injections."

"So you know, then, that people who have taken steps to

medically transition are on the restricted list for vampirification." He stares at me over his wire-frame glasses and old pla-
sticky laptop. Slowly, his lips purse. "The nurse gave me your
stats. I'll have to report this. I'm sorry, I'm required by law."

I squeeze my legs together and lean forward, trying to
appeal to his human side while I still have one. "Look," I say
softly. "I need help, okay? This is the only clinic I even feel
safe coming to for trans stuff."

"Mr. Hall, this isn't trans *stuff*, this is vampire *stuff*. And
there's a reason the two don't mix; we don't have conclusive
studies on how vampirification affects atypical bodies." He
starts typing, again.

I've seen the Federal Vampire Commission's list of *atypical bodies*. It's trans and intersex folks. Disabled and neu-
roatypical folks; the F.V.C. even provides a list of prohibited
surgeries and medications. Never mind those who can't afford
the required physical exams and application fee. And heaven
forbid you're a woman of childbearing age who "might want
to have kids someday; *how can you be sure you won't want to?*"

"As I'm not versed in vampire anatomy—" Dr. Treggman's words buzz like a fly in my ears. "—I hesitate to make
any recommendations—"

I clench my hands into cold, white fists and punch them
down on top of Dr. Treggman's shitty laptop. His tan, hairy
arms tremble where they stick out from the keyboard. I lean
over the wheelie desk and bare my growing fangs. If I breathe
deep enough, he smells like dinner.

I lean my full weight on the shattered laptop, crush-
ing him in a hand-sandwich between layers of circuits and
plastic.

"Finley." His voice is hoarse and shaky. "Finley, please,
you're hurting me."

"Finley!" Andreas's sea glass voice turns my head.

"What," I ask, slowly, "are you doing here? You're supposed to be asleep."

"Good thing I wasn't. You need to let the doctor go. He's just doing his job."

"You know how many doctors I've met who are just *doing their jobs?*" The one who asked if I was really, really sure, because I didn't seem very masculine. The one who suggested psycho-sexual therapy as if my kinks disqualified me. The one who told me no cis gay men would want to sleep with me.

"I know." Andreas snakes an arm around my waist and pries me off the laptop.

Dr. Treggman squeaks relief and Andreas looks into his eyes and says, "You will wait quietly." The doctor slackens, suddenly unconcerned about his injured hands or the one and a half vampires fighting in his exam room.

"I can't go like this." I gesture over my un-reproductive organs.

"So, buy some new clothes. Here." Andreas thrusts a few bills into my hand.

I hate that he's so easily solved my problem. I want to stay angry. I'm still angry. I'm still *bleeding.* "How did you know where I—"

"I can smell you." Andreas taps his nose. "Now, I'm going to convince the doctor not to report us for this mess. You will meet me outside."

"I didn't even think you could go outside at this time. I thought I'd ditched you."

"Yeah, well I'm old and soon you'll be young, so don't ditch me for a few more centuries. You have a lot to learn."

My "Ugh!" is a bratty growl as I slam my fist into the doorframe and leave. If this is my life, now, bring on death.

Andreas meets me in the back alley and pushes me against the brick so hard it cracks. Notably, I don't.

"What were you thinking?" he asks. "Are you trying to get us euthanized?"

"I was thinking you don't understand how my body works and I needed to see someone who does." I try to pry his hands off my shoulders but he's got millennia on me. I haven't even managed to die, yet.

"Dr. Treggman doesn't know more about vampirification than I do. Besides, if you're really concerned, we have vampire doctors."

"Any trans ones?"

"What?"

"Do you know any transgender vampire doctors?" I ask slowly to drive home my point.

Andreas's lips twitch, revealing a flash of white. I wonder if he has emotions or only teeth.

"Didn't think so." This time, I brush him off easily. "You're welcome to feel doubly stupid, by the way. Turning someone without an application—a someone who also happens to be trans. It's not even legal!"

I get halfway down the alley before he says, "I thought you smelled different. Not enough to deter me. Actually, not bad at all. Just different."

"I'm flattered." I suppose that's the vampire equivalent of "Wow, I'd never have guessed you were trans," or "But you look so normal."

I put my borrowed sunglasses back on and pause at the shade's edge. "Let's go home so I can die, already."

Andreas catches my shoulder before I can step further into the sunlight. Smoke rises from his hand before he jerks it away.

"I thought you were old," I snap, still unable to control my temper.

"I am." Blisters swell on his otherwise unblemished skin. "Just because I don't catch fire wearing SPF 70 in the shade, doesn't mean I can lie out on the beach in June."

I cross vacations off my list of future plans. A list that seems to shrink every hour.

"Look, Finley, don't let this ruin your last day."

I walk backwards across the line of light, watching

Andreas grow smaller. He doesn't offer any more wisdom. He doesn't even stay.

Don't let this ruin my last day. It's not really my last day. My last day was pizza and burnt French fries, strobe lights and pulsing bass. Drunk pissing.

I stand at the top of St. Paul Street and watch cars fly past. They disappear between skyscrapers and the orange glow of sunset. I should care that this is my last sunset—at least for a few centuries.

I cared when it was my last night with breasts. When I faced losing erotic sensation. Never arching under the hard pinch of rough fingers or the wet suction of a man's lips. I didn't want the mounds, but I had them my whole life. And, then, I didn't.

I cared before my voice dropped. When I faced losing my ability to sing. "Most guys can't," the Internet said and no voice coaches worked with trans men, only trans women. The drop was sudden and uncomfortable. I strained and pushed to sing The Kinks and The Beatles and cried when I couldn't. I hadn't lost my ability to cry, yet.

I care that this is my last sunset.

◉ ◉ ◉

The sky is black and blue when I show up on Andreas's doorstep. His bandaged hand and heavy eyelids are my fault. He glances at the back of my canvas and my small kit of paints and brushes, as if he expected more.

"I probably won't see another sunset like that." Not that I have to justify my time to him. He probably expected I'd visit with family or friends, vomit up a last ditch attempt at a favorite drink or meal. Maybe I should've. Too late, now.

"No, you probably won't." Andreas steps aside so I can set my things in the guest room and kick off my shoes. "Ready?"

"Yeah." I roll up my pink and orange stained sleeves. "I'm ready."

Andreas leads me into the basement. It's unfinished. The

rough cement floor cools my feet; the air chills my exposed skin.

"You don't have to take off your clothes, but you should," Andreas says.

"Why?"

"Death is messy. You don't want it sticking to you."

"Fair." I don't ask for further details. Despite stabbing myself with a needle every two weeks and going through surgery, I'm not particularly good with gross body stuff. Surprise-menstruation was enough to last me an eternity.

I leave my shirt and jeans in a pile, half-folded. Andreas lifts up a metal hatch, exposing soft, freshly tilled soil underneath.

"No coffin?" I ask. Vampires aren't exactly forthcoming about their reproductive process. Secrets are power and they've already given over so much to humankind.

"No," he says. "Just you and the earth." His cheeks flush with recently-drunk blood. He's jealous. He stares at the loose dirt like a lover he wants to wrap himself around.

"You can join me. If you want."

Andreas shakes his head. "You don't want that. You want to be alone. Trust me. There'll be other nights."

I don't tell him I don't want to be buried alive and alone. I don't want to taste dirt. Don't want it matted in my hair, packed up my nose—the crumbs rolling up into my brain. If I'm barely breathing, does it even matter?

Andreas offers his hand. I let him help me into the earthen grave because no one's done anything like that for me since I was a girl.

I sink a few inches when the dirt gives beneath my weight. Andreas's grip tightens to keep me from falling. Mine tightens with hopes of pulling him in with me. But he doesn't stumble, doesn't follow. When he lets go, I clasp my hands in front of me.

"Lie down." Each of his words is a nail in my imaginary

coffin.

I dig myself a space, lie down, and close my eyes. When Andreas pushes the first mound of dirt over my feet, I panic. But my body's not setup to panic, anymore. I have no racing heart or nauseous stomach. My deep breaths mean nothing. I suck air in, but it sits there until I push it out.

"Relax." Andreas covers my legs next. He doesn't pack the soil tight. I assume so that I can get out. I hope.

He unclasps my hands and lays them out beside me. Even corpses get to hold themselves in death. But I'm left exposed to the dirt Andreas piles on my chest and over my arms. Over my neck and ears.

I blink up at him, nothing but a pale face amongst black-brown soil. A waning moon in the night sky. Andreas bends and presses a soft kiss against my lips. It doesn't mean anything. I almost wish it did. We don't love each other, don't long for each other's touch or look forward to some eternal romance. I didn't even pick him. He bit me. I didn't get a say beyond turn or die.

Andreas climbs out of my grave and disappears from view. When he returns, he's holding the wooden handles of a dirt-filled wheelbarrow. "I'll be back for you." And with that, he dumps it over my face. I feel him pat its cold weight over my head and body. Hear the squeaky hinge on the metal trapdoor and its bang shut.

Dirt fills my mouth when I scream.

⊛   ⊛   ⊛

Starving.

Starving and dried and thirsty.

Thirsty and hungry are the same. My body is a desert. I swallow bits of dirt with the rush of blood I suck down. The source is hot against me. Hard against me. My jaw is rigid, eyes wide on those of the man who feeds me.

"Finley." His voice is underwater. My name ripples to the surface.

He rips the source away. I lunge after it, but he pins me on a cold cement floor. I run my tongue over the sharp line of my teeth and cut it on my fangs. They taste like him. My wandering eyes settle on the source. The source has a name. His name is Andreas.

"Finley."

That's my name. I know because I chose it.

"Finley, can you hear me?"

I cough up dirt and blood. Spit it on the cement. "Yes." My voice is smoother, darker, fuller.

"How do you feel?" Andreas asks.

"Starving and dried and thirsty."

He smiles with closed lips. "Let's get you in the shower and some blood in your system. How does that sound?"

My answer is a low growl—one that's conceived in my chest and born through my throat. I chase the feeling with another. Andreas pulls me off my feet and into his arms as if I am his pet. I press my nose against his shirt and sniff his blood through the layers of cotton and flesh.

He sets me on my own feet, again, in the shower. It's big enough for three, no curtains blocking us in. Showerheads hang from the ceiling, raining hot water onto our cold bodies. Andreas rips his clothes off and tosses them into a sopping heap on the rug. I'm already naked—I forgot.

Starving.

I feel every drop of water that strikes my skin like a match tip catching fire. Mud rolls over my muscled arms and unsticks from the dark curls between my legs. I'm not bleeding, anymore.

Andreas offers his wrist. I latch onto his neck, instead. His laugh resounds through my jaw. The blood jostles, choking me for a moment. I pull back and crack my neck, let the rush settle in.

Nerves in my chest prickle to life—nerves that died under the knife years ago. I squirm where Andreas slides his hand down my back, where he rests it under my ass and squeezes, pressing our bare bits together.

When I bite him again, my teeth light with as much pleasure as my cunt—more, even. Like there are nerves in my new fangs.

"There are," Andreas says, confirming my thoughts. "And it's so much better than sex."

My body pulses with blood like that first rush of testosterone. Andreas doesn't taste like one person. He isn't a varietal vintage. He's the blood of everyone he's drunk. Like the house blend, I drink him until he stops me.

I know it's blood; I can taste the iron. But it recalls words like silky and juicy, the swirl of red in a glass, and roll over the tongue.

"Enough," he says with fangs exposed.

I didn't expect the lust part of bloodlust, but Andreas looks different with my undead eyes. I can see the lines of severity in his expression, the flare of his pupils, feel his subtly shifting muscles.

I reach between us and grab Andreas's erection, rub my blood-engorged clit against it and moan. "I want you," I say.

"You want blood."

"I want both."

Andreas smiles. "I'll give you both."

We fuck with my forehead pressed against the slick tiled wall, Andreas's mouth hovering against the back of my neck. Even amidst the steam, his breath is hot, tongue strong and wet. I want him to feed on me again, like that night in the alley. Only this time we both want it and it is so much better, this way.

His cold fingers shock my nipples hard, rolling and pinching them. In only a few hours they've regained the sensitivity they lost under the knife, two years ago.

With his other hand he covers my mouth. And while I relish the bondage, the stifling of my growls and moans, I know it's an offering. I sink my teeth into his wrist and draw the color from him.

While his blood rushes through me, turning me, resurrecting me, Andreas pushes his thick cock into my cunt. I steady myself against the wall while he lifts me with one arm—the arm not lodged in my mouth—and thrusts.

It's not long before he comes, trembling inside me; his body pins mine to the wall. I'm so close, so full, probably saturated. Andreas reaches between my legs and rubs my clit. I close my eyes, lick the wounds on his arm, rest my weight on the full feeling in my groin.

If he weren't propping me up, my orgasm would knock me to the shower floor. It radiates through my blood stream. It wakes me up.

Andreas has to rip his arm away from me. "Careful," he whispers in my ear. "Your body is adjusting. You don't want to be sick, again, so soon."

He rinses us off, takes my hand, and together we lie on the shower tiles, their orange-pink marbling a farce of sundown. I rest my face against his pec, over his juicy heart, and kiss the skin. Andreas chuckles and holds me there while the water pounds over my blissed out body.

"I'm still hungry," I say.

"I bet you are."

"When can we hunt?"

"We can't."

"Why not? You did."

Andreas flips his body on top of mine. "I'm old, Finley. Too old. I've followed human history for millennia. I've met believers and skeptics. Warm beds and pitchforks. Somehow, I never expected assimilation." He relaxes onto his side, rests his head on his hand. "Never expected to go mainstream."

"'I'm Andreas. I was a vampire before it was cool,'" I say, mocking him.

His smirk is sharp and quick; I almost miss it. "You think

you're going to be the vampire that breaks the rules. That fights the normalization of our culture. That doesn't register with a government that's existed as long as my last haircut.

"Your laws don't really matter to me. But for some reason I went along with them. I figured, why not try something new? Live in the open for a change, make friends, furnish an apartment, get a hobby.

"Wasn't so bad at first. Bagged blood is like your Diet Coke. Not as good as the real thing, but you get used to it—so much, sometimes, that you get a sugar rush if you revert." Andreas traces a finger down my jaw, over my neck and chest, swirling it around one of my swollen areola. "I wanted to hold a live body in my arms and feed while it wriggled against me, struggled for the life I sucked hot out of it."

I squeeze my legs together and rock my hips while lust washes over me again.

"You like that." He smiles.

"I do."

"We can't feed on humans."

"But I get it, now." I sit up straighter. "I feel—"

"Forget how you feel, now. Remember how you felt, *then,*" Andreas says, squeezing my hand with a strength I can almost match.

Remembering back a few days ago seems impossible, like seeing into someone else's mind. But I close my eyes and use the white noise of the running water to go back. Even then my human memories feel like facts rather than experiences. "I was angry that you took my choice away."

"Right. Remember that, even if you have to write it down, every morning."

"Okay, but what if we get a donor—a certified blood donor—whose choice it is to give us their blood?" I bat my eyelashes.

Andreas leans over my chest and licks my nipple. "I'll consider it."

I moan and arch up to meet his mouth.

His lips brush my sensitive flesh while he speaks. "When you prove you can control yourself enough not to kill anyone, I'll consider it." He sucks the hard nub between his teeth and presses his fingers between my legs.

Control myself. Just once I'd like to control my own damn body.

◎   ◎   ◎

We feed on blood bags, together. Andreas "convinces" my landlord to break my lease early and without penalty—just like he "convinced" Dr. Treggman not to report us—so I can move into the guest room. He buys me a real bed and a mug that says "Blood: it's not just for breakfast, anymore."

During the first week, we eat and fuck. I'm still not in love with him—don't expect to be—but he lets me feed on him in the shower to ease my bloodlust.

I stumble out, naked and wet, still unsteady on my changing legs. My muscles thicken and shape the more I drink. My facial hair fills in thick and dark where it was patchy before: a fine, perfectly groomed layer on my cheeks and neck. I always thought vampires looked like more beautiful versions of their human selves, though I can't imagine a duller Andreas.

"Stop staring at yourself in the mirror," he teases.

"Stop staring at myself?" I rub a towel over my hair. It rests shiny and perfect without any help. "I've never been happy with the way I look until now. And I'm not supposed to stare?"

Andreas's smile is so subtle, I'd have missed it with human eyes. He lifts me onto my new Ikea bed.

"Can vampires cut their hair?" I ask, diverting Andreas's mouth from its intent.

"What? Why? You just said—"

"When we were talking earlier, you said our government was as old as your last haircut."

"We can make small changes over long periods of time. If

you cut it all off, it would grow back while you slept. Mostly, I was being facetious. Bit of vampire humor." He glances at hair. "Why, you weren't thinking of changing . . . anything, were you?"

I wasn't. Not really. But knowing I can't? What if prosthetics or surgery become so advanced—I'm going to live to see that. Doctors will be able to grow you a dick using stem cells or someone will invent a CyberCock that pairs with a brain implant. In a future where trans people will be able to customize their bodies, I won't be able to. Mine will reject and revert. Beautiful but stagnant. No implants, no surgeries. Not even a haircut. This is why trans people aren't allowed to undergo vampirification.

It's still better than dying.

Will I feel that way in a hundred years?

"Finley?"

"Uh, no, not planning to change anything. Sorry."

"You okay?"

"Yeah. Just . . ." I focus on the body I have, on the things I can control. Like my current arousal. "Just get back to it." I force a smile when I recline. The smile sticks.

The particleboard rocks under the force of our weight, knocking over the canvas I leaned against it. Andreas dives between my legs and sucks on my clit. It's grown like a satisfied tick. And I'm hornier than I was during my first six months on T.

I twine my fingers through Andreas's shiny curls and hold his face against my crotch. He's happy to oblige, trailing his kisses over my abdomen and up my chest. Ever since I turned, I can't get enough of his mouth and fingers on my nipples. I missed them. I missed them and now they're back, healed by his venom.

He pulls away, leaving my slick, wet chest cold and exposed.

"Don't stop," I whisper.

Andreas looks between my chest and my face then back to my chest. "Something's wrong," he says.

"What? Nothing's . . ." I pat the bare skin and wince. Tender dimples of breasts poke out. "What's happening to me?"

Andreas swallows a hard lump in his throat. "Your body. It's—I don't know."

I skitter back until I hit the headboard, until I can't run any further away from my own chest. "Make it stop," I say. When Andreas doesn't move, I shout. "Make it stop!"

He hisses at me for silence.

"Please," I whisper. "Please, make it stop." Something warm rolls down my face, red drops splatter on the growing mounds of my chest.

Andreas growls as he rips the covers off the bed and flings them into the air. The colorful cotton drifts slowly to the floor between us. He bites his bottom lip leaving a thin red line that drips down his chin.

"I have an idea."

"What?"

"I'll be right back." But before he can get too far, he turns back. "*Don't* move."

I shake my head. "I won't."

I can't and I don't.

I stare at the pattern on Andreas's manufactured quilt. The colors are intense, even in the dark. Red too bright for blood. Yellow too clear for the sun. A sun I won't see again until I'm god knows how old, and only then from the shadows.

The quilt doesn't warm me like I wish it would. My body's cold now. It used to be warm. Testosterone runs warmer than estrogen. I stopped wearing a sweater to work. Wonder if I'll start, again.

The door clicks shut. Andreas appears in the doorway; he slows to a human pace mid-step. I can see the change, now. It looks like slow motion. How slow must walking feel to him after so many years.

"Drink this." Andreas crawls onto the bed and wraps an arm around me. He rests a blood bag against my lips.

I push it away. "I'm not hungry."

"You're hungry for this. Trust me."

I purse my lips before accepting the bag. My fangs pierce the thick plastic so easily, I have to concentrate on not ripping it open over the mattress.

"How do you like it?" Andreas watches me.

I don't like when he watches me. I look inexperienced—I am, but that's not the point. Andreas makes vampirism look casual, like a lifestyle. Like vegetarianism.

I carefully back off the bag, long enough to really swallow, to run my tongue over my teeth and let the blood absorb into my body. My temperature rises. A warm euphoria radiates from my skin, swarms my brain, swells between my legs.

"This is good."

Andreas smiles.

"What'd you do to it?"

"Vampire venom enhances what it finds: clear voice, luxurious hair, firm muscles—"

"Remaining breast tissue; I get it." I grit my slippery teeth. "What did you *do* to this?"

"Injected it with testosterone." He looks thoughtfully between me and the bloody bag. "I didn't think, when I drained your blood, that I'd depleted any hormones you may've injected. Most humans' bodies keep producing whatever they need."

"Mine doesn't."

"I know that, now. Thought I'd reintroduce what you need. Steer your new vampire body in the right direction."

"Not bad, Dr. Andreas."

I crush the bag against my mouth and suck it dry. The plastic crinkles until it's raisin-like in my hands. A drop spills over my chin and tickles my neck. Andreas leans over and licks it away.

I growl and toss the empty bag onto the floor, accepting Andreas's mouth against mine. He avoids my chest, though I feel the mounds press against his shirt when he climbs on top of me.

※   ※   ※

I wake up horny. Andreas sleeps beside me, still, his hand draped over my chest to protect me from it. My consciousness stirs him. When he flexes his hand, it brushes my side and I push it away. It's too much. I can't stay in and fuck away the bloodlust for the rest of my life.

"Hey." Andreas props himself up, eyes only half-open. He stares at my body. "They're gone."

I look. I don't want to, but I have to, and he's right. The area's not as hard and defined as it used to be. Andreas gently touches the puffy skin. I gasp. The air feels strange in my lungs, like a lump in my throat.

I quickly expel it and sit up. "I need more of that blood."

※   ※   ※

I burn through T like a bodybuilder. My old dose is not going to be enough and Andreas warns me against trying to visit a human doctor, again.

"They'll report you. They'll report me!" He follows me to the front door.

"Why do you even care?"

I pull the door open and storm into the night like an angry teenager. Heat builds under my cold skin. Cis people are all the same: human or vampire.

Andreas grabs my arm gently, by his standards. I pause out of respect—and rather than dislocating one of our shoulders.

"Is it so wrong to want to feel normal for once?" he pleads with me.

I see an ancient monster against canary yellow walls, glossy wood floors, and ergonomic furniture. He tried. He's still trying.

"I'll be back." I leave, running as fast as I can, which is still not faster than Andreas, but hopefully fast enough to lose him and his questions.

Normal. I slow to an acceptably human speed outside the Center Street Clinic. It's closed. Obviously. Nothing discourages new vampires from visiting like hours that end before sunset. Perfectly legal. Perfectly gross.

I watch patrons drinking in the bar next door, while I walk around it and into the alley. I've yet to ask Andreas how long until my body can handle alcohol. Seeing how fast it absorbs hormones, it'd probably take a lot of booze to get me as drunk as the night we met.

I race up the fire escape and crack the glass with my elbow. The clinic is empty. At home in the dark, I easily navigate the clutter of chairs and narrow hallways in search of the pharmacy.

A sign stops me: "Ask about subsidized hormone therapy, today!" Center Street is a good clinic. What kind of asshole robs a pharmacy?

Me. I'm the kind.

There are dozens of bottles of T, here. They'll know if I take one, so I might as well take what I need for the next six weeks. The clinic can order more.

I load the little boxes into my backpack, grab some needles and syringes for good measure, and climb back out the broken window. Halfway down the fire escape, I consider that Andreas would have found a less obvious and destructive way in.

I jump from the second floor, landing on wobbly feet in the alley. Drunk blood wafts past me from the bar. I hurry away from it, so I won't be tempted to rip a beer out of someone's hands—or the jugular out of someone's throat.

I still smell the alcohol when I pass the gym. Fast-pumping blood, still hot from working out, burns my nostrils. I drag my tongue over my fangs, imagining how one of these late-night meatheads would taste.

"Hey." A solid, wide-jawed man nods at me. "You're out late."

"No." My razor teeth show through my smile. "You're out late." I hear his heart pump faster, smell his adrenaline spike. I bet he tastes even better turned on.

He runs a hand through his sweat-slick hair while he swaggers towards me. He lowers his voice. "I've never fucked a vampire, before."

I press a hand against his abdomen and linger on the over-developed muscle. "You're subtle."

"Wasn't getting the feeling I needed to be."

"You don't. Come with me."

⊛   ⊛   ⊛

Andreas isn't home when I-still-haven't-asked-his-name and I get in. I sit my backpack carefully on the bench in the foyer then kick my shoes into the middle of the hall.

"Bradley," the man says between kisses. "My name's Bradley."

"Finn," I say instead of "I didn't ask."

"This your place?"

"Something like that."

He peers down the hall into open rooms as I pull him into mine. Probably wants to know what a vampire's lair is like. Apparently it's like the inside of a Swedish furniture store. Sorry to disappoint.

Bradley tugs his shoes off and leaves them behind the bed. He smashes his mouth against mine—a move I assume is sexier to someone who can't literally bite his face off.

But I go with it. I relax. I let him push me against the mattress—even pretend he's pinning me there. His sweaty shirt sticks between us when he pulls mine off over my head.

"You feel like marble."

Big vocabulary for a gym rat. "If that's a problem, I can put my clothes back on."

"No, no, no." He kisses down my chest. "I like it. It's just . . . different. You're cold."

I snake my hand down the front of Bradley's drawstring pants. He's already hard. My hand glides easily over his sweaty cock.

He moans against my lips. "You want that? Want me to warm you up?"

As cliché as his lines are, his arrogance gets me wet.

"Do it," I say, helping his clothes off. I accidentally rip his tee shirt. His pants slide off unharmed. His swollen cock bobs near my face and I fight the urge to suck it. Bad idea, teeth.

"Hey, you should know . . ." I trail off. I could kill him and I'm still afraid to tell him our genitals don't match.

"What? This your first time?"

I shake my head.

"Afraid you're going to hurt me?"

"No—well, a little, but I—I'm trans."

"What?"

"I'm transgender."

"You have a dick?" He pulls my briefs down, throwing me off balance.

"Excuse me!"

"Are you kidding? I find the only fucking gay vampire with no dick?"

"Didn't think I'd need one for what you planned to do."

"I'm not putting anything in your pussy."

I tense up at the word. "Please don't call it that."

"Whatever."

"I have another hole, in case you missed it."

Bradley shakes his head and reaches for his clothes. "I'm not into girls."

I grab his arm and flip him onto the bed. "And I'm not into transphobic douchebags, but I'm hungry so I'll make an exception."

My fangs lodge easily into his neck. My tongue slides over his salty skin and I overwhelmingly realize why Andreas bit me. I can't even blame him.

Bradley doesn't taste like Andreas, though. He tastes like steroids and adrenaline with a hint of alcohol. He doesn't fight me or he stops fighting me. His heat floods my veins.

The front door clicks its quiet, controlled click shut. Andreas's eyes meet mine in the dark. He doesn't speak. He walks slowly, at human speed even though no one's around to judge him, and kneels at the foot of the bed.

"He smells delicious," Andreas says.

I swallow a mouthful of Bradley's thick, heady blood, then pull out. "Want to share?"

Andreas kisses me, his tongue flicking against mine for a taste. He licks the corner of my mouth, cleaning me up. I'm a messy eater. I'm a monster.

"No thanks," Andreas says. "Once was more than enough." He bites his wrist and lets his blood drip into Bradley's wounds.

"You didn't do that for me."

"You're not even close to draining this man, Finley."

The effects on Bradley are instant; the ragged holes in his neck stitch themselves back together. Seamless.

Bradley opens his eyes on Andreas's.

"You and Finley had a good time, but it was a one-time thing. He's not really your type."

"Yeah," Bradley says.

I roll my eyes.

"Why don't you head home and shower off that gym stench," Andreas says.

"Good idea," Bradley agrees, robotic.

When the jock's dressed and gone, Andreas says, "Get what you need?"

I stretch my jaw and crack my neck. Slide my tongue over my teeth to get the last of the taste. "Mostly."

"Let me help you."

Help me. How is an old cis vampire supposed to help me when he doesn't understand the first thing about my body? My eternity?

I ask, "Do you have any nails?"

⊛　⊛　⊛

Andreas leans against the threshold, sipping blood while he watches. His skin is pale, but not pallid. His pose casual, but precise. "Little more to the left," he says. "There. That's it."

I walk backwards until I bump into him. He hands me the mug and I take a sip. "Not bad," I say.

My last sunset hangs over the bed. With my new eyes, I see the thick texture of paints where the colors blend and my brushstrokes overlap like waves. Apricot, wine, and golden-rod blur together, each clearer and more real than anything printed by a machine on one of Andreas's quilts.

"Small changes over long periods of time, you said?"

"Yes," Andreas says. "Why?"

"Just making sure."

I imagine what a real sunset will look like when I'm old enough to experience one. If they'll still exist or if smog will cloud the skyline. The only thing that won't change is me, my body, my canvas. "What about a tattoo? You know, to remember." Blood drips from the corners of my eyes.

"Possible. It'll hurt, but possible." Andreas tightens his hold on me. "Are you sure you're okay?"

"Yes," I resolve. "Haven't cried this much since—before, you know. It feels good."

"Since before I turned you?" he asks.

"No," I say. "Before I turned myself."

END

Clearly Lettered in a Mostly Steady Hand
Fran Wilde

Entrance

There's a ticket booth on my tongue.

Don't look in my eyes, don't plead curiosity, you won't get anywhere with that. Try it and you'll see your reflection in my sea-green gaze: your shadow sprinting through the heavy glass doors. You'll smell a whiff of brine, perhaps something more volatile. You'll be caught and held, while your likeness departs. You don't want that.

No one wants to be pinned between an entrance and an exit, unless you're part of the show.

Here's what you do instead: drop your dime on the rose carpet, just there. Don't pick it up. The carpet's sticky. Don't ask why. Stare at my lips, my hands clasped over my velvet skirts, what rests below that, and wait.

If you're worthy, I'll say the word. Your dime gets you a look and a souvenir. Your hands are beautiful, did you know that?

         ❀   ❀   ❀

Welcome

Three steps backwards: follow me. See the boiserie panels,

carved with nymphs and satyrs and stained just so? See the seam between the boards? Push on that, right there, until it parts. You can see the hinges now in the shadows between the nymphs. Hold the door open and let me pass through. The wood feels warm to the touch, your fingers brush a leg, a horn.

Wait there. Let me light the way before you. Phosphorous hisses against air, kisses the kerosene lamp wick. We've had electric since the collection began, but most of us feel gas is easier on the eyes. It was our first disagreement with the curator.

A shadow ducks low, then high. You hear soft breathing, a giggle. Curious?

You're too big to fit through that small hatch. Most guests are. You'll have to crouch, chest to knees, head down so you can feel your lungs press your spine.

Now duck-walk, your fingertips dragging on the rose carpet, until red lint clings to your cuticles. Move beyond the nymphs, into the wood, the wall.

You think you'll be able to straighten once you're through the door, but the ceiling's too low. Keep your stoop. Bend your knees and wish, only for a moment, that you were smaller. Notice the mirrors, set high in the walls, like eyes.

Don't worry, I'll stay right behind you.

⊛   ⊛   ⊛

A Hallway of Things People Have Swallowed

Observe: here are several obvious groupings: fishhooks (seventy, mostly steel, a few bone), one hundred fifteen clam-broth marbles. Glass cases of them, lining the walls. Pencil nubs, matches, rows upon rows of teeth. Don't touch the glass just yet.

Yes, those are butterflies. Someone always tries to eat a butterfly. It tastes like dust.

There are three hundred fifty worms there, the longer ones rolled up in apothecary jars along the wall. Here are the instruments used for removal. Notes on the amount of time each extraction took. The state of the patient before and after, clearly lettered with a mostly steady hand.

Don't miss the cases, their drawers of pins and needles, thimbles too, as if we could sew ourselves back together from the inside. The jacks and rubber balls, the charms, for good luck. That last drawer contains beetles. They are a particular delicacy, especially the large ones. They taste like solder and licorice, but don't eat the claws.

Come this way, the ceilings grow higher in the next room. You won't have to stoop much longer.

❀   ❀   ❀

A Radium Room

Stop there, your feet within the box marked with black tape. Stay very still. The X-ray device hums as it warms up, but don't let it worry you. The technology is very safe. Hold still. Let me slide a film in and I'll take an image of your soul. Hold *Still*.

Your cellulose shade and shadow came out beautifully. You may move now. A few streaks of still-pure hope run the film's darkness. Unless that's bone? I can cut that out if you like.

No, you can't keep the image. It goes in our collection with the others. Careful of your fingers, we don't want prints. Neatly write your name on the tape at the corner. The date too. These details are important.

Silly, you thought that was your souvenir?

We spread the souls on the floor sometimes, during staff breaks. Look at them, debate their merits.

Keep moving. Through that doorway. Watch your head.

❀   ❀   ❀

A Room of Objects That Are Really People

Here, straighten up now. Hurts, doesn't it, all the tiny bones settling back into place? We have pins, if you like, to help hold you together.

Maybe take this chair. I'll push you around. The wheels squeak on the wood floor, and the chair is really more of a bin. Don't mind the parts in there with you, the arms bent at angles, some screws missing; the legs, still braced, the leather straps, the metal bits and the plastic... remember, plastic's newer and we don't really respect anyone who's turned on by that. Comfy?

I wish you could see yourself. Slouching! You're becoming a mess. Mouth wide open. And that stare. At the glass cases, at me. Surely you've seen us before, on the street? In a shop? Surely you haven't gaped quite so much. Is it the ceiling? Impressive, with all the mirrors?

Perspective. The angle you choose, how you observe us, makes everything change. You're nearly lying down now, which is fine. Relax. I'll push you along.

You see, I can walk just as quickly as you, despite what the posters say. You're wondering how. You're imagining what's beneath my skirts. You think you can guess at me. You think you hear scales scuffing the old wood floor.

You might. But see here, the cabinets here are so nicely illuminated. They're walnut, you know. Brass fittings. Take a moment to stare at them. You paid your money, you might as well have a look.

Don't be shy, the cabinets are here for your comfort. It's like looking at dolls, as the posters say. That's why you came. For the strange dolls in the grotesquerie. The Oddities.

We're keeping the lights low. Any brighter hurts our eyes, bounces off the mirrors. You can still see the finer details, if you lean really close. We've left the glass off the fronts, just for you. Touch the sutures, the pins, if you like. Try to push aside the velvet skirting to see the workings below. We're all like dolls here, with some spare parts. Interchangeable. May I take your hand?

That's right. Good.

Let me catalog our alphabet of differences for you. Here

are the heads, the horns, the holes where they tried to let out headaches. Here are the spines, curved like serpents. Here, the jars of jellies with heads too big to be human. A pair of burly palms like beetle's claws, skin tight over bone.

Here are the doubles and triples, the cephalics, their two legs supporting so much thought. The twins, wrapped around one another like trees. Here is the stone baby, we found him in the trash. See his marble skin, worn away where someone had been touching him too much? We've been teaching him his letters.

⊛   ⊛   ⊛

Our Curator's Special Collection

Through here, the lights are brighter. I can't fit your bin past the door, but that is the curator's desk, his chair. His coat, hung neatly, his stethoscope, the rubber gone a bit rot. He always kept very good notes. Paid well, too.

He'd seen the Royal Collection in Denmark, the walls crowded, the glass containers and the formalin. He'd once wondered aloud what such a display might cost. But he wasn't cruel. He wanted to fix us. Or, at least pin us still so he could study us, like you're studying the articulated skeleton in the corner. It was for posterity. Never confuse good intentions for malice. A friend told me that once. He's not here now, not really.

Am I holding your hand too tight? No? You can barely feel it? Good. We'll keep moving, then. More to see.

⊛   ⊛   ⊛

A Room of Objects That Are Very Sharp

Lie still, this is what you paid for. I can't push any faster. Heavy bins are difficult to pivot around corners, as are tails. You could be more considerate.

You might recognize these cases. Medical tools, some very old. Many rusty hinges. Of course that's rust. Ancient. You all love the tools so much. The spreaders, the extractors, the mechanical leeches.

Open the drawers of Items We've Let Touch Us Because Someone Just Like You Said It Would Make Us Well. The hooks and saws, the foul tastes and that stuff that made us gag and didn't make us any better. You all wrote neat words down about each experiment anyway and that made *you* better. Details matter, like on the X-ray. Angles, perspective. Lie back. Hold my hand again. You see the mirrors? They're too high for us to see ourselves in, always. But we can see you with them, no matter where we are.

We can see you, and you can see us as we really are.

Remember the way we turned to bone and stone when you looked at us on the street? Froze, waiting to see what you'd say? Imagine the pain of it, the hardening of each joint when you thought that word, the non-scientific one, the one that rhymes with *eek*. You feel it, don't you. That chill down your spine, the hardening? Yeah, we know. That's why you pay your dime.

So we'll stay quiet and let you look.

⊛   ⊛   ⊛

The Hall of Criminals and Saints

One more room. Through this arch. Don't worry about my skin, it flakes now, when I'm too long out of water. The scales fall from me like coins and people swallow them.

Here are my last loves. I'm always one for the bad boys, the good ones too. The first name's blurred, damp, but you can see he was strong. Broad brow, firm jaw. He wasn't really a criminal, but his skull matched the phrenologist's map. They locked him up behind glass, just to be safe. This one was a criminal, but they didn't catch him. He came here on his own, looking for us. See how similar his skull is to my love's? To yours?

Here is my best friend, her black and gold wings tacked to the wall with seventeen #7 steel mounting pins, her gilt-flecked glass eyes, so like marbles, focused on the ceiling. Wore out her blue eyes, she did, trying to find differences among our guests. You are all so alike. We used the best marbles. Don't look at her eyes. You haven't earned that yet.

You've earned admission. A catalog. A touch of seams, of beetle's claw. A place on the floor, no more. Not our eyes.

Look here, my children, bone and dust. You didn't think I could have those? Neither did we. They were a surprise, the small fish, their mouths so beautiful before they were hooked.

Stay quiet, it will be over soon—

❦   ❦   ❦

This Way to the Exit

Stay quiet. The lights dazzle your eyes too now. We'd never tell you that you all look odd to us. That would be rude. We'd never stare. But the truth isn't kind: you're all kind of boring, really. Identical eyes and matching limbs, smooth faces and parts all in the same order every time you come through. The curator was boring too, once we looked close enough.

But you're changed now, at least a bit. A touch of chitin, those beetle hands. They look good on you. They match your soul: Luminous and opaque.

Would you like to stop at the gift shop? No? Would you like a pill, a potion? There's a taste on my tongue, like brine. Something volatile. Here is a kiss to remind you. Here is a story to take home. A parting gift. A souvenir.

Your kind always leaves so terribly, gaze darting from seam to seam, then to sticky carpet, to my sharp eyes, my tongue, then, finally, the exit. You crawl and stumble: building up speed, tapping your ineffectual hands beautifully against the glass.

***

A Human Stain
Kelly Robson

PETER'S LITTLE FRENCH NURSEMAID was just the type of rosy young thing Helen liked, but there was something strange about her mouth. She was shy and wouldn't speak, but that was no matter. Helen could keep the conversation going all by herself.

"Our journey was awful. Paris to Strasbourg clattered along fast enough, but the leg to Munich would have been quicker by cart. And Salzburg! The train was outpaced by a donkey."

Helen laughed at her own joke. Mimi tied a knot on a neat patch of darning and began working on another stocking.

Helen had first seen the nursemaid's pretty face that morning, looking down from one of the house's highest windows as she and Bärchen Lambrecht rowed across the lake with their luggage crammed in a tippy little skiff. Even at a distance, Helen could tell she was a beauty.

Bärchen had retreated to the library as soon as they walked through the front door, no doubt to cry in private over his brother's death after holding in his grief through the long trip from Paris. Helen had been left with the choice to sit in the kitchen with two dour servants, lurk alone in the moldering front parlor, or carry her coffee cup up the narrow spiral staircase and see that beauty up close.

The climb was only a little higher than the Parisian garret Helen had lived in the past three months, but the stairs were so steep she had been puffing hard by the time she got to the top. The effort was worthwhile, though. If the best cure for a broken heart was a new young love, Helen suspected hers would be soon mended.

"We had a melancholy journey. Herr Lambrecht was deeply saddened to arrive here at his childhood home without his brother to welcome him. He didn't want to leave Paris." Helen sipped her cooling coffee. "Have you ever been to Paris?"

Mimi kept her head down. So shy. Couldn't even bring herself to answer a simple question.

Peter sat on the rug and stacked the gilded letter blocks Bärchen had brought him. For a newly-orphaned child, he seemed content enough, but he was pale, his bloodless skin nearly translucent against the deep blue velvet of his jacket. He seemed far too big for nursery toys—six or seven years old, she thought. Nearly old enough to be sent away to school, but what did Helen know about children? In any case, he seemed a good-natured, quiet boy. Nimble, graceful, even. He took care to keep the blocks on the rug when he toppled the stack.

She ought to ask him to put the blocks in alphabet order, see how much his mother had taught him before she had passed away. But not today, and probably not tomorrow, either. A motherless, fatherless boy deserved a holiday, and she was tired from travel. The servants here were bound to be old-fashioned, but none of them would judge her for relaxing in a sunny window with a cup of coffee after a long journey.

They *would* judge her, though, if they thought she was Bärchen's mistress. She would be at Meresee all summer, so she needed to be on good terms with them—and especially with Mimi.

"We traveled in separate cars, of course. Herr Lambrecht is a proper, old-fashioned sort of gentleman." Helen stifled a laugh. Bärchen was nothing of the sort, but certainly no danger to any woman. "The ladies' coach was comfortable and elegant, but just as slow as the rest of the train."

Still no reaction. It was a feeble joke, but Helen doubted the nursemaid ever heard better. Perhaps the girl was simple. But so lovely. Roses and snow and dark, dark hair. Eighteen or twenty, no more. What a shame about her mouth. Bad teeth perhaps.

Helen twisted in her seat and looked out the window. The Meresee was a narrow blade of lake hemmed in tight by the Bavarian Alps. Their peaks tore into the summer sky like teeth on a ragged jaw, doubled in the mirror surface of the lake below. It was just the sort of alpine vista that sent English tourists skittering across the Alps with their easels and folding chairs, pencils and watercolors.

The view of the house itself was unmatched. Helen had been expecting something grand, but as they had rowed up the lake, she was surprised she hadn't seen Bärchen's family home reproduced in every print shop from London to Berlin, alongside famous views of Schloss Neuschwanstein and Schloss Hohenschwangau. Schloss Meresee was a miniature version of those grand castles—tall and narrow, as if someone had carved off a piece of Neuschwanstein's oldest wing and set it down on the edge of the lake. Only four storeys, but with no other structure for scale it towered above the shore, the rake of its rooflines echoing the peaks above, gray stone walls picked out in relief against the steep, forested mountainside. Not a true castle—no keep or tower. But add a turret or two, and that's what the tourists would call it.

No tourists here to admire it, though. Too remote. No roads, no neighbors, no inns or hotels. From what Helen could see as she sat high in the fourth floor nursery window, the valley was deserted. Not even a hut or cabin on the lakeshore.

She'd never been to a place so isolated. Winter would make it even more lonely, but by then she would be long gone. Back in London, at worst, unless her luck changed.

When she turned from the window, Peter had disappeared. The door swung on its hinges.

"Where did Peter go?" Helen asked.

Mimi didn't answer.

"To fetch a toy, perhaps?"

Mimi bent closer to her needle. Helen carried her coffee cup to the door and called out softly in German. "Peter, come back to the nursery this instant." When there was no answer, she repeated it in French.

"I suppose Peter does this often," Helen said. "He thinks it's fun to hide from you."

Mimi's lips quivered. "Oui," she said.

"Come along then, show me his hiding places."

The nursemaid ignored her. Helen resisted the urge to pluck the darning from Mimi's hands.

"If I were newly orphaned, I might hide too, just to see if anyone cared enough to search for me. Won't you help me look?" Helen smiled, pouring all her charm into the request. A not inconsiderable amount, to judge by the effect she had on Parisian women, but it was no use. Mimi might be made of stone.

"To hell with you," she said in English under her breath, and slammed the nursery door behind her.

It was barely even an oath. She knew much filthier curses in a variety of languages. Her last lover had liked to hear her swear. But no more. That life had cast Helen off. All she had left in Paris were her debts.

The clock chimed noon. When it stopped, the house was silent. Not a squeak or creak. No sign of Bärchen or the servants, no sound from the attics above or the floors below. She padded over to the staircase and gazed down the dizzying stone spiral that formed the house's hollow spine. Steps fanned out from the spiral, each one polished and worn down in the center from centuries of use.

"Peter," she called. "Come back to the nursery, please."

No reply.

"All right," she sang out. "I'm coming to find you."

Who could blame the child for wanting to play a game? Peter had no playmates. She could indulge him, just this once. And it gave her a good excuse to snoop through the house.

    ◈   ◈   ◈

By the time Helen had worked her way through the top two floors, it was obvious that the servants were outmatched by the housekeeping. The heavy old furniture was scarred and peeling, the blankets and drapes threadbare and musty, the carpets veiled with a fine layer of cobwebs that separated and curled around her every footstep. The surfaces were furred with a fine white dust that coated the back of her throat and lay salty on her tongue. After a half hour of wiggling under beds and rifling through closets and wardrobes, she was thirsty as if she'd been wandering the desert.

In old houses, the worst furniture was banished to the highest floors. As Helen descended, she expected the furnishings to become newer, lighter, prettier, if just as dusty. In the main rooms, the ones Peter's mother would have used, the furniture was the same: blackened oak carved into intricate birds, fish, and beasts. The sort of furniture that infested Black Forest hunting lodges, but raw and awkward, as if one of the family's great-uncles had taken up a late-in-life passion for wood carving and filled the house with his amateur efforts.

Still, if she could get the servants to clean it properly, she might adopt the large sitting room as her own. She could teach Peter just as well there as in the nursery. It would save her from climbing up and down stairs all day long. And though the sofa was backed by a winding serpent with a gaping maw, it was still a more likely setting for seducing a nursemaid than a drafty nursery window seat.

Under one of the beds she found a thin rib from a rack of lamb, riddled with tooth marks. Somewhere in the house was a dog. She'd have to take care to make friends with it.

Still no sign of Peter. Perhaps he was a troubled child, despite his placid looks. If so, this summer wouldn't be the holiday Bärchen had promised. She'd found him in a booth at Bistro Bélon Bourriche, downing himself in cognac. Within five minutes, he'd offered to pay her to join him for the summer at his family home and teach his nephew English. It would be easy, he said. Bärchen knew how badly she needed money. He was always so kind—famous for his generosity among the boys of Montparnasse and Pigalle.

Helen tapped the rib in her palm as she descended to the ground floor. There, the staircase widened and spread into the foyer, forming a wide, grand structure. At the back of the foyer, the stairs continued through a narrow slot in the floor. To the cellars, no doubt. Exploring down there would be an adventure.

Helen's trunk still sat by the front door, waiting for the steward to bring it upstairs. On the near side of the foyer, tobacco smoke leaked from the library. It smelled heavenly. She hadn't been able to afford cigarettes for months. She'd almost ceased yearning for the taste of tobacco, but her mouth watered for it now. Bärchen would give her a cigarette, if she asked for one. But no. She wouldn't disturb him. He had kept a brave face all through their journey. He deserved some time alone with his grief.

She padded into the murky parlor opposite the library

and pulled aside the heavy green drapes, holding her breath against the dust. The sun was high above the mountains. The lake gleamed with light. Dust motes swarmed the air. The sunlight turned the oak furniture chalky, the heavy brocade upholstery nearly pastel. The walls were festooned with hunting trophies—stuffed and mounted heads of deer, wild goats, even two wolves and a bear. Their glass eyes stared down through the cobwebs as if alarmed by the state of the housekeeping.

She skated her finger through the dust on the windowsill. P-E-T-E-R, she wrote in block letters. When she began the boy's lessons there'd be no need for work books and pencils. Any flat surface could be used as a slate. It might embarrass the servants into doing their work.

Stepping back from the window, her foot jittered over a lump on the floor. Two tiny bones nestled under the carpet's green fringe—dry old gnawed leavings from a pair of veal chops. She tucked them in her pocket with the lamb bone. Then in the dining room she found a jawbone under a chair—small, from a roast piglet. She put it in her pocket.

Helen found her way to the kitchen at the back of the ground floor. An old woman chopped carrots at the table, her wrinkled jowls quivering with every blow of the knife. Beside her, the steward crouched over a cup of coffee. He was even older than the cook, his skin liver-spotted with age. They watched as Helen poured herself a glass of water from the stoneware jug.

"Peter likes to play games," she said in German. "I can't find him anywhere."

The cook began fussing with the coffee pot. The steward kept to his seat. "We haven't seen the boy, Fräulein York."

"I hardly expected bad behavior from him on my very first morning at Meresee."

"The boy is with the nursemaid. He is always with the nursemaid." The steward's tone was stern.

"How can you say that? He's certainly not with her now." She brushed cobwebs from her dress. "I've searched the house thoroughly, as you can very well see."

"You must continue to look for him, Fräulein," the steward said.

The cook bit into a carrot. Her jowls wobbled with every crunch.

They were united against her, but it only made sense. They were old country people and she was just an English stranger in a dirty, dusty dress. Raising her voice would win her no friends.

"Could you bring my trunk up to my room?" She smiled brightly. "I'd like to change out of my traveling clothes."

"Yes, Fräulein York," the steward said.

The cook went back to chopping carrots. The steward sipped his coffee. Did they expect her to retreat now?

"There is still the matter of Peter," Helen said.

The cook's knife slipped. Carrots scattered across the floor.

"The French girl takes care of the boy." The cook's words were barely understandable, some kind of antique form of Bavarian. "He's not allowed in the kitchen."

The steward's mouth worked, thin lips stretching over his stained teeth.

"Is that true?" Helen asked the steward. "Why not?"

The steward covered the cook's hand with his own. "The boy's welfare is your business now, Fräulein."

⊛   ⊛   ⊛

Helen found Peter at the back of the freezing cellar, hunkering in front of a door set deep into rock. The walls were caked with frost. The boy's breath puffed like smoke.

"Aren't you cold?" she asked. "Come back upstairs now."

"*Bitte*, miss," the boy said. He wedged two fingers under the door, then crouched lower, head bobbing as he worked them deeper and deeper. His hair was neatly parted, two blond wings on either side of a streak of skin pale as a grub.

Whatever he was up to, whatever he thought he was going to find on the other side of the door, he was fully engrossed by it. Helen let him have his fun for a few minutes while she poked around the cellar, ducking under the low spines of the vaulted ceiling. On the wall opposite the door, bottles were stacked into head-sized alcoves in pyramids of six. She wiped the dust off a few labels. French, and not that old. Champagne, Bordeaux, Burgundy. More than three hundred bottles. Enough to last the summer.

The cellar smelled salty. It must have been used for aging and preserving meat, in the past. The cold air's salty tang flooded her dry mouth with spit. What she wouldn't give for a piece of pork right now, hot and juicy. Her stomach growled. Perhaps the cook could be persuaded to let her explore the kitchen larder.

Helen wandered back to the boy. "Come along, Peter, that's enough. Mimi is waiting for you."

The light from her candle jittered across the brass plate bolted to the door's face. The tarnished metal was crusted with frost. She stepped closer, lifting her candle. It was a shield—griffins, an eagle, a crown.

She nudged Peter's foot with her toe. "Time to go back upstairs." He was stretched out on his belly now. "Peter, come along this instant." An edge came into her voice. She was tired of being ignored by everyone in the house.

He pulled something from under the door and put it in his mouth.

"Stop that." She grabbed Peter's collar and hauled him across the cellar to the stairs. He pitched forward onto his hands and knees. The object popped out of his mouth and bounced off the bottom step.

Helen picked it up and turned it over in her palm. It was a tiny bone, slender, fragile, and wet with spit.

She stared at Peter. "That's disgusting. What are you

thinking?"

"Mama," he sobbed. His thin shoulders quivered under the velvet jacket. "Mama."

Remorse knifed through her. She tossed the bone aside, scooped him into her arms, and hauled him upstairs. "Hush," she said, patting his quaking back as he sobbed.

Tobacco smoke leaking from the library had turned the air in the foyer gray. Her trunk still crouched by the front door.

Helen lowered Peter to his feet. He was heavy. She couldn't possibly carry him up to the nursery. She'd be gasping.

Helen squeezed his bony shoulders. "You're a good boy, aren't you?" He wiped his nose on his sleeve and nodded. "Good, no more crying."

She lugged the trunk upstairs and dropped it in her room. Then she took the boy's hand and called up the spine of the staircase for Mimi.

When her pretty face appeared at the top of the spiral, Helen shooed the boy upstairs.

"Take care of him, won't you?" Helen said. "There'll be no lessons today. Not tomorrow, either. Then we'll see."

"Oui," Mimi said.

⊕   ⊕   ⊕

When Bärchen came to dinner he was already drunk. The scarlet cheeks above his brown beard were so bright it looked like he'd been slapped.

"So many letters. My brother's desk is stuffed to bursting." Bärchen offered Helen a cigarette. "I can't understand them. I have no head for business, Mausi."

Helen blew smoke at him. "You always say that, but you seem to manage your own affairs well enough."

"I must go to Munich for advice. I'll be back soon, I promise. Two days at most."

"Don't stay away too long. You'll come back to an empty

wine cellar and a pregnant nursemaid."

He giggled. "If that happens, it must be God's will."

Helen opened her mouth to make a joke about the furniture, but managed to stop herself in time despite the free flow of wine. The dining room chairs were particularly awful. Each one was topped by a sea serpent, thick and twisting, with staring eyes faced with mother-of-pearl. Under it was a rudely-rendered pair of human forms, male and female. And beneath them were thumb-sized lumps the shape of fat grubs. They dug into the small of Helen's back.

Portraits glared down at the table from the surrounding walls. Wan blond children with innocent, expressionless faces. Handsome, smiling men and women, brown-haired and robust just like Bärchen. And sickly-looking older people, prematurely-aged, with smooth gray skin and straggly black hair framing hollow, staring eyes.

When the clock struck seven, they were halfway into the third bottle of claret. Bärchen was diagonal in his chair.

"Time for me to play *pater familias*." He called out, "Mimi! *Ici!*"

Mimi appeared at the door, clutching Peter's hand.

"Now, Mimi," Bärchen slurred in French. "Is Peter behaving well? Is he in good health?"

"Oui," said Mimi.

Helen watched close as the girl spoke. Yes, some of her teeth were missing, but how many? Helen pretended to yawn, making a dramatic pantomime of it and sighing ecstatically.

Mimi's eyes watered as she tried not to yawn in response. When her lips curled back Helen caught a quick glimpse into her mouth. Her front teeth were gone, gums worn down to gleaming bone. Candlelight glinted on metal wire twisted through her molars.

Mimi clapped her hand over her mouth. Helen reached for a cigarette and pretended she hadn't noticed. Poor girl. Nothing more sad than young beauty in ruin.

"Peter, come here," Bärchen said.

With rough hands, he examined Peter's fingernails and scalp, looked into his ears, then pried opened his mouth and poked a finger along his gums.

She knew what that felt like. Her father had done the same. His fingers had tasted of ash and ink.

One of Peter's front teeth was loose.

"You're losing your first tooth," he said. "Does it hurt?"

Peter shook his head.

Bärchen wiggled it with the tip of a finger. "Let's pluck it out now, and be done with it."

Peter ran to Mimi and hid his face in her skirts.

"Oh come, Peter." Bärchen laughed. "I'll tie it to the doorknob with a bit of string. It'll be over in a moment."

Peter clutched Mimi's waist.

"No? Then we'll get an apple and you can bite into it like this." He mimed raising an apple to his mouth and chomping down. "You can do that, can't you?"

"No, Uncle." Peter's voice was muffled against Mimi's hip. The girl had backed against the wall and was inching toward the door. Bärchen was taking this too far.

"It's late, Herr Lambrecht," Helen said. "Let the girl take Peter to bed."

"Well then. The tooth with fall out on its own and then this will be yours." Herr Lambrecht put a silver coin on the table. "Miss York will keep it for you."

Mimi and boy slipped out the door.

"How was my performance?" Bärchen asked. "Was I convincing?"

"Very. I can hardly believe you never had children."

"God forbid." Bärchen shuddered and drained his wine glass. "Did I ever tell you about my nursemaid? Bruna was her name. She was devoted to me. You would have liked her. Very pretty. But like Mimi, not much of a talker. Not like you."

"Nothing can keep me from saying what I think." Helen reached into her pocket and set the bones on the stained tablecloth. "For example, your servants are lax," she said.

He shrugged. "What can be done? They're old. Who would choose to live here, if they could be anywhere else?"

⊛ ⊛ ⊛

After dinner they took their wine out the front door and onto the wide front terrace. Evening stars twinkled above looming mountains and a lakeshore veiled in mist. The three sides of the terrace stepped straight down into the water, like a dock or jetty. The skiff bobbed alongside, tied to an iron ring.

That morning, the water had been an inky sapphire, the color so brilliant it seemed to cling to the oars with Bärchen's every stroke. Under the darkening sky it was tar black and viscous. In the distance, a dark object broke the surface, sending lazy ripples across the water. Helen squinted.

Bärchen followed her gaze. "Just a log, that's all. I have a present for you."

He pressed a silver cigarette case into her hand. It was her own—she'd pawned it for rent money three months ago. And it was full—forty slender cigarettes, lined up with care.

She grinned. "If we were back at the Bélon Bourriche, I could put on a pair of tight trousers and sing you a song, as many a young man has done. But you don't want me sitting in your lap any more than I want to be there. So I'll just say thank you."

"It's nothing. Will you be happy here, Mausi?"

"Of course. It's so beautiful. Though I'm not sure how long I can stand to live in a place where nobody appreciates my jokes."

He laughed. "Meresee is beautiful, but it can be a little confining. I'll show you." He led her to the edge of the terrace to peer around the side of the house. Its walls jutted straight down into the water, raising the house's profile far beyond the shore. Behind, the steep mountainsides advanced on the lake, threatening to topple the house into the water.

"You don't want to fall in. It's deep, and so cold it'll knock the breath right out of you." He braced himself against the wall with an unsteady hand.

"I suppose this was a fortress, once," said Helen. "Holding the border of some medieval Bavarian principality."

Bärchen patted the wall. "A fortress, yes, but it never protected a border. It protected the salt."

"Your family had salt mines?" Helen asked. No wonder Bärchen was wealthy.

"The mines belonged to the Holy Roman Emperor. The crown owed much of its wealth to Meresee. More precious than gold, once, this salt. My family protected it."

Bärchen peered over the edge of the terrace. The water clung to the sides of the house. A shadowed stain crept up the foundation.

"Don't fall in," he repeated. "In winter it's somewhat safer. When the ice forms, you can ski across the lake, or skate, if the snow has blown away. But even then, you must be careful."

She laughed. "You've convinced me. I'll be careful to be far, far from Meresee by winter."

"Of course, Mausi." Bärchen forced a chuckle. "Naples for the winter. Neapolitan widows like tall Englishwomen like you. Or Athens, if you please. The world is open to us. We are rich, happy, and at liberty."

Bärchen was trying too hard to be jolly.

"Your new responsibility is eating at you, isn't it, Bärchen?" She threaded her hand through the crook of his arm and drew him gently away from the water's edge. "Why worry? Send Peter away to school. In England, many boys are sent away at his age."

"Maybe you're right. After the summer, if you think he's ready. I'll take your advice."

"What do I know about children? Next to nothing—I

told you so in Paris. You couldn't find a less experienced fraud of a governess."

Bärchen patted her hand. "You're a woman. It will come naturally to you."

"I doubt that very much." Helen pulled her hand away. "But how much damage can I do in one summer? I'll teach him a little English at least."

"That's fine, Mausi. Do your best."

She grinned. "Are you sure you're not his father? Peter favors you."

"A family resemblance." The last trace of dusk drained behind the mountains, and Bärchen's mood darkened with the sky. His gaze fixed on the floating log. "If you think I'll develop a father's feelings, you're wrong." Bärchen's deep voice rose to a whine. "It's not fair to shackle me to a child that's not mine. And it's not fair to the child, either. He should have a mother's love—devoted and selfless."

"What happened to his mother?"

"It was grotesque. She swelled larger than this." Bärchen held his arms out, encircling a huge belly. "How many babies can a woman's body contain? Twins are common, triplets not unheard of. I can't imagine how women survive even one, can you?"

Helen shook her head. Sour wine burned the back of her throat.

"My brother's fault. He should have been more careful than to get so many babies on his wife."

"I don't think it works that way," Helen said.

"It does in our family. One is fine. They should have been content with Peter and stopped there. But no, they had to have more children. And now they've all joined our family in the crypt."

Bärchen stared at the house's foundation stones. Helen followed his gaze.

"Do you mean there are tombs in your cellar? The door

in the cellar leads to a crypt?"

He nodded. "I'll go there too, eventually. Not soon—I'm still young." He shrugged his broad shoulders. "I try not to think about such things. Paris makes it easy to forget."

A chill breeze stirred the water. She put her empty wine glass down and chafed her arms. "And your brother?"

"My brother couldn't live without his wife. He had to join her."

"Let's go in, it's getting cold." Bärchen shook his head. "I can't leave you out here alone," she insisted, pulling on his elbow. "You're too melancholy."

"Don't worry about me, Mausi," he laughed. "I have no urge to join my family. I love my life in Paris too much to give it up yet."

At the door she stopped, half in, half out of the house.

"Do you know what happened to Mimi's mouth?" she asked.

"I heard it was an accident," he said, and turned back to the lake.

⊛   ⊛   ⊛

Bärchen left at the first light of dawn. Helen's pounding headache woke her just in time to spot him from her bedroom window, rowing across the lake in the skiff, pocking the water's surface with each frantic pitch of the oars. She'd never seen him move so quickly, put so much of his bulky muscle to work. It was as though he were escaping something.

Anxiety wormed through her breast. If she called out to him, he'd turn around and row back. But the window latch was stuck, the claw cemented into the catch with years of dust and grit. She struggled with it for a minute, and then gave up. Her head throbbed, her mouth was coated in grit, and her eyes felt as though they'd been filled with sand. She crawled back to bed and shoved her head under her pillow.

When she finally ventured up to the nursery in the afternoon, Mimi was sitting in the window seat, needle and thread idle in her lap. The boy was nowhere to be seen.

Helen joined Mimi in the window seat. "How long have you been caring for Peter, Mimi?"

The girl shrugged.

"I suppose when you first came here, you ransacked the house every time he hid from you."

"Oui," said Mimi.

"But you're tired of it. He's older now. He should know better."

Mimi hung her head. One lone tear streaked over the rose of her cheek and dropped to her collar, staining the cotton dark.

Helen longed to wipe her knuckle along that soft cheek, lift the dregs of the tear to her lips as if it were nectar. But no. That might be fine in a sodden Pigalle bistro, but not here. She'd only frighten the girl.

She rested her palm on Mimi's knee, just the lightest touch. "Stay here, I'll get him."

Helen found Peter sitting on the edge of the terrace, legs extended, trying to reach his toes into the water. He leaned back, balancing on his arms, and squirmed closer to the edge.

Helen's heart hammered. She bit the inside of her cheek to keep herself from calling out—a sudden noise might startle him. She crept closer, poised to run and grab him if he fell. When the boy turned his head toward her, she kept her voice low and calm.

"Come here, Peter."

He ignored her. She slowly edged closer.

"Come away from there, please."

When he was within reach she snatched him up, hauled him to the front of the house and set him down on the doorstep. She gripped his arms firmly and bent to look him in the eye.

"Peter, you can't keep running off, do you understand? It's dangerous. What if you'd fallen into the lake?"

"*Bitte*, miss." The boy scuffed his foot. The light bouncing off the lake seemed to leach the color from his skin.

"*Yes, Miss York.* That's your first English lesson. Repeat after me, *Yes, Miss York.*"

"Yes, Miss York," he said.

"Good," she said.

He raised his hand to her cheek. He gave her one brief caress, and then snaked two of his fingers into her mouth.

Helen reeled backward. Her arms pinwheeled. She grabbed for the door handle but missed. When she fell, she raked her shin along the doorstep's edge.

Peter stood over her and watched as she keened in pain, clutching her leg and rocking on the ground like a turtle trapped on its back. She rolled to her side and wadded her skirt around her leg to sop up the blood.

When she could stand, she grabbed his hand and yanked him upstairs, lurching with every step and smearing blood in a trail up the steps. Mimi met her on the upper landing. Helen shoved the boy into her arms, dropped to the floor, and raked up her skirts. Blood poured down her leg and into her shoe. Her shin was skinned back, flesh pursed around gleaming bone. She fell back on one elbow, vision swimming.

Mimi guided her to a chair and lifted her skirts. Helen flinched, but Mimi's touch was soft, her movements quick and gentle. She ran out of the room for a moment, then returned with rags and a jug of water. As Mimi cleaned her wound, Peter cowered in the window seat. Helen kept a close eye on him. He was crying again, silently, his mouth forming one word over and over again. *Mama.*

Mimi put the final tuck into the bandage, then squeezed Helen's knee and looked up, her brown eyes huge.

"Merci," Helen breathed.

Mimi smiled. Lips peeled back over gaping gums. Wire wormed through pinholes in her back teeth. Helen recoiled. She grabbed the edge of the table and hauled herself to her feet. She stumped over to the window seat, grabbed Peter's shoulders and shook him hard.

"That's enough," she yelled. "No more games. No running off on your own. Understand?"

The boy sobbed. She lowered her voice, trying to reach a source of calm, deep within her. "Don't be afraid, Peter. I'm not angry anymore. What do you say?"

"Yes, Miss York."

"Very good. I understand you miss your mother and father. It hasn't been very long since they died, but it will get easier, with time."

"*Bitte*, miss," the boy said. "Mama and Papa died many years ago."

⊛   ⊛   ⊛

The cook and steward blocked her questions. In between their one-word answers, they commented to each other in an impregnable Bavarian dialect, gossiping about her, no doubt, as if she weren't even there. And why shouldn't they? She was acting like a madwoman, limping around the kitchen, waving her arms and yelling at them in every language she knew.

Helen took two deep breaths, and tried again.

"A few days ago, in Paris, Herr Lambrecht told me his brother had just passed away. He had to travel to Meresee and take responsibility for his nephew, the house and the family finances. Is that true?"

"Yes, Fräulein," said the steward.

There. Everything was fine. The knot in Helen's chest loosened. "But Peter just told me his father and mother have been dead for years."

"Yes, Fräulein," said the steward.

"How can you say that?" Helen longed to grab him by the throat, shake him until he rattled. "How can both those things be true?"

The steward ran his tongue over his stained teeth. "It's not my place to contradict either Herr Lambrecht or his nephew."

It was no use. She stumped up to the nursery. Mimi and Peter stood in the middle of the rug, waiting for her.

"Peter, play with your blocks. I want to see them in alphabet order when I return." She pointed at the blocks. "*Ah—bey—tsay.*"

He knelt on the carpet and began stacking the blocks, obedient for the moment. She didn't trust him, though. She wedged a chair under the handle of the door, trapping them both inside. Then she stumbled downstairs to the library. It was locked, but one stubborn shove and the lock gave way.

The desk was abandoned, cubbyholes dusty, drawers empty except for old pen nibs, bottles of dried ink and a silver letter opener shaped like two entwined sea serpents. *So many letters, I can't make sense of them*, Bärchen had said. Had he taken everything away to Munich?

It made no sense. Why would Bärchen lie to her? He knew how desperate she was. No more friends to borrow from, nothing left to pawn. She would have followed him across the world. She had no other option.

She lit a cigarette and pulled hot smoke deep into her lungs. By the time it had burned down to her knuckle, she was sure the mistake was nobody's but her own. It was typical of her—always too busy searching for the next joke to listen properly. Bärchen had said his brother was dead, but not newly dead. He said Peter's mother had died in the spring, but not this spring. She'd made assumptions. Hadn't she?

There was one way to find out.

"The crypt key." Helen held her hand out to the steward, palm up. "Give it to me, please."

"I don't have it, Fräulein."

"Of course you do. You're the steward. Who else would have it?"

He flipped his jacket open and turned his pockets inside out. "I only have this." A blue and white evil eye medallion spun at the end of his watch fob. "You should have one of these, Fräulein. It keeps you safe."

Helen ransacked the house for keys and limped down the cellar stairs. Her mouth began watering as soon as she smelled the salty air. She lit a cigarette. It dangled from her lips as she tried each key in turn. None fit the crypt's lock. She leaned on the door with all her weight but the heavy iron hinges didn't even shift. She squinted through the keyhole. Only darkness.

She lowered herself to the floor and threaded her fingers under the door. A feathery shift of air drifted from below, ruffling her hair. It smelled delicious, sea-salty and savory, like a good piece of veal charred quickly over white-hot coals and sliced with a sharp knife into bleeding red pieces.

Her fingers brushed against something. Forcing her hands under the door, she caught it with the tips of her fingers, drew it out. It was a tiny vertebra, no bigger than the tip of her finger. Helen held it close to the candle flame, turning it over in her palm. It was brown with dried blood. The canal piercing the bone was packed with white crystals. She picked at them with her fingernail. Salt.

There was something else under the door, too—a tooth coated in a brown blush of blood. A tendril of frozen flesh hung from its root.

Helen limped upstairs. The chair she'd leaned against the nursery door was wedged so tightly the feet scratched two fresh scars into the floor as she dragged it away.

Peter waited in the doorway. Mimi was curled up in the window seat.

"Is this yours?" She showed him the tooth.

"No, miss." He skinned his lips back. His loose tooth hung from his gum by a thread.

"Where did it come from, then?"

He blinked up at her, eyes clear and innocent. "*Bitte*, miss, I don't know."

Tall as he was, in that moment he seemed little more than an infant. His voice was quite lovely. The effect of a slight childish slur on those German vowels was adorable.

"Do you know where the key to the crypt is?"

"No, miss."

"Have you been inside the crypt?"

"No, miss."

He was just a child; children had no sense of time. Did he even know the difference between a month and a year? She'd gotten herself worked up over nothing. The steward and cook had taken a dislike to her, but it was her own fault. She should have taken care to make friends with them. But no matter. Bärchen would be back in a few days, and the summer would continue as planned.

⊛   ⊛   ⊛

Helen brought Mimi and Peter their dinner, barricaded them in the nursery, then helped herself to a bottle of claret from the steward's pantry. She set it on the dining room table beside her dinner plate. No corkscrew, and she hadn't found one while searching through the house for keys. The steward must have had hidden them. She hadn't seen any cigarettes, either. She'd have to ration the ones in her cigarette case until Bärchen came home.

She called for the steward. When he didn't come, she fetched the silver letter opener from the library and used it to pry the cork from the bottle. She lifted the bottle to her mouth like a drunk in a Montparnasse alleyway. The wine burned as it slipped down her parched throat.

Helen put the letter opener in her pocket and took her plate and the wine bottle out to the terrace. The air was fresh with pine. The first evening stars winked overhead between clouds stained with dusk. A hundred feet off the terrace, the floating log bobbed. Slow ripples licked the terrace steps.

She had almost drained the wine bottle when the log was joined by another. The breeze carried a whiff of salt. The two logs seemed to be moving toward her, eel-sinuous. Starlight glistened off their backs as they slipped through the water, dipping under and then breaking the surface in unison like a pair of long porpoises.

The bottle slipped from her hand and smashed on the terrace. Shards of glass flew into the lake.

The logs turned to look at her.

Helen scrambled into the house and slammed the door. She ran to the parlor and began dragging an oak chest across the floor, rucking up the rug and peeling curls of varnish from the floor. She pulled it across the foyer, scraping deep scars across dark wood. By the time she'd barricaded the front door, she was dripping with sweat. Her wounded leg throbbed with every shuddering heartbeat.

She crept to the parlor window and peeked between the drapes. Only one creature was visible, floating just beyond the edge of the terrace. It looked like a log again, but she knew better. She'd seen them. Two long, inky serpents raising their heads from the water, their maggot-pale eyes hollow and staring.

Just a log, that's all.

The log flipped. Water poured across its back. Its mouth split open. Starlight revealed hundreds of teeth, wire-thin and hooked.

Just a log, that's all.

Bärchen was a liar.

⊕   ⊕   ⊕

The cook and steward sat at the kitchen table, heads down over their dinner, one candle burning between them.

"I suppose you'll tell me there are no serpents in the lake. Herr Lambrecht says they're logs, and it's not your place to contradict him." She threw her arms wide. "If one of those monsters bit off your leg and Herr Lambrecht said it hadn't, you'd agree with him."

"Would you like another bottle of wine, Fräulein?" the

steward asked.

"Always." She pounded her fist on the table, rattling their dinner plates. "But I'd rather know how badly Herr Lambrecht lied to me, and why."

The steward shrugged and turned back to his meal.

Helen ransacked the kitchen drawers and piled instruments on the table—knives, forks, even a slender iron spit—everything she could find that was long and slender and strong. She wrapped them in a rag, grabbed the candlestick from the table, and lugged everything downstairs.

Delicious, salty air roiled out from under the door, stronger than before. Helen's stomach growled. She lit a cigarette and rolled up her sleeves.

The white coating on the walls and door wasn't frost; it was salt. She scraped the crust off the eye of one of the griffins. It wadded up under her fingernail, dense and gritty.

Helen licked the salt off her finger and slipped a filleting knife into the keyhole. She could feel the latch inside, and bumps that must be a series of tumblers. They clicked as she guided the knife tip back and forth. The blade sawed at the corners of the keyhole, carving away fine curls of brass. But the knife was too wide, too clumsy.

She tried the iron spit next. It left a patina of sticky grease on her palms. She attacked the lock with each instrument in turn, whining with frustration. She knocked her forehead on the door, gently, once, twice.

A chill played over her bare skin. Gooseflesh prickled her arms. Sour spit flooded her mouth.

Finally, she drew the letter opener out of her pocket and fed its tip through the lock, leaning into the door as if she could embrace its whole width. She peeked into the keyhole, hand by her cheek like an archer with a drawn bow.

She licked salt from her lips. The lock clicked. The door opened an inch, hinges squeaking.

A little wet bone bounced across the floor and hit her

foot. She turned.

Peter was right behind her.

Candlelight flickered over his round cheeks and dimpled chin, the neatly combed wings of pale hair framing his face. He was just a child. Orphaned. Friendless. She'd already given him her sympathy. Didn't he deserve her care?

"Hello." She kept her voice gentle. "How did you get out of the nursery?"

"*Bitte*, Miss York. The door opened."

The chair must have fallen. She hadn't wedged it hard enough.

Peter stared at the crypt door. She should take him back upstairs, tell Mimi to put him to bed, but he would just come down here again. And wasn't this his own home?

"Do you know what's behind this door, Peter?"

"Mama," he said.

"Yes, that's what your uncle told me. Not just her, but your whole family—all of your ancestors, in their tombs. Do you know what a tomb is?" He shook his head. "A big box made of stone, usually. Or an alcove in a stone wall, sometimes. Usually family crypts are in cemeteries or churches. But your family—"

She hesitated. *Your family is strange*, she thought. She needed to find out exactly how strange.

"Are you sure you want to see your mother's tomb?"

Peter nodded.

The air that rushed out as she opened the door had a meaty, metallic tang. Her stomach roiled with hunger; her vision swam. She shielded the candle flame with her body. Peter took her hand and led her into the crypt.

Helen had seen crypts before. They didn't frighten her. At age five she'd seen her mother shut away in a Highgate Cemetery tomb. She'd kissed her first girl in the crypt at St Bride's, after stealing the key from the deacon. And she'd attended parties in the Paris catacombs, drank champagne watched by thousands of gaping skulls.

But this was no crypt.

The passage opened into a wide cavern, its walls caked with salt crystals and honeycombed with human-sized alcoves, rough indentations hacked out of the rock with some primitive tool. Some were deep, as if they might be passages, some gaped shallow and empty, and others were scabbed over with a crusted mess the color of dried blood, leaking filth down the crystalline walls. One of these was just over her left shoulder. Tiny bones were embedded in the bloody grime. It smelled like fresh meat.

A few—just a few here and there—were furred over with cobwebs the same bloodless pale pink as Peter's skin.

At the bottom of the cavern, a wide pool of oily water quivered and sloshed.

"Mama," Peter said. "Papa."

"I don't think they're here, Peter," she whispered, pulling him back toward the door.

His hand slipped from her grasp. He ran to a cobwebbed alcove and plunged his hand deep inside. She grabbed his jacket and pulled him away. The strands clung to his arm, stretched and snapped. When his hand appeared, he held tight to a squirming grub the size of his head. His fingers pierced its flesh; the wounds dripped clear fluid.

Its eyes were dark spots behind a veil of skin. Its tiny, toothless maw opened and closed in agony.

"Brother," Peter said. He raised the grub to his lips and opened his mouth.

Helen swatted it out of his hand. The grub rolled across the floor of the cavern and plopped into the pool.

She ran, dragging Peter behind her by his elbow.

Helen slammed the door and braced it with her shoulder, throwing her weight against it as she jabbed the lock with the letter opener. Getting the door open had been sheer luck. She'd never get it locked again, not if she worried at it for a hundred years.

She couldn't believe her stupidity. Opening doors that should stay shut. Going places she didn't belong. Trusting Bärchen, as if she actually knew him. As if he were human.

"Stupid, stupid, stupid," she said under her breath.

The lock clicked. She fell to her hands and knees, weak with relief. Pain shot up her leg. Her vision darkened.

Peter lifted the candle. "Yes, Miss York?"

She sucked air through her teeth and wrenched herself around to sit with her back against the door. She would get away from Peter, run as fast and as far as possible. Into the mountains, into the forest, anywhere but here. But she didn't think she could stand. Not yet.

"Do you remember your mother? Your father? Do you know what they are?" Monsters, with hollow staring eyes. Her voice rose to a shriek. "Do you know what you are?"

"No, Miss York. I know you."

He sat at her feet and slipped his hand into hers. His fingers were sticky with fluid from the grub. It stank like rot, like old meat turned green and festering with maggots. Her gorge rose once, twice. She took two convulsive gasps for air and then the stench changed. Her stomach growled. She raised Peter's fingers to her mouth and licked them clean, one after another. Then she sucked the last of the juice from his sleeve.

There was more on the other side of the door, puddled on the stone floor. She could open the door again. But Peter looked so tired. His eyelids were puffy and the skin under each eye was stained dark with exhaustion.

"Come here," she said, and the boy climbed right into her open arms.

⊛ ⊛ ⊛

Helen watched Mimi undress Peter and tuck him into bed. When the nursemaid tried to leave the bedroom, Helen stopped her.

"No. We're staying here. Peter can't be alone. We have to

take care of him."

Mimi hung her head.

"Do you understand?"

"Oui."

"I don't think you do. You let Peter go—every time. You don't even try to stop him. Why don't you care for him? He's just a child."

The boy watched them, hands folded between cheek and pillow. Mimi stared at the floor. A tear streaked down her cheek.

"We have to keep Peter safe, you and I, so he can grow up healthy and strong like his uncle. And then like his parents, out in the lake." Helen sighed. "I wish we could talk properly, you and I."

"Oui."

"Wait here," she said.

Helen ran to fetch a pencil and paper. When she returned, Peter was asleep.

"Tell me why you let him go."

Mimi fumbled with the pencil. She couldn't even hold it properly, and the only mark she could make on the paper was a toppling cross inside a crude shape like a gravestone.

Mimi's lower lip quivered. A tear dropped onto the paper. Helen took the pencil from Mimi's shaking fingers. "It doesn't matter," she said.

Mimi climbed onto the bed and lay beside Peter.

Helen pulled a heavy chair in from the hallway and slid it in front of the door. It might not keep him from getting out, but if he tried to drag it away the noise would wake her. Then she kicked off her shoes and climbed onto the bed, reaching around Mimi to rest her palm on Peter's arm.

The girl was crying. Her back quivered against Helen's chest.

"It's all right," Helen whispered, holding her close. "Everything is going to be all right."

Mimi cried harder.

Helen expected to be awake all night, but Peter was safe, the room was warm, the bed cozy, and Mimi's sobs were rhythmic and soothing. Helen slipped into sleep and tumbled through slippery dreams of inky shapes that writhed and grasped and tore at her skin. When she woke, the moon shone through the window, throwing the crossed shadows of the windowpanes over the rug. Her leg throbbed. The clock struck four. And Peter and Mimi were both gone.

On the pillow lay two bright pieces of copper wire, six inches long, worried and kinked, their ends jagged. The pillow was spotted with blood.

Helen ran down to the kitchen and fumbled with a candle, nearly setting her sleeve on fire as she lit it on the oven's banked coals. She plunged downstairs, bare feet on the freezing steps, and when the smell hit her she stumbled. She slipped on a bone and nearly sent herself toppling headfirst.

She panted, leaning on the wall. The smell pierced her. It coiled and drifted and wove through her, conjuring the last drip of whiskey in her father's crystal decanter, the first strawberries of summer, the last scrap of Christmas pudding smeared over gold-chased bone china and licked off with lazy tongue swipes. It smelled like a sticky wetness on her fingers, coaxed out of a pretty girl in the cloak room at a Mayfair ball, slipped into a pair of silk gloves and placed on a young colonel's scarlet shoulder during the waltz.

The smell was so intense, so bright it lit the stairwell. The air brimmed with scents so vast and uncontainable they poured from one sense to the next, banishing every shadow and filling the world with music.

Helen fell from one step to the next, knees weak, each footstep jarring her hips and spine. Her vision spun. The cellar brimmed with haloes and rainbows, a million suns concentrated and focused through a galaxy of lenses, dancing and skipping and brimming with life.

The only point of darkness in the whole cellar was Mimi.

The nursemaid crouched in front of the crypt door. She humped and hunched, ramming her face into the wood as if trying to chew through it. The threshold puddled with blood.

Mimi's jaw hung loose. It swung against her throat with every thrust. Her nose was pulped, upper lip shredded, the skin of her cheeks sloughed away.

The remains of her teeth were scattered at her feet.

Helen grabbed her foot with both hands and heaved, dragging her away. Mimi clawed at the floor, clinging to the edges of the stones with her shredded fingernails.

"Miss York?"

At the sound of Peter's voice, the air cottoned with rainbows.

Peter stood at the head of the stairs, lit by a euphoria of lights. It cast patterns across his face and framed his head in a halo of sparks.

Mimi threw her head back and screamed, her tongue a bleeding live thing trying to escape from a gaping throat, a cavitied maw that was once the face of a girl.

Mimi lunged up the stairwell. Helen chased her.

"Peter, run!" Helen howled.

Mimi threw her arms around the boy. The huff of breath through her open throat spattered the walls with blood. She lunged down the hall, dangling Peter like a rag doll. Helen pitched after her, grabbing at the nursemaid's hair, skirt, sleeves. In the foyer she caught hold of Peter's leg and yanked the boy away.

Mimi dug her fingernails into the heavy chest and pulled. It scraped over the floor, throwing splinters across the foyer. She yanked the door open and turned. Blood puddled at her feet. Her tongue wagged from deep in her throat. She raised her arms, as if yearning for Peter to enter her embrace.

Helen clutched Peter to her chest. She forced his head

against her neck so he couldn't see his nursemaid's pulped face.

Mimi yowled. Then she plunged out the door and clattered across the terrace. At the edge of the water she teetered for a moment, arms wheeling. In the moment before she fell, an inky shape welled up from the water. Its jaws welcomed her with barely a splash.

❦ ❦ ❦

The boy knelt on the nursery window seat beside Helen, his nose pressed to the window pane. Two sinuous forms floated in the lake, lit by the pale rays of dawn poaching over the mountaintops.

"Come sit over here." Helen patted the stool in front of her.

When the sun broke over the peaks, Peter's mother and father were gone, sleeping the day away at the bottom of the lake, perhaps, or in the crypt pool, keeping watch over their precious, delicious children.

Helen kept Peter by her day and night. She barely took her eyes off him, never left his side. To him she devoted all her care and attention, until her lashes scraped over dry and pitted eyeballs, her tongue swelled with thirst, and her ears pounded with the call from below.

The scent slipped into her like welcome promises. Lights spun at the edge of her vision, calling, guiding her down to the cavern.

At night, the serpents tossed back and forth in the waves, dancing to the rhythm shuddering through the house. She didn't have to look out the window to see them; every time she blinked they were behind her eyelids. Beckoning.

Helen made it three days before she broke. When her pen turned clumsy, when her handwriting dissolved into crude scratches, she was past caring. The crypt was all she could think of. Hunger gushed through her, overflowing and carrying her down each flight of stairs as if floating on a warm river to the source of everything left in the world worth wanting.

Her hands were too clumsy to open the door, but it didn't matter. She could eat her way through it. The scent itself was nourishment enough. Every bite was a blessing. She drowned herself in it. Gave herself over until her mind hung by a thread.

Her world collapsed into pain when Peter pulled her out of the cellar. She resisted, a little, but she couldn't fight him. Not if it might hurt him. When he got the wires through what was left of her teeth and jaw and twisted them tight, the light abandoned her, the call receded, the house darkened.

"Will you be all right now, Miss York?" Peter asked.

"Oui," she said.

- End -

Biographies

Richard Bowes has published six novels, four story collections and over 70 short stories. He has won World Fantasy, Lambda, Million Writer and IHG Awards. A new edition of his 2005 Nebula shortlisted novel *From The Files of the Time Rangers* will appear later this year from Lethe Press. His 9/11 story "There's a Hole in the City" got a very nice review in the *New Yorker* and is online at *Nightmare Magazine*. He's currently writing chapters for a fix-up novel about a gay kid in 1950s Boston. Recent and forthcoming appearances include: Queers Destroy Fantasy, *The Doll Collection* and *Black Feathers*.

Jonathan Brazee is a retired Marine infantry colonel, now a full-time writer living in North Las Vegas with his wife, two cats, and twin baby girls. He published his first short story in 1978, then switched to non-fiction until writing his first novel in 2006 while deployed to Iraq.

He started writing in earnest in 2012 and now has 68 titles, 43 being novels. He writes primarily military fiction, military SF, and paranormal. In addition to his Nebula finalist novelette, his novel Integration was a 2018 Dragon Award finalist.

Jonathan can be reached via *jonathanbrazee.com.*

Matthew Kressel is a coder and speculative-fiction writer whose work has been a multiple-finalist for the Nebula Award, the World Fantasy Award, and the Eugie Award. His fiction has or will appear in *Clarkesworld, Lightspeed, Tor.com, Analog, The Year's Best Science Fiction and Fantasy 2018 Edition*, edited by Rich Horton, and *The Best Science Fiction of the Year: Volume Three*, edited by Neil Clarke, as well as many other print and online publications. His stories have also been translated into six languages. As a software developer, Matthew created the Moksha submissions system, which is in use by many of the largest speculative-fiction publishers today. And he is the co-host of the Fantastic Fiction at KGB reading series in Manhattan alongside veteran editor Ellen Datlow. Find him at *matthewkressel.net* or @mattkressel.

Sarah Pinsker's stories have won the Nebula and Sturgeon awards. Small Beer Press published her collection *Sooner or Later Everything Falls into the Sea* in early 2019, and her first novel, *Song For A New Day,* will be published by Ace in late 2019. She's also a singer/songwriter with three albums on various labels. She and her wife live in Baltimore in a hundred year old house surrounded by sentient vines.

Vina Jie-Min Prasad is a Singaporean writer working against the world-machine. She has been a finalist for the Nebula, Hugo, Campbell, and Sturgeon Awards. Her short fiction has appeared in *Clarkesworld, Uncanny Magazine*, and *Fireside Fiction*, and you can find links to her work at *vinaprasad.com.*

Rebecca Roanhorse is a Nebula and Hugo Award-winning speculative fiction writer and the recipient of the 2018 Campbell Award for Best New Science Fiction and Fantasy Writer. Her novel *Trail of Lightning,* Book #1 in the *Sixth World Series* (Saga Press), is available now. Book #2, *Storm of Locusts,* is out April 2019. Her epic fantasy *Between Earth and Sky* drops in 2020. She lives in Northern New Mexico with her husband, daughter, and pug. Find more at *rebeccaroanhorse.com* and on Twitter at *@RoanhorseBex.*

Kelly Robson is an award-winning short fiction writer. In 2018, her story "A Human Stain" won the Nebula Award for Best Novelette, and in 2016, her novella "Waters of Versailles" won the Prix Aurora Award. She has also been a finalist for the Nebula, World Fantasy, Theodore Sturgeon, John W. Campbell, and Sunburst awards. In 2018, her time travel adventure Gods, Monsters and the Lucky Peach debuted to high critical praise. After 22 years in Vancouver, she and her wife, fellow SF writer A.M. Dellamonica, now live in downtown Toronto.

Hugo and Nebula finalist **K.M. Szpara** is a queer and trans author who lives in Baltimore, MD. His debut novel, *Docile,* is coming from Tor.com Publishing in Spring 2020; his short fiction and essays appear in Uncanny, Lightspeed, Strange Horizons, and more. Kellan has a Master of Theological Studies from Harvard Divinity School, which he totally uses at his day job as a paralegal. You can find him on the Internet at *kmszpara.com* and on Twitter at @kmszpara.

Hugo and three-time Nebula Award finalist **Caroline M. Yoachim** is a prolific author of short stories, appearing in *Asimov's, Fantasy & Science Fiction, Clarkesworld,* and *Lightspeed,* among other places. Her work has been reprinted in multiple year's best anthologies and translated into Chinese,

Spanish, and Czech. Yoachim's debut short story collection, *Seven Wonders of a Once and Future World & Other Stories*, came out in 2016. For more, check out her website at *carolineyoachim.com*

Jamie Wahls started writing stories about his friends at the age of 9. He once named a character by looking at the keyboard until inspiration struck; her name was Tab. His brutally minimalist website can be found at *jamiewahls.com* and he technically has a Twitter, @JamieWahls.

Martha Wells has written many fantasy novels, including *The Books of the Raksura* series (beginning with *The Cloud Roads*), the Ile-Rien series (including *The Death of the Necromancer*) as well as YA fantasy novels, short stories, media tie-ins (for *Star Wars* and *Stargate: Atlantis*), and non-fiction. Her most recent fantasy novel is *The Harbors of the Sun* in 2017, the final novel in *The Books of the Raksura* series. She has a new series of SF novellas, *The Murderbot Diaries*, published by Tor.com in 2017 and 2018. She was also the lead writer for the story team of *Magic: the Gathering*'s Dominaria expansion in 2018. She has won a Nebula Award, a Hugo Award, an ALA/YALSA Alex Award, a Locus Award, and her work has appeared on the Philip K. Dick Award ballot, the *USA Today* Bestseller List, and the *New York Times* Bestseller List. Her books have been published in eleven languages.

Fran Wilde's novels and short stories have been finalists for three Nebula awards, two Hugos, and a World Fantasy Award, and include her Andre Norton- and Compton-Crook-winning debut novel, *Updraft* (Tor 2015), its sequels, *Cloudbound* (2016) and *Horizon* (2017); *Riverland* (Abrams 2019); and the novelette "The Jewel and Her Lapidary" (Tor.com Publishing 2016). Her short stories appear in *Asimov's*, *Tor.com*, *Beneath Ceaseless Skies*, *Shimmer*, *Na-*

ture, and the *2017 Year's Best Dark Fantasy and Horror.* She holds an MFA in poetry, an MA in information architecture and interaction design, and writes for publications including *The Washington Post, Tor.com, Clarkesworld, io9.com,* and *GeekMom.com.* You can find her on Twitter, Facebook, and at *franwilde.net.*